A TOWN CALLED TAXI

Stephen Rose

Copyright © 2025 Stephen Rose
ISBN: 978-1-923078-55-0

Published by Vivid Publishing
A division of Fontaine Publishing Group
P.O. Box 948, Fremantle
Western Australia 6959
www.vividpublishing.com.au

A catalogue record for this book is available from the National Library of Australia

All rights reserved. No part of this publication may be reproduced, stored in a retrieval system or transmitted in any form or by any means, electronic, mechanical, photocopying, recording or otherwise, without the prior written permission of the copyright holder.

Dedication

I dedicate this book to all those people who enjoy the escapism that is found in science fiction. To all those who like to think outside the box and are not afraid to expand their horizons in all directions. This story is for you to enjoy, a spicy journey of fantasy and imagination. Please come along and join me on this crazy trip.

Prologue

Great, what now?

As the cloud of red dust settled, I looked up to get my bearings. Glancing around at the sparse, silver-green scrub, I noticed that there was a small, rusty road sign partially hidden by a mulga tree with a dirt road next it. Many on the highway would not even notice the inconspicuous sign pointing to Poison Valley Road, but it drew me in; I had heard that name before. Below that, it read, *Taxi: 30 miles.*

Taxi?

I checked my GPS, but there was no sign of a town by that name on the screen.

Weird.

Next, I googled it, but there was nothing about a town near here called Taxi online, either. Poison Valley Road was there, but no Taxi.

I had to know more. Was this the kind of place I had been searching for? I recalled the dream that had haunted me the last few nights.

* * *

She floated a few feet off the ground: a stunningly naked woman with golden skin that seemed to constantly swirl, as if it were alive and independent from the rest of her body. Her face was unclear, but her arms were outstretched and beckoning to me.

"Come back to me, my eternal love," she begged.

* * *

I refocused my eyes and peered down the long, shimmering highway; mirages featuring pools of water appeared to float across the blacktop. My gaze flickered to the little sign pointing to Taxi. My brain insisted I continue straight ahead, but my heart demanded I turn.

She is here.

Taxi already had me hooked.

1

A Town Called Taxi

I love an Aussie road trip, and I have had a few. This time, I wanted to do something different: something off the beaten track, deep in the outback, west of nowhere. I was searching for my next story. The first step was finding a town that no one goes to and getting in touch with the local vibe to try and understand why the people there lived so remotely. Australia fascinated me; it was so diverse in so many ways, yet comforting and homely, too.

In my youth, I had done the whole east coast thing: searching for the perfect wave to surf or the perfect girl to spend a night with. Then I explored the spectacular Nullarbor Plain and the west coast. From Cactus to Esperance, then up the west coast all the way to the Kimberley and the Pilbara, our land is amazing and so beautiful. I felt blessed to embark on that trek for myself. I learned much along the way: breakdowns and other vehicle troubles, blurry one-night stands and women with sadness in their eyes that I could not help. I learned more about myself, too. I also learned how to write—not like somebody famous or anything, but I got through and sold a few short stories to magazines and newspapers. I found that the best way to find a story was to get out there, experience life, and then put it down.

I was a loner for most of my early years. It was something that I grew used to since I had a single mum who had no time for a boy born out of love. I would sit on the cracked wooden floor at the age of four with nothing but a dirty teddy bear. I had to invent adventures to keep myself busy. So, Ted and I were fearless champions. My imagination was endless. There were many places to go, and so many things to do.

My mother never showed me much affection because I reminded her too much of my father. She stayed out late and forgot to feed me, so I would help myself to whatever I could find in the nearly empty fridge or the cupboards that were more often than not bare. Ted and I would share stale bread and eat vegemite straight out of the jar. Sometimes I got sick from eating it and Mum would get angry, yelling and throwing stuff. We would hide away, but she always found us, and then I would get in real trouble and locked in my room. One day, she was so angry that she tried to take my teddy away and grabbed his little arm. She yanked it completely off, and his inner stuffing flew everywhere. I was terrified, and poor Ted had only one arm from then on; his stuffing often fell out, but I always tried to push it back in. That made me stronger, and helped me learn to accept pain, to deal with it and live with uncertainty. For so long that little teddy was my only friend; he was my home when nothing else was.

Mum's negligence instilled in me a sense of survival, an awareness of danger, and a way to live in a world where everyone was out to get you—or a piece of you at least. However, she also showed me the frailty of life, how everything could be ripped apart and torn from you in an instant. This proved to be an invaluable lesson, one that was hard to define and that took me some time to internalize.

I headed north along the Bruce Highway in Queensland all on my own. The brilliantly blue Coral Sea was on my right. The ocean smells filled my nostrils. It was the middle of June and quite mild in the tropics, which meant cooler nights and milder days with not a cloud in the deep blue sky: perfect for traveling.

I arrived in Townsville, and after a hearty burger from a truck stop, I headed north a bit and found a free park just off the highway next to Bluewater Creek. I found a nice, shady spot to roll out my swag and sat down to check my old, crusty maps.

Time to head inland.

I would have to go back toward town, then get on the Ring Road, and then on the Flinders Highway to Charters Towers, and from there head straight on through. A place out there was calling me.

I had been on the road for hours, so I decided to take a short nap. I lay back in the shade of an old gum tree; a eucalyptus breeze rustled the leaves above me. I closed my eyes and fell asleep within seconds.

* * *

I could feel her love. She was pulling me along, dragging me to her. Her golden skin seemed alive and shimmering, and her big, emerald eyes glowed like inviting pools.

"Find me, Danny. I need you again. This life has been empty without you."

I could feel her electricity drawing me in like a magnet. She floated a few feet off the ground, stunningly naked; her arms were outstretched, begging me to hold her once more. I stumbled and she was gone.

* * *

I suddenly woke up. I'd had this weird dream before, but I remembered it clearly this time. She seemed familiar, but out of focus; she felt so real.

Who was she? I don't know her.

I quickly packed up my gear and headed west. Two hours later, I pulled up to Waverly Hotel in Charters Towers.

Next door I entered was a beautiful, turn-of-the-century Aussie pub and said to the barman, "Schooner of Great Northern. Thanks."

"No worries, mate," he replied as I picked up a menu off the counter and scanned it for something simple. Before I knew it, he set the beer down. "Here you are."

I swiped my card, ordered battered mackerel and chips, and paid for everything.

"No worries, champ," he said, and then disappeared out to the kitchen. About thirty minutes later, he brought out my steaming hot fish and chips and placed a bottle of tomato sauce on my table. "There you go."

"Thanks, buddy." I glanced up at the flat-screen TV that hung above the bar; Aussie rules football was playing.

I never could play football very well. I never seemed to fit in. My teenage years were tumultuous, and I always carried the feeling of not belonging, of not being comfortable with who I was. I was a façade, a fake, and when all the other guys started dating, I was left out. I felt that the girl for me was out there, but never where I was. She was far away, so far that I feared I may never find her. But she was there, and she was looking for me, too. Somehow, I was certain that we knew of each other's yearning.

I eventually fell in love with a girl, Janet, and she loved me, too. We got engaged, and she was everything at the time, but not *that* girl: the one who was searching for me. No, there was someone else; I could feel it. Maybe my golden girl. Nonetheless, Janet and I were married a year and a half later, and within two years, little Robbie was born. We were a happy little family, but nothing lasts forever.

I downed another ice-cold beer and then jumped back into my truck and headed southwest. An hour a half later my Triton suddenly came to a standstill, I looked up and noticed the small sign. Poison Valley Road. Taxi.

Here. Turn here.

My truck started straight away so I turned off the highway and soon rounded a bend, startling a large flock of white cockatoos that screeched at me angrily as they took off in a sea of white and yellow and a cacophony of earsplitting noise. Flying off in every direction, they alerted other native animals to my intrusion on their territory.

About six miles later, I came to an old, high fence topped with rusty barbed wire that was mostly obscured by dense scrub. The fence stretched out on either side of the track and into the distance. It had massive gates that were wide open. I noticed a security camera, high up on a pole as I entered.

Who's watching me?

Why such big gates out in the middle of nowhere? Is that to keep people out, or something else in?

The road could barely be considered as much; the corrugated surface made the sound of my tires passing over it more like a drum beat. It couldn't have been used often, given its state of disrepair, but once I was on it, I felt there was no turning back. The foul stench of death filled my nostrils, a familiar smell on outback roads. On either side of the track, kangaroo and emu carcasses rotting under the midday sun were covered in hungry blowflies fighting over the spoiled flesh.

I felt drawn in for some reason, and my tension grew with every mile I traveled, wondering if the little sign was right and that this was indeed the road to Taxi.

My truck was having issues; it was five years old, but running well until that turn onto Poison Valley Road. Then it started playing up, and seemed to be overheating and losing power. I needed to stop, or carry on and risk permanent damage.

Eventually, the road became asphalt again, and I was relieved when I saw a gas station just inside the town limits of Taxi.

2
Bart's Truck Stop

Bart's Truck Stop
Stay a while, and we will look after you! You are everything to us.
Taxi: Home of Taxidermy in North Queensland!

The sign over the station baffled me—who knew there would be a taxidermist way out in the middle of nowhere—but my tank was getting low, so I thought it would be a good opportunity to fill it up. I turned off my truck and scanned the parking lot. It seemed so desolate and rundown with only one other filthy car out front. An old Slim Dusty song played over the rusty speakers as the pump slowly filled my tank. I put the nozzle back and headed inside to pay. Opening the creaky door, I was confronted by an unusual smell. Suddenly, a huge barn owl spread its wings directly in front of me, and I ducked instinctively.

A sweaty, domineering, old man sitting behind the counter snorted gruffly and slowly stood, scratching his stubble and nodding. "Heh, gets 'em every time."

I took a closer look at the bird and straightened back up when I saw the bird was stuffed and tried not to be embarrassed. The man took a stained, white-and-black rag from his pocket and wiped dust from the counter as he peered at me through round, thick, smudged glasses that sat crookedly on his hairy, bulbous nose.

I could not put my finger on it, but this place gave me the creeps. I peeked into the attached diner I'd just noticed and saw a few people sitting down with food in front of them and steam rising from their coffee mugs. The light from the afternoon sun streamed through the narrow blinds, illuminating the suspended dust particles and making it hard to distinguish anyone else's features.

"Howdy, traveler, how you doin'? I'm Bart," the man growled at me.

Apart from the music playing in there, it seemed deathly quiet; an eerie silence surrounded the occupants of the diner.

Bart rang me up for the gas. "That will be ninety-five dollars. Anything else strike your fancy? Where are you staying? Gertie has a nice place down River Road that will suit your needs: Gertie's Bed and Breakfast."

"Who, said anything about staying?" I asked.

"Oh, I can tell the stayers from the goers. You're a stayer," he replied, staring into my soul.

"Right, okay, then. I'll see you around," I answered.

"That you will," he replied with a creepy grin before motioning to the people in the diner. "I'll be right with you folks."

Funny—I didn't hear any of them ask for anything.

The patrons' faces were still obscured by sunlight beaming through the blinds, but I swore they hadn't moved since I walked in. Was that a spiderweb stretching from one guy's shoulder to the table? Surely not. They creeped me out; they had to be mannequins, but if that was the case, why did they have hot coffee?

As I left, Bart called out in a menacing tone, "Welcome to Taxi!"

There were no taxis in Taxi, and as I drove down Main Street it became apparent that life there was slow. The locals sitting outside some of the quaint little shops were watching the sun go down behind the distant mountains, staring off into the distance. I supposed I needed to stay the night since the next town could be miles away. Reluctantly, I took Bart's advice and headed down River Road to find Gertie's. The drive was eerily quiet as the shadows stretched out and the sun turned everything a reddish hue. I didn't pass a single car and had to wonder if everyone was just having dinner at the same time or something. I was hungry myself, and hoped my destination had some food.

Opposite a bend in the river, I could see Gertie's. I was more than slightly impressed by the homely, turn-of-the-century dwelling that may have once been a hostel or a hospital. From the outside, it was clearly well-kept and tidy. It had a commanding view of the broad river, a few cars parked out front, and lights on inside. As soon as I came to a stop, I clambered out of my dusty truck and grabbed my bags.

I could smell food, which just ramped up my hunger to the point that I felt as if I could already taste the food and licked my lips in anticipation. I was about to ring the doorbell when I noticed a small sign that read, *Beware of Gertie*. Confused, I rang the bell anyway. I opened the front door and was immediately confronted by a huge emu. It had to have been six feet tall, and was glaring at me menacingly. I stopped in my tracks, petrified and gasped.

"I see you've met Gertie," a warm voice called from within.

Beyond the sentry at the door, I could see the walls of the hallway were lined with all manner of stuffed creatures: snakes, fish, an owl, an eagle, the head of a water buffalo, a cat, and two dogs.

Wow, these people must love their taxidermy.

"Quite a collection you h-have here," I stammered. "Hi, I'm Daniel Starr. I'm looking for a room for the night. Just me—I'm traveling alone."

"Hi, I am Betty. This is my place…oh, and Gertie's. Come on through to the office and we will find you a spot. Are you hungry?" Betty bustled out from what must have been the kitchen, wiping her hands on her apron.

"Yes, please," I shook her soft hand briefly, but all I could feel was pain. My rheumatoid arthritis was acting up, and I feared that soon it would take over and my very soul would scream in agony. "Your cooking smells great. What's on?"

"Kangaroo stew: one of my favourites," Betty said, staring at me as if she was going say something else.

"Sounds great. I've never had 'Roo.'"

"I'm sorry, but do I know you?" Betty bluntly asked.

"Er, no I don't think I have ever met you before, and I've never been out this way, either. Pretty sure I'd remember that charming smile of yours."

I smiled at her, but she looked down at her computer screen and pressed some buttons.

"Sorry, you just kind of look like someone I used to know." She quickly changed the subject. "Yes, 'Roo is one of those meats that is considered roadkill in the outback. You must get over that *death* thing and cook it correctly if you want to get the true flavors of the meat. It's quite gamy and lean."

The fantastic stuffed animals in the hallway came to mind, as well as that owl and those folks in the diner. I had never seen such realism; they were amazing recreations of their living selves. Getting over death could be hard. After all, how long had it been since my own life changed beyond recognition? Seven years, and yet it felt like only yesterday. The loss cut so deep when they passed. I doubted I'd ever just get over it.

"Can I take it to my room? I am tired and need some rest."

"Sure, I will bring it over. Would you like a bottle of Shiraz? That goes great with 'Roo." She handed me a key. "The rooms are out by the car park on your left."

"Yes, that sounds great, thanks Betty."

Do I know you?

Betty seemed vaguely familiar to me, as if I had met her before, but I doubted it. I was probably just exhausted—dead tired, even. I headed out toward my room, my head swimming with so many emotions.

I checked the number on the key in my hand and kept walking until I came to my room: lucky number seven. By then, memories I usually tried to keep buried flooded my thoughts, and tears flowed down my cheeks. We never forget tragedy, I realized. It followed us like shadows. We tried to shrug it off, but we couldn't. It embraced us until it *became* us.

Before long, there was a tap on my door. "Hey, it's Betty. I have your dinner."

I opened my door and found Betty balancing a huge tray filled with a beautiful, home-cooked meal. The aromas that filled my nostrils making my mouth water. "That looks amazing and smells great! Thank you, Betty."

"No problem—enjoy! You can leave the tray outside your door, and I will swing by later and collect it. Please fill in your breakfast form, too."

"Thank you, Betty."

She grinned and walked off; I watched her for a few moments, then shut my door.

Famished, I sat down at the small table in my room, opened the wine, poured a healthy glass, and took a sip. I pulled the plate close and took in the big chunks of meat, potatoes, carrots, pumpkin, and peas, all in a thick, dark gravy with a hunk of buttered, crusty bread. I dove in and was not disappointed, it was delicious; Betty was a great cook. The kangaroo was so tender it melted away as I chewed it.

When I'd eaten the whole lot and finished off the wine, I was fully satisfied and ready for bed. It had been a long day. I undressed and climbed into the double bed, which was soft and comfy and smelled of fabric softener. My watch stated that it was only seven-thirty.

It was so quiet—almost too quiet. The whole town must've been asleep. In the city, I was always bombarded with all kinds of activity.

As I started to drift off, I heard the faint rumble of a truck—no, two trucks slowly approaching the bend out front. I opened my eyes and looked toward the window, expecting to see headlights bouncing off the trees, but there was only the dull glow of moonlight. The sound grew louder, as if they were right out front, but still no lights. Jumping up, I raced over to the window and pulled the thin curtain aside. The road was dark; none of the streetlights were on, but in the glow of the moonlight, I saw two identical white trucks with no markings and no lights slowly making their way toward town. Once they were out of sight, I went back to bed.

Lying there with my eyes open, I wondered what was going on in this quiet little town. It was probably nothing, but it still seemed a bit odd. Something felt off, but I could not put my finger on what that was, and I got the distinct impression that I would have to be very careful as to how I investigated it.

* * *

I was in the car with them; we were driving down the road where it happened.

I knew what was coming, but I could do nothing. I was screaming on the inside, but nothing came out of my mouth.

She smiled at me just as he came around the bend on the wrong side of the road and hit us head-on, spinning us, flipping us over. We slid into a massive eucalyptus tree, crushing the roof. The car burst into flames; we were already dead, but I could still see everything.

* * *

I woke up in a cold sweat and sat straight up. It was four o'clock in the morning,

I heard the trucks again. When I looked outside, I noticed that this time, they were heading the other way: out of town. But, just like before, their lights were off and the drivers maneuvered slowly and stealthily.

It took me a while to get back to sleep after that, but once I did, I did not wake until the sweet smell of bacon wafted from Betty's kitchen.

3
The First Day

"Knock, knock!" Betty sang outside my door at eight o'clock that next morning—the exact time I had written on my form Luckily, I'd already had my morning shower and dressed.

"Good morning, Betty." I beamed as I opened the door.

There she stood, the sun behind her creating a golden halo around her. She was a delightful, almost ghostly apparition in a flowery dress with a tray full of delights. My golden girl dream from yesterday suddenly flashed through my mind, but then it was gone.

"Good morning, Daniel. Hope you had a good sleep." The smell of bacon and eggs filled my nostrils, but as Betty moved closer, her perfume wafted over me. She smelled like a field of summer flowers, yet also spicy and inviting. "How was dinner last night?"

"Yes, it was amazing. You should be on *MasterChef*! Now, what is this? Here, let me take that; it looks heavy."

And it was. I lifted the tray and took in one of my favorites: an English breakfast, complete with a mountain of bacon, scrambled eggs, baked beans, sausage, sautéed mushrooms, fried potatoes with green onions, and a huge fried tomato with cheese. A glass of freshly squeezed orange juice and a black, steaming coffee were also there for me to wash it all down with.

"Enjoy!" she said, and I just knew I would.

"Thanks again!" I started to take the tray into my room, eager to tuck in, but paused. "Oh, Betty, I decided to stay a few more days. Is that okay?"

"Of course, Daniel. I had a feeling you would; this little town has a lot to offer. Have a look at the brochure on the side table. Oh, and don't forget to fill out your dinner form for tonight. See you!" She waved and strode off.

I tried to remember if I'd seen a brochure the night before, but decided to look after breakfast; my food was going cold.

Betty's cooking reminded me of a trip I took to England twenty years ago, during which I stayed at a small bed and breakfast in Colchester: Joan's B&B. Those people went above and beyond expectations. Joan would greet us every evening with, "How was London, dears? I've run a nice, hot bath for you, love. Your dinner will be ready when you've finished." Dinner was always this unreal, home-cooked perfection, and I could tell that Betty was just as passionate about cooking as Joan was. I could feel her love in every mouthful. I hadn't had a breakfast like that in years, but thought to myself that I could eat her cooking for the rest of my life.

I snuck outside for a quick cigarette—why, I had no idea. I'd quit months earlier, and I didn't even enjoy it then. Lightheaded, I went back inside to find this brochure Betty spoke of.

I opened the drawer of the side table and found what appeared to be a freshly printed document.

TAXI: OUR TOWN, YOUR TOWN.
The tours of the old gold and silver mines our forefathers worked have made our town famous! Ring this number to book: 555 495 101

Our biggest industry is taxidermy, hence our town name. We have one of the largest taxidermy facilities in the area; be sure to visit Taxi-Home-Museum, which houses one of the largest collections of taxidermy in the southern hemisphere, it is a true wonder. Everything on display is stuffed and available for immediate purchase, Ring this number to book: 555 495 102

We also have an exciting graveyard tour that is absolutely jam-packed with the fascinating history of our little town. Ring this number to book: 555 495 103

So, relax and enjoy all that Taxi has to offer—we are here for you!

The mines that supposedly made Taxi famous were not even on an online map, but I couldn't wait to go explore. Still, after what I saw the night before, I knew there was more to discover; the town's secrets would not be fully divulged at a taxidermy museum or even a graveyard tour. I'd have to dig in order to find the dirt.

I examined the simple map at the bottom of the page. I had to start somewhere, and the mines were at the top of the list. I rang the number and booked a tour for that same day that would begin in just an hour.

Arriving at the designated spot, I realized I was the only one on this tour. My guide, a redheaded Irishman, was dressed like a miner from the old days.

"Hi, I am Shaun," he said. "Welcome to our Gold and Silver Mines! Just be open minded and take part in this experience."

I was open, but now that I was there, I was also a bit dubious. What could possibly make these mines so special?

Shaun led me to an old, wooden building nestled against a large hill and unlocked a huge door with a silver key. It creaked loudly as he pushed it open. He entered and flicked a switch, illuminating about two hundred feet of an ominous-looking tunnel that stretched out before us. We headed in.

"1890 was a good time in this area. Gold and silver were being dug up in mines all over the place, and Taxi was no exception. A deep stream of silver was discovered in 1864, and everything changed—especially the locals. Folks killed each other over claims on the precious metal, and unrest churned among the indigenous populations. So many died, but they found more than just gold and silver."

"Wait, *what*?" I said. "What did they find?"

"Now, let's not get any further ahead of ourselves or I will get in trouble. All in good time," my guide assured me. "Come have a look in this tunnel; all the tools and equipment is exactly as they left it one hundred and thirty-six years ago."

"Why did they just leave it?" I questioned.

"Oh, there you go with all your questions; you are so smart! I will tell you everything eventually," he said with conviction.

I examined everything; my curiosity grew by the minute. It seemed to me that they just up and left one day without taking anything, even though some of these tools would have been expensive to replace. My questions multiplied, but I bit my lip. He had said he would get in trouble if he got ahead, but with whom?

"The silver was shipped out on these old tracks, and ours was a bustling town back then. People came from all over to work here, and we were a thriving community!" Shaun certainly had the enthusiasm of a tour guide who didn't often get the opportunity to do his thing. "Alright, let me tell you about the accident. It was the morning of the seventh day of July in 1892. Thirty men were down the southern shaft, or what is now the sealed shaft. Suddenly, one of the miners broke through a vent, and toxic gas and water soon filled the shaft. Twenty perished, while ten escaped only to die later from the poison. Back then, they couldn't retrieve the bodies, as they had no means of safely entering that contaminated shaft. It wasn't until late 1919 that they sent in a team in special underwater suits to retrieve the remains."

"Oh, wow! Is it still full of water?"

"Yes, apparently there is still some toxic water in there. The whole area around the southern shaft is completely closed off even now due to fears of contamination."

"Did they find any bones after twenty-seven years?"

"Yes, thankfully they found them all. They are now buried in our cemetery."

"Fascinating—I don't think I've never heard of this story before."

"Oh, I doubt ya would have," he said, brushing off my concern. "An accident like this is not something you advertise."

Actually, this is not something you downplay.

"Come, Daniel, here is the highlight of the tour."

He flicked a switch on the wall and pushed open a partition door. As more lights came on in the tunnel, I saw a glass divider, behind which there were no less than ten figures: miners posed and dressed to look as if they were hard at work. They had shovels and picks; some were bent over as if examining the rocks, a few appeared to be taking a break, and one was even having a nap.

"They all look so real! Someone went to a whole lot of trouble with these. Are they wax?"

Shaun glowed with pride, "Yes, and the artist even found some photos of the miners to copy." He pointed to photos hung near the display. "This is them outside the mine back in 1890."

"Most of them look quite young."

"Yes, they were—such a tragedy. It hit the town very hard. Many families left after that." To my surprise, he had a tear running down his cheek as he pushed open the door and then shut the light off." Come on, let's get some sunlight."

As we headed outside, I found myself looking forward to the cemetery tour even more.

"Thanks for the great tour, Shaun. See you around." I said as I turned to get in my car.

"See ya later Daniel."

I seemed to always be hungry, so I headed back into town for some lunch. It was only eleven-thirty in the morning, and I was only one of two cars on the quiet road. I found a spot called Bb and Kitty's Café. A bell above the door announced my arrival, but I paid more attention to how good it smelled in there: coffee, pastries, bacon, and eggs. I could almost taste it.

"We'll be right there!" a singsong voice called out. I scanned the menu, torn between eggs benedict, a steak sandwich, or battered fish and chips. In seconds, a server appeared. "Hi, traveler, how can we help you? I'm Bb and this is my daughter, Kitty."

"Er, hi. I'm Danny." I gestured at the menu. "Any recommendations?"

"Our club sandwich is outstanding," she boasted. Kitty nodded in agreement.

"Perfect, with some fries?"

"Absolutely. Chicken salt?"

"Yep, sounds perfect."

"Coffee?"

"Do you serve it iced? No cream?"

"Yes, no problem." they nodded, Bb headed to the kitchen, Kitty started on my coffee. I already loved this place. Bb and Kitty were delightful, and the perfect hosts. I looked forward to my meal as I sat and sorted out my thoughts and impressions of the town thus far.

There was whole lot going on in the background—stuff people weren't talking about—of that much, I was sure. I just couldn't put my finger on it. My mind raced, but everything else seemed to move in slow motion. Outside, the streets were deserted.

Is it me? Am I going crazy? What is this place? Where is everyone?

"Here is your iced coffee. Your club will be out shortly. We aim to please," Kitty said with a wink.

Corned beef, sauerkraut and Swiss cheese: the club sandwich was perfectly presented with top-quality ingredients. If this place was in a city, they would always be busy. I was so impressed that I was taken back in my memory to another time, in another place. We were in San Francisco; it was 2015, it was late around 11.30 pm we had driven from Las Vegas and we were starving. We entered a small diner across from our hotel. I ordered a club on rye. It was so good, and I could not wait to order it again.

"Bb and Kitty, thank you for that, it was delicious," I said as I finished up.

"We're glad you liked it," they chimed, smiling at me from behind the spotless counter as I left.

I jumped in my car, deciding to take a drive around town, which took less than five minutes. There was a grocery store, a butcher shop, a bakery, a newsstand, a general store, an old cinema that looked like it might have been closed, a funeral home, a doctor's practice and pharmacist, a tiny school, a sweet, little church, another fuel stop and mechanic's shop, two cafés, a haberdashery, a large corner pub called The Dermy Hotel and the most impressive Taxi-Home-Museum. The remainder of town was mostly rundown houses, and I saw a few locals on their porches, motionless under the afternoon sun. I passed a black van with dark windows; red letters on its side read, *TAXI+*, and the A floated in a drop of bright blue water. Soon, I came across a cluster of about a dozen immaculate houses that looked totally out of place in such a small town. I did notice there were hardly any signs, but a lot of trees; the little valley seemed very fertile for somewhere so far west.

The river that ran past Gertie's was about twenty feet across, but it appeared to be quite deep, and it flowed slowly over beautiful granite rocks and boulders. There was one small sign that pointed down River Road, past Gertie's, that said, *Airstrip: No Through Road*. I decided to have a look, but didn't get very far since the road was blocked off with road works signs and barriers. As I pulled up, I noticed a camera mounted on a tall pole that seemed to be tracking me as I approached. I backed up and made a three-point turn, knowing the camera still watched my every move.

Slowly I drove back to Gertie's, my mind working hard to digest Taxi's secrets. Just as I pulled up to Gertie's, a small jet flew overhead. Looking out my driver's side window and through the trees, I could see that it was a Citation XL, and that it was slowing down with its wheels out, ready to land.

Fancy little jet for a place like this. I bet it's owned by some rich bastard. or some big corporation, but what would they be doing out here?

It was just midafternoon, but I was getting weary; my poor bones were aching. People didn't often realize that rheumatoid arthritis affected your whole body. It was a constant battle, one that couldn't be won—just managed, barely.

Once I was back in my room, I stretched out on my bed for a power nap and drifted off almost immediately.

* * *

Sitting in rows, they stared: glass eyes, everyone neatly dressed. The movie played over and over, and nobody blinked. They sat staring in silence, they were perfect, their skin was perfect, but they could not breathe. They could only stare as I walked down the center aisle. I stopped halfway down, and as I did; they all turned their heads toward me. I saw that their glass eyes had been replaced with cotton, and their cotton eyes mocked me, repulsed me. I ran out, but as I passed a mirror, I stopped and looked. My own eyes were also gone, their sockets full of cotton. I screamed.

* * *

Jolting awake, I checked the time and realized that I had slept for nearly two hours, although it felt like it'd only been five minutes. I sat up and scratched my head. Dinner was at six-thirty, so I had two and a half hours to kill. I went out to my truck and grabbed the case on the back seat, then walked down the road to the park next to the river and sat on the first bench I saw and opened the case.

My Mavic Pro drone was neatly folded in its cradle. I took it out, unfolded its arms, flicked its switch, and placed it on the ground in front of me. Retrieving the controller, I placed my phone in its clamps and found the Mavic app. The 4K camera was working perfectly, but I did a few checks with the controls anyway. Then, I took it up about forty feet above the river. I had it slowly pan around and record my surroundings. This place was stunning. As far as I could see was untouched, bushland. The Torrens River disappeared between rolling hills, and in the distance, blue misty mountains loomed. I flew the drone out until I could see the barrier in the road, but stayed high enough to avoid being detected by that camera. I could not go much further, though, as soon my drone would be out of range, but I didn't see any actual construction going on. This didn't surprise me.

I glanced around to make sure no one was watching me, then let the drone hover as I stood up and casually walked about fifty feet down the riverbank. I sat again, keeping one eye on my case on the bench and the other on my screen. I had the drone fly higher and travel another thirty feet along the road.

In clearing the trees, I could see the airstrip, which looked well-kept and tidy. There were two small jets: the one I saw earlier and a larger cargo jet with four engines and a single engine turboprop. There was also one helicopter, and a large hangar had been built into the side of a hill. It stood next to a small control building and two other buildings that were partially hidden by trees. Further along the road, I saw three large, brick buildings; one had a high chimney with smoke billowing out. The two white trucks from the night before, which had piqued my curiosity about this town, were backed up to a loading bay alongside a few cars. They were mostly hidden by trees, so there could have been more. Moored to a small jetty nearby was a fancy, fifteen-foot cabin cruiser.

Deciding I ought to bring the drone back before I get caught, I pushed the home button; the drone spun around and came straight back to me within minutes. I picked it up, folded its arms in, and switched it off as I went back to where I left the case.

Back in my room, I poured some Jack Daniels in a cup, sat down at my little table, plugged my phone into my laptop, and uploaded the footage from the drone. I pushed play and went to full screen. The camera on the drone was great, not to mention very clear and stable. The river came into view, beautiful and crystal clear. The scrub was dense and green; I figured this area would be classified as subtropical.

When I thought about it, I realized that the roadwork signs were most likely meant as a deterrent for nosy people like me. But why would an airstrip and a factory be off-limits? I examined the jets and the runway on the screen. Even the helicopter was high-end. Among the ten cars, I noticed two black vans and what looked like a hearse. I turned my attention to the factory: three buildings, side by side, and one was a lot smaller than the others, all made of brick and quite old by the looks of them. What was cooking in that largest one with the chimney?

Then again, perhaps I was reading more into it than was actually there. Still, it had my imagination running, and I liked that.

I shut it all down and went to take a shower and shave before dinner. I decided I'd eat with Betty in the dining room that night. I dressed and poured another slug of whiskey. My thoughts were slowly settling down, and I reminded myself to be careful and to keep my ideas to myself and my ears open.

In the main entrance, I gave Gertie a light pat on the back. "Hi, Gertie."

"Hi, Daniel," Betty replied from down the hall.

"Hey, Betty. Hope I'm not too early."

"No, go on in and a grab a seat. Our two German guests are already seated."

"Okay, thanks," I replied, intrigued by the idea of German tourists. I went past all the amazing animals and entered the dining room. "Hello."

Two well-dressed men were already eating, but they looked up at my greeting and nodded.

"Hello, I am Eric. This man with his mouth full of steak is Gus," one of them said warmly and with a thick accent. "Gus does not know much English."

"I'm sorry for interrupting your meal—please carry on! I am Daniel. Mind if I join you?"

"Go ahead," he said as he shoved some steak into his own mouth and Gus nodded.

I sat as Betty came in with two more beers for Eric and Gus.

"Here you are, gentlemen. Everything alright?"

"Yes, thank you."

"Good, good. Daniel, what would you like to drink with your fish: wine or beer?"

"I will have a beer, too. Thanks!"

"Is Great Northern okay?"

"Yes, that will be fine. Thanks."

She returned with my beer in a flash, only to head right back out as she called over her shoulder, "Here you go, love. Your barra will be out in a few minutes."

"No worries, happy to wait. Your cooking could hold its own in a city restaurant."

"Thanks for saying so, Daniel."

The other two were eating like they were starving Vikings and gulping down the beer between mouthfuls, so I let them eat in peace and looked around the dining room. There was a lot to take in, and once again that included plenty of taxidermy. It was like sitting in a museum for dinner. Betty had some pieces that were like works of art, like the large owl swooping down on his next meal: a rabbit that would never get away from those talons. There was a dingo curled up in the corner on a mat as if he was sleeping peacefully near the fire. There on the mantel was a big, green tree frog posed as if it were launching itself off a branch, and a beautiful Lyrebird with its plumage on display.

Betty came in with my fillet of barramundi with crispy skin, a pile of crunchy chips, and a fresh salad.

"Looks and smells great, Betty!"

"Thank you, dear. Can I get you gentlemen anything else? Some dessert?"

They had just finished their meals and were downing the last of their beers.

"No, thank you. You are a very good chef. We thoroughly enjoyed our meals and are quite full, so we will be off now." Eric said as he and Gus stood up. "*Danke.*"

"See you, and thank you," Betty replied.

The two well-dressed men left the room, chatting in German as they admired the animals in the hall. They went outside; Betty watched them from the door of dining room. I tucked into my food, and Betty left and then returned with a small plate of salad, some fish, and two more beers. She placed one in front of me and sat down on the other side of the table.

"Mind if I join you?"

"Go for it; chefs need to eat, too. The fish is delicious and perfectly cooked, and the chips and salad are all good, too!"

"Thanks, Daniel. How was your day?"

"I had a great day. Betty, why are you here? In Taxi, I mean. I know that sounds rude, but seriously! You could run a restaurant or motel in a big city with ease."

"Well, thank you, but really? I don't know. That is different."

"You are a great cook! Everything you have served me is worthy of five stars. You could set up shop in Sydney and be prosperous in no time. I know you could do it."

"Oh, you are so nice, but my place is right here. You don't get it yet since you just got here, but you will."

"I'm sorry. I didn't mean to offend you. It's just that, with your skills, you could make so much in Sydney or even Melbourne." I finished off the last of my dinner.

"It's not about the money. I love it out here; sure, it's a little weird sometimes, but like most country towns, it's also serene. I love it."

I realized I was staring at Betty while she talked about her hometown, so I quickly averted my eyes. In another place, or maybe in another time, I felt she could have been a big part of my life.

Don't go there. You are only passing through, and you are no Casanova.

It was true; at forty, I had very little to offer. My career was nearly dead and I had little in the way of savings.

When she was done, Betty stood up, took my empty plate, and scurried out the room. "Care to join me for a stiffer drink, Daniel? I could use one tonight." I heard her rummage through a cupboard down the hall before she evidently found what she was looking for. "Ah, here you are!"

I heard the rattle of glasses and her rushed steps before she bustled back into the dining room with two shot glasses and a bottle of Jack Daniels Old No.7. I was impressed.

She placed the glasses down and pulled a chair up close to mine. She poured and we drank. Another soon became another, and we chatted away about everything. She was funny and full of stories about local hijinks, so we laughed and laughed. I hadn't realized how much I really needed that until we finished the whole bottle. And I realized that less than forty-five minutes had passed.

"Excuse me for a second. I have to pee," she said dramatically, but with a laugh. "Be right back."

Soon, the toilet down the hall flushed, and after I heard more scrambled noises from the kitchen, Betty returned with another bottle and some pretzels, nuts, and sea salt chips. I laughed, thinking that she and I had more in common than our liquor preferences.

"More Jack?"

"When you say it like that, how can I refuse?" I said. I could've kissed her right then and there. I had been alone for seven years with only sadness and frequent nightmares as companions. Betty's company was like a balm to my soul. "You have found my weak spot."

We laughed a whole lot more and ate tons of nuts and chips before the topic of conversation got serious.

"So, I noticed you aren't wearing a wedding ring, but you've got a tan line where it once was."

I knew those questions had to be coming, but that didn't make them any easier to answer.

"I was married for fifteen years. Seven years ago, my wife was on her way home with our son Robbie in the back seat of the car. This drunk guy came around the corner too fast and on the wrong side of the r-road," I stammered. My eyes were full of tears. I could see it all playing out again as I blinked. I took another shot before continuing. "The car flipped over, slid across the r-road, hit a tree, and burst into flames. No one could help, no hope for t-them."

"I am so very sorry, and I swear I didn't mean to upset you by asking."

Regret was plain as day in her eyes as a tear ran down her cheek. I was instantly sorry that I had shared my past. I hardly knew Betty, but now there was no going back.

"I'm sorry, too. I don't usually share so much. I have tried to overcome my loss, but it is hard; they were everything to me. It's okay, though. Don't fret about me. I will be fine."

Betty looked into my eyes. "My heart goes out to you. Give us a hug, please."

Her arms stretched as wide as they could possibly go. How could I not give her a hug? She was so very warm; I could feel her heart beating against my chest, and she smelled of a dozen different flowers and spices, but somehow, they all blended well together. That moment lasted forever, but in reality it was only maybe a minute. In that instant, it was as if I had always known her. Something good stirred inside me.

"Thank you, Betty. You are so sweet, and you make me feel safe."

"You are more than welcome. You poor thing! Please accept my condolences and know that I will always have an open ear for you. If I can help, I will; even if it's just another hug."

I found it hard to let go; Betty felt so good in my arms. She had a warmth that I had forgotten. But, eventually, we awkwardly parted.

"I had better get going. Thanks for the JD; I owe you one."

"That's okay, it was my treat tonight. Thanks for your company."

I stood slowly and looked down at her; she seemed so vulnerable, but I needed to go. "Good night, Betty. I appreciate your honesty and humor.

We should do this again."

She looked up, teary and clearly doubtful. I, too, felt doubtful and sad. She had a beautiful soul; it only took me one day to realize that.

"See you tomorrow, Danny."

"Yes, Bett, mind if I call you that? I'll see you at eight for bacon and eggs. Hash browns, too?" I asked hopefully.

"Sure, love, most of my friends call me Bett, I'll see you then!" She smiled warmly at me.

I headed off to my room, berating myself the whole way. Why did I talk about them? Probably because I missed them so much. I couldn't help myself, and Betty was so easy to talk to.

I could still smell her sweet perfume on me. Who was this woman. She was so down-to-earth: an old soul, wise and somehow familiar. As I undressed and climbed into bed, my thoughts lingered on Betty, and I drifted off to sleep.

* * *

I heard laughter and saw my golden girl up ahead, running naked into the water, her arms in the air as she jumped and spun around like a ballerina. She called for me to join her.

"Come on, wuss!"

"I hardly know you."

And yet, I took off my clothes and dove into the cool water.

"Come on over here, my Danny boy. Give yourself totally to me."

4
Day Two

Slow: everything about Taxi was slow. I waited and waited, but the internet connection was lousy. I gave up, and tried ringing for the museum tour but the phone rang out so I tried ringing for the cemetery tour, which I booked for nine-thirty that morning. I showered and dressed and headed off to breakfast. The two German dudes were just leaving.

"Hi, Betty," I called as I patted Gertie.

"Good morning, Daniel!" she called from the kitchen.

The luscious smell of bacon and fresh coffee filled the hall. I went into the empty dining room and sat in the same chair I occupied last night. Within a minute, Betty entered the room with a tray of food and two cups of coffee. She carefully put it all on the side table and placed my plate in front of me. I could feel her eyes peering at me through her slightly messy hair.

"How did you sleep? Do you have a hangover?"

She was glowing and her smile was so sweet.

"I slept like a baby, and no, my head is all good. I *am* hungry, though, and this looks amazing. How about you?"

"Here's your coffee, love. Just so you know, I don't usually drink alcohol with my customers, or even that much. I had a good sleep, too, and a couple of Panadol when I woke, so I'm all good now." She winked and sat down with her coffee. "Where are you off to today?"

"I'm going on the cemetery tour, then I'll check out Taxi-Home-Museum. These eggs are seriously good! So light and fluffy, yet so creamy," I said as I stuffed more eggs into my mouth.

Betty smiled at me over the top of her mug. "Are you coming back for lunch, dinner, or both?"

"Only dinner, I reckon. I might drive up into the hills out west for a bit of sightseeing. You know, tourist stuff."

"That sounds nice. There is a lookout up there, and on a clear day you can see all around for miles. I kind of wish I could tag along, but today is all booked up with motel stuff: cleaning rooms and a lot of cooking."

"Maybe we could go for a drive some other day, when you are not so busy," I suggested.

"Thanks, Daniel, I will hold you to that."

With that, she stood up, gently rubbed my shoulder, and breezed out of the room. I was flattered; no woman had shown me any interest in years. I couldn't stay much longer, but I was falling for her charm. She deserved more than just a fling or a one-night stand. My mind was churning, just as my mouth was churning. I took another sip of coffee and mentally berated myself for jumping the gun. She only wanted to go for a little drive. She was probably just as lonely as me.

When I was full, I finished off my coffee, I decided to take my dirty plates to the kitchen. Betty was standing on the other side of the room, looking out the window as she talked quietly on the phone. I cleared my throat so as not to startle her, but I did anyway.

She whirled around and said to whomever was on the phone, "Just a second." To me, she added, "Oh, thank you. Just put them there. Such a gentleman!"

I put them down, waved, and mouthed my apologies. She smiled at me and turned back to the window, and I saw her smile disappear as she did. I left as quickly as I could, embarrassed.

The cemetery was a short drive out of town to the east. I could see only one other car there and figured it must have belonged to the guide. It was a big cemetery for such a small town, and it looked old, but well-kept. An older gentleman approached me through the rows of tombstones, his mop of gray hair and his long, gray beard standing out like a beacon. In his hand, he held a large, straw hat and some papers.

"Hello, you must be Daniel," he called as I retrieved my Akubra hat from my back seat.

"Hi, yes. Pleased to meet you."

"My name is Paddy, and I'll be your tour guide," he said with great pride.

We shook hands and proceeded through the gates, both of us donning our hats since the sun was already quite warm. Paddy started his spiel; he must have done this a thousand times.

"This cemetery opened in 1870 with just two graves: that of Abby and Norman Hood, just here on your left. They were killed when the horses pulling their buggy were startled by a snake and ran straight off the Hood Cliff, which was named after them posthumous. Our cemetery has grown steadily bigger ever since that day. Here we have a section of miners: thirty-eight graves, including eight wives who died before or after their husbands—very sad."

I took my time while Paddy sat on a bench and let me look at all the headstones. Some of the plots had small bunches of fresh flowers.

I slowly walked over and sat down next to Paddy.

"Gee, half of them were only teenagers," I said hopelessly.

"Yes, that is correct. Sixteen were younger than twenty, and the youngest of them all was only fourteen. Did you see them at the mine? Seven of the young ones are in that display, very clever how they did that."

"Yes, I did see them, that display is very well done." Paddy stood up and motioned for me to follow him, "Let's go see the bushrangers. When you have gold and silver changing hands, you're going to have outlaws. They decided way back then to keep them separate from the good folks even in death." We came to a low fence with a rusty gate. Twelve plain crosses with names scratched into them stuck up from the ground. "We had these cement plaques added later with more information for their descendants. The crosses are cement copies of the original wooden ones."

"Who's this guy?" I asked, pointing at the last one, which bore the name Johnathon Starr.

"Oh, he's a bad one: gunned down by seven troopers after four stagecoach holdups and the murder of five innocent souls. They never found his loot. All their stories are similar, really."

"Mind if I take a photo for research?" I was fascinated.

"Go right ahead."

I took a couple of shots, and we moved out of the bushranger's area to one behind a wire fence.

"These are the indigenous plots. Back in the day, they had to be separated from everyone else to pacify the racists," he said matter-of-factly.

"A lot of graves in there," I said without meaning to.

"Yeah, they never got any medical help from the white folks who brought in some of the diseases and sickness and alcohol in the first place. We pretty much wiped out the whole local population in this area in just a few decades."

"That is terrible."

"The black fellas called it white man's curse." Paddy led me to another section of the cemetery. "This over here is the ashes wall, all the folks who get cremated go here. Seems to be the trend lately."

The wall was about six feet high and curved around in a half circle that was at least thirty feet across and had rows and rows of small plaques on both sides: hundreds of them.

"*Wow*. There are heaps of people here. Well, their ashes at least. Where is the crematorium?" I asked.

"Oh, it's down at the end of River Road." He added, "It's not open to the public, as all the funeral services are held in town."

"Oh, I went down that road the other day, but it was closed off for construction. I wanted to have a look at the airstrip," I said, hoping to get more out of him.

"You can't do that; it's owned by the mining corporation. They basically own this town."

That the jets, the chopper, and the boat were all likely owned by the mining company made sense, but if the mines were closed, why was the mining company still so influential?

"Who owns the crematorium?"

"Who do you think?" he asked.

"The mining corporation? Who exactly are they?"

"If I told you that, Daniel, I'd have to kill you." He stared me down with a menacing look, then roared with laughter and carried on for ages. I, on the other hand, was not amused. "Come on, there is more to show you. You need to see the mausoleum and the crypts."

"Wait, *what*? There's a mausoleum? Really?"

He looked at me as if I was stupid. "Of course there is."

Why the hell not? You're full of surprises, Taxi.

He led me down a winding path through a grove of trees. An old ornate building loomed ahead, surrounded by smaller, individual crypts.

"This is amazing! Can we look inside?"

"Unfortunately, we cannot enter without the consent of the relatives of those who are interned here. There are four generations and three separate families in here, each with their own crypts within."

I was fascinated; it was such a big, beautiful structure. I would have loved to see inside.

"And over here we have twenty smaller crypts, all owned by locals. Some are named, but others preferred to remain anonymous. Most are sealed, but some are only locked due to the circumstances of entombment."

I looked at him. "What does that mean?"

"If the casket is sealed correctly, it can be viewed by family. It has a lot do with our water. If it's not, the whole tomb has to be sealed off. Otherwise, it would get quite stinky around here."

"Oh, I didn't think of that." *A lot to do with their water?* I let it go.

"Well, that is about it. I thank you for coming on this journey of enlightenment and allowing me to share some of Taxi's history with you. It has been a pleasure," Paddy said as he held out his hand.

I shook it enthusiastically. "No, thank *you*! That was great; you know so much about Taxi's past." I glanced down at my watch; surprisingly, I had been there for more than three hours. "Wow, time flies! Paddy, it has been a pleasure spending this time with you."

"Good luck, Daniel! Do the right thing and you will be okay. She will be good for you. See you around!" He turned away before I could reply, walking between the graves.

How did this random man know about my already complicated feelings about Betty? It was a small town, but really, how much did people talk?

I had so many more pressing questions, though. These tours had opened Pandora's box, and it felt as if it could not ever be closed. I had a whole lot more research ahead of me, but I was looking forward to it.

By one o'clock, my stomach was growling. I headed back to town to try Shazza's Café. There were no cars along Main Street, as had been the case since I got to Taxi. I came to a narrow shop front, next to a beautiful little raised Queenslander home with an immaculate flower filled garden. I parked and clambered out, not bothering to lock the car. Why would I? My nostrils suddenly filled with sweet perfume from the flowers. I stopped and took it all in as it suddenly reminded me of Betty.

Glancing around, I noted at least three CCTV cameras mounted nearby on this street. I went in, and the quintessential bell above the door alerted anyone inside to my arrival. It was a nice café, with booths along the wall in a sort of fifties design and some quiet jazz playing in the background.

"Hello, traveler!" a sweet voice called from the back.

Traveler?

"Hi!" I called, leaving that question for another day.

She came flying in. Customers must have been a rarity, and she was eager to please. Immaculate in a rock and roll dress that looked like it'd come straight out of the 1950s, a silk hibiscus in her perfectly coiffed hair, long lashes, and red lipstick, I felt as if she had stepped out of a time machine.

"Hi, Daniel! I'm Sharon, but you can call me Shazza. Welcome to my little café. Here is our menu. We don't have a lot, but what we do have is really good. Can I get you something to drink?"

"A cup of Earl Grey would be good, for starters," I said, looking down at the menu. "Oh, and a house burger with chips. That would be grand."

"Okay, no probs," she said before she left to put in my order.

A younger lass soon came by with a glass of water; I assumed she was Sharon's daughter. Three minutes later, smiling broadly she brought over a cup of steaming Earl Grey.

It occurred to me then that Sharon knew my name even though I didn't give it. Did they broadcast my arrival or something? *New guy in town! The traveler, Daniel: watch out, he's a wise guy!*

At this point, I wouldn't rule it out. This place was slightly off, but I couldn't work out why. In fact, Sharon's daughter was the first young person I had seen in Taxi.

I looked around while I waited for my food. There were a few knick-knacks for sale over to one side and a few small bunches of fresh flowers that must have come from her garden next door. There was a refrigerator with a glass door that contained what looked like homemade jams, sauces, and a few cakes.

"Here's your burger and fries. Can I get you anything else?" Shazza asked as she put a plate down in front of me.

"I wouldn't mind a beer if you have any."

"Of course we do! Is Great Northern, okay?"

"Yes, that would be great," I replied.

Once again, I was impressed by the food in this town. *Immaculate*. Could a mere burger be that? It had everything a true Aussie burger should have: a runny egg, beetroot, bacon, pineapple, lettuce, a thick slice of tomato, a chunky, beef patty, sauce oozing out slightly, and a bit of mayo. This was seriously my dream burger. Sharon's chips were on par with the best: twice-cooked in some delicious kind of oil and so very crunchy. They seemed to have the best cooks out there, and the best ingredients. How was that?

I finished up with lunch and felt totally satisfied, as I had been with every single meal I'd had there. Betty, BB, Kitty, and Shazza all cooked better than anyone else in Outback Queensland.

"Thanks, that was delicious—very nice."

"Oh, my pleasure, Daniel. Please enjoy your stay here in Taxi. We always welcome new travelers; our town is small, but our hearts are big and our skin is thick."

"Er, okay. Is that a saying out here or something?" I asked.

"Well, we do all have thick skin, yes, yes, we do. Our water makes the difference—yes, sir."

"Okay, not too sure what you mean, but your food was excellent. Thank you. See you."

"Oh, yes, I will see you again, Daniel. Bye, now!" she said with such certainty it was hard not to believe her.

Her food might have been amazing, but I wasn't so sure about her mind. What was she on about? Thick skin and water? What did that have to do with anything? I went out to my car and sat for a while, trying to digest that conversation. Our thick skin, our water: I'd heard something about the water before somewhere, so I figured I needed to find out more about that.

In the meantime, I could feel a food coma coming on. Perhaps a nap when I arrive back at Gertie's was in order.

You old bastard.

* * *

The water filled my lungs. It was killing me, but it was much more than that. What was it doing? My skin tightened and then relaxed. I was dying, but I felt like I would stay there forever. I was dead as a doornail, and yet I looked alive; people would be looking at me forever.

* * *

Once again, I awoke drenched in sweat. What was that about? These nightmares in the daytime didn't make much sense. It felt like a few seconds passed, but I fell asleep more than two hours earlier.

I needed some fresh air. I jumped in my truck with a bottled water, snack bars, a Coke, and an apple. Yeah, I was a regular survivalist. Hopefully there was no apocalypse coming anytime soon, because I would die within twenty-four hours for sure.

I headed out west, toward the hills, and forgot about the all-important Taxi-Home-Museum tour I was supposed to take. I wanted to see the countryside, and out there, at that time of year, it was beautiful. I took Poison Valley Road toward Torrens Creek, then went up to the lookout. Betty was right. A vista was spread out before me; our country was so beautiful, so full of color. The valleys below were beautiful and full of beauty with wildflowers all in bloom. The red soil contrasted with the green and silver scrub. Tall gums and eucalyptus trees were everywhere. The air was filled with the distinct smell, with many in full bloom with a wide diversity of color. In the distance a chorus of kookaburras sang their unique song. I wished Betty was there to share it with me.

Damn, do I? Yes, she seems special to me. I don't even get it, but it couldn't work between us. I'll be out of there soon…right? Damn it. Stop!

From where I stood, I could see the airstrip; it was far away, but I could see it. It was buzzing with activity. I retrieved my binoculars in time to watch a jet land, another being loaded with some kind of cargo, and trucks and cars were all over the place. What was going on? I cautioned myself not to get caught up in their politics or start kicking any hornet's nests, but maybe it was drugs. That's what it was—drug cartels disguised as mining corporations! A fake crematorium that is cooking Meth or growing marijuana in the mines under grow lights!

No, chill. This town isn't rife with drugs. These people seem so nice. So, what, then? And who is this mining corporation? Why do they still have interest in Taxi? Why so busy at the airstrip, what are they loading or unloading?

Taxi was one big, complicated riddle, and it shouldn't have been. It should have been a quiet, little town with no questions.

At two o'clock that afternoon, there was still enough time to swing by the Taxi-Home-Museum; it was open from nine in the morning to five in the afternoon. I jumped in my truck and headed back into town. As I pulled into the car park, I saw cameras mounted up high on the streetlights, watching me. At least, I felt as if they were.

I pushed open the door; the air was thick with something that smelled like incense, as if someone was trying to mask some other odor. The space was huge, brightly lit, and felt like a showroom from the early 1920s. There was a classy vibe to the way the taxidermy was displayed. With ornate Art Deco cabinets, Peacock feathers and fancy lamps. Two elderly people sat at the desk in front of me, quietly drinking tea and eating biscuits. They looked up and seemed slightly startled by my appearance.

"Hello," I said. "Mind if I have a look around?"

They looked at each other, then back to me, and the man stood up, "Er, hi, yes, of course. Welcome to Taxi-Home-Museum. This is one of the largest collections in the southern hemisphere—even bigger than the largest one in Western Australia. I am Rueben and this is Hanna, my wife of fifty years."

Hanna stood slowly. Her purple hair was stunning, and not a hair was out of place. She smelled like sweet roses and her voice sounded like velvet when she said, "Hello, traveler."

"Hi, I am Daniel. It's nice to meet you both. I tried to book a tour ahead of time, but I couldn't seem to get through. It's okay if I can't get a formal tour. This place looks amazing."

"I will come with you and explain a few things, so it won't really be a tour, just a bit of friendly banter," Rueben said.

I thought it was really cool that, even though he wasn't expecting me, he was willing to show me around. "Thanks, that'd be great."

I nodded to Hanna and smiled as Rueben walked off to the first stop on our informal tour. I quickly caught up and finally started to take in the majesty of the art form. It was something, especially when it was arranged like this. As far as I could see, there were creatures of every kind, all beautifully presented and frozen in glorious poses. I was in awe.

"This is fantastic. How many artists are responsible for all this?"

"Well, that is a hard question to answer. Many of these items are quite old. A few are new, but most are from before my time, made with love and dedication to the craft. We still have plenty of artists here now, but most of their work gets shipped out, so we don't get to see it."

Shipped out? To whom? Aloud, I said, "Old? They look like they were made yesterday."

We continued down the aisles, looking intently at all of the critters. They were so varied, and so beautiful. Birds, mammals, reptiles, fish, insects: they were all present, and there weren't just Australian breeds there. Animals from all over the world, big and small, had places on the shelves.

"Here are the hybrids: combinations of animals that come straight from nightmares. Some folks love this aisle."

There was definitely a steampunk feel to those pieces. Foxes wore suits and sported owl wings, fish and monkeys came together as alien creatures; they were all very wild, yet clever creations.

"Their skin makes it look as if they are still alive," I mused incredulously.

"It is all part of the unique process they use here. It has to do with our water."

There it was again: the water. Maybe this was how I would get to the bottom of this town phenomena.

"Rueben, please tell me about your water."

5
Their Water

"The poison water comes from the southern mine shaft. I am allowed to tell you that much," he said ominously.

Okay, what? Poison water? The water that killed the miners?

"Rueben, please tell me a little more." I hope I didn't sound like I was pleading with him, even though I was.

He sighed heavily. "On that fateful day back in July of 1892, when one miner broke through a wall and into that seam of gas and water, he unleashed something miraculous. The gas and water created a formula that would change everything to do with taxidermy." Now he really had my attention.

"While this so-called poison water kills any living thing it encounters, it also has the ability to preserve any type of dead skin. Once immersed, a chemical reaction occurs in the skin. After it dries, it is impervious to rot and degradation and insects—practically anything. It remains pliable and almost as if it were still alive. All these critters on display here have been treated with our water. They don't age and don't need to be treated to ward off vermin. Our water is truly special. This is Taxi's secret, and it stays here and cannot be shared. You understand me?"

"Why did you say you are allowed to tell me this? Who allowed you?"

"No, no, don't ask me that." He looked worried.

"But this is a fantastic discovery. Its preservation quality is something the whole world needs to know about," I said, ready to launch into a thousand reasons why.

"No, Daniel, I could only tell you because they knew you would not tell a soul."

My back was up almost immediately. "Oh, really? How on earth would *they* know that?" *This may be the biggest story to come out of outback Australia in years.*

We had made our way back to the desk at the entrance and Hanna. Rueben looked into my eyes and said solemnly, "Because of your wife and son."

"What?" I yelled, unable to believe what he had said.

"Please, Daniel, I am only the messenger. I know hardly anything; I just say what they tell me to say. I'm sorry, but you should leave now." I suddenly noticed he was wearing a weird looking hearing aid. I slowly looked around and sure enough there were two cameras pointing directly at me, I glared back. *Who are you? Why are you watching my every move? Why tell me your fantastic secrets if you are worried I am going to tell the world?* Ruben and Hanna were watching me closely. My excitement had turned to anger and frustration, and what did *they* mean because of my wife and son, was that a threat? How do *they* even know about them?

"Okay, fine. I get it and I'm sorry, but just about everything you've told me and everything I have seen here has rocked my boat, and I am sinking fast. Goodbye."

"See you around Daniel," they said in unison.

What on earth? What the actual fuck was up with this place? I jumped in my truck and just drove.

I had so many questions. *What is the connection here? How do they know about my past? My darling and my boy. You fuckers, stop messing with me.*

This was too much. I needed to stop and work it out. Shit—I needed a drink and to talk to Betty. Did she tell them about my wife and son? It was nearly four in the afternoon, so she would be starting to prep guests' meals, but I had to see her and find out what she knew.

Once I arrived back at Gertie's, I nearly ran inside. At the door, I called out a generic greeting as I passed by Gertie herself.

"Hi, Daniel," Betty's replied from the kitchen, "Come on down. You're the only one here tonight. What do you want for dinner? I have…" she started, but trailed off as I raced into the kitchen. Her smile dropped when she saw me. "Oh, Danny, whatever is wrong? Come here."

Shit, do I look that bad?

She'd spread her arms invitingly once more, and I needed a hug so badly. I fell into her embrace, and my troubled life faded away. As if she knew I just needed a moment, some love without words, she said nothing, and I was grateful. We pulled back and stared at each other for a bit. There was something about Betty that was genuine and true, and in her green eyes, I could see honesty and a longing for something more.

"Hey, do you have bourbon on the menu?" I asked in what I hoped was a fairly innocently tone.

"My boy, I have anything you want," she said so sweetly.

My mind and heart shifted gears *Why is she so nice to me?* She quickly headed to her stash in the cupboard. She nearly threw a bottle on the table, then found two tumblers, put them down, and turned off the main light. The atmosphere instantly changed. The ambient light coming from the hood above the ample stovetop cast a warm glow across the kitchen.

"That is better," she said warmly as she sat down. "Come on, I can see you need to talk and have a drink with me."

Beauties like Betty rarely came waltzing into my life, and I felt like I needed to catch my breath because I certainly did not expect Betty. She was everything I hadn't had in a long while, and that made me nervous. Betty poured enough for four between our two glasses.

"Oops," she said with a laugh. I sat down and she drew close, until her knee was touching mine. "Here's to today."

She motioned with her glass, so I raised mine as her share of bourbon disappeared down her throat. I swallowed mine in a second.

"Again?" she asked even as she was already pouring out our second helpings.

She downed hers quickly, then grabbed mine and downed it, too. Before I could react, she reached out and grabbed me by the back of my neck gently, but with intention, and pulled me toward her. I could not resist her as our lips locked. It felt so good. I could feel her longing to be loved; I could taste the bourbon. Betty kissed me with so much passion that soon I was all but twitching with excitement.

"Whoa," I said as we pulled apart.

"I get that your day went to shit, but I am so happy you came here to Taxi and into my life. I will help you get through this if you are willing to try and understand what Taxi is about."

We kissed some more in between drinks and talking about nothing, and I realized I was already falling for this beautiful woman. She moved closer, her knees between mine, her hand gently squeezing the back of my neck. I felt lost in her beautiful gaze, she smiled gorgeously, winked and closed her eyes. Her head rested on my shoulder. She smelt so good; I held her tenderly for what seemed an eternity but it we had only been sitting there for an hour.

"Bett, I must go. Don't worry about dinner or anything. I just need to be by myself. Sorry—you are so nice to me, but I need some time. Thanks for the drinks and for the support."

"I understand. Please be careful and don't poke around too much; let them come to you. I will always be here for you, and I can feel your needs. Rueben may have told you too much, but it is all part of their plans. I'm sorry, but they have warned me. I want to tell you more, but you need to trust me. If you can do that, then eventually, you will understand everything."

I trusted Betty, I did, and she was my kind of woman. But as I went back to my room, I was more confused than before. I poured another glass of JD since nothing was making any sense anyway. What was all that about her being warned? Who was doing all this warning? Then there were all these feelings about the woman herself swirling around in me. Lost love: was that what I was feeling for her? Yes, I was sure it was love for Betty, but I hardly knew her. I never expected this, or was even looking for it, but somehow, she was consuming me. At about five thirty I fell asleep, exhaustion overwhelming me.

* * *

We wept; our lives were over. They came and took our skins, for they had a plan, a way to incorporate themselves into our society. Blank, shining eyes: at that moment we felt doomed. They walked among us. They were us, and although we could not see them, we knew they were there. To us they were obvious, and they were everywhere, wearing our skins.

* * *

I awoke suddenly from my nightmare; half an hour seemed to have passed like a second. How did that even work? What was that dream? I didn't remember much about it, but I knew it was important. Rueben had rocked my world, and now his words were haunting my dreams.

The fucking water.

I told myself to slow down and take a breath. The dream, Betty and Rueben, and this place was somehow all rolled into one, but why? I was searching for a reason not to find Betty so enticing, but I knew I also seemed so desperate for love, so willing to accept it. Betty showed me such beauty, the kind I'd only dreamed of, and I felt that our journey had yet to begin.

I slipped back into my dreams, hoping to find clarity.

* * *

You have made it easy. We searched every kind of planet to carry out our simple plan. Take the skin and wear it. This way we can survive. You people have no idea: senators worn, prime ministers worn, your dead friend, worn. We have no limits. Our eyes are vacant and yet we shine so brightly as we wear you. You are mere children, but you have made our survival easy. Your skins fit us so perfectly, and we are grateful.

* * *

What was I seeing? I had no idea. Was it a vision, or just a dream? Fantasy or reality? The words kept repeating over and over in my head: eyes vacant, we wear you. What on earth were those weird dreams about, and why did they start after I arrived in Taxi?

I stood up and went to the bathroom. At the sink, I took handfuls of water and splashed my face, soaking my shirt in the process. I grabbed a towel to dry myself off and then changed shirts.

Deciding I needed some fresh air to clear my head, I left my room and crossed the road to the riverbank, then sat on the bench. For the first time, I was not hungry; I sat and watched the sun slowly sink behind the hills that surrounded Taxi. My mind was full of images from the Taxi-Home-Museum; every kind of animal, all perfectly crafted in death, was not an art form that everyone could embrace.

I heard a jet taking off in the distance and wondered yet again where do those jets I spied on the other day went. What did Rueben mean when he said I would never tell because of Jan and Robbie? Did *they* know about the accident before or after I told Betty? Is Betty innocent in whatever was going on in the town? Surely she was; I was determined to trust her. Then again, she said *they* had plans. What was that about? Why would they share their fucking secret with me anyway, if I, the wanna-be writer, couldn't share the biggest story I had ever come across?

I looked at my watch, it was nearly seven thirty, *might as well go to bed*. I stood and turned back toward Gertie's, and there she was. Betty leaned against my door, smiling at me with a bottle of Jack Daniels in one hand and two glasses in the other. As I slowly walked toward her, she raised a finger to her lips as if to stop me from talking. I hesitated in front of her, she came forward, leaned in, and kissed me with so much passion I had to stop and catch my breath.

"Do you mind if I come in for a while?" she asked coyly.

Damn if I would say no to her, and good God, she smelled beautiful. I knew where this was headed, and I was excited but scared because I had not been with another woman since Jan passed. I opened my door and let her go in first. She poured out two measures of whiskey, handed me one, and then put her arm around my shoulder and raised her glass to mine. We tapped glasses, took a sip, and then both went on the side table as we embraced, kissing each other for all we were worth. She pulled back, grabbed the strap on her shoulder, and pulled it aside. The other followed, and then her dress fell to the ground. She stood there for a few seconds—totally naked and smiling at me—before we nearly fell into bed together.

There was no talking. We were frantic, but also gentle and passionate; her warm body against mine was so comforting. We had both been denied intimacy for so long that our lovemaking was intense, overwhelming. It consumed us, and afterward, we could not let go of each other. We lay there together, just staring at one another with admiration for ages. Finally, she broke the silence.

"Jack?"

"No, I'm Daniel," I answered, winking at her.

We both laughed and grabbed our drinks.

"Cheers to us," she said with a brilliant smile.

"Yes, cheers to us," I replied, downing my drink.

Before I could even set my glass down, Betty was all over me again.

6
Day Three

I awoke to Betty gently stroking my face. "Good morning, Danny. I have to go get ready and prepare breakfast."

I looked at my watch and saw that it was five o'clock. "Oh, okay."

She kissed me, climbed out of the bed, and stood there naked with her hands on her hips, looking down at me with that smile of hers and her head tilted to one side. Her body was stunning: slim and fit, yet curvy and with beautiful, full breasts. My pulse raced as I pulled the sheet back. She looked at my stiff penis and then jumped back in. She guided me inside her and slowly started rocking. She never took her eyes off me, and her face hovered inches from mine the whole time. Her kisses drove me wild.

Eventually, she jumped out and threw her dress back on. After combing her messy hair with her fingers, she blew me a kiss and said, "I really must get going now."

"See you, Betty, and sorry if I made you late."

"That was absolutely my pleasure. See you at breakfast. The usual?"

She left in a whirlwind as soon as I agreed.

Whew, what a woman.

I took my time in the shower, enjoying the warm water on my back. I had only been there a few days, but it seemed like a hell of a lot longer. I couldn't stop thinking of Betty. How did that even happen? Everything with us seemed so natural and effortless, but I never expected anything like last night or this morning to happen. She felt right, and the way she looked at me had me spellbound every time. It seemed like I had known her for a millennium.

I turned off the tap, dried off, shaved, and dressed. I still had an hour and a half before breakfast. I heard a rumble outside and looked out the window just as a semi went down River Road. It lugged a refrigerated trailer with no markings or words on it. A large tanker followed from about two hundred yards away. I wondered if it was full of their miracle water. I walked out across the road to the edge of the river and watched the water flowing gently over the smooth rocks. A few small fish swam around near some algae. It certainly looked like normal water. I faintly heard another jet taking off.

I suddenly felt as if I were being watched, so I sat on the bench and very casually looked around in front of me. When I didn't see anything out of the ordinary, I stood up and stretched, twisting my head this way and that as if I was just cracking my neck. Sure enough, perched above the streetlight was a small, black dome: the type that usually housed a moveable camera. Then I recalled that first night with the vans with no lights; there were no streetlights, and yet there were light poles set up all the way down the road. I looked in both directions, as one does before crossing the street, and every second pole had a dome, too.

I went to my truck and started it, eager to see if they were all like that. I went for a slow cruise through town and found that every second pole was indeed armed with a camera. Someone could track anyone anywhere in town with a system like that, and they were probably doing just that, wondering what I was up to. But who was doing the tracking?

I pulled up at Shazza's Café and went in.

"Good morning, Shazza! I'm just after some flowers," I called.

"Hi, love! How are you? You look different somehow, but I can't put my finger on it," she said as she came out from behind the partition, smiling at me. "Take your pick, but I only have these three today: Aussie natives from my garden, ten bucks per bouquet."

"Lovely, I'll take these." I handed her a ten-dollar note.

"Good choice! Betty loves the Sturt's Desert Pea," she smiled warmly, pointing at the peapods. "No one has bought her flowers in years and years, so good on you, Daniel."

I smiled and thanked her and jumped back in my car before I realized she'd accurately guessed that the flowers were for Betty. How did she know? Did they live stream our night together to the whole town?

Jeeze, I am getting paranoid.

I was almost back at Gertie's when it dawned on me that when I flew my drone down River Road, they would have seen it all through their own lenses. Considering I seemed to be the only traveler in town, they wouldn't have much else to keep an eye on. I would have to be more careful going forward.

I pulled into Gertie's just as two cars with tinted windows pulled out, tyres spinning.

"Hello, Betty," I called down the hall, as I patted Gertie.

"Hi, but I'm not Betty," a new voice answered. "She had to step out for a minute. I'm Rita, her offsider."

"Mind if I come into the kitchen, Rita?" I asked.

I was getting nervous. *She had to step out? And since when did Betty have an offsider?* She wouldn't have stepped out, not this morning. She told me herself that she had to prepare breakfast.

"Yes, that is fine," she replied.

I walked in with the flowers still in my hand, although I felt foolish for having gone to the trouble when Betty wasn't even there. "Er, these are for her."

"Don't fret, Daniel, she can handle herself. She told me to tell you not to worry before she left," Rita said as she retrieved a vase for the flowers and filled it with water. "Please don't ask me where she is, though. She will tell you when she returns, okay?"

Evidently, they had thought of everything I would ask, but were those her words or *theirs*? And why this morning? I couldn't help but wonder if this sudden meeting was because of me.

"How long will she be gone?" I asked.

"Well, I suppose that depends, but they won't hurt her. They would never do that."

My mind reeled with the possibilities. "Thanks, Rita, but I just remembered I have to go," I said as I turned to leave.

"Don't do it, Daniel. Do not go anywhere; I will make your breakfast. Betty is relying on you to not do anything rash."

"What does that mean? Is that a threat?" My anger flared at the mere insinuation.

"I am not your enemy; I am just the messenger."

Another friggin' messenger.

Then I noticed her small hearing aid. Or was it a different kind of earpiece, through which they could tell her what to say? *Damnit!*

"Okay, I hear you loud and clear. I will obey your wishes and stay in Taxi for now."

I turned and left the kitchen without waiting for a reply. I was sick of all their messengers. I was so worried for Betty, but what could I do?

Be careful and not compromise her safety.

I went out and sat in my car, but then I started to wonder if my car was bugged or if it had been fitted with a tracker while I slept. The former was more likely, as a tracker was probably not necessary given all their cameras. I headed to the lookout, knowing they were watching me go.

I jumped out the car and sat on the tailgate, looking off into the distance. I glanced around for a camera, and sure enough, there was one on top of the light pole. I got back in my car and parked it directly under the pole and out of the lens's field of vision. At last—some privacy.

When I googled Taxi before, the town didn't exist on any map. I found Poison Valley Road on google maps and Torrens Creek was there, as were the hills and valleys, but no Taxi. How did one wipe a whole town off every map online? I took out my phone and googled taxidermy, and there was so much information out there that my head started to spin. Fascinating and a little creepy at the same time. First, the subject animal was measured, and then the skin was removed and dried. Usually, all the bones and flesh were discarded, but sometimes the skull was kept, or the taxidermist held on to the femurs and used them as a true indication of height. Once the skin was dry, any remaining flesh was scraped off, and the skin was scrubbed with borax and then washed again. That part could take a while. An armature was constructed out of wire or wood, and once cured, the skin was placed over the armature and stuffed with cotton or straw before it was stitched up. The eye sockets were filled with clay, then the glass eyes were inserted.

Rueben had said that the poison water kills living but preserves the dead, and that the many creatures in Taxi-Home-Museum were perfectly preserved despite their being so old. Then it hit me that the miners' bodies were recovered in 1919, and they would have been preserved perfectly because of that water. That display could have been real. Their bodies preserved so perfectly, their skins used and placed over armature, just like all the critters. Oh, hell—those folks in the diner, the dusty ones, could they have been stuffed, too? What about all those folks on the porches staring off at the distant sunset? Was the real secret of Taxi that they were stuffing *people*? This is insane, no wonder Taxi is invisible to the world. This is a huge secret, bigger than I thought.

I needed to think; I needed to save my Betty. They knew my every move. They had my girl. They seemed powerful, with international reach thanks to those jets. They were always a step ahead, so in order to save Betty, I needed to talk to them. I didn't want to, but it was the smartest plan I could come up with on the fly. They will definitely be smarter than me, I must stay grounded and believe in myself.

7
Bring It On

I drove back to Gertie's, then clambered out of my car and walked to the park across the road.

I stopped at the bench, turned, looked up at the camera, and clearly said, "We need to talk."

I stood and waited for about twenty minutes. Finally, just as I was thinking I needed a new game plan, three black SUVs tore down River Road. I told myself to keep calm and stay in control and everything would be fine, but what did I know?

The SUVs came to a screeching halt less than fifteen feet from me—talk about a dramatic entrance—but I stood still as a statue. The drivers exited their vehicles, not in black suits as I expected, but they were mostly wearing black and didn't pull any guns. I was still intimidated.

One with a deep voice said, "Please get in the second vehicle. Mr. Rage wishes to talk to you."

I climbed into the vehicle, expecting a hood to be placed over my head, but I was allowed to keep my eyes peeled as we drove down River Road, past the construction signs, and on to the crematorium. We pulled up, and one goon opened my door.

"This way, Daniel," he said, "follow me."

We headed inside the first building; it looked like a factory and was quite noisy. He opened another door, and we entered a brightly lit boardroom that was obviously soundproof. There was a large mahogany desk in the middle of the room, which was surrounded by eight leather chairs.

"They will be with you in a moment," The goon pulled out a chair, so I sat and looked around. He moved back against the wall silently watching me. There was a large photo of the miners on the wall, the same one that was in the actual mine. There was an old photo of a man in a diving suit, holding his big, copper and bronze helmet under one arm. On the far wall was a large wedding photo, that looked like it was taken in the nineteen twenties. The couple were immaculate in Gatsby attire and obviously very well to do. Under that sat a sideboard filled with ornate whisky decanters and glasses. Standing proudly next to them was a beautiful little fox. Who looked so alive, I felt as if his piercing glass eyes were staring into my soul.

After several minutes, I get to meet *them*. Three men entered the room, all dressed in business clothes. I stood up politely, and the first guy extended his hand to shake mine.

"Hi, I am Conner Rage, CEO of Taxiplus. These are my executives, David and Pete. I'm pleased to meet you."

"Pleased to meet you." I tried to sound confident as I shook first his hand, then those of the other two.

Rage motioned for me to sit down. "Let me first say that Betty is fine, and that she came here by my request and of her own free will. I could have asked you, too, but sometimes I like to make a point. I am sorry if I angered you yesterday with what I told Rueben to say to you, but no, Betty didn't tell me about your past. David ran a background check on you when you first came to town, our standard procedure with travelers." I nodded, and he continued. "Our town is sacred. It means everything to those who live here. Our water must remain *our* water. If our secret gets out, we'll lose the one thing we have."

"Please explain why you told me about it, then."

"You don't know the full story yet; there is so much more, and it is good. The man in this photo here is my grandfather, Justin Rage." Rage pointed at the picture of the man in the old-school diving gear. "He went into the southern mine in 1919 and retrieved all those perfectly preserved miners. He was a part-time pearl diver, but he was also a chemist, and a goddamn hero because he worked out the secret of our poison water and how we could use it in taxidermy. He renamed our town, which was formerly just known as Miners Camp 107. So, you can see why I am invested in this place. And so is my daughter Betty."

He raised his eyebrows at me as the pieces came together in my head. The guy in charge of *them* is her father.

My head was spinning, but all I could manage was, "Oh, okay, that is, er, that is interesting."

"I need to know what your plans are. She will not leave Taxi, and she told me today that you mean a lot to her even after only two days. So, what are you up to? I'll tell you right now that you don't get to break her heart. My Betty means everything to me."

They were all waiting for my response but I drew a blank. I had no idea what to say to him. This man, her father, owned this town; he was the boss. I needed to choose my words carefully.

"Sir, I will not hurt your daughter. She is very special to me. But whether I stay or go will probably have a lot to do with what you are willing to tell me about Taxi. I get your secrecy, but if you want me to answer you honestly, then you need to be honest with me, too. it's not just animals that you are stuffing, is it? Those miners in the display are not waxworks, are they? That is their actual skin, that is quite macabre, if those miners are taxidermy."

"Wouldn't that be far less macabre than putting a dead person in a wooden box and burying them six feet under so they can slowly rot and be eaten by worms? *That* is macabre." He was serious as he went on. "There are currently tens of thousands of Taxiplus-crafted individuals in people's homes all over the world. It's one of the best-kept secrets on the entire planet. And now, you," he pointed at me, "are in on that secret." I suddenly thought of Jan and Robbie's funeral, his small casket being lowered into the earth. It was the saddest day of my life. But I could never sit with their taxidermy treated remains. Their bodies were burnt beyond recognition. Even if they weren't I prefer to remember them as they were before they passed, not after. "Don't look so shocked; it is not for everyone, but for those who have lost someone special. They can go and spend time with them, and they will never change. Our process means they never rot, never age, don't smell, are impervious to insects, they don't turn blue or gray and their skin remains supple. In fact, depending on the armature used, they can be posed or repositioned in any way."

I stared at the photo of the miners, letting it all sink in. My life will never be the same again, that is for sure.

"Is everyone in Taxi in on this? Do they all know?"

"Absolutely. They live here because they all have a role to play in Taxiplus; this entire town is employed by me. We only have a population of one hundred and seventy-seven. Most of the homes here are empty because, as our production process became more automated, we required fewer people to run the factory. There are three scientists working on our plans for the future. We have eighteen artists who work on the finishing touches and the animals. We have six doctors for the dissections of the cadavers after they are skinned for medical studies, and organs can be perfectly preserved and sent off to medical schools and universities. Some of the skins are designated as Study-Skins, which are packed in flat containers and left unstuffed with no glass eyes; some of these are not even stitched back up." I was certain he was talking about my nightmares; I was sure I have dreamt of these Study-Skins. "For all other commissioned projects, the remains are cremated once the skin has been removed. I will show you through the plant sometime if you are up to it, it is very confronting to some the first time, but for now, Rita can work at Gertie's for a few more days so you can get to know Betty better." Rage's phone kept lighting up, he glanced at it and flipped it over. "Perhaps try camping in our hills or go wherever you want around here; you probably need to spend some time with her. She definitely needs some time off, and if you have more questions, Bett should be able to answer them."

When he finished his spiel, it was quite clear that he was done with me for the time being, so I stood when he did and quickly shook his hand.

"Thank you for trusting me with all of this information, Conner. I'll see you gentlemen later, I'm sure."

Then I was ushered out to the car park, where Betty was patiently waiting for me. Her face lit up when she saw me, and she ran forward for a hug and had a quick kiss.

"So, you met my dad. He can be pretty intense at times; this really is his town, and he is so proud of what he has achieved with Taxiplus."

"I'm good, but what about you? I was so worried when I walked into the kitchen and Rita greeted me. The only thing I could think of was your safety. I felt helpless."

"Oh, Danny, come here and give me a real kiss." She pulled me in and kissed me hard, and there it was again—that feeling of want and need.

We jumped into the company car they had sent for her and headed back to Gertie's. We went to my room, grabbed the bottle of Jack, and walked over to the park to sit by Torrens Creek. It was about eleven-thirty in the morning—early to start hitting the hard stuff, sure, but it had been a hectic morning. We downed the first couple of shots in a few minutes. It wasn't long after that, though, that we suddenly became aware of unexpected cars coming down River Road. A black SUV from Taxiplus followed by, *what is that?*

"Now what?" I asked as I turned to see a brand new, top of the range, Maui camper pull up alongside the SUV.

The driver of the camper came out and said, "Compliments of Mr. Rage, this is fully stocked and ready to go. He advised that it would be best if you did not go further than White Mountains National Park, but he hopes that you relax and have a good time."

With that, he got into the SUV and left. We looked at each other, then burst out laughing.

"I think he likes you, Daniel. Let's have a look."

We walked around the outside of the camper first. According to what was painted on the side, Betty's dad had had named it Horus; there was a picture of a falcon above the name as well.

"What's with the name?" I asked.

"Dad likes Egyptian mythology, and Horus is the god of healing and protection of the sun and the sky. He was often represented with a falcon's head."

We walked around and opened the door; it was brand new, and beautiful. A steaming hot bag of burgers and fries waited for us on the table, a note on the bag said 'Hope you have a nice break in the hills. Enjoy, love Shazza.' The vase of flowers I'd gotten for Betty had somehow ended up next to the bag of burgers. There was a bar with a dozen bottles of spirits, cupboards full of supplies, and a map of camping spots with GPS coordinates.

"I got these for you, though I'm not sure how they ended up here," I said, gesturing at the flowers.

"Oh, Danny, how sweet! They are beautiful. I love them."

"It looks like they've already grabbed some of our stuff, which is a bit creepy, but okay. Let's just go up to the lookout, eat these burgers, have another drink, and plot a destination," I said, glad to be in charge for a second after feeling so adrift all morning.

"Okay, let's go," she agreed with a sparkling wink.

How was I supposed to resist her charm?

The burgers from Shazza's were delicious, as were the fries, she was seriously a great chef. We washed them down with a beer each and studied the map, which showed Taxi, the mines, Poison Valley Road, the lookout, and a few camping spots in the hills. It also showed two other mines and a spot where the river was dammed.

"Here," I said, pointing at the area around the dam. "That is only about twenty minutes away, but it's off the beaten track."

"Okay, that sounds good, I remember that lake, I haven't been there in years," Betty said enthusiastically.

I punched in the coordinates and the GPS immediately mapped it out for me. Twenty minutes later, we arrived at a large clearing next to a lake the size of a football field and surrounded by hills with trees full of noisy birds.

"Here we are: heaven," I announced.

Betty had already poured a drink for us both and set up two deck chairs. We sat by the lake for a bit, drinking and talking about nothing important, even though there was plenty of that on my mind. We did indulge in plenty of healing laughter, and I couldn't help but wonder how that woman made me feel so comfortable with myself?

"Time for a swim." Betty stood and peeled off her clothes, standing in front of me naked again and downed her drink. "Come on, wuss!"

"Okay, but the water will be freezing," I said even as I took off my clothes.

She ran into the water, and I chased her in. When I resurfaced, she was fifteen feet away and gasping for breath as the cold water took her breath away and made my genitals retreat into my body. Still, it was so refreshing, so revitalizing, and that was all that mattered: the here and now with Betty.

"Crap, this is freezing," I called, but Betty laughed it off.

"Stop your whining, Danny! Freezing our toots off is so good for the soul." She swam over effortlessly and wrapped her legs and arms around me like an octopus. "Come here, you city slicker. I'll warm you up."

With her mouth on mine, I was instantly warmer.

"You make me feel like this is home," I said later as we sat by the little fire I made and drank some more whiskey.

It was nearly dinnertime, but I was so tired from her lovemaking, first in the lake and then on shore…then a little more in the camper. Betty was insatiable, but so was I. I needed her as she needed me, but I needed to know more of her story, so I planned to ask her more about herself the next day. I was thankful for today.

"I will cook you one of these amazing steaks. You have the night off, young lady," I said.

I just wanted to make her happy, so I cooked, and she ate with gusto. That meant the world to me.

A short time later, she asked if I wanted dessert and pulled off her dress, revealing that she was totally naked underneath it. I just looked at that beautiful woman in awe and appreciated the fact that she loved being naked and was so confident with herself.

"Damnit, you beat me to it," I said, "but yes, please."

She went into the camper, grabbed a big rug, and graciously spread it out on the grass before she kneeled in front of me and pulled down my shorts. She grinned up at me gorgeously.

"But first, let's have some bourbon." She gently squeezed my cock and then grabbed the bottle to pour out two glasses for us. "Cheers, my Danny boy, I love—er, sorry. I mean you…you mean a lot to me, Danny, and I just want to be with you so badly right now!"

With that, she grabbed me, and we fell onto that rug to do what people who love each other often do. I realized that I did already love Betty as we came intensely at the same time.

A good while later, we lay there on our backs naked, staring up at the heavens. Our eyes were fully open to the millions of stars. The moon was a thin, silver sliver over the hills, stunningly beautiful and serene. The night was not cold, but when the breeze picked up, there was a slight chill in the air. The liquor kept us warm on the inside, and our hands were tightly but gently clasped together between us. The small fire provided some warmth and glowing security; I had not felt so calm or relaxed in years.

"The stars are so beautiful tonight—just like you, Bett."

She squeezed my hand. "You are very sweet, Danny. Oh, look—a shooting star!" She pointed out the bright streak flying across the sky, then sighed. "We should probably go inside to bed; it is nearly one o'clock, and I don't really like the idea of sleeping out here in the open. There could be dingoes or snakes around when the fire dies down completely."

She stood up and finished off her glass. I did the same and tipped some sand onto the fire to put it out. Still naked, we went inside.

"Left or right?" I asked.

She looked at me and smiled. "On top."

We laughed, but then lay there looking at each other in the glow of the stars coming through the window until we fell asleep.

* * *

I opened my eyes only to be temporarily blinded; there was a circle of bright light around our camper, coming from above. Betty was not next to me

I raced outside and saw her staring up with arms spread and her eyes were glowing, as if she were in some kind of trance. I took her hand, intending to pull her away, but as soon as I touched her, my skin went numb. The sensation traveled up my arm and then I blacked out.

When I woke up, we lay together on blue grass. The sky was purple with green clouds, pink and red trees swayed in a warm breeze, and two small moons hung in the sky alongside two dim, red suns. Then I realized we were being watched. There were people all around us in a circle: humans like us, but all with the same jumpsuit and standing at the same height. They were looking at us, some pointing and speaking in hushed whispers. Betty was still unconscious, but breathing steadily. I fell back asleep.

8
Day Four

I smelled bacon and sat up, disorientated. That's when I remembered we were in the camper. I looked over to the stove area, where Betty wore an apron, but nothing else, so her nice, round bum was on display.

"Well, hello, lovely. Very cute look you have going on there," I said.

"Why, thank you, sleepyhead," she replied with a wink and a broad smile. She was so friggin' cute, and her apron barely covered her nipples. "Are you hungry? We have bacon and fried eggs on toast with a cooked tomato."

"Yes, please. I am starving! Must be all this great sex I am getting now."

She laughed and pulled the side of her apron back to flash me a breast.

"Oh, very nice." I sat at the little table. "Can I do anything to help?"

"You can take the teabags out of the cups for me."

"Can do. Oh, that looks great—the bacon I mean, not that sweet little ass of yours. That looks fantastic," I said as I patted it.

"Here you go—service with a smile! Gosh, I am hungry, too," she said as she sat next to me. "Here's a teacloth to put in your lap, I would hate for you to drop any food on *that*. You might burn yourself, or I might mistake it for a wiener and poke it with my fork!"

She made stabbing motions with her fork toward my lap, causing us both to laugh.

We ate quietly with only the occasional sound of appreciation coming from either of us. We drank our tea, sat back, and took a deep breath at the same time.

"That was delicious, baby."

"Why, thank you. I'm full now. I think I'll go lie on that rug and get some morning sunshine on my pale ass."

"Sounds like a great plan. We can work out what activities we can do today. But first, I'm going to take some shower gel and go and freeze my nuts off in the lake."

"Good idea! I'll join you. Where did they hide the towels and toiletries?" She started opening cupboards, and I got up to help. "Oh, we have fishing rods, a cast net, and inflatable paddle boards. Cool!"

"Over here is a deck of cards and some board games. How old do they think we are?" She laughed at my joke as I continued the search. "Oh, wow! Bows and arrows, a couple of big hunting knives, and what appears to be a safe with a combination lock. Is that for a handgun?"

"Yes, Dad always has a sidearm for protection. The combination will be 1892."

Sure enough, that was the winning combination and there was a small handgun inside with boxes of ammo.

"Hey, that is my gun from Gertie's."

"You have your own gun?"

"Sure, and I'm a good shot. I've had heaps of practice on the range. Dad says it's a necessary evil."

She reached for it, and within about thirty seconds she had it in about fifteen separate pieces, all laid out neatly on the table.

"Wow, how did you learn to do that so quickly? This is the first time I've ever even held a gun." She had it back together by the time I had finished talking. She was much more than met the eye. "I'm definitely, not messing with you! God, dressed like that, with a gun in your hands." I shook my head, then caught sight of what we'd been looking for in the first place. "Ah, here are the bloody towels and the gel."

"Good, please put this back and let's go and have a wash. I'll beat you into the water!" She said as she stood, pulled off the apron, and sprinted away.

"Oh, no, you won't!"

I promptly gave chase, but she was way faster than me. I tried to catch her, but she'd already dove under and come back up spinning.

"Chuck me the gel, I'm first, kiddo!"

I was only five feet from her and threw the bottle gently; she caught it and started to lather herself.

"Come here and I'll do you in a second."

Yes, you can.

I watched the frothy goddess in front of me lather up her hands and then squirt me with the gel.

"Go where it's a bit shallower. I must make sure I don't miss anything." she said, her hands still sliding everywhere.

Soon, I was a bubble-man standing in ten inches of water with an erection, but I couldn't help that. I had to have looked ridiculous.

"Now, where is my camera? You will look great on Dad's conference room wall."

She laughed so hard as she ran for her towel, but I ran the opposite way and dove all the way under, just in case she had her phone there with the towels.

We lay on the rug so the sun could warm on our bodies after being in that freezing water.

"Do you think it is safe to lie out here naked? What if someone comes by all of a sudden?" I asked.

She looked at me squarely. "Oh, Danny, you still don't understand this place, do you? My father would never allow anyone to disturb us. He will have had all the roads closed and sentries posted. All of Taxi will know we are staying up here by now. He would have made sure they were told to grant us privacy. There is only one road up to here, anyway, and the road into Taxi is usually closed for construction; sometimes the gates are locked, and he orders them to remove the Poison Valley Road sign for most of the year. Nobody knows we exist. Living out here segregated from the world has taught me so much, especially about myself and my needs. I learned how to find happiness, when I thought I never would. Danny what is truly important to you? It should be obvious what is important to me lately."

"You know what that is already: love and being loved, Betty you are more important to me than anything. I love you."

Oh, shit—I said it. But I knew it was true; I could not imagine being away from her. Only four days to fall in love? Yes, it could happen even quicker than that, I was sure.

"Oh, Danny, I think we were meant to meet, that our pasts led us to this moment. I feel exactly the same as you do, and we are so alike. I know I am in love with you, desperately in love even after so few days. What really matters is love and family, not money or possessions. We can lie here butt naked for as long as we want, or until Dad rings and asks us to bring back his camper." She leaned over and kissed me, then snuggled up and threw a leg over mine. "Ask me anything, and I will do my best to answer so you can know me better."

"Okay, I would like to know a little about your past, even if it hurts. You have pain; I can feel it."

She squirmed uncomfortably. "I was married to a man named Harrison—or, Harry, as I called him. He was my childhood sweetheart, and we got together when I was fifteen. We married here in Taxi twelve years ago; within a year I was pregnant with little Joe. I was happy, but then Joe became sick, very sick. He was only a year old, and he had brain cancer. We went to Brisbane to see the best doctors, but they could not help him. The tumor was growing too fast, and they explained that it was hereditary. They did tests, and, sure enough, Harry had a brain tumor too, He died only three months after Joe, He died heartbroken and I was a mess for years."

By the end of the story, she was bawling, and tears flowed down her face.

"It is okay, darling, let it out. I am here." I hugged her and held her in my arms for what felt like a lifetime, her body heaving with each sob.

"My father didn't even ask me," Betty said a while later. "He just went ahead and did it. They are in there, side by side in the damn mausoleum for all to see. He said he did it for me, but Joe was his grandson, so I knew he did it for himself. My mom, his parents, and his grandfather the diver are all in there. He goes often, but I don't ever visit that sad place. Their skins are only shells; all the skins are only shells. Photographs from the past. My dad thinks he is doing God's work, but I have never agreed with him, and he knows it. He thinks you will stabilize me. That is what he's said around my friends in high places." She was angry now, but thankfully not with me. "How could he do that to them? He knew I was messed up, on the edge. When I found out, I nearly went over that dark edge, but I didn't want to end up in there, too: another shell. He would have done that to me even if I'd said no. I love him, but that side of him is way too dark for me. I want more of what you have: freedom to live life to the fullest. Yes, I have seen your background check, but it is what you have shared these last few days that's made me decide to stretch this break out for as long as he lets me. I am loving every minute with you—honestly loving it."

With that, she jumped up and went in the camper. Bon Jovi's "Living on a Prayer" started playing so loudly, and she came running back out with a bottle of whiskey in her hand. She sang along at top of her lungs; *she can really sing!* Threw her arms in the air, and danced naked in between taking swigs from the bottle. She offered me some as she danced around me. and I took my own gulp straight from the bottle.

Conner must have had his hands full with you, and so will I, but I am looking forward to it. You are the challenge I have been searching for.

Creedence Clearwater Revival blared through the speakers next. Yes, I was a "Fortunate Son." I started dancing, too: a weird, white, naked dude running around like a freak, drinking liquor from the bottle, and singing as if it were part of some pagan ritual. Betty and I waltzed around for ages, carrying on like teenagers until we collapsed on the rug in a heap of laughter. Our nakedness meant nothing; we were just two people out there in the outback, having a fantastic time.

At one o'clock in the afternoon, we realized we hadn't had anything since six that morning.

"Sandwiches?" Betty said, and I agreed because they would help soak up the alcohol.

We hastily made sandwiches with ham, cheese, tomato, and salt and pepper. We took them out to the deck chairs with a bottle of Pinot Gris and two wine glasses.

"Look at us: day drunk on our second day of the holidays. We are hopeless," I said.

We had decided to get dressed since we suddenly thought we were being inappropriate by lounging around naked. Betty donned her bikini, and I pulled on board shorts.

"Betty, I know we are eating, but I need to know. Who skins the cadavers for your father's company? I mean, who could possibly do that day after day?"

This was totally inappropriate for lunchtime conversation, and I blamed the alcohol for allowing me to let it slip. The thing was, I knew Betty would not mind my asking.

"There used to be a guy who did that job all by himself, but in the end, it killed him." She winked, obviously proud of her dad joke and attempt to lighten the mood. "Seriously, though, now Taxiplus have this machine that does it very efficiently: the Danny-Dee Glover."

I chuckled. "No."

"Yeah, no, it is called the D-glove 101. That is what it does; it pulls the glove off." Despite the morbid topic at hand, it was kind of cute how she shoved the second sandwich in her mouth like she hadn't eaten in days. "Every day, ten to twelve hours a day. Thousands a week."

"Really? That many?"

"I don't get it either. How can so many people like this crazy shit?" she asked, but I did not have that answer.

"Where do all the cadavers come from?" I asked.

"From all over the planet. USA, Russia, China, Dubai: they all love it. Medi-Corp is one of our biggest clients; they supply all their own cadavers, and they take almost all of the Study-Skins for research."

"Where do they get so many organ donors?" I asked.

"It's not our place to ask, Danny. We can never ask those questions of our customers. It is part of our code of conduct. There are many aspects of the business that I don't get involved with. I am part of it, but not really."

But you are, Betty; I can see your conflict, poor girl.

"I think we need to stretch our legs. Let's go for a walk."

We put on our sneakers and headed up into the hills with a couple of bottles of water in a backpack. It was so beautiful, and the Australian outback had much to offer when it appeared untouched, like it did out there. I had Betty's hand in mine; we followed the creek as it flowed down the hill we'd just climbed. We came to a small waterfall, and the sound of it was perfection. We sat for a while, getting our breath back.

A nearby kookaburra called out to his mates, and then they started up with a crazy bush chorus, chiming all around us. On the other side of the creek, a couple of young kangaroos hopped up for a drink, but, on seeing us there, quickly left. The beauty was astounding, and the water bubbled away. I glanced at Betty; she was staring at me.

"What?" I asked when I noticed her eyes were teary, "It is so nice here, huh?"

"No, Danny, *you* are so nice. Thank you. I needed this walk, and it seems like you always know how to fix me. For years, I thought I was broken, but you have opened my eyes to what it means to live again. No, you can't sing or dance, but that is why I find you irresistible. Come here and give us a kiss, you big lug."

She kissed me with that beautiful urgency of hers, and I discovered that when she was that vulnerable, her beauty increased tenfold.

"Come on," I urged her, "there is more to see here."

The hills and valleys were stunning. We headed up the next path to the crest of the highest peak around.

"Look at this vista," she said. "How stunning!"

Our view of the mountains was amazing; we could almost see all the way to Charters Towers from there. The red hues, the blue, hazy mountains, and the overall serenity were incomparable.

Betty turned and hugged me, then planted the biggest kiss ever on my cheek. She tugged at her bikini top and removed it, tucking it in to her briefs as she started off in the wrong direction. "Let's go back now."

"Wait, beautiful, it is this way," I said as I grabbed her arm, but she had other ideas.

"Come here, you beautiful man, and make love to me. I need you right here, right now."

She pulled down my shorts and pushed me down onto a fallen tree, then mounted my stiff cock, sitting down slowly as I entered her. It was grand: two people in love and simply cherishing the moment.

We headed back to camp and jumped in the water to freshen up. Then, we dried off and dressed in normal clothes, as it was getting quite cool.

"JD?" I said, grabbing the bottle. "I just need it to warm up a touch."

"Sure. What do we feel like for dinner?" Betty opened the fridge and had a look around. "We can knock up a couple of pizzas in no time. We have lots of toppings."

I grabbed the two bases from the cupboard and threw them onto the table, then found the sauce. Betty retrieved some salami, ham, and mozzarella from the fridge.

"What a team!" Betty said with a laugh. "Pineapple?"

"Ham and pineapple: I'm a Queenslander, after all," I replied, turning on the oven.

We built those pizzas in less than five minutes and had them in the oven as soon as it was up to temperature. Betty opened Spotify and found a slow, jazz mix that was perfect for dinnertime. We set the table and opened an expensive bottle of Shiraz: a Grange Bin 95 that likely went for about five grand a bottle. The irony of drinking it with five-dollar pizzas did not escape us.

"Your dad must have a killer cellar," I said, looking at the back of the bottle.

We poured two small glasses, both of us reluctant to indulge in this type of excess. However, it was exceptional and made our cheap meal that much better. We shared two more small glasses, but resisted the urge to finish the bottle of bliss. I had never had wine of this caliber before.

"I grew up on this extravagant grape. I had my first taste on my eighteenth birthday," she said before she downed that second glass.

"You do know how it sounds, right? Conner must have spoiled you." As soon as the words left my mouth, I knew I'd said too much. "I'm sorry, I didn't mean to sound bitter."

"You know, my father had to try and be my mom, too. She passed when I was only three, He was everything to me until Harrison and I got serious. He used his money to fill my life with happiness, and I was none the wiser about where it came from until I turned eighteen. I never dreamed he was stuffing dead bodies; I hated when he told me all about Taxiplus. From that night on, I could not trust him; he had lied to me my entire life. I thought he worked as a taxidermist. I know how it looks—how I look—but it's how I grew up. Please don't judge me."

"*Shit,* sorry. I'm not judging you; I will never do that. Can you forgive me?"

"Oh, of course I do, Danny. You did not offend my hard ass; I am thick-skinned."

I felt a whole lot closer to her than before. So, we finished off that bottle of cheap piss because the price meant nothing to us.

At one point, Betty pulled out the deck of cards and started to shuffle. "Let's play."

"I don't really know any games," I admitted.

"I will teach you. Twenty-one is a good place to start, and if you don't like it, just say so."

Betty was such a great teacher. We played the game for hours and laughed as she kicked my ass more often than not. I won a few games, though, so I didn't feel like a total loser.

"Did you let me win those?" I had to ask.

"No, you did that. And I must say, well done. Did you like this game?"

"It's great. Thanks for showing me. I really needed this escape. Can I get you anything? Do we have anymore whiskey?"

She went back into the bowels of the camper and emerged holding a bottle of Sinatra Century. "We have a few of these."

"Damn, I love you. That is impossible to find and so expensive."

Betty found two glasses and poured us a round, then clinked her glass with mine. "Cheers to us Danny."

"Cheers, babe. Thank you for a great night," I said as she reached down and started rubbing my manhood.

We retreated to the bed, undressed, and climbed in on top of each other. Our lovemaking was intense, but gentle as we moved together in a perfect rhythm. We climaxed as one.

Later, totally satisfied, we slept.

* * *

The light was back, and it was so bright. I remembered this light being all around us before.

"Betty, are you okay? What is happening?"

The light faded to purple, and once again there were two dim, red suns in our sky. It was late in the day, and they were trying to reach out, to talk to us, but we didn't understand.

Slowly, so slowly, I made out, "Help us, you of the many skins. Please Daniel, Betty, you: only you two can help."

9
Day Five

I woke to the sound of my own name ringing in my ears.

"Hello?" I called out, not really awake.

"Danny, how are you, my sweet?" Betty said softly in my ear.

I felt her warmth as she snuggled up to me. "Betty? What did you say?"

"You must have been dreaming. I said nothing except your name, but you were saying things I could not understand: almost like you were speaking another language. It was a bit weird."

I didn't want to worry her, but I felt I should explain. "Okay, I have been having these weird dreams and nightmares lately—ever since I got to Taxi, actually. They feel creepy, and when I wake up, I can't remember anything, but I feel as if I am missing something important and terrifying. I'm sure it's nothing to worry about, though."

"I'm sorry, to hear that, Danny. I hope it is not me giving you bad dreams."

She snuggled up even closer, entwining our legs as her hand gently slid down my chest to my navel, gently scratched my pubic hair, then ever so slowly trailed back up to my chest.

"As if you could cause bad dreams. Wet dreams, maybe." I winked at her.

This time her hand went further down until she found what she was looking for.

"Hmm, this is hard," she whispered as she squeezed me and then climbed on.

She moved slowly and rhythmically, kissing me. Soon I could feel the tremor rising within my beautiful woman, her back arching. She let out a deep moan as we climaxed together. Her shuddering went on, followed by another deep, continuous moan.

When it was over, she opened her eyes and looked down at me as if amazed, still breathing hard. "That was unbelievable. It was like having at least four orgasms, one after the other. I've never had that before."

I held her face close as she kissed me all over my face. "You are amazing and beautiful, and you mean everything to me."

We lay there for another hour, kissing, laughing, and chatting.

"Swim time?" I pointed toward the lake.

"Yes, for sure."

We jumped up and went out into a glorious morning, where there was not a cloud in the sky. We grabbed the towels and the shower gel. The chilly water invigorated us as we swam around for a while. Then we stood in the shallows and washed ourselves.

"I could get used to this lifestyle."

Betty nodded, "Yeah, me too."

We dried up and went back into the camper.

"How about toast with Vegemite and a slice of cheese on top? We can also have my nearly famous black coffee?" Betty looked at me as if she expected rejection. She held up the Vegemite jar and waved it near my face, took the lid off and held it near my nose. She grinned as saw my reaction.

"Yes, ma'am, I'm all in for that." I replied.

Our production line went into motion. I threw on my boxers while Betty threw on that tiny apron. We operated like a well-oiled machine, only sexier.

"This bread looks amazing, and it smells like it was freshly baked." I couldn't help myself as I shoved my nose into a slice and inhaled deeply.

"It probably was on the morning they delivered the camper; it's from Jean's Bakery. She makes the best bread and pastries. We are lucky to have the best employees here in Taxi: all handpicked by the big guy, you know. Now, are you going to eat that now that you've had your nose on it?"

She smiled as I stopped breathing in that beautiful smell and then shoved the entire slice in my mouth.

Within about six minutes, we had everything on the table. We sat and admired our handiwork before tucking in. We devoured our toast, and when we started in on our coffees, I decided to ask about something she'd said.

"He chooses everyone?" I looked at her as she nodded, not needing me to elaborate on what I was asking. "Did he choose me?" She appeared to be thinking, trying to form an answer. "Betty…did he choose me for you?" I stood up, feeling disappointed and used all of a sudden. "Did you know?"

"Danny, wait, it's not like that. How could it be? You turned on our road by yourself; it was random., wasn't it? How could it not be"

Confusion clouded her eyes. I wanted to believe her, but considering everything I'd seen and heard since I got there, I couldn't help but wonder if this was this all another façade. Part of the plan: she had said as much herself. Was my background check run before or after I arrived?

"If I was handpicked, does that make me an employee?"

"Please don't do this, Danny. I am on your side. I love you, Danny." She was sobbing, and it broke my fucking heart that I was doing that to her. I sat back down and grabbed her hands, but could not say a word as she tried to work through it herself. "I did not even consider that he might have somehow orchestrated this. If he did, I will leave with you tomorrow. His power stops here and now. I have not felt this kind of love since I held little Joe in my arms. Not even Harry compares; he was very nice, but he was not you. I feel like we're meant for each other."

"Okay, I really want to believe you Bett. I see it in your eyes. We will sort this out together." *I would do anything to know the full truth. Conner Rage has some explaining to do; his power means nothing to me.* "Betty, I need transparency from you right now."

"Yes, just ask me and I will tell you what I know," Betty said earnestly as she looked deep into my eyes.

"I felt compelled to come out here. I can't exactly put my finger on it, but somehow, maybe someone planted the idea in my head after my car kind of stopped, or broke down on the highway, right where the Poison Valley Road sign is. If I had not seen that, I probably would not have turned down here. Is Conner powerful enough to pull off something like that?"

"Frankly, yes, I think he could be. But Danny, you need to be so careful. Don't go and question him or anything like that. I've heard stories that, at one time, I dismissed as hearsay, but I fear what he may be capable of."

Betty's phone pinged with a message. We'd had zero contact with anyone for two and a half days, and at this crucial moment, her phone reminded us of life outside of our bubble.

"Sorry, it's Dad." She looked at the message, and a look of dread came across her face. "There has been an accident. A random light aircraft crashed in Taxi and the pilot is dead. Dad asked me to come directly to HQ and for you to go to Gertie's immediately. We must do as he says."

"That is terrible, but at least no one else is hurt. Let's go."

I started packing up, and we left in less than ten minutes. I had no idea what was in store for either of us, but I did not feel it would be anything good. I dropped Betty off at the crematorium and kissed her.

"I love you. Be strong."

"You, too. I'll see you soon," she called over her shoulder.

I drove solemnly back to Gertie's, went into my room, and turned on the radio to listen to the local news and scrolled the internet on my phone to see if I could learn anything more about the accident. There was nothing yet, but maybe it was too early. But, as the hours slipped by, I heard nothing from Betty, and there was no news of any crash. Doubt crept in once again. Was there even a crash, or was it an excuse to get us back here?

Finally, four hours later, the story started to filter through on the radio; a light aircraft crashed just outside of Charters Towers, and the pilot was killed. But this crash was nowhere near here apparently. What exactly is going on here. It had nothing to do with Taxi…or did it? For Betty's sake, I hoped Conner hadn't done anything he may regret later.

Did he even have any regrets? He seemed like such a cold, emotionless bastard the one time I met him, and someone I shouldn't mess with. I could feel it coming, though, and sometime soon.

My phone pinged with a text from Betty.

Can't talk, in crisis meeting with Dad and co. Grab some food from Shazza's or BBs for yourself. I will be there later. Love you. xo

I suddenly realized I hadn't had a thing to eat since that morning, and it was two-thirty in the afternoon. I rang through to BB's and put in an order for a steak sandwich and some fries.

"Okay, it'll be ready in fifteen," she sang.

I had a quick shower, then headed into town. I swore I could feel eyes on me, and as I pulled into BB and Kitty's, a couple of SUVs and a large van tore down the street.

"Hi," I called as I entered the cafe.

"Hi, Daniel! Here you go, love." Kitty handed me a bag. "Bit of a stir going on here today, isn't there? Trucks flying around and all."

"There is, for sure." I didn't want to say too much more than that. "Keep the change."

I hurried out and drove back to Gertie's, took a beer from my fridge, and walked across the road to sit on what had already become my favorite bench by the river. I knew the camera was following me. I'd only been there five days, but it seemed like it'd been way longer than that.

The sandwich was great, as well as the chips. All handpicked, I'd bet. All chosen by him: Mr. Big. He might have even chosen me for Betty. We were so suited for each other, it was uncanny. I was so sure he had; he was devious and had unlimited resources. How was his daughter so natural and unspoiled? She had none of his qualities of that I was certain. Regardless, I was glad for it.

I finished off that delightful late lunch and washed it down with the remainder of my beer before heading back to my room. I grabbed another beer and lay back on the bed to watch the news. A sixty-eight-year-old man died when his plane crashed in a remote spot and burst into flames. An eyewitness came forward, stating that he heard a loud bang and looked up to see the aircraft plummeting and then bursting into flames when it struck the ground. He ran over, but there was nothing he could do. What a mess; nothing was discernible, and a large, blue tarpaulin covered the pilot's remains.

A short time later, I drifted off to sleep.

* * *

A billion stars and colorful nebulas filled my vision. I was flying through space at an incredible rate. My skin was golden and glistened in the starlight.

I didn't know where I was, what I was, or even how fast I was going. It was unbelievable.

It was just me—no, not just me. Someone flew right by my side. Then, two dim red suns and two bright moons loomed ahead. We had arrived.

* * *

"Hey, sleepyhead. Wake up." Betty gently tapped me on the shoulder, then pointed at the local news still playing on the TV. "How did you manage to sleep with all this going on? Let's take the camper back up to the lake; we need to talk. Rita has cooked a big pot of Bolognese for us to take. Are you up for it?"

"Are we allowed to go? Did Pops approve it?" I asked.

"He suggested it since we will just be in the way here. I'll explain what I can when we get there."

She hurried off to the kitchen while I checked on the camper. Looking inside, I immediately noticed that it had been tidied up and fully restocked. Well, dear old Dad sure did think of everything. Betty bustled in with a big, cast-iron Dutch oven, and just like that, the aromas of Italy surrounded us. I quickly took it and placed it in the sink, which seemed like the safest spot for something so hot. Betty also had two fresh baguettes wedged under one arm.

"Ready to go, baby? That smells delicious." I smacked my lips. "I'll find some tunes."

"Apparently our road up there will be closed off after we enter due to a serious rockfall." Betty shrugged and winked before pointing ahead. "That way!"

I put Horus in gear, and we headed down River Road. When we turned left onto Poison Valley Road once more, we passed more SUVs than I had seen yet.

"Dad is preparing to go into stealth mode to hide our entire town from any outlets that may be snooping around after the crash," Betty said matter-of-factly. I looked at her incredulously. "Just be patient, Danny. I need a drink, and we're nearly there."

"Sure, yeah, patience after you mention casually that Taxi is going into *stealth mode*. This town is crazy."

"You got that right!" Betty exclaimed.

When we had arrived, we camped closer to the trees for cover; Conner had installed a portable toilet for us under the trees in case the one in the camper filled. There was firewood stacked by a dedicated firepit, and a tank of fresh water despite the lake's proximity.

"Hey, babe, you all good? I'm starving," I said as Betty organized our dinner.

"How does this look?" she asked, serving up the pasta.

I nodded to indicate that she'd put enough on my plate and furiously buttered the baguettes. I was so hungry. Betty had a bottle of Grange Bin 95 on the table; she opened it skillfully and poured out two glasses. Damn, even then, I was so angry with that bastard but so thankful at the same time. Conner organized all of this, and I was glad for the perfect moment, but only because I was with Bett. At the same time, she was my connection to Conner.

We drank and ate that delicious pasta. I stared at Betty without meaning to.

"You need to talk at some point, babe—whenever you're ready, of course."

"I know, but there is a lot to unpack." She looked me in the eye; we had finished eating, but we each had a full glass in front of us. Betty drew a deep breath and let it out. "Okay, I will tell you everything I know, which is more than I am allowed to share, mind you. The pilot was flying close to our airstrip and suddenly lost power. He tried to land, but crashed at the start of the strip. We have measures for this kind of thing, which have been rehearsed a thousand times. He was dead, so Dad had to relocate the crash."

"Wait, what?" I was already so confused.

"Danny, please, I know you have many questions, but just listen to the full story first. Otherwise, I will be talking all night, and neither of us wants that." She smiled. "Dad decided to relocate the crash. Unethical? One hundred percent. Illegal? Yes. Immoral? Yes. But he did it to protect his town. I know how that sounds, and I was shocked too, but I get it. My dad is a survivor, and he wants Taxi to survive, too. So, he arranged for the plane and the body to be shifted one hundred and twenty miles from here and closer to Charters Towers." Betty was talking, but my mind was racing. "Did you notice the face of the witness? It was David, Dad's offsider. Acting, in one of his most important roles. He confirmed that this new site is where the crash took place. And I can see it in your face; I had nothing to do with any of this. Dad includes me when he feels it is necessary. They destroyed any evidence of the change in venue with the explosion. They lit it up, Danny, destroying any evidence. I know this is horrible, but please try and understand Conner's way of thinking. His thoughts are of protection: protecting his town, his people, and his family. That is everything to him, and shifting the crash will help protect Taxi's secret—hopefully. Now, please grab the whiskey."

"Betty, what has he done?" I stood and grabbed the Sinatra Century, then handed her our glasses. "Here you go, sweet."

She poured a slug, which we promptly drank since we kind of needed it at that point.

"My dad is relentless. He never seems to stop or let up with anything. Watch out."

"Hey, baby, I am not worried. I will be careful, but I am who I am."

"You really do need to be careful, especially after all this." She patted my knee and gave me a light kiss on the cheek. "As far as Taxi stealth mode goes: I'm not sure if you noticed the gates when you turned down Poison Valley Road, but they have been closed and locked. On those big gates, the signs say, *Miners Camp 107, keep out, no admittance, private property, offenders will be prosecuted.* The sign to Poison Valley Road has been removed again, too, so there will be no access from that for at least a week, possibly two. The town has gone into full lockdown. Curfew is at seven o'clock every night, and then the lights go out all over town. No one leaves for now, and no one enters. Everyone has to be off the streets. Phones and internet will be limited. It's all for our own security, and you need to try and understand that, please."

"Conner shifted an entire accident site within four hours. How is it that he can do that, Betty? He could go to jail if anyone found out."

"Er, Dad has never worried about the law—only his law. He does what he wants." Betty looked at me intently. "Our airstrip has been cleared and has tree trunks and dirt all over it so no planes can land. Taxi is off the grid. Taxiplus is offline. He also has men in Charters Towers, spreading rumors, staying alert for any new information, making sure the story sticks."

"You need to settle down, Betty. I can see this has you rattled."

She looked at me earnestly. "Danny, you have not even heard everything yet. Sometimes, my dad is like a raging bull. He will do anything to protect Taxi. I sometimes think he would kill to protect Taxi. I have nothing but my feelings, but I feel he is capable. It scares me when I see and hear him like this, it really does. This bubble he has us in is sweet, but his control is all around us. He sent us up here into the hills like this, almost his prisoners. He still has complete control. Never mind, I absolutely adore being a cellmate with you Danny."

It took a while to sink in, but Betty was right. And one other thing was certain; we needed a plan to get out of this mess.

"So, what is our next move?"

"You, stay away from him, you hear me? I know it will be up to you and him at some point, but he is very strong, Danny. Do not go head-to-head with him. He will beat you, hands down, please believe me. Outsmarting him is our only option, but I know we can do it. I have your back, too. I love you baby." She leaned forward and planted a kiss on my cheek. "He gave me the papers to the camper. It is mine now—ours."

"*Shit*, now I hate him and love him at the same time," I said passionately. "If we try to leave Taxi, would Conner let you go?"

"Well, that will depend on how we go about it. We can't just go. You know that, right?" She regarded me with her eyes wide and her eyebrows raised. "He would hunt us down and drag us back. No, he must allow us to leave, and right now he expects me to stay; I am his only family."

"I thought as much. We will need to convince him that it is the best thing for you. Our timing will need to be spot-on, too. We can't approach him now with all this shit hitting the fan."

"No way, all this will have to blow over first. So, we have a while to formulate a plan."

"But Bett, would you really leave here?"

10
Conner Rage

Conner had been through some tough times, but this was right up there with the toughest. He remembered back to his childhood, when his dad was so hard on him. If Conner stepped out of line or said something wrong, his father's belt would often get involved. Conner learned to do things right the first time. Mistakes were very costly and painful.

His dad taught him to play chess when he was seven years old. It was important to Conner senior that his son learn tactics and defensive maneuvers. He was a busy man, but he took the time to groom junior just as his father had done with him.

"That move is useless—a wasted sacrifice," Senior would say. "If you sacrifice anything, make sure it will be worthwhile in the end."

Senior took him through the plant when he was only six years old. He carried him and talked softly in his ear the whole way through that bloody and terrifying tour. Nothing was omitted, and Conner had nightmares for weeks.

A month later, Senior took him again, carrying him in his arms and explaining everything quietly. Junior sobbed through the entire tour, but Senior would not allow him to close his eyes. If he did, he would pinch him hard until his eyes opened again, and then they would move on. Conner soon learned to pay attention and to tolerate the sight of death and the skins.

As he grew up, he developed a sense of belonging; Taxiplus was part of his life it and in his blood. Conner took over when his father passed, and even at twenty-one years old, he was fully prepared to do so. Changes needed to be made, customers needed to be sourced carefully, and he needed an heir to the empire.

Conner had had many women, but none worthy of his long-term attention. Finally, he settled for Joanne. She was nice, with good hips for childbearing. So, he married and hoped for a boy to carry on this legacy. Betty, his beautiful little girl, was born less than ten months later. He loved her dearly, but Conner needed a son to perpetuate the family name. Two miscarriages followed, but then, during the fourth pregnancy, they learned that a boy was on the way: Justin the second. At last, the day arrived. Conner had the best hospital and doctors lined up for the birth, but in the end, none of that mattered. Joanne and Justin died in childbirth. Heartbroken, he shipped their bodies back to the factory and had them treated and placed in the family mausoleum. It was over.

Conner became ruthless, expanding exponentially, and decided that Betty would be his savior by giving him a grandson. When she was only nine years old, he found the perfect future husband and made sure Harrison was in all of her classes. He influenced them in every way he could, and as she grew into a woman, he encouraged Betty.

"He is perfect for you. I can tell he loves you."

Later they married, and before too long, Little Joe was born. Finally, he had an heir.

Conner's bliss did not last long enough. When Joe became sick, he spared no expense. He spent hundreds of thousands of dollars trying to save him, but money did not help. He was doomed, as was his father. When they were both gone, Conner was lost. He forgot about his Betty, who really needed him. She was nothing more than a failed chess piece in his mind. Had Senior been there, he would have felt that belt once more. They, too, were treated and placed with the rest of Conner's family, and he spent every night in the mausoleum., ignoring Betty who was in agony. She was lost and broken and for her it lasted years.

Shifting the crash site was not a simple task—far from it. It required no less than fifty employees, all trusted and practiced in messy cleanup. There had been accidents nearby before, but not a plane crash; investigators would be thorough. There was no room for mistakes, so he was present for all aspects of the move. The new site was chosen with great care: isolated, far enough away not to draw attention to Taxi, but still accessible. The explosion went according to plan, and all evidence of the shift was destroyed.

Major roads were closed, but they were quiet roads anyway. David had told the police officers his story and waited for the reporter crews to arrive, wiping his sweaty hands on his pants. He knew he would be looked after for the remainder of his life by Mr. Rage. Conner waited for the storm that was coming, but he was ready.

My Taxi is safe, and it is not too late for Betty. Daniel may be my last chance for an heir.

He had been chosen carefully. Conner's best scouts worked for years on this pairing, but he was a wild card. It would take some work to move his queen to a position to call checkmate.

11
Dark is the Night

It had been a long day, and Betty and I were tired after the bourbon, wine, and pasta, so we decided to hit the sack early. After undressing, we climbed into bed and curled up in each other's arms.

"Good night, sweetheart," I said after kissing her head.

"Sleep well, my love."

Sleep embraced us both within minutes.

* * *

Darkness enveloped me, but it was not the darkness of night. There was no escaping it as it closed in like murky water slowly rising. Dark, dark was the night, and it was taking me away, far from here. Drowning in it—I was drowning, gulping and gagging. The darkness was terrifying, and I didn't understand it.

Then, through the murkiness I saw a billion stars slowly come into focus. The darkness fell behind me, and ahead there was a billion points of light, all slightly different, a bright pink nebula, and magenta clouds. Here is where stars are born. They were so close together they formed a bright, cloudy mass. With ominous black voids within. The stars that surrounded me were white, yellow, and red; some were even nearly black. Then, directly ahead, there were two dim, red stars: a binary system, my destination. I slowed down as a young newly formed planet slowly appeared in front of me with two small moons flanking it. It was so familiar, like home.

"This is where we live, Daniel," a voice said.

"But I am asleep."

"No, you are home. This is our home, and you are soon awakened"

* * *

Betty nudged me. "Are you okay? Wake up, Danny."

I was fully awake then. "What's the matter? Are you okay?" I was worried about her.

"I'm fine. You were talking in your sleep again. I was worried."

"Are we home?" I asked, confused.

"My sweet, go back to sleep. No more dreams," Betty whispered.

"Oh, okay…"

* * *

"Betty, don't leave me here."

"I am right here," she said. "Relax."

I looked at her; she was a flat skin, a Study-Skin, and empty of everything. She lay beside me with her flat hand in mine, her missing eyes staring at me.

"Come home," she called. "I am right here in the dark night, among the stars."

* * *

"Danny, wake up! Please, you're scaring me!"

I fell out of our bed and woke up startled. "What the fuck? What happened?"

Betty was breathing heavily, she sat next to me, looking down, she had one hand on my cheek and the other gripped my hand tightly; her face full of concern. "You were having a bad dream again. It seemed really bad."

"I'm sorry. That scared me, too. I won't tell you about it now, but these nightmares are all connected to this place somehow. I will work it out."

"I'm alright; I was more worried about you. We'll talk about this more tomorrow. For now, fall into my arms and feel my body on yours, my heartbeat next to yours, my legs around you. Relax into me. Time your breath to mine," she whispered in my ear.

My breath slowed, and I listened to her heartbeat so I could try and time mine with hers. I felt every part of her body on mine, and I slowly drifted into a peaceful sleep.

* * *

"Danny, I am here, by your side. Dark is the night, but I am right here: your golden light. Hold me tight in your arms, and don't worry, my love; I have you now as you have me. Together, we have this world in our hands. Our love will survive it all. Our love brings light to all."

Our golden, swirling bodies flew naked through space, hand in hand. We would survive an eternity together. The Old Ones were together again.

* * *

As we slept, the dark, moonless night carried on. The stars were so very bright but we did not see them. Trails of brilliant light crossed the sky; some were natural, and some were not, but they all went unseen. Distant howls of dingoes searching for companionship, fruit bats fighting battles in trees, curlews screaming like babies wanting to feed in the early hours, a cow mooing: we were oblivious to nature's cacophony. We finally found peaceful sleep wrapped up in each other.

12
Day Six...I Think

Seriously, was it? It felt like we'd spent weeks there, though I was not sure why. My days with Betty had been magical. Every day was so diverse and amazing, even the wild ones that rocked my concepts of normality.

I stared at the goddess lying next to me in the morning light, gently stroking her cheek with my finger. I didn't want to break this perfect feeling of bliss, beauty, and love.

"Hey, you," she said softly without opening her eyes.

Her hands slowly moved under the sheets, gliding over my body, and feeling as though electricity came from her fingertips. A woman with superpowers: her electricity awakened my soul, making me feel alive.

"Hey, you," I answered with a moan as her fingers slid all over me. She moved closer, her lips on mine, tenderly kissing me, and her hand wandering, taking hold of my cock, making me hard. She had glided on top of me effortlessly, in full command of her body and mine. I looked into her eyes, which seemed to peer into my very soul. "Betty—"

"Hush, my love, feel me. Feel my heart, my love, my body on you. We are one."

"Oh, Bett, I feel you. Oh, hell—how do you do that?"

She was tightening and then releasing me; I struggled to form words. The gentle rhythm slowly built until we reached the crazy crescendo of our epic symphony; it was far more than anything Bach or Beethoven could ever envisage. We heaved in erotic joy together as our notes slowly died down.

"Girl, you will give me a heart attack if you keep that up, but I don't even care if that's how I die. I am in love with everything you are, baby. You have awakened a passion in me that has been lost for such a long time. You make me hungry."

Betty slid off of me and grinned. "I know, I can feel your passion and your hunger. I can feed you, my love."

She winked that wicked wink and gave me that alluring, irresistible smile. I kissed that beauty so gently and warmly, but I was worried because I remembered something all of a sudden.

"Hey, sorry about last night. I remember some of it. I did not mean to scare you."

"There is no need. So much has been going on, so it is not surprising your mind is in overdrive."

"Betty, there's more to my dreams or nightmares than that. My dreams are all tied to the heavens, and I keep seeing a place with two moons and two dim, red suns."

"Really? Danny, I have been having dreams about a place with two moons and two suns. I thought I was going crazy, especially when I heard you talking in that strange language. I thought I could understand it; it was so foreign, yet so familiar. What is this all about?"

"Are you friggin' serious, Bett? Are you are dreaming about the same place as me? How is that even possible?"

"This is creeping me out. Let's take a swim and wash up, then talk about this some more over breakfast. I think we need to write down what we remember from these dreams, separately, and then confer with each other. Maybe we can get to the bottom of this crazy shit together."

Betty stood, found the shower gel and towels, and grabbed my hand. "Come on Danny, I'll race you to the other side of the lake—whatever stroke you like."

We walked to the edge of the water hand in hand, letting the morning sun warm our naked butts. We dropped the towels and sprinted into the cool water. We dove in at the same time, and our swimming felt synchronised; our arms rose and fell rhythmically, and we were neck and neck all the way across. We stood and looked at each other.

"Draw," we both said, then laughed.

"Race you back!" I said, but she had already turned and dove back in.

She had a two-yard head start. I swam furiously after her, but she was too quick this time. God, I loved her strength and fitness.

"Ha, I beat you!"

She was jumping up and down in the shallow water with her arms raised above her head, clapping her hands with such a sweet smile. Water splashed everywhere. She was so happy, and so was I. We washed and dried ourselves off, threw on some clothes, and put the kettle on.

"What should we do for breakfast?" I asked.

Betty thought for a second and said, "How about I whip up some eggs Benedict with smashed avocado and bacon? We have fresh sourdough bread, so that will be perfect."

"Isn't hollandaise a pain to make?" I asked.

"Oh, hell no. I've done it a thousand times, and a few minutes is all I need. You can get started on the bacon; toast the bread on one side in the bacon fat after, okay?"

Betty really was a great cook. I watched the ease she showed in pulling together the whole dish in awe. By the time she was done, it looked so damn good that it was practically begging to be eaten.

"This meal belongs in a five-star restaurant, not out here in the bush! I am so grateful you are so blessed with this ability. This is amazing," I said.

She smiled. "I studied hard to become a chef: four years of agony I was top in class. You didn't know that did you?"

"Er, no, that was conveniently omitted from your resume," I said with a laugh as I tucked in. "You are truly full of surprises; I love it!"

The breakfast was delicious; I would have to start calling her *chef* whenever we were in the kitchen together. We loaded every dish into the dishwasher and turned it on.

"How about a walk to help all this protein digest?" I asked.

"Sure, I'll just go to the toilet first and get changed into something suitable for a hike."

I put on my walking shoes and grabbed some water and energy bars, then loaded it all in a backpack. I went outside and looked up. A few big, beautiful clouds milled around, but the day was warm. My phone's weather app said it was eighty degrees Fahrenheit with eighty percent humidity, which was typical for late June in northern Queensland. I loved the tropics and hated the cold because it messed with my bones.

Betty came out of the camper in a beautiful, sky-blue bikini I had not yet seen, joggers on her feet, and a thin shawl type of thing around her waist. I couldn't find the words to tell her that while her outfit wasn't really suitable for hiking, it looked so good on her.

"I'm ready," she proclaimed.

"Wow, beautiful! You can lead the way." I smiled like a fool and checked out her butt as she took the lead.

"Watch where you walk. Don't just stare at my ass or you will fall over."

We set off, talking and having a great time. The path led us around the side of a big hill, and we slowly climbed and wound our way through the sparse scrub. Betty was powering ahead.

"Hey, slow down and keep an eye out for snakes. They often come out onto paths in the winter to get warm in the sun," I warned her.

Sure enough, she stopped in her track's mere minutes later. Up ahead was a big scrub python: harmless, but scary. This one was about thirteen feet long and as thick as my arm.

Betty ran back and grabbed my arm. "Er, that is massive."

"I can see that, but he is also harmless to us. Still, we had better go around. He may be slow to move, as it is morning and his blood still cold, but let's not tempt fate."

"Good idea. Lead the way."

I laughed, but agreed and took her hand. We worked our way through the scrub off the path and came to a clearing that was as big as a football field. There were no trees around, and the ground was different there—almost like it was dead. A sealed road led into the clearing, and the whole place seemed so familiar.

"Do you know this place?" I had to ask.

"Yes, we have been here before," she answered.

"When?"

"Not sure, but it was recent."

"Okay, I'm not so sure." We stopped for a moment, and I looked at her. "How is this happening? What were we doing here—wherever here is? Is Conner messing with our minds? That must be what is going on. Does he have anything that could possibly do that?"

"I don't know, that sounds far-fetched. What could even do that?" She appeared to search through her memories. "I can't recall him having anything that could make us forget a place. That seems too crazy to me; maybe I came here years ago, with my dad. Yeah, that's got to be it."

"Okay, let's get going. This is creeping me out," I said as I pulled on Betty's hand so we could continue on in the direction the path led.

We continued our walk with no more surprises except for unintentionally startling a mob of kangaroos grazing on the side of our path. They all turned in our direction, froze, and then bounded off, crashing through the scrub.

"Oops!" Betty exclaimed.

We turned back after another few miles and slowly made our way back to camp. We had a quick swim to freshen up, and it was so invigorating.

"Hey, you hungry?"

"Yes, one hundred percent! What do you feel like?" she asked. "I'm thinking burgers. We can have them on our plates in ten minutes."

"That sounds great, chef! Let's do this."

Betty started on the meat, and I took all the fixings from the fridge and started buttering the buns. I toasted them while Betty cooked the meat. I sliced and peppered the tomatoes while Betty threw in some sliced jalapenos and finished off the burgers. They looked amazing, but way too big for any human mouth. We devoured them anyway, washing them down with a few Coronas. We cleaned up the kitchen and went outside to the deck chairs with some bourbon, pads of paper, and pens.

"Okay, just write anything that you remember from the dreams, no matter how trivial, let's just take our time.

Betty handed me the pad and a pen, then poured out two hefty shots of bourbon to help jog our memories. We balanced the pads on our knees, which was awkward to say the least, but we made it work.

- The skins, I dreamt of the cinema full of skins
- Blue grass, purple sky, two moons, two dim, red suns
- Green clouds
- Pink trees
- Humans, or were they skins? They were watching us.
- Someone asking for help?
- Traveling through the stars but no spaceship, just me and you?
- My cock is golden with swirling patterns, and it is way bigger.
- A flat skin version of Betty holding my hand was the worst.
- Flying naked
- My home is not here, but there?
- Two balls of lightening in front of me.

Betty's page contained the following:
- Deep sadness, a lost community
- Displaced people, looking for home
- Two small moons in the sky
- Everyone in jumpsuits, staring, human?
- Two dim suns and they are red, purple sky
- Danny you are standing in a field of blue grass?
- I dream of you with a golden, sparking, glowing cock, swirling with colors it is huge.
- Dark, dark nights and brilliant stars brighter than here, everywhere.
- You Danny standing holding up something important and all around are joyous
- A feeling of total satisfaction, I can't see this, but I feel it deeply and it comes from you Danny and those all around us, but I don't know who they are.
- Flying naked in the sky and space.
- And I've seen a huge statue of your cock: fifteen feet high.

We had sat quietly for more than an hour, sipping our drinks and trying to remember everything we could. We did not say a word to each other the whole time.

Bett was so pensive, and I had no idea she was going through the same shit I was.

"Right, let's swap pads and work through this," Betty said. "Feel free to write notes about anything else that comes to mind and speak your mind. This is the only way we're going to work this out."

13
The Awakening

"Bett," I said as I kept rereading her points. "What the fuck is going on here?"

After a minute Betty looked up at me, aghast. The blood had drained from her face, leaving her skin deathly white. "I don't understand. How can this be? This makes no sense."

"Do you really see me in your dreams, or do you think you just know it's me?"

This was important to me for some reason.

"No, I see you like I see you right now. This is real, isn't it?"

Her question was not as crazy as I might have thought before all of this, but I was eager to reassure her, so I dropped to on my knees in front of her. I put my arms around her and pulled her in for a hug. She embraced me openly, obviously needing to feel me as I needed to feel her.

"It had better be real. Look, I don't have the answers to this shit, but I know I love you."

"I have no idea what is going on, but I love you, too."

She kissed me on my ear before we pulled back and looked into each other's eyes.

"Okay, we need to throw some ideas around. Some of the things we wrote were nearly the same. It seems like we are seeing another planet, but that could also be symbolic of something else, couldn't it?" I asked.

"Absolutely. Hear me out; if a race or whatever could not really communicate like we do, they might try to influence our thoughts. This could also be paranormal activity."

"Whoa, ghosts, lost souls? I hadn't even considered that, but thousands of skins coming through Taxi every week has to count for something. I have never believed in ghosts, but here it seems like anything goes."

"That sounds like something we could make a song about. Yeah, in Taxi, anything goes," Bett sang beautifully.

I appreciated that we could still smile and laugh in spite of what was in front of us: what a team.

"Okay, what do we do? Are we being abducted by aliens when we go to sleep? Maybe we should pull an all-nighter, where we do not fall asleep?" I suggested.

"We could try that, but what is going to happen tomorrow? We have to sleep sometime," Betty pointed out.

"What if we stagger our sleep tomorrow so we can keep an eye on each other? That way, we can wake each other if we notice something weird."

"Okay, I am up for this," Betty said. "But how are we going to stay awake all night if we can't even make it past nine?"

"Easy: very little alcohol, copious amounts of coffee, and some games that keep us focused."

"We should nap now or soon to help with tonight. My dreams come during the day, too, but a nudge or some words in my ear may help with that."

"Lie down, my sweet. I will look after you," Bett whispered.

So, we lay down on the rug under the filtered sunlight. I closed my eyes while Betty gently stroked my forehead. I fell asleep within minutes.

* * *

"Am I dreaming? I am. Bett? Are you here? Where are you? I can feel you; you are close, but I am falling into that place that's far away from here. Two doors, they are pulling me through one, but you are pulling me back. I can feel your strength. You are stronger, way stronger. We got this."

* * *

I woke up, startled.

"It's okay. I am right here." Betty's soothing voice calmed me.

"How long was I out?" I asked.

"An hour and a half. You started squirming around in the last twenty minutes, though, and I talked to you the whole time you were in REM sleep. I'm glad you are back. Do you remember what you dreamed?"

"I felt protected by you; I could feel your presence the whole time. Okay, do you think you'll nap now or soon?"

"I doubt it. I never fall asleep on a whim."

It was my turn to subdue, I held Betty's hand and kissed her extra tenderly. I told my girl how much I loved her and stroked her hair. She soon fell into a deep sleep.

* * *

"Daniel, I am not ready! I'm falling I have no control, down through the stars— I'm not ready for this, stop it! Where am I going? Danny, please!"

"You are safe; I am here. We are in complete control. We got this. We are the Old Ones."

* * *

She roused slowly, but immediately found my eyes. "I am right here, and I'm okay."

"Bett, I've been thinking that this almost seems like a telepathic connection between us, not ghosts. Seriously, do you feel that?"

"Yes, I know what you mean. I could hear you, but I was asleep. You pulled me back, and I'm so grateful you did."

"You could hear me? But I didn't say a word. Honestly, I was watching you and willing you to be safe. You looked scared, you know you slept for the whole hour."

"What? An hour? That's crazy. It felt like a few minutes."

"If this is all about telepathy, not aliens or ghosts, perhaps our connection is causing all this, I don't know how or why or what it all means. What do you think?" I said as I reached for my drink while Betty considered my question. She mentioned that the dreams had intensified for her as well over the last few days. "Yeah, same here."

"Danny, I didn't say anything, but I was thinking exactly that!" Betty exclaimed.

"I could have sworn you said the dreams had gotten more intense for you, too." I was confused, but then Betty stared at me intensely, and I could clearly hear her voice in my mind without her moving her lips. "You want me to give you a big kiss on the cheek. Right?"

Yes, she thought. *Now you try.*

How about you come here, sit on my lap, and give me a real kiss on my lips?

She smiled, pulled the sheets back, sat up, and straddled me before leaning down and planting the sweetest kiss on my lips. "How's that baby?"

Perfect. This is astounding, but how is this possible, Bett?

"You are perfect, too. I have no idea what is going on; I can hear you in my head as if you were speaking out loud. I can't read your mind, though. I'll admit that I did try, but when you form words, I hear you."

Same: I tried to see into your head, read your secrets, but that doesn't work. This is amazing! God, you are more beautiful than ever this morning. Want to fuck?

I thought you would never ask.

I laughed, and my cock was rock hard as she deftly maneuvered onto me. She moaned in my head, that was so erotic, and her gyrations slowly increased.

You are incredible.

"Thank you, my lover. So are you," she whispered in my ear as her moans grew louder and she picked up the pace. *Yes, oh, hell yes!*

We were as one now, in total unison as we cried out together. Betty collapsed onto me totally and deliciously, exhausted. We relaxed as we caught our breath, breathing deeply.

"Are you okay?" I asked.

Oh, fuck yes, Danny. I have never felt better.

A short while later, we took our first showers in the camper, but we were mindful and conserved water. Having warm water to wash in felt luxurious. We sat at the little table and stared at each other for ages without thinking or saying anything. Then, we both smiled at the same time and had the same emphatic thought.

Jack time and food time!

"This is so weird! We are talking and thinking exactly the same thing, but it's still different. Like two halves of a whole," I said as we stood up at the same moment to get the Jack and the glasses.

When we realized what we were doing, we burst into laughter.

Betty said, "Well, this is going to be interesting. Two peas in a pod like twins…but not related, thankfully. Soon we'll be finishing each other's sentences." She poured out two hefty shots. "Cheers! We should eat. Are we still staying up all night?"

"I am hungry, but I've been thinking about our new ability. I wonder how well it works with distance. Can we do a quick test?" *I'll go for a short walk and we can talk to each other the whole way so we'll know if it cuts out.*

Just don't go too far. It will be dark soon.

I'll just go as far as the lake.

We continued our conversation, and I told her when I'd reached the water.

I hear you loud and clear, Danny. This is incredible!

Okay, that is about sixty yards, I am by the lake. I am coming straight back. Tomorrow we should try even further, but I'm starting to think it will be unlimited.

Yes, I feel that, too.

This was so strange. I never would have dreamed that I could be telepathic, and the whole Taxi thing was already doing my head in. Then there was Betty, the best thing that had ever happened to me. It was like a brilliant light bulb had been turned on in my mind, and my heart had doubled in size. I was so glad I found Poison Valley Road that day.

When I returned, Betty was making some hot dogs for dinner in her cute apron.

I must be the luckiest man alive. Her body is so beautiful.

Hey, big boy, I heard that! Thank you. You are beautiful, too, and we are the luckiest pair alive.

"Oops, I need to be more careful with my thoughts," I said out loud.

Danny, thoughts like that will get you laid, so keep 'em coming. She grinned, winked, and flashed a tit again.

I love this woman. "That smells delicious, Bett."

"It's just a couple of hot dogs with the lot and fries," she said modestly. "Here you go, darling."

She placed the plate in front of me, and on it was another masterpiece. The bratwurst sausage was hanging out each end of the toasted bun, and I could see and smell bacon, chilli beans, jalapenos, and heaps of cheese.

Oh my god, Betty, this is amazing! Thank you, my love.

You're welcome. Enjoy, Danny.

Oh, I will. I love you. Ha, now I can talk and eat at the same time! That's cool.

We finished our dinner and sat back with a glass of Shiraz to relax. We thought the day was nearly over, but there was a whole lot more that we didn't see coming. We were casually chatting, trying to work out if it would be advantageous to stay up all night like we'd planned when we felt it.

What is that? We looked at each other.

"Bett, get some clothes on. Can you feel those vibrations? They're barely noticeable, but I feel them in my bones."

Betty ran to the bedroom and threw on a dress and panties. I pulled on some shorts. "Listen with your mind. There are people talking. That is weird. Listen Danny—shh."

They are awake. Be careful, they might hear us now that they have fully awoken. They know we are out here now. We feel they are not scared of us; They need not fear us, they know we are friends; they will love us, like they love each other.

Wait, what did they just say? This is creepy. I peered through the curtains, but couldn't see anything.

They think we are creepy; we need to show them we are just misunderstood. We are your friends. Please come outside and into our light. Your time for enlightenment is now. We have much to tell you. We are Ishta.

"Betty, close your mind to them." *Do you think we need your gun?*

Honestly, no. I don't think that is a good idea.

Hunting knife?

"No, I think they are okay. Let's go out and see. Grab a torch and put the spotlights on."

"Okay, let's do this." I pushed the door open and we walked out into the night, but it wasn't dark. We could see two people standing about twenty feet away: Normal looking people, a man in his late twenties and dressed neatly in business clothes, and a girl who was maybe twenty and in neat jeans and a sweater. They just stood there motionless. They both had dark sunglasses on, but it felt as if they were staring at us. We moved forward slowly, slightly terrified of why they were there and what was going on.

They spoke in unison in our heads with telepathy. *Hello, we are Ishta, and we are two as one, like you. We are binary like you. You understand us now that you are fully awake. Before this time, we could not talk to you, but the awakening removes your fear of Ishta. We are the influencers, who guided Connerelle to get you back together because we need you as one again. We assisted your awakening. Your kind is rare; in this timeline, you are the last two.*

They each held up their hands as if to hold up an apple in their palms towards us; it would have been almost comical. But it was their way to show us we were the last two, we understood clearly. We could hear them just clearly, even though their mouths did not move at all, and why those dark glasses on at night?

Hello, Ishta, we thought together, somehow knowing what we both wanted to say. *We are pleased to meet you, but we do not understand what you're saying. Can you please tell us more about this awakening? Why have you come to us out here and in the middle of the night, it disturbs us, we were not expecting visitors? Where did you come from? You look like us, and you talk in our heads. Why do you refer to Conner as Connerelle?*

I tried to keep my thoughts to myself after that, but I was struggling against what felt like someone scratching my scalp with a hard brush. It was unnerving, to say the least.

Please, don't close your minds and we will answer your most pressing questions, we did not expect you were strong enough to hide thoughts from us. Your joining is meant to be. You have been together before, many times; you are the Old Ones, but now you have much to learn. You are the children with amnesia due to resets, and we are the teachers, influencers, and guides. It was necessary to get you two together again: vital. We ensured Connerelle made it happen. It was the only way. As you are BettDanny two as one, soon Connerelle, will be two as one. We say your names as one, you are whole, when you are together. We are from all places and all times; this is of no matter to you now. Connerelle has no idea what we do, only that we purchase his skins, and we hide our eyes so as not to scare you with our true forms. The awakening that you have experienced is a gift from long ago that was given to so few; it means that you can now speak the lost language of your minds. We showed you our haven through thoughts to assist in your awakening, but we did not abduct you. You felt as if you were there, but you never left this place, this is how we wake you. We show you. We must leave now, but you will remember tonight, not like other nights. Ishta is happy you are awake. We will return tomorrow after the midday sun has crossed over for the start of your enlightenment.

They turned away simultaneously and walked off. The light faded, and they disappeared into the night. We stood motionless, stunned, and then that low hum returned; it was a vibration so deep in my stomach that I was not sure what it could be. It grew in intensity, but then that, too, faded away. Numb, we went back to Horus.

14
Fully Awake

"What the actual fuck was that about? There is a lot for us to unpack before tomorrow. Were you scared of them at all? I didn't feel threatened, but this is freaking me out. Binary they said, like us; they see us as binary, whatever the hell that means."

I googled the term. 0 or 1 binary code for all computing systems, only two possible values. One true, one false. They live together as one, needing each to survive, without they would die. A couple can be referred to as binary, two parts to be whole, two by two, each half necessary to the other.

"Were they some kind of artificial intelligence thing? And what were they implying when they said we were together again, or that they need us as one again? Have we been together before in previous lives. Is that what they were saying?"

Betty just stared straight ahead trying to comprehend all this information. "Should we revisit the alien theory? Is that what they are?" she asked.

They could be, Bett. My love we have no idea. They could be humans for all we know from our future or our past, or maybe even another dimension. They could be robots. The list goes on.

I understand, but this is all too much. Can I have another drink?

Are you okay, babe?

Yes, but come over here and put your arm around me. I need your warmth even though I am not cold. I was terrified but calm the whole time. Oh, Danny what is this?

"Here's to our awakening." I held up our newly filled glasses and looked into Betty's troubled eyes. "Hey, nothing changes more than change itself. I have no idea where I heard that, but it sure applies to us right now."

We clinked our glasses, but I could see Betty was still worried.

"So, what is our next move?" she asked. "And what about the resets they spoke of? Did they mean resets of civilization like through biblical floods, huge comets, volcanic destruction, solar flares, the Younger Dryas, or ice ages? Ancient lost civilizations."

"If it is, and if everything Ishta said is true, then I wonder why we didn't live through all that stuff," I said.

Betty turned and stared at me; I could feel how deeply troubled she was by Ishta's revelation. I didn't blame her; it was batshit crazy.

"Do we live, fall in love, die, and then repeat all that over and over? That is so terrifyingly sad. And if that's the case, I don't understand our existence, our purpose. Conner sold Ishta their skins, but I doubt he has any idea that they wear them and who the fuck is Ishta anyway? Does Conner know who he is selling the study skins to? What are they, and where are they actually from?"

"And how many like Ishta are walking around right now, influencing our decisions or even our governments? Ishta didn't talk out loud, so maybe they can't. Maybe that is why they need us. They said themselves that they are influencers. I'm not sure I want to be influenced by them, or anyone for that matter."

Danny, they didn't give us this ability, they just helped bring it out, we had it in us all the time and we can shut them out as needed. That may help us a lot.

Yes, I agree. Do you think they had a spaceship, and that's what caused that vibration when they arrived and left? Bett, who is Elle? They had said Connerelle soon would become two as one.

"I have no idea; Dad is way too busy for a woman. Certainly, no Elle's in Taxi. It makes no sense. Danny, I have an open mind, but to think we may have just had a conversation with aliens is insane."

"I know," I said as I reached for the bottle. "This will turn us into alcoholics."

I poured out two more shots, and we downed them in unison. I poured again so we could have something to sip on. With my left hand wrapped firmly around the chunky glass and my right arm on the back of the seat, I gently massaged Betty's shoulder. Her right hand held her glass, and her left was on my leg, gently rubbing my knee. We sat for ages, quietly lost in our thoughts.

Eventually, and without discussing it aloud, we stood and went to the bathroom for a quick wash and to pee, then climbed into bed and curled up in each other's arms. We kissed tenderly; I brushed Betty's hair from her eyes.

"Good night, Bett. Sweet dreams or none at all, okay?"

Good night, Danny boy. Sweet dreams of me or none at all.

I smiled and closed my eyes.

* * *

"Daniel, I see you," Betty said.

I opened my eyes and there we were, standing hand in hand on a beautiful beach.

"Where are we?"

"Does it matter?"

"No, it does not matter at all. You look different somehow. I have never seen you like this, all golden and glistening."

Betty let go of my hand and stepped back. "Watch this." She lifted off the ground effortlessly, her arms moving gracefully while she twirled as if she was dancing a ballet. Higher and swirling around. "Come and fly with me."

I thought about it, then looked down to find myself rising into the air. I followed Betty as she soared higher. We could see for miles across the dazzling ocean; the warm sun made our golden bodies glisten. I reached Betty and held her close; her body immediately melted into mine. She felt amazing as we flew on together. Below us in the ocean, a hundred whales followed us, singing a fantastic song of love.

"Oh, Danny, this is wonderful. This is pure bliss."

Betty's heart pounded against mine, strong and beautiful.

* * *

I opened my eyes and Betty was right there in my arms, just as we were when we fell asleep. One of my arms had gone numb from being pinned under her all night. She opened her eyes, and her huge smile lit up the bedroom.

"Good morning, gorgeous," I said as I kissed her on the cheek.

Good morning, golden boy. "Did we share the same amazing dream?"

"We did. How is that possible?" I asked.

"I want more of that. It was beautiful, and it seemed so real."

"I wonder what new revelations today will bring."

"Danny, have you looked at the time? It's nearly nine o'clock. We slept ten hours straight."

"What? That is a first for me, but I feel great. You up for a swim?" Betty was up grabbing for the towels.

"Yeah, sure, I must go to the loo first. I'll meet you out there."

Betty went into the little bathroom, while I headed outside. There wasn't a cloud in the sky. I ran out to the cool water, diving in. I stopped swimming to wave to Betty as she came out of Horus in a green bikini.

Very nice.

Ha, I heard that. Thank you.

I laughed. *I keep forgetting about our new superpowers.*

We swam for a while and then lathered each other up with the shower gel. Bett took off my shorts and threw them to shore, followed by her lovely bikini went flying.

So damn cute, you are making me hard.

Come over here and give me some slippery sex, bubble dick. Betty laughed hard at her own joke.

Watch out. If I squeeze you too hard, you'll go flying, Bett.

After that slippery encounter, we dove back in and then dried off on the shore. Walking back to Horus, we started talking about Taxi and wondering what was going on with the crash.

"I'll turn on the radio and see if we can catch the morning news."

"Okay, Danny, and I will fix us something for brunch. I feel like bacon, eggs, and maybe some baked beans on toast. Sound good?"

Sounds great! There was news about the local football team's historic win over a team from Townsville. *Must be a big news day here.*

Betty laughed from the kitchen just as the anchorman said, "In other news, investigators are still trying to determine the cause of the plane crash that occurred outside of Charters Towers on Thursday afternoon. Allegedly, there was a minor explosion while the plane was still in the air; it banked sharply before hitting the ground and bursting into flames. The pilot, a sixty-eight-year-old local man, died at the scene. The only eyewitness to the crash, a tourist on holiday from Tasmania, has been reported as missing, with authorities unable to locate any trace of him or his vehicle. Now, onto the weather—"

I switched the radio off. In the kitchen, Betty was in her apron once more.

"Can I help?"

"I'm nearly done, but you can grab us drinks. There's apple juice in the fridge, and you can fill the kettle and put it on for a cup of tea later. Thanks."

"No problem, sweetie. You know I love that tiny apron."

"Yes, and that is why I wear it. That, and it keeps me from getting food getting all over my body."

"We can't have that now, can we?" I smiled as I poured the juice. "Is that all part of the plan? David going missing?"

"I'm pretty sure he is either hunkered down in Taxi, or Conner has whisked him off overseas for an impromptu holiday. He could be in Italy by now," Betty said matter-of-factly. "Okay, all done. Here you go, my good man!"

She handed me the plate of love, and it was full of love; Betty's love of cooking was as clear as the love she held for me.

"Thank you, my dear. That looks and smells delicious as always. Now plant that sweet little butt right here next to me and tuck in." My fork was already headed into my mouth. *That hits the spot, thank you, baby.*

My pleasure darling, enjoy.

We ate without verbally speaking, chatting away in each other's heads as if it was what we had always had done.

Betty, you are too good for me. I'm a loser: always have been.

Now, Danny, please do not doubt yourself. You and I have made an incredible connection, one that apparently lasts through the ages. It would be cool if we could remember some of that stuff.

Perhaps there's a reason we can't. The trauma and sadness of this one life is enough to shoulder. If we've lived many lives, it may be too much for us.

I did not consider that side of my life and I should always take it into account. Thank you, darling.

We were getting better; we could communicate clearer and faster than before, and later, we learned that we could do so from great distances. At two miles apart, we could still hear each other perfectly. I suggested we try blocking our thoughts to use that against Ishta, if needed, but that was difficult to test. Finally, we used the cards. I would pick up a card and look, then concentrate on not saying what it was in my head. It worked eventually, but it took hours of practice. We felt stronger, more ready to deal with Ishta, although we still had so much to figure out.

"What questions do we ask them? How much do we think they will they tell us?" I said.

"At first all I could think about was the supposed resets, but we may be better off not knowing about that just yet. I think it would be more advantageous to find out what's coming, not what was behind us. We can't change any of that."

"I agree, but how do we prepare for what lies ahead? You know, they may not be willing to tell us the truth about our future." *They have the upper hand.* "Okay, so what else can we ask? Can we have a look at your ship?"

"Yes, I do want to see that," Betty said.

"They had said it was vital that we reunite, but why? And to whom: us or them? Is Ishta part of the watchers our overseers? Or whatever that is all about. All these conspiracies are now carrying some weight. Especially with all this disclosure on UAP's and UFO's coming from the government."

Bett then said. "We should have them tell us about Roswell and UFOs and UAPs."

"Hell yes, good question." I looked at Betty, and she smiled and winked. She was still the same girl I'd come to love, but we had already changed so much. "We could ask if we will develop any other abilities."

Yes, I was wondering that myself. Let's also ask how many others like them are here on earth right now, and how many humans are like us. I wonder if they can speak verbally at all?

"I'm sure that whatever they tell us will raise even more questions," I said, retrieving a couple of beers from the fridge. "Beer?"

"Why not? I think I will need a few before my next alien encounter," she admitted with a nervous laugh.

"Yeah, maybe a few stiffer drinks, too. Damn aliens—if that is what they are—got me rattled. Hey, do you want to go fishing? We have a few hours to kill before the freak show. We can sit and talk and drink like we are now, maybe catch a barramundi for dinner."

"That is a great idea, Danny: some fresh barra cooked over the campfire. Yum!"

Betty stood and grabbed the rods, the barra lures, a net, and the large tacklebox from the cupboard. I retrieved the JD, glasses, some ice, and the Esky. I threw a bag of chips in and clipped the hunting knife to my board shorts. We took the deck chairs and walked up the river until we came to spot that looked like a place a barra would hang out.

"There are a few logs in the water. They love that," Betty said, pointing to some submerged branches and tree trunks.

Have you done much fishing, Danny?

Yeah, when I was younger, but I haven't held a rod in years and I never fished specifically for barra—only in the ocean.

"These lures need to keep moving to trick the fish into thinking they are live prawns. These are small fish, so once you cast out over that way, make sure to reel back in slow and steady."

"You good with knots?"

"Yes, all good, let's do this."

Drinks poured, we clinked our glasses, took a swig, and then got down to some serious fishing. I had one on my line within thirty minutes, but lost it after a brief struggle.

A short time later, Betty screamed in delight. "There you are! Watch how the pro does it!"

Betty leaned right into it, reeling when she could. Her rod was being pulled down forcefully, but she knew when to let up a little.

"Look at it jump!" I called, so excited for her.

He's a brute. Come on, big fella.

"You got this, Betty. It's big, its body just flashed on the surface, go easy." I reassured her.

"I have to wear it down slowly, or he'll break the line."

I stood there watching Betty, I was in awe, I had put my line down and took out my knife. *Get it on land and I will kill it for our dinner.*

Patience, my man, I am getting there. Have the net ready, then stab it behind the eye; that is the quickest and most humane way to kill them. Then, cut just behind the gills to bleed it out quickly. Here it comes!

The barra put up a mighty battle, but it was no match for my Betty. She carefully reeled it in, exhausted, and I barely get the net under it. It was at least thirty inches long. I dragged it up and away from the water, pulled it out of the net, and took my knife to its brain. It died instantly, and I pushed my knife into the flesh just below the gills and cut through, then turned it over and did the same thing on the other side. I held the barra in the water while it bled out. Then, I scaled the fish on the banks of the Torrens River and proceeded to gut it.

Nice work, I would employ you in my kitchen, Danny.

I looked up. "This is enough for a few nights. You are amazing, baby."

"Thanks, Danny. I'll fillet it here. Give us that knife, please."

I handed the hunting knife to her; she immediately spun it around her index finger, threw it spinning into the air, caught it with ease, and deftly sliced through the fish's flesh—off with its head.

Damn girl, you amaze me.

Thank you, my love. Bett gave me another of her wicked winks. Slicing back the flesh, she created two immense fillets. It looked like enough fish for six people, or three meals. "I have the perfect recipe for tonight. Two chunks will go into the freezer, and four in the fridge. We'll cook two tonight on the campfire, and the other two will be for a green curry I'll make in a couple of days."

She sliced off an extremely thin piece, cut it in two, and handed me one of them. "Here you go: fresh sushi." She put her share in her mouth, so I did the same. It was seriously delicious. She winked once more and spoke. "It is all about the cut, Danny: the right spot on the fish and the thinnest slice possible."

"I can't wait for dinner tonight, baby. Thank you for just being you."

"My pleasure, Danny. That was fun. Do you want to catch and release for a while?"

"Sure, I'm not arguing with a girl who has crazy knife skills like yours."

"Check this out." She held my knife by the blade, turned, and threw it hard at a tree about fifteen feet away. It hit the center of the trunk and stuck.

"Are you serious? Did you go to a school for CIA candidates, or are you some kind of secret agent? You never cease to amaze me, my girl."

"Thank you, Daniel. You are very special to me, too. As for where I got these skills, there is not a lot to do in Taxi, so I learned all kinds of stuff every chance I got. I had the best trainers Dad could afford."

"Well, I am so glad you are on my side, Betty."

I wrapped my arms around her, hugging her as I lifted her off the ground and spun her around and around.

"My girl, thanks for just being here with me. This is perfect. You, baby, are perfect."

"I honestly love you with all my heart."

Betty kissed me, and it was a moment I did not want to end, maybe even a defining moment for us.

I'm never letting you go, Bett. Never.

I will never let you down, Danny. Ever.

15
The Lloyds

After catching and releasing four more barra—though none as big as that first one—we headed back to our camper. I'd learned a few new skills, and Betty showed me some more tricks with the hunting knife. She tried to teach me knife throwing, but I had a long way to go with that.

We sat and waited for Ishta. At around four-thirty-five, we felt the vibrations slowly grow, then nothing. Even though the sun was nowhere near setting, the light changed; it became lighter out rather than darker. Ishta came into our clearing, followed by two elderly women. These two were also in typical clothing for their age, and they wore dark glasses just like Ishta. They stopped about twenty feet away from us.

We are Ishta; these are the Lloyds. They are here to talk as well.

Hello Bettdanny we are the Lloyds we are here to talk with you also. It is a good thing that you have awoken: very important to all. Your timing is crucial to what is imminent. We have waited patiently for this, with much anticipation and as did Ishta, and we invite you to your next level. We will try to make it easy and understandable. Know that you must be confident your planet will survive, as it does time after time. We are here to try and assist you, as we believe in you as a species. If you listen, we speak as we see it. You Bettdanny are two will who guide the survivors; you will bring them into the new world. This is the law. Lloyds are glad to have spoken. We will talk again before the trouble has arrived. Farewell.

When all four turned to leave, I found my voice.

"Wait, you don't just go, are you serious? What is going on? Who are you? Bring who to the new? What the hell is that, anyway? You don't own us, so do not tell us about our destiny without explaining anything, and do not underestimate us. You may be influencers, but we have the power, don't we? That is why you need us"

The four stopped in their tracks, then slowly turned back to us and walked forward.

Uh-oh. Betty, close your mind now. Sorry for that outburst.

It's okay, Danny. We got this.

The Lloyds then spoke in unison. *Do not presume too much. You are mere infants. Your newfound skills are good, but you are a millennium behind us. This has nothing to do with power, and everything to do with the survival of your human race. There is much to do; your time will arrive soon. We are here to guide, not conquer. You have only just achieved the awakening. Enlightenment will come to you in stages, for which we prepare you slowly so as to ease the stress on your minds. As for your many questions: resets happen to all planets, they are inevitable, and no two are exactly the same. One approaches this timeline, so we must prepare. You will survive, as you have before. No, Roswell is not about us; other races have been visiting this planet for eons. They have much to learn from you. They come now before the reset because they are aware of it, too. Our craft is off-limits to you now because, in your current form, you would not survive even just entering it. There are other sentient species that also live on this planet and they must survive this event, but we have time and will advise you on this later. You have other interstellar friends that will assist you. You still have much to learn. The time of artificial intelligence is upon your kind, and it is inevitable, expected. Your reunion was important to all, your love shared is so important, it will bind this planet, you have no idea how vital it is. You have a strength you have yet to discover, but it will come to you soon. No, you are not superheroes, but you have gifts that will aid in the survival of your species. We will help your development, but you must trust us. Connerelle also has a role to play in this story. We will communicate soon.*

They turned and walked off; the light changed again, and the vibration could be felt once more. They were gone.

Close your mind. They heard our questions. Maybe they can hear us now.

No, Danny, no, if we stay closed, they will not hear us, I am sure of it. They may be way ahead of us, but apparently, we have been around for a while too. We have had time to grow and get stronger. They know it, too. They're not scared of us, but it sounded like they have plenty of respect for us. They answered many of the questions we planned to ask. They must have heard our conversation, so when we talk about them, we need to stay closed and talk in our heads.

Yes, I agree. We need to think like spies and be clever.

I was glad that I spoke up, although it was done spur-of-the-moment.

Danny, what you said was nearly perfect. It demanded their attention, and the Lloyds said a lot that we need to unpack.

We stood together and pushed each other out of the way like kids trying to grab the same toy. I let her get the Sinatra Century while I grabbed the glasses. We sat back down, and Betty poured. I leaned toward her, and she leaned into me and gave me her lips so genuinely and sweetly. The kiss was everything to me; it felt pure and real.

To anyone watching, we would have looked like two people sitting in total silence sipping on drinks, staring at each other, touching each other, and occasionally laughing out loud at the sheer ridiculousness that our lives had become.

So, we have a role to play in the survival of humanity. Us? Out here in Taxi? In the middle of nowhere? Resets are inevitable on most planets, but we will make it through this one. That is a big deal, Danny. Well, except if you factor in that they told us everything we discussed asking. Is this even truth? How the fuck would we even know? We are the infants, they said. We need to rethink everything we think we know about them.

Yeah, I think there is way more to this, stuff they are not telling us. But if we are infants in the darkness, how do we get to the light?

Maybe if we concentrate on only that conversation, we'll gain some insight. We are truly awake, alive in the now. Danny, are you okay?

Yes, babe, I'm good.

We were still totally silent as we discussed everything. Not a word from our lips except the occasional giggle or laugh, which was a bit weird considering the gravity of what we had been told, perhaps we were slightly nervous about all this information.

The Lloyds mentioned trouble was due to arrive. Do you feel anything about that?

It seems a bit cryptic. Maybe a solar flare will take out electronics and the internet, sending us into the dark ages. We had a big one back in 1859—the Carrington Event, I think it was called. It took out a bunch of telegraph poles, sending a huge surge through the lines. Telegraph poles sparked up all over and started fires. An event like that now would be devastating, especially to internet servers. Imagine if you could not access your money for a few weeks. Fuel would not be available, and there'd be no lights or phones. How could we possibly do anything to help with something like that?

We would be in serious trouble if any of that occurred, for sure. And apparently Conner has a role to play in this. Because of the skins? No. Maybe. They also mentioned AI. Maybe we're headed for a judgement day by way of the Terminator. We're not that close to having sentient computers, are we?

I heard a rumor in Taxiplus, but I thought it was way too fantastic to be something possible but now I'm not so sure. Imagine for a second that you are terminally ill, but there's a way you can live forever, but you must die first. Before you die, you upload your brain into a memory stick, which is then placed into a humanoid robot covered in your very own treated skin. You now have the potential to live forever or do as much as travel through the stars with no need for oxygen or food.

Wait, is this a thing yet?

Not as far as I know, but I am sure they are working on it. It makes sense as the next stage of human evolution. It doesn't sound ideal to me, but to some, maybe it does. They are still very basic now, but in a few years, what about twenty or fifty years, will we be able to tell a difference if it's our own skin covering a robot?

Jeez, Betty, you are starting to scare me with this talk.

Danny, Taxi is a small community and sometimes lips are looser than they should be, I have heard things that make me shudder to think I am even a small part of this.

And I thank you for sharing that. It could be very important soon. By the way, can I just ask where you think they got their crazy names? They don't look like Lloyds or Ishtas. Between our chuckles, I decided to switch to verbal communication. "Hey, we have nearly finished all of the Sinatra Century. It's already been an hour and a half of silence."

"You must be starving, you poor thing! Can you get the campfire going and some lights on out there? I will prep the barra. Oh, and grab another bottle from the stash, please."

"Yes, Chef Betty."

I hustled out of Horus and relit the campfire, then adjusted the hot plate and put a few small logs under it. We had some solar-powered lights rigged around the campsite that would last a few hours. It was a warm night, and we had such a great, secluded spot by the lake. I brought the deck chairs out and spread the picnic rug. I placed the Sinatra Century on the bench and poured out two hefty glasses. For good measure, I also poured two glasses of Pinot Gris to go with the barra. Betty came out of Horus in her tiny apron and with a big tray in her hands; I raced over and took it from her.

"Bett, I think you're overdressed."

"I searched and searched for something to wear for this meal, but ended up in this. Hope you don't mind."

I laughed so loudly. "This is perfect, you know that."

"I do," she said with a wink. She took the spuds wrapped in foil and carefully tossed them into the fire, then adjusted their position with a stick. She quickly adjusted the fire under the hot plate, poured some oil on it, and threw on two ears of corn that were covered in melted butter and sprinkled with chili powder, cotija cheese and lime juice. The fish had to wait a bit, as it would be quick to cook, so Betty took the opportunity to pass a glass of whiskey to me and raise hers. "Cheers to us, and to another day spent together in love. That honestly means way more to me than the survival of humanity."

"Cheers, babe. You are everything, and whatever happens with all this crazy shit, I am so glad I am doing this with you. I am glad they brought us together, or whatever it was they did."

"Absolutely."

We clinked our glasses and gulped them down, the liquor warming our guts nicely. The campfire was so nice, like being at a school camp or watching an old Western movie. The delicious smells coming from the fish just added to the bliss. Betty placed them on the hot plate, skin side down.

"What is that smell? What is on the fish? Cajun spices?"

"Sure is, Danny."

She flipped the fillets, then retrieved the spuds and carefully opened them to fill them with sour cream and spring onions. Then she placed the corn on our plates and smothered those with even more butter, Cajun spices, and cheese. Lastly, she plated the fish.

"Here you go, check this out, Cajun smoky barramundi with spicy corn and a baked potato. Not what I originally had in mind, but it should be okay," Betty said modestly.

"Are you kidding me? You are amazing, and it smells delicious. You have outdone yourself. The smell of the fire and your Cajun feast goes perfectly together, and we can't forget the sight of your little apron that I get to enjoy."

"Oh, Danny, you are so predictable, but I do love everything about you."

"Oh, Betty, this is a beautiful meal. I absolutely love the heat of those spices; it's not too much, but just right. The fresh barra is forefront of everything. Yum!"

"Why, thank you, cowboy. The fresh barra is delightful: nice and flaky."

"The skin is perfect, too, and the spud and this corn are next-level!"

We finished off our dinner and sat back, staring at the fire as our thoughts turned from scrumptious meals to the more serious matters at hand.

What is to become of our beautiful planet? How many innocents will die? And what the actual fuck can we possibly do to help? I can cook and love you and run a B&B, but I just can't see myself saving lives. You're the writer; can you see it?

Yeah, nah, Betty, I think they've got the wrong people. How could we possibly contribute anything helpful to all this?

Have you ever heard of the Sumerians or the Anunnaki or Nephilim?

Er, yeah, I have no idea what you are talking about.

Okay, Danny, we can go down that road later if it's necessary, but not now. You know, there are so many remnants of ancient foundations that have survived in this world. Some structures defy logic, like Saqsaywaman at Cusco in Peru. We can't pull things like that off even now. They can't even work out how the Great Pyramid of Giza was built. Danny, we do have amnesia. Baalbek, the Trilithon in Lebanon, another site, we cannot explain. There are so many others in Japan, and China: similar examples of architecture all over the world that no one is willing to talk about or try and connect. It's funny, but it also makes sense now. There was a purpose to these structures that we may never know, but there's no way they were just tombs.

Betty, where are you getting all this from? Because it sounds like, I don't know, crap?

Danny all these things are reminders. From our past, things that have endured the test of time. Just listen with your mind; they are still there. They are part of the universe, as are we. Our atoms and molecules are the same as the stars, and we are all linked. Humans are like grains of sand on a huge beach: insignificant as individuals, but a beautiful beach together. But that beach is on one continent on one planet of a billion planets, we are tiny compared to the universe, and yet we are of the stars. Our hydrogen molecules come from the combustion of the suns. Are we the universe trying to express itself, trying to learn who it is? We are part of the whole. Do you feel that, Danny?

Yes, I do feel a connection with everything. I don't fully understand it, though. There is so much more to our existence than we are currently aware as a species. We all tend to live in the moment, and that is fine, Carpe Diem, or seize the day, live in the moment. Fantastic to most, but this is almost a delusion that keeps us from considering our past or our future, both of which are very important to our present. We are here, right now because of the sum of our past, and this is so relevant to now. Betty, I do know you. I feel it deep down, which is why we've had this connection all along. I have known you for a long time, it seems, and we have seen so much pain. It is overwhelming; do not open yourself to that.

Danny, it is too late; I have seen it, all that loss, the death of humanity repeated, many times over. The most recent incident was nearly 12,000 years ago during the Perseids, a meteor shower that returns every year. On this occasion, it rained hell on earth, plunging us into an ice age. Massive flooding through the American Midwest and eastern Washington State, now called the Scablands, caused by the northern ice sheet melting in a flash, the floods took over the northern parts of America and scraped the land bare. All of the mammoths and megafauna died in that maelstrom as did most of the population of this planet. They called it the Younger Dryas and still debate over whether it even happened. More Jack?

Ha, you read my mind.

That event changed the planet. Humanity went underground for survival, and then Egypt started fresh with all those pyramids sitting there, waiting to be claimed by the first king who had the balls. Khufu was the first, and he scratched his name on all artifacts he found, according to the practice of claiming property in Egypt back then. This is how they date stuff, Daniel. You get that these artifacts are way older than that, don't you?

"Yeah, but they hide this truth from the masses," I said. "It feels like we are standing on a precipice: a new dawn, the next event to change humanity. As humans, we tend to think that we are currently seated at the culmination of our history, that we are the alphas, the smartest people that ever existed on this planet, but we aren't, are we?"

What I don't understand is how we have lost whole swathes of our history how does that get completely wiped from existence? Or is that something Ishta and the Lloyds are responsible for? Is there a hidden council or group that runs the earth behind the scenes, controlling governments like puppets? I bet they are prepared for whatever lies ahead. Hey Danny, I just remembered my dad talking about prepping for the future. He never said anything to me directly, but I'm sure he has done something, he is always thinking ahead. There has been a lot of activity out at the northern shaft, and he seems like the type to build a bunker or something.

Ha, Conner the doomsday prepper. I bet he has an arsenal of weapons, down there too. Dad has many friends in high places. Someone in the know might have told him something that's relevant to all this. And what better place to hide from an apocalypse or a zombie horde than in the middle of nowhere? I mean, with all his money, he could go anywhere, but here we are: one hundred and fifty miles from any other town in the middle of the outback, and with a twenty-foot, barbed wire fence surrounding us. Taxi may be one big bomb shelter from the coming storm.

The fire was nice and warm, as was the Sinatra Century in our bellies. The night was still, but we could hear the occasional curlew crying out across the lake. The heavens were alive with a trillion stars. Soon, though, we became aware of the Ishta in our heads.

Bettdanny, do not be afraid; we are Ishta. We are not near you, but we ask that you put the fire out and go inside your transport. Do not fear, all is well, but we sense other visitors are about to fly over your campsite. They are not here to harm, but they do not need to know you are here just yet, and you are not ready to meet them. While you are in the vehicle, we can hide you from them. Go now.

We quickly did as they asked and waited, peering up through the windows.

How weird is this, Danny? Other visitors? Wait, can you feel that?

Yes Bett, and that low hum is not natural. Look!

An oblong orb slowly passed over us. It had a faint holographic, swirling surface, with an almost golden glow, so it was hard to tell exactly how big it was, but it must have been at least fifteen to twenty feet across. It paused over the lake, then went straight down and fully submerged itself. Its glow could still be seen on the surface of the water. It stayed there for about five minutes, then lifted slowly while it appeared to be spinning extremely quickly. Suddenly, it shot straight up and disappeared.

You are free to go outside once more; they have left your atmosphere. They only wanted some water, that is all. The many different species that visit this planet do so for various reasons. Most are observers, but some are mere drones sent by travelers who are passing through this system. We will leave you in peace now. Good night, and rest well.

Well, Danny, that was new: Ishta looking out for us and a strange orb from space collecting water from our lake. Could you feel them in that craft?

Their bodies were weird, like jellyfish or octopi, but nearly all water.

Yes, that's what I thought, too. We are ninety-five percent water, but they seemed more like ninety-nine percent. Where are they from? A water planet, or the depths of our own oceans? I felt no fear or malice from them. Ishta must have gotten the same impression, but maybe not at first.

Yeah, Betty, I can feel that too, this has me thinking what else can we feel? I feel your love for me, Bett; it is tangible, it is healthy, and beautiful, but I can feel something more, too. There is way more to you. You have a secret; you have not told me, but now I see them. Oh, Bett, you are pregnant with twins, aren't you? I can already feel their presence. They are telepathic, too. This is amazing.

Oh, Danny, I-I don't get it. I love you so much, so I don't understand why I couldn't tell you. I was embarrassed, vulnerable, and scared. So much has been going on.

Hey, this is a lot for both of us, but this is so beautiful. I love you, my Betty. Come and give us a hug.

I gave Betty the biggest hug, then stood back and pulled up the shirt she was wearing to place my hands over her womb. I could sense them in there: a boy and a girl.

"This is fantastic, but a little scary, especially with all this weird stuff happening. I've got you, Bett. Don't worry."

I stepped back and went down on one knee, holding her hand and looking into her eyes. She had tears running down her face and I hadn't even asked the question yet.

"My darling Betty, will you marry me?"

"Oh Daniel. Yes, I will, yes! Come up here and kiss me, please."

I stood up, and we embraced each other tightly as we locked lips. Our kisses became more excited, and Betty started tugging at my shorts until they fell to the ground. I pulled her shirt off, and we fell into the bed. Our lovemaking was as intense as ever. Betty was so passionate and so full of joy; we knew how to make each other very happy by that point.

When we were thoroughly satisfied and exhausted, we just stared at each other and grinned until we fell asleep.

* * *

We floated above Earth, our golden bodies orbiting around our fabulous, blue bowling ball. The sun was rising: on the east as city lights were going off in the west. Another glorious morning in Australia.

A spacecraft zipped by at an incredible rate of speed. We could tell the occupants were three Grays. Small, hairless, large heads with big black oval eyes. They were mere vessels, beings bred to carry nonphysical entities though space. An oblong, white, glowing craft came into view and headed toward Antarctica, then disappeared from view. This carried three tall, blonde humanoids, but they were not from earth. We turned to our moon just as four small saucers zipped around the far side. Looking to our sun, we saw a black object the size of a planet approach it. A filament came from it and appeared to draw plasma from the sun. We could not sense anything coming from it; it was as if it was shielded from our minds. It hung there, motionless apart from the wavering filament for about ten minutes. Suddenly, it withdrew the filament and zipped off.

Our minds were drawn to these objects as if we were searching for something, but could not find it. I looked at Betty; her naked, golden body floated perfectly, and with Earth behind her, she looked like a goddess. Her normally dark hair was now golden and swayed in the vacuum of space, and her eyes glowed the brightest emerald green and sparkled like the stars around us. The liquid gold of her body glistened in the sunlight as she reached for me and took my hand. We flew down through the atmosphere and soared through the clouds like two golden eagles, twisting and turning, enjoying the joy of flight. She squeezed my hand, and—

* * *

We were back in our bed with the morning sun streaming through the window, with the sheets pulled back on her naked body, so the early sunlight turned her skin a gorgeous golden color. Betty gently squeezed my hand.

"Good morning, my beautiful man. That was another incredible dream." She smiled so warmly, so sweetly.

"I had no idea there were all those different kinds of beings from different places visiting the Earth. Who do you think *we* were looking for?" I asked.

"I have no idea and why so many aliens? how about a swim and a wash? Then we can get the fire going and make some brekky," Betty suggested.

"Sure thing, my golden goddess."

Betty winked and slapped my butt as I walked by. "I'll see you out there, Danny boy."

16

Day Nine

I headed out to the campfire, stoked it up with wood from the pile, and lit it. The fire immediately took and grew, its warmth comforting. I stepped back, turned and sprinted into the lake and started swimming freestyle to warm up. I didn't understand it, but my bones had been great lately; my rheumatoid arthritis appeared to have gone into remission after I met Betty. Maybe all her positive energy was rubbing off on me. Or is it something to do with the awakening?

Betty emerged from the camper in all her naked glory, carrying the towels and the shower gel. She ran effortlessly to edge of the water, dumped the towels, sprinted in and swam alongside me in perfect rhythm.

What a beautiful day.

Yes, it's amazing, the sky seems bluer and clearer, and this water is as smooth as glass.

We swam around for another ten minutes and then made our way to the shallows; Betty retrieved the gel and we washed each other, splashing around like kids, kicking water at each other, and laughing our heads off.

Back at the camper, Betty donned her skimpy apron, and I threw on some board shorts. I turned on the radio to catch the local morning news bulletin. There was nothing important or about the crash, so I changed the channel and found some relaxing music, then turned it down so we could barely hear it. I found Betty in the kitchen.

"What can I do to help, chef? What are you making?"

"Just a simple omelette with ham, cheese, and tomato."

"Sounds great, darling."

"Danny, can you pour us some juice and get the kettle on for a cup of tea, please?"

"I'm on it, babe, no problem."

Betty constructed two omelettes and folded them over with the filling inside and melted cheese on top with a smattering of spring onions in less than ten minutes.

"Mm!" I snorted as the first mouthful went in. "Thank you, Bett, delicious once again! Although, all your meals are delicious—as are you."

"You are too kind, Danny."

We finished off our meal with a cup of peppermint tea.

"Mm, that hit the spot. It's always good to get some protein first thing in the morning. What's on for today, Bett?"

"I think I should call my dad; I haven't spoken to him since we came back here, so it'd probably be a good idea to touch base."

"Of course, I agree totally. I do think we should take it easy the rest of the day. The last couple of days have been quite intense. Don't you think?"

"They sure have been, considering we are supposed to just be out here camping. We can relax by the fire, fine-tune our skills, digest all that has happened, think about our wedding and the children's names—oh should I tell Dad anything yet?"

"Er, I'm not so sure. Maybe not yet, perhaps gage his mood, the pregnancy is still very early."

"Okay. You don't mind if I go outside, do you? I have no secrets from you, it's just force of habit, I guess. I have always talked to him alone."

"Go ahead, I trust you completely."

"Thanks. I won't be long."

Betty retrieved her phone from the bedroom and stepped out, still wearing her tiny apron, I smiled as I watched her sweet, round bottom leave. How could I have possibly become so lucky? Betty was a priceless gem; one I could never afford but stumbled into Taxi and there she was in front of me, in love with me and carrying our offspring. It was hard to believe all of this had happened in only nine days.

Then there was everything else piled on top of that, unbelievable, even the dreams, they were so real and fantastical. It was incredible, a little like being on a huge roller coaster for the first time: terrifyingly exciting, with unexpected twists and turns. Conner would become my father-in-law; he was so intimidating. I'm not sure how I feel about that, hopefully we can find some common ground so we can get along

I stood up and loaded the dishwasher, thankful that this luxury had been installed in this beautiful camper. I wondered how things were in Taxi, and if they were still under a lockdown, or stealth mode as Betty called it.

At that moment, Betty came back into Horus. "Dad would like us to come into town briefly so can talk to us together. He seemed to be in a good mood. I did not say anything just yet. I thought it may be more appropriate to tell him we're engaged in person."

"Bett, is it okay if I ask his permission to marry you? I feel he is kind of an old-school dad who would appreciate that, what do you think?"

"I do think he will like that, but I will tell you telepathically when and if it is okay to proceed. It will have a lot to do with whatever it is he wants to tell us. I tried to get it out of him, but he simply said he would tell us when we arrive. He did say we can stay up here as long as we want, and that he will organize more supplies if we need them. He asked if I am happy, if we are happy, and he never asks me that kind of thing. I did tell him that we are deeply in love, and he said that is great news."

"I'm happy that he is on board with us," I said.

"I'll ring Davo at The Dermy Hotel and order some of his famous lamb shanks for lunch," Betty said as she looked up his number.

"That will be nice to have some pub food, and I haven't been to The Dermy yet."

We tidied up the camper and camp site and headed back into Taxi. When we parked in the car park next to the second building in the crematorium complex, one of the Taxiplus goons was waiting for us. "This way, please." He opened the same door as last time for us. Once inside, Betty took the lead. This time we went directly to Conner's office, and Betty rapped on the door lightly.

"Come on in, guys." Conner called from within. He and Betty shared a hug, then he shook my hand. "Thanks for coming. Please take a seat. As you have heard it has been a very busy few days here in Taxi. We learned this morning that the crash investigation is winding down. The cause has been determined to be a poor maintenance record and a leaky fuel line. I have made an anonymous donation to the poor fellow's family, and others have raised more than half a million dollars to help his widow and their three children.

"In the last week, we have had to pull double shifts focused on the Study-Skins because Medi-Corp has nearly tripled the number of cadavers they are supplying."

Uh-oh! Betty glanced at me from the corner of her eye.

"I am starting to question this contract. The bodies are all in excellent condition when they arrive, but I am tempted to have autopsies conducted on them even though their contract prohibits this. However, there is another strain of Covid running rampant as we speak, so they might be taking advantage of that. The skins do freeze and thaw out perfectly, so perhaps they'll go into storage. Anyway, because of this, we have had to reemploy fifteen staff members that were let go. They started a few days ago." He had barely stopped to breathe, but he continued. "You may see more trucks coming and going from the northern mine at the airstrip. I have been having some major restoration work done there, and we recently discovered that this mine is connected to a massive cave system with truly massive caverns. We haven't even found the end of it yet."

Betty leaned forward and frowned. "Are you planning on moving in?"

I thought Conner might get angry at the question, but he burst out laughing instead, Betty and I looked at each other in surprize. "Well, that would be a last resort—literally. I always taught you to be prepared for anything; well, this is my insurance policy. I have been quietly working on this for many years now, and I think you'll be surprised when I give you a tour in a few weeks. Only our people have been inside, and everything we need is being delivered to the airstrip since the mine entrance is hidden in one of the buildings there."

Trust me, Betty. "Have we missed any important news while we have been camping? Like a coming apocalypse or something?"

He smiled broadly. "No, I would be the first to know about anything like that. I have connections all over the world who look out for me and my family. Betty, I must say you look so radiant this morning. Is it all that fresh air you two have been enjoying?"

Betty blushed. *Ask him*.

"Er, excuse me, sir, but I have another question."

"Go on then, Daniel." He sat back, waiting, but for a moment I just stared at him like a fool.

"Yes, well, I—*we* are in love, very much in love. So, I would like to ask for your permission to marry your daughter."

Well done. Betty smiled at me in admiration; she knew I was terrified of Conner.

"Before I answer that, I need a few things from you." He hadn't flinched at my request, but he looked menacing then, like a lion about to pounce. His steel blue eyes were focussed on mine, it felt like he was peering into my soul. Betty stopped him.

"Daddy, stop playing around. It is a yes or no question."

He looked at her, surprised and maybe even a little hurt. Well, that is what I felt coming from him. I suddenly realized I could sense his emotions; this was something entirely new. "I apologize, but that is one question I have never been asked. I respect and admire you for that, Daniel, and I look forward to the pleasure of having you as my son-in-law." He stood and came around the table to hug both of us. He seemed like a different person as he walked over to his bar and poured out three glasses of Sinatra Century, beaming the entire time. "Congratulations on your engagement!"

"To family," I said, and they replied in kind. Conner stepped back, and I saw him look at Betty's ring finger. "Sir, I'm sorry. I haven't had time to—"

"No, son, don't be. This is perfect. Betty, I would be honored if you would please accept your mother's engagement ring to wear until Danny replaces it with whatever you both decide on. You can keep it and her wedding band. I know you will look after my little girl, Daniel, and I will look after you both with all my heart and money. But please, I wish for grandchildren before I get too old and grumpy."

"We are working on it," Betty said out loud by mistake.

"Oh, lordy that is way too much information, my girl! Now, I have done a full restock of the camper, and I've added a few extra surprises.

Go celebrate this great news, you two. You have made this old man very happy indeed. I will be in touch if necessary, but I will try not to bother you."

"See you, sir and thank you," I said as I left, thinking they might want a moment together without me.

Betty gave him a quick hug and whispered something in his ear.

He smiled and kissed her on the cheek. "I love you too," he said as warmly as Conner ever could.

We went to the camper in silence.

"To The Dermy?" I asked as I got behind the wheel.

Yes, lunch first and then we need to talk about all of this silently when we get back to camp. I don't want Ishta or the Lloyds hearing us.

Yeah, sure. So, that went well.

Of course it did. Danny, this is what he wanted all along. He is a devious schemer, after all. Are we just playing into his hands?

Pretty much. Let's see how it all pans out, okay?

17
Taxi's Dermy

The Dermy had a very old school feel to it. I learned that it was erected in 1914, and was made entirely from timber. It was very ornate, as was everything that was built back then, it seemed. This was well maintained and quite beautiful. There were big windows, but the overhanging porch cast a shadow on everything inside. I guessed that was kind of the idea since it kept the place cool. Most of the large windows were open, and huge ceiling fans stirred a comfortable breeze inside, too. As we entered, our eyes had to adjust to the dimmer lighting.

"Howdy, Betty! And you must be Daniel, the traveler," a voice called from down the far end of the long curved wooden bar.

"Hi, Davo," we said in unison.

Once I could see properly again, I took in the majesty of the taxidermy on display. There were stuffed animals everywhere, even hanging from the ceiling.

"Woah! This is incredible! Even better than the museum."

Davo came with two pints of ice-cold beer and followed up with a large carafe of cold water with two glasses. He set them down on the wooden bar which seemed to stretch off into the darkness. "Here you go, you lovely folks. Your lamb shanks will be ready in about ten minutes, I reckon. Conner called ahead and said this is all on him."

Betty smiled at what I'm sure was my baffled expression.

"Wait, what?" I asked.

"Forever his shout for you two here, that's what I was told." He repeated.

"Well, okay then, Davo, but we can still tip you, can't we?"

Davo rolled his eyes and looked at Betty for some support. "Don't worry about any of that. Conner looks after everyone who does right by him. That's how it is here in Taxi. Everyone here basically pays nothing for anything. They do the work, and he gives them whatever they need, which is hardly ever money because Conner provides."

With that comment, Davo turned and left us to check on our lunch.

I did not even think to explain this. I thought you understood how it works here. Sorry, Danny. But, once you are in, you are in.

Oh, shit. Am I in a cult now?

Don't be silly. We only sacrifice the elderly.

What?

I eyeballed her warily, but quickly recognized that she was totally messing with me. Still, this revelation troubled me. Conner had complete control over these people as well as his daughter, but she didn't see it. Was everyone corruptible?

Betty chuckled, "Come on, Danny. Relax. Could you please pour me a glass of water, you can have my beer."

I looked around and started to feel overwhelmed by the décor. Foxes, owls, bats, deer, a huge crocodile, dingoes, kangaroos, kookaburras, platypuses, rats, mice, potoroos, quokkas, and every native bird in Australia were all present and accounted for in the pub. My hands were sweating as my eyes darted around. I was trembling as I reached for my beer.

Your head is working overtime; this is like a panic attack, Danny. Look at me. I've got you, and I love you. Come back and relax with me.

I am okay. Thank you, Betty.

"Hey, lovebirds! Here are your shanks, veggies, and mash. Enjoy." Davo put it all down in front of us and walked off.

More than anything else, the overwhelmingly good smells bought me back to reality. The meat was so tender it fell apart under the first prod of my fork, and steaming hot to boot. The mashed potatoes were superb, with a little garlic, heaps of butter, pepper, and something else: something crunchy, yet soft. I only looked up when two waitresses approached us, each holding a glass of red wine.

"Hi, Bett and Danny, I'm Delores and this is Billy. Pleased to meet you, Danny. Here are two glasses of Grange Bin 95 for you from Mr. Rage. It'll go perfectly with the lamb. Cheers."

They smiled down at us and placed the glasses down. Delores winked at Betty, while Billy looked into my eyes and flashed me a huge, flirty smile.

"Betty, how does he do stuff like this?"

"I think you made a good impression on him today. I don't think I have ever heard him talk like that. I hope his good mood lasts."

"Me, too." I said as I turned back to my food. Betty swapped her full glass of wine with my nearly empty glass, and took a small sip.

"Yum," Betty said as she finished up, rubbing her tummy and looking so sweet.

"Bett, let's go and get naked, have a swim, and relax."

I snuggled up to her, rubbing her tummy and cradling her face in my other hand. I kissed her on the cheek, and I could tell she loved the attention.

Let's go, lover.

"Thanks, Davo, everything was delicious. See ya!"

"Thanks, guys, see ya." He waved as we left.

18
Glamping in Our Sanctuary

We were headed for our sanctuary, our little camp in the hills, our place to unwind, but also full of wonder and weirdness. We hadn't looked at the extra surprises Conner mentioned were included with our supplies; we would wait until we arrived.

As I pulled up, Betty went into the back of the camper. I was engaging the hand brake when she came back totally naked and sat on my lap in the driver's seat. She smelled like a thousand flowers; holding my head still, she planted the sweetest kiss on my lips. Then, she stood and buried my face between her breasts and swung from side to side. I had no idea what was going on. She pulled up her Spotify playlist and pushed play, then proceeded to sing Fleetwood Mac's, "Dreams" at the top of her lungs while dancing like Stevie Nicks in front of me: twirling around, her arms in the air, beauty embodied. She smiled her wicked smile and danced over to the stash to retrieve a bottle of Jack Daniels, but I walked over and kissed her with all the passion I had. Betty trembled with excitement, already on the edge of bliss. The bottle landed on the bed as she pushed me onto the bed and practically ripped my clothes off before all but jumping on my stiff cock. Her passion was intense and forceful; she was in total command and loving every second of it. The explosion that followed was like a bomb that detonated a few times and in quick succession. She was full of electricity and joy, and her whole body moved in time with mine as she squeezed me so tight. We were in ecstasy together, and in love.

"Bett, that was amazing. Can you dance around the campfire tonight?"
Betty giggled. "I love you; you perv."
She kissed me again and again as we drifted off.

* * *

Purple clouds gathered strength as the breeze intensified. The pink trees were in motion, and Betty and I were lying on the blue grass once again. An intense storm was coming, this was a planet wide storm. People were running, but they had nowhere to go. They started screaming when the wind picked them up and carried them up into the atmosphere. They cried out for help, but we couldn't do anything.

The storm blew over us and we found ourselves totally alone. They were all gone.

* * *

It was three o'clock in the afternoon. Betty still slept peacefully next to me. She looked like an angel: so beautiful. I reached over and carefully turned the music back up, then lay there staring at my angel for about fifteen minutes when she suddenly gasped and opened her eyes.

"Danny! Their planet! Did you see that?"

I woke up a little while ago and watched you sleep. You were still on the grass after they were all blown away, but that was it on my end. I wake up. I'm sorry I should have woken you too.

Yes, Danny you disappeared; I was alone. Their planet was slowly ripped apart. I felt its pain, and it was horrible. What was all that? What did I see?

Oh, Bett, I can feel your pain. Do you have any idea whose planet that was?

No, but we need to step back and wake up, then we can debrief on what has occurred today. Maybe you can have a drink or two.

Yes, darling, that sounds perfect.

Danny, can you light the fire, too, please?

Great idea. Do we have a boom box, or something similar?

Yeah, in the bottom drawer over there.

I found the Bluetooth speaker and two whole cases of Sinatra Century. I took a bottle and a glass and a bottle of sparkling water for Bett outside.

At some point, a large, camo tent had been pitched by the firepit, but it was no ordinary tent. This was a friggin 'Glamping tent', fancy as fuck. It had fly screens everywhere which would keep out any mosquitos and we would still see the lake and fire. and was filled with thick mattresses and a soft, comfy stack of huge pillows. There was a solar fridge filled with Bollinger champagne. There were two big outdoor couches next to solar lights and a large charger as well. The fire was soon lit and giving off warmth. I, even though it was not cold to begin with, but a campfire brought it all together.

Hey, you. Betty emerged from the camper wearing a see-through orange shirt with only two buttons done up.

Why even put that on? I mean, it does look fantastic on you.

Ha! I got you; I thought you would like it. "What is all this?" she said when she saw the tent.

"Conner has been busy. Check out how cool this is!"

Betty jumped on the mattresses. "Wow, this is even nicer than the camper. Oh, crap, he has Bollinger and Moet in here, Danny, please get some glasses."

I handed her one, and she gingerly set them on the small table before deftly opening the champagne with a loud pop. Betty poured out two small glasses and handed me one.

This must be heaven.

Yes, you are my heaven. Thank you for everything, darling.

We went outside with our glasses and sat on the couches to look out across the lake. It was so serene there, and such a beautiful place.

I believe Conner. Do you? Did you feel his emotions? He was overjoyed. I didn't think he had it in him.

Of course, Danny. Everything he said was the truth. I could sense his happiness for us too and his love for me. You know, I have never felt that before. I never really knew that he loved me so unconditionally. He has never showed it. When he looks at me, he is reminded of my mum and he is so grateful. Danny this is not what I expected. He hides all his emotions so well and never lets on anything but it is there, deep inside his façade.

I didn't get all that from him, just glimpses, but I too was somewhat surprized. He has built a wall around his emotions and that is how he copes with all the stress of Taxiplus. You know, I'm not sure if I could be locked away in a tomb for however long in Conner's escape tunnel, even to escape an apocalypse. The idea is great, but really, could you be locked up with family and friends in a hole in the ground? Especially now if we can sense others feelings, we will need to control what we take in somehow. Otherwise, it could become overwhelming.

Betty nodded. *I know what you mean, people's emotions are all over the place, I can't imagine what it will be like in a crowd. We should just try to focus on one emotion, maybe love. That seems universal and not hurtful. Perhaps we guide by focusing on love. This will be hard as one day shelters like his might be all over the planet, with individuals and governments thinking they will survive underground. We can't even agree about taxes. How will humans survive the next catastrophe in such close quarters?*

Yeah, I'm starting to accept your dad, more each day for who he is, and I think he's had to struggle a lot to get where he is. but I'm not sure if I could be locked up with him for years.

We will cross that bridge when it comes—if it does.

I looked over, and Betty had her glass poised at her lips to take a little sip. Her beauty was poetry that sprang from her vulnerability, her innocence, her strength, her needs and desires. She was my woman, and she had the strength to survive whatever was headed our way.

"Didn't Conner say the northern shaft was at the airstrip?"

Yes, I went in there once. I was about twelve years old, exploring with some friends. We should not have been in there at all, and when we had only gone in about fifty feet, I froze with fear. Panic overtook me, I had to get out. It was like I could sense something…evil. Not ghosts or anything like that, but it was ancient, and it scared the crap out of me. I refused to go any further and convinced my friends we should turn around and leave. So, when Dad said he was turning it into his very own doomsday shelter, I felt a wave of dread. I'm not sure if I could go back there.

That is interesting. Now I want to go in and see what I can feel. If we went in together, we may be able to figure out what caused that reaction in you all those years ago. You are an adult now with telepathic skills. Perhaps you only feared what you did not understand.

I'm not so sure, but I am willing to go if you'll hold my hand.

Okay, deal.

I went over to the small fridge, opened it, and noticed there was a tray with cheeses, meat and antipasto. I placed the tray between us and poured myself some more champagne.

"Oh, that looks nice," Betty said as she picked up a slice of Swiss cheese.

We had better keep this conversation to ourselves, Betty— especially the bit about Medi-Corp.

Yes, when Dad said that, I was shocked. Why do they need so many skins? Are they planning to take over our planet? That could amount to a thousand skins a week or more. And where are they getting the cadavers? Surely they are not killing people. These are questions we need to ask them. They did tell us to trust them.

Yeah, but we don't even know them or where they are from, all very mysterious.

I feel we might be able to learn more from these fantastical dreams we have been having if we could only control them a little bit more, allow us to search and find some answers. So far, they are doing the opposite of that; we are totally confused with what we are experiencing and wake up with a heap of questions. Maybe someone or something else is guiding us telepathically in the dreams, only showing us snippets of the bigger picture for fear of overwhelming us?

Why do you say that?

Because I can feel another presence when we dream together. I think that is what I feel, anyway; it is comforting, like being hugged, or watched, constantly by something benevolent.

Okay, tonight, immediately before bed, we should have another chat like this to see if we can influence our dreams to show us something we can use.

Yes, Daniel, that is a good idea. For now, do you mind if I put some Crooners like Sinatra on Spotify? I am in a slow kind of mood and not that hungry. How about some sausages with some bread later?

"Yeah, that sounds good," I said just as Moon River came on the speaker. It was nearing sunset, and the shadows slowly stretch out. "Do you want to take a slow stroll by the water? I feel I need to walk off some of that champagne." Betty was in the middle of a huge yawn, so I laughed and added, "That is a no."

Betty stood up, surprised me by doing a few star jumps, and said, "Nope, let's go."

The last rays of sunshine warmed our backs; our shadows were about twenty feet long and walked in time with us. We were in no hurry. All the events in our lives had led us to that point in time. We embraced each other and kissed as the sun descended behind the hills.

Sometimes, life manifested turning points, and this moment was one of them. We perched on the precipice of some unknown disaster, with no idea of what turmoil would proceed. We were engaged in hope and believed that we could survive this, but everything seemed tumultuous and unfathomable to us both, we felt lost in a maze of the unknown. A road that lead over our horizon. Beyond our understanding, with beings we could not comprehend or understand their existence, yet they were right there in front of us. And that was why it had all been concealed from us, our past hidden. Forget Betty and me; our species was not ready for this.

There was so much to learn, so much about our past that remained hidden. We were a civilization with amnesia, consumed by normality: buy a new car, pay off the house, sell it and move to Byron Bay. Money was the downfall of society; to get it, you had to borrow, then pay back what you owed. Then you were owned, until the pay off day. When that day came it was nearly too late, twilight set in for most before that could be achieved, and some didn't even see the light of the following morning.

Betty and I were ready. Our minds and hearts were open to the universe and what it had to offer. This was how we would learn: by listening. Our universe spoke to us, and we were awake to hear it.

Betty held my hand, our eyes locked, and we knew we were definitely a force to be reckoned with. We looked out across the water and imagined our future. It was full of surprises, death, and wonder, but we were in it together.

"Hey, Bett, do you feel like something that's not part of us, something external is giving us power?"

I do, Danny. There is something else at play here. I feel like it is saying over and over that it has never left us.

19
The Dream of Five Million Nights

I threw some more wood on the fire and set the hot plate in a good spot.

"Let's go for quick swim."

I turned in time to see Betty dropping her shirt next to the water. I pulled off my shorts and ran after her. This was our joy, swimming naked in cold water. Well, more like freezing my balls off.

Betty stopped swimming and turned back to me. We were treading water, looking at each other from about a foot away, but suddenly I felt her firmly grasp my balls.

Can't have these babies freezing off now, can we?

She kissed me, and we forgot ourselves and went under the water.

I came up sputtering. *Oh god, I nearly drowned.*

She laughed in my head. *Oops, sorry.*

Eventually, we headed back toward our camp, feeling refreshed and so alive.

Time for tunes and snags!

"I'll get the food; you organize the tunes, Bett." I headed on up to Horus and took the sausages from the fridge, noticing just how much food they had given us. I grabbed some bread, margarine, sauce, chillies, onions, and another bottle of Jack. A familiar riff from the start of "Crazy Train" by Ozzy Ozbourne played loudly from the tent.

I love this song!

Ha, I got you again!

Betty was messing with my head. She was way ahead with this telepathy thing than I was. I needed to concentrate more.

As I approached the tent, I could see her dancing around with no clothes on, singing into her glass in perfect time with the song. Her voice is pitch perfect; she can really sing.

Concentrating I thought, *this is my girl, I love her.*

You tried, but I still got you! Her voice in my head was loud and clear. How did she do it?

You are so powerful, my girl. I can't do that.

You can, I know it. Watch this; I learned this today.

She lifted her hand toward the firepit outside. The flames grew and swirled and became a small tornado of fire, then subsided. I thought that was it, but suddenly the couches overturned and then landed the right way up.

What was that? You now have the Force or something! When did you learn this? I have been with you nearly all day.

That half hour in the camper when you lit the fire. I was choosing my shirt, thinking about what you would like you to see me in, and the shirt I had on earlier suddenly, flew out of the cupboard and landed in front of me, and I thought, I did that! Then I tried to lift things, and it is so easy. I know this is crazy. Watch.

She held her hand out toward the bottle of Sinatra Century; it lifted in the air smoothly and glided across the tent gently into her hand.

"Dragula" by Rob Zombie came on, and interrupted our thoughts, in a good way. Bett started dancing like she was possessed. In fact, she seemed different, on another level. "Paranoid" by Black Sabbath came on next, and she was still dancing naked and looking at me. Her performance was so beautiful, but it was as if she was on another plane. I was not sure she was even aware of her present anymore until her voice sounded in my head.

Tonight is special; I feel it in my soul. Please come and dance with me.

"Break On Through" by The Doors came on. Not the type of song I would ever dance to, but not tonight. The lyrics seemed to fit the mood perfectly—my moves, not so much.

Still, we were attuned to each other. When "Blitzkrieg Bop" by the Ramones and then "White Wedding" by Billy Idol came on, Betty took off like a rocket. I was enthralled by her elegance and enthusiasm. I had asked her to dance for me earlier, but this was next-level, and not at all what I expected. Her timing was perfection, and her moves were executed as if she had been practicing.

The song ended and she said, "It is all about frequencies."

"Bett, you sound so distant. You okay?"

"Suddenly I feel like I have many things going on at once. Sorry, but I don't know how to explain it except to say that it's like there are many dimensions in my head. I thought I saw hundreds—no, thousands of me all dancing together, like in a mirror. I don't know what that means."

I wish I had seen that, too.

"I Wanna be Sedated" by the Ramones came on, and Betty let go again. Had she somehow opened a space between dimensions when she worked on her powers? She seemed to be toeing that fine line between sanity and insanity. In my head, she repeated the same list of seemingly unrelated words over and over.

Hathor, Pleiades, Maia, Pleione, Dreamtime.

"Ramble On" by Led Zepplin snapped me out of my musings. But now my mind was suddenly full of other thoughts. Thoughts that had somehow come to me from the owners of this land. They filled my mind.

* * *

You are part of our Dreamtime from long ago. Your story will be added to the new Dreamtime; our heritage calls to you, and you are awake for our smoking ceremony, just as are we. Sixty thousand years, and now this is our slow dawn for all humanity, to be added to our future's past. We are grateful for your respect to our fathers; you have always been with us through our Dreamtime, for you are the Old Ones. You respect our elders, and Gondwana rejoices; you have returned.

* * *

The haze lifted from my mind and we came back to reality, the music was low and we stood by the hotplate, Bett smiled at me but everything seemed surreal, confused. We tossed the sausages on the hot plate with the onions. Betty prepared the bread as if nothing out of the ordinary had happened. Before, she was somewhere else, far away, but she was back and right there with me, buttering bread and squeezing the sauce and mustard. I kept looking over at her, though, unsure, but she smiled as we cooked our dinner, and nothing else unusual transpired. When the sausages were cooked, we worked together and put them on our plates and we sat on the couches by the fire. We ate in silence, and neither of us felt the need to talk just for the sake of talking. The crackling fire was the only sound apart from our quiet munching.

Then I noticed Betty staring at me again.

Tonight, my Danny, is the next stage of enlightenment. You and I—oh, this is something else.

Bett, what is it?

Just you wait. I feel something awesome is just ahead of us. Seven is so important, as is the Systran and Dendera in Egypt. I'm not sure what all these things mean, but very importantly; Hathor plays a huge role in all this: seven goddesses to aid humanity and the Pleiades cluster. That is clear.

What on earth are you on about, Betty? Hathor and Pleiades cluster? Dendera: I have heard of that place: a beautiful temple that Napoleon rediscovered in Egypt. But Pleiades is that to do with those seven stars?

In Egyptian mythology, seven Hathors came from the Pleiades star cluster to protect and guide this planet. The Australian Aboriginals have a similar myth of the seven mothers coming from the seven stars. Hathor is the mother and the lover, the goddesses adored by all, who lived at Dendera, and was the mother of Ra, or the daughter of Ra. She is the mother of dance, sex, song, music, make-up, perfume, flowers, and beauty. Hathor can have the head of a lion or a cow, and Sekhmet Hathor (as she was also called) is a cosmic mother of dance, fertility, love, and death. She is a protector of women and a guide of the dead. Her name refers to the house of Horus. Our camper is Horus.

Oh, shit, Betty, this is all going in circles, isn't it?

After all of that, we were tired and decided to lie down. We headed into the tent, and Betty wrapped her legs around me. We soon drifted off into blissful slumber.

* * *

Our liquid, golden bodies floated high above the Earth.

"Hey, Bett?"

"I am here, Danny. Look, our Earth is below, and it is spinning backward."

"Yes, what is going on? We are going back in time!"

"Hello, our children," a benevolent, but multifaceted voice said all around us. "We are glad you are here with us; we wish you both all the glory of fertility. You are blessed with two who will be amongst the first teachers of the new world, but you will be blessed with four teachers in total, who will help humanity survive. We are compelled to show you a tiny slice of your history, a piece that has been hidden to most, as many cannot comprehend it."

"Who are you?"

"We have many names, but you may call us Hathor. We are the seven who have always been here: the watchers, and humanity's true mother. We gave Earth its moon to provide it with stability and strength. We have helped humanity genetically, and guided you through many storms. We cannot stop events from happening, but we can aid you in your recovery. Now we show you the last event so you can better understand what this event may bring. Look at your true past. Twelve thousand years ago, as we looked upon Earth, we saw a mighty civilization, one that we did not know of, but that covered the planet, it had lasted five thousand years . Yes, there were many areas where there were still hunters and gatherers, untouched by sophisticated civilization, but the cities were huge even by today's standards. There was no carbon-based power, no gas or oil or petrol, and no electricity poles. Everything ran on magnetism and frequencies and vibration. There was no smog or pollution, and no cars; but vehicles floated through the air effortlessly. Made of timber, reeds, and sometimes stone, they were elegant and stylish. They turned massive trees into exquisite, sturdy structures intricately carved, that locked together without the need of nails. These races had survived an ice age, and lived south of the ice sheets that stretched three miles tall and covered the northern hemisphere. It was a global civilization of connected races that had contact with species from other worlds and dimensions. They had worked out how to open gateways and pass through to other realms. They had interconnected pyramids covering the globe that supplied power to all. Architects were held in the highest regard for using technology to meld and shape and lift stone effortlessly, no matter the weight. All of this was below us. Above us, there were the stars and one point of light that grew brighter as it neared the planet. Many objects came into the atmosphere one day at incredible speeds. The impacts were terrifying: North America, Greenland, Europe, and China.

Millions of tons of ice were vaporised in an instant. A wall of flame covered the northern hemisphere as a tidal wave of melted ice and rock raced south at a thousand miles an hour, scouring any traces of humanity that survived the initial blast. Dust and smoke quickly surrounded the entire planet."

Betty and I looked at each other in horror. How could anyone survive this?

"This cloud would last for a hundred years and plunge Earth into another ice age for a thousand years. The entire population was reduced to a few hundred thousand individuals, and there was no trace of civilization left except for a few megalithic foundations and structures. The hunters and gatherers were the ones who knew how to survive; those from the cities did not, they had no skills to survive, and many perished in the years that followed. A few escaped to live among the stars. Many also went underground and lived for years in caves and hidden shelters. You were here during this time, but your memory has been wiped so you do not have to live with the anguish of this time. Your role was always to reestablish order through guidance, love, and joy; your empathy is your strength, and your power is your will to survive.

"Our gift of telepathy and telekinesis is to aid you. Together, your love is the binding force of humanity. Your journey has taken only a few steps; there is a long road ahead. Your offspring will travel the globe, restoring humanity. We allowed Ishta and the Lloyds to contact you; they are our helpers, but they do not live in this system. They, too, are going through a catastrophe on their home world. Human skins are their only means of survival, so please give them any help you can.

"We seven Hathors are here for you both. The coming event will not be as the last, but the outcome will be similar. You have much to discuss. We grant you peace and love, and we are here to help you and feed on your love. You are our beloved children, reborn to help humanity. Share your erotic love as much as you can. Your love is our nourishment. Now, a new morning awaits you."

* * *

We opened our eyes together; we were inches apart, embracing each other as the morning sun turned our bodies golden.

Betty smiled and winked as she squeezed me. "Does that make you my brother? Ew!"

"Ha, I hope not." I kissed Betty sweetly, looking into her beautiful green eyes. "Bett, we know most of humanity will die sometime soon, but we can't say a word, can we?"

"Truthfully, how would that help anyone? We would likely just cause chaos, and that's if anyone believed any of it."

"No, my dear, nobody would believe us, so forget that idea they would likely think us crazy. Is Hathor really a god? I mean seriously an Egyptian goddess?"

"Yes, and the Egyptians gods are not that old in the grand scheme of things. They are just not who we thought they were—more like a presence than a being. But this is early days they may show themselves yet. I feel like Hathor is with us all the time. We just need to reach out to them if we need them. You know, she was not always the nice mother. At first, she was Sekhmet Hathor: the destroyer. Her father Ra became upset with humanity's lack of faith and sent Hathor to punish them. She came with great rage and killed all before her, crushing every city she came to. The other gods were concerned there would be no humans left alive, so they told Ra to stop Hathor, but she'd grown too powerful. Ra devised a plan to get her drunk on the strongest beer, dying it red so Hathor would think it was blood. At Dendera, her temple she drank it all until she fell asleep and woke as Hathor: the benevolent. She was devoted to protection, joy, love, sex, dance, music, motherhood, and above all, gratitude. Hathor also guided the dead on their journey through the afterlife. Isis took over and absorbed Hathor's attributes, but the Seven Hathors then arrived and became the deciders of destiny at the birth of all human children. I'm sorry, that's a lot to digest at once. Dad's enthusiasm for Egyptian history has rubbed off on me slightly."

"Er, yeah, you are full of surprises, aren't you? Surely, we weren't talking with the original Hathor…were we?"

"Seriously, they are impossible to read. I have no idea who we spoke with, but if I was to go with my gut, I would say yes, that was the true Hathor. Who else could they be?"

"Well, whoever they are, they could be playing us. We are thousands of years behind. Maybe they are here for a big feast, and humanity is on the menu."

"Danny, they can hear us."

"Good. I am over this." I stood and poured myself some whiskey. I went to pour Betty one, but she placed her hand over the second glass.

"No, thank you. The twins." Betty smiled and gave me one of her beautiful winks.

"Oh, babe, I love you—all three of you." I blew her a kiss and grabbed her a bottle of water from the fridge.

Generations of our children will be teachers, leading survivors into a new dawn.

But who teaches them? Us? We need to do some serious research and study, Danny!

Yes, Bett, we need to learn all aspects of our civilization.

No, listen to your heart: nothing about our civilization, nothing at all, but everything about survival and finding their own direction. We help with shelter and guidance and love; we can't repeat previous mistakes. Each time this happens direction changes, a new path emerges, and they need to find it. We must learn how to open up their possibilities; every avenue must be open to them. They will need to learn agricultural practices, so we need to stockpile seeds. Dad can help with that, since he is all about prepping. We will need to work out some form of transport for our offspring. There is a lot of planning ahead.

Okay, but I'm going to need your help, too.

I've got your back, baby. Whatever gets thrown at us, we can get through it together.

The city folk won't make it, will they? All I can think is how I am still technically one of them.

No, you are with me, and we are special.

20
Hathor's Gift, Conner's Dream

*D*anny, they have not mentioned when this planet is going to shit. They don't seem to be in too much of a hurry, do they?

It could be five years or even only a few days. But if it is that soon, we have zero time to prepare. Do these gods have any concept of time? I doubt it. Actually, they are aliens, aren't they?

I guess they are. Hathor said they placed the moon, so perhaps that is where they watch us from.

Well, that would make sense, wouldn't it? They said they placed the moon to provide stability, but how does any civilization bring or place a friggin' moon? That is just crazy. You know, there are a lot of conspiracies that have to do with our moon.

I have heard quite a few, Danny and I hate to say it, but it kind of makes sense. Yes, I know how weird that sounds.

Betty, nothing is weirder than everything that we are going through right now.

You got that right.

We were still lying on the mattresses in the tent, looking at each other intently.

"I gotta pee," Bett said.

"Yeah, me too. I'm also kind of starving."

"Then I need to feed my man. I'll be right back."

Betty jumped up and nearly ran to the outdoor toilet. I went out to find a tree. Standing there, I looked around, taking everything in. Judging by the sun, I guessed it was about eight o'clock. I looked at my watch, and I was right. I'd always had a sense for time like that, but how important would that be in our future? Sometimes, it made no difference to a person's day, but sometimes every single second was crucial. Minutes can pass like hours, and vice versa. What would we teach our future children about time? In regards to survival, dates and seasons were important to planting crops. But lunchtime? No, we'll just eat when we're hungry.

"What lessons? You want to eat, babe?"

Your mind is strong, babe, I said in her head.

I know, I feel it, she said silently.

English breakfast, darling?

Yes, let's do it babe.

Scrambled eggs, bacon, sausage, baked beans, fried tomatoes, sautéed mushrooms, and fried potato bits: we had it all on our plates in less than ten minutes. What a team, and what a luxury. I figured we may as well make the most of it since that could be our last meal like this. We sat down in front of our TV and watched a documentary on preppers while we ate.

"Oh, crap, these guys know?" I said out loud.

Betty looked at me with some doubt. *These shows have been around for years. Have you never seen one?* I studied the screen; they were showing off their backyard bunker. Featuring shelves full of tinned food. Enough for six months they said.

Why would I have? I've never seen the need to sit and watch a bunch of crazies.

Okay, but do they seem so crazy now?

Er, well, no.

Conner Rage has always been a devoted prepper. Hopefully he can help us prepare, but we can't tell him what is really happening. He can't know… can he?

I really don't know the answer to that, Betty.

I feel he needs to know so he can help us properly prepare for this.

We will know the answer to this question soon, Betty. I can feel it.

We cleaned up our dishes and headed down to the lake for a swim.

"I'll race you to the other side," Betty said, already advancing through the shallows. "Go!"

I tried my hardest to catch her, but she was way ahead of me. I didn't mind; I liked that she pushed me to try harder, to go faster. Betty was essentially my personal trainer as well as everything else she'd become to me. I had been thinking about us, out here in the middle of nowhere. Our isolation was manageable. A major city like Sydney had too many people and nothing to survive on; chaos and anarchy would take over in the event of a disaster. We'd be doomed within a week. People become crazy when there was a lack of food. Kill-or-be-killed mode would set in and take over all other instincts.

Yes, we'll stay away from high-density areas, which is what we're doing anyway.

How prepared is Conner?

He has been at it for years now. Remember what Ishta said that they sent him down this path and got him started on the whole prepping thing. We do need to talk to him and see what he has built in that mine, but it shouldn't be too hard to do that and not say too much. Really, what the fuck do we even know about when, where, or even what is going to go down?

A quarter of the planet probably thinks something big will happen sometime soon, anyhow. We have a head start only because we have insider information.

We need to get a move on: target practice with the bows and guns, knife and hatchet throwing, any survival skills like living defensively. This is not going to be easy, Danny. We need to stockpile some books, too. I must tell Dad to do the same. There will probably be no internet, so this is very important. We need rifles and lots of ammo. People will go crazy and kill each other without mercy. They said our strength is our love, but we will have to survive.

Yes, my Bett, everything you just said is true. I will try my hardest to live up to your expectations since you are such a badass. I think we should tell Conner we want to get married soon, and about the twins and the books. We can also see if he will show us through his bunker, so we can gauge whether or not it's big enough to fit all of Taxi inside.

Do we do it today? We do need to get things rolling. Perhaps organize a few items from the armory, while we are there.

Can we get Hathor to show him something? I don't know what, but it wouldn't need to be much since he's already all about preparing for the worst.

We went into the tent and lay back on the soft mattresses. It was ten o'clock in the morning, so we weren't tired, but we both knew we didn't need to actually fall asleep to make contact, so we simply closed our eyes.

* * *

We opened our eyes and found one Hathor casually sitting on a huge chair. She was a beautiful, tan woman with long, golden hair. She was dressed in a white gown with gold trim, and she had the ears of a cow and a crown with long horns on either side of a glowing disc. She smiled, and the disc glowed brighter and vibrated in time with her speech. Her full bosom was almost fully exposed, as the gown was open to her navel.

"Thank you for thinking of us. What can we show Conner Rage? What will help you?"

Betty looked at me, then back at Hathor. "Can you give him a dream?"

"Yes, of course. If he sees some of the last reset, it should encourage him to help. His next sleep cycle will be vivid. You and your children will be in his thoughts the whole time, and this will be enough to guide him."

"Hathor, please do not scare him or make him worry too much."

"We understand. We love you and are here to help you, our children. You are beautiful souls."

"Wait!" Betty cried, knowing Hathor was about to leave. "When will this event happen?"

Hathor looked from Betty to me and said simply with a finality, "*You will have enough time to prepare.*"

* * *

We'd officially begun playing chess with Conner—a dangerous game, yet one that had to be played for the sake of humanity.

Betty jumped up. "Time to get moving. Let's go for a jog around the lake."

"Er, okay, just go easy on me," I said, hoping she didn't want a race.

Bett found the smallest shorts, a tank top, and some joggers. I threw on some board shorts and joggers, and we headed out. She kept up a brisk pace, but I was keeping up.

"I kind of wished I could see the look on Dad's face when he's given that dream," Betty called.

"Yes, I think he will be shocked. We were," I answered. *What about our wedding Bett? What do you want to do?*

Let's keep it simple and small. I know Dad will want something fancy, but now is not the time. Our priest, Father John, is very nice and has a great sense of humor. He can marry us in the Taxi Church of Christ, and the reception can be in Gertie's rear gardens, which are quite spectacular, if I do say so myself. We should ask Dad when is suitable for him.

That sounds great. Perhaps you should call him and tell him we would like to see him today? I know he's busy, but this won't take long. Are you going to tell him about the twins?

Yes, and he will be over the moon.

We ran for another half an hour; I huffed and puffed as we neared the lake. Betty and I stripped and ran into the water to cool down, just floating on our backs under the midday sun.

I smiled at the thought of marrying her soon and reached for her hand, which was already stretching toward me. We floated there for another ten minutes, holding hands and smiling like a pair of galoots. We eventually swam back to shore and dried off, and then Betty sat with a towel around her waist on one of the couches. She held out her hand, and her phone lifted from the mattress in the tent and glided out to land gently in her palm. I didn't know if I would ever get used to seeing her do that. Then her other hand rose, and her bottle of water floated over to her.

Betty rang Conner, and I went into the tent and poured myself a glass of whiskey. Then, I headed to Horus to pack a few things for our trip back to Taxi. I wondered how Conner would react to all of this news.

We can go as soon as we are ready. "Hello, my darling," Betty said, dropping her towel to the floor and embracing me before planting a wet kiss on my lips. "Right now, I need to get dressed and clean up, and so do you. We'll have plenty of time to mess around later, I promise you." *We only have about fifteen minutes with Dad. He is totally stressed because of the demand for the Study-Skins from Medi-Corp. If only we could tell him that the skins are for the survival of a race of doomed beings; that would really get him charged.*

Can he deal with what we want to tell him right now? Could it push him over the edge with everything he has going on?

No, my dad relishes a challenge, and this whole scenario is the ultimate game of chess, one he will embrace with every asset he owns. If he doesn't own what he feels he needs, he will acquire it. This is right up his ally. He is a planner and a winner; I know he will not give up for anything.

Okay, now you are scaring me a little.

Are you ready? Let's go.

We climbed into the cab, put our seatbelts on, and headed into Taxi once more. The road was clear of roadblocks since everyone knew not to bother us up here. When we arrived in town, there were vehicles everywhere for the first time since I had arrived.

"What the hell?" I mumbled.

Trucks and vans traveled up and down River Road. When we arrived at the crematorium, we jumped out of Horus and found a goon waiting for us as if we didn't know where to go. Nevertheless, we followed him into the heart of Taxiplus and Conner's office. Betty rapped on the door as if we didn't have a daunting task ahead of us.

"Come on in," Conner called from within. We entered somewhat gingerly. "What can I help you with?"

"Daddy, Danny and I are going to have twins," Betty blurted out so suddenly and so decisively that even I was shocked. Conner was motionless and seemed unable to speak, so Betty continued. "We would like to get married as soon as possible and have a reception in Gertie's gardens."

Conner abruptly stood up, and I braced myself for the worst until he said, "Twins? That is fantastic news! Come here, baby." He grabbed Betty so hard I thought she would break. "Thank you, Betty, and you, too, Daniel! Come here, son, and give us a hug. I will cover your wedding. You know that, right?"

"Dad, we want a small wedding. You know me," Betty said with conviction.

"But this is the biggest wedding Taxi will have seen in years. I will try to keep it small, but everyone is invited. You understand the dynamics here in Taxi."

"I get it, but Danny doesn't know hardly anyone here."

"Well, I guess this will be your chance to meet everyone, son. I will keep it as simple as you wish, but we will have some seriously good food and drink, including the finest mocktails for Betty. This is the best news I have heard in such a long time. Thank you both for coming in today. Let me make this all happen as soon as possible; I will talk to Father John today."

"Thank you, Daddy, I love you," Betty said.

The man appeared to be close to rapture, maybe even lost in a new dream of his future. But that dream was truly lost, because a whole new future awaited. That night, he would see humanity's true destiny.

We left Conner to the rest of his day, and Betty headed to Peter's office. His door was open.

"Hi guys, how can I help you?" he asked warmly.

"We need a few things, er, from the armory and the cellar."

"Sure, just write it all down here and sign there. I will organize it all while you are having lunch and bring it to you."

"Thank you, Peter, we'll be at Gertie's."

We jumped in Horus while Betty rang Rita to let her know our plans. As we drove through Taxi, everything seemed slightly different, but perhaps it was because I knew this era was coming to end. Soon, life as we knew it would change drastically.

We pulled into the car park at Gertie's, where there were a few new cars out front. We headed in, and both of us patted Gertie as we passed by.

"Hi, Rita," Betty called down the hallway.

"Hey, guys, come on through." We entered the kitchen; Rita and another woman were in full swing for lunch with about four meals going at once. Still, Rita paused what she was doing to give us each a hug. "Your pasta will be ready in about fifteen minutes."

"Hi, guys! You must be Danny. I'm Penny." She had her arms full of dirty plates, which she placed in the sink. "Congratulations on your engagement, you two!"

"Thank you, and don't stress about our lunch. We are in no hurry. I want to show Danny the back gardens, anyway."

"Good timing. The gardener was here yesterday, and he did a great job. It's immaculate," Rita said, looking out the window as she cleaned a pot in the sink.

Betty poured me a big glass of Shiraz and found the nonalcoholic V. No Patritti for herself. She took my hand and led me outside. Rita was correct; it was immaculate out there.

"Wow, this is beautiful and huge! There are so many flowers and native trees." I was in awe; the grassed area was as big as two tennis courts, and had been mowed perfectly. "This is stunning."

"This will be perfect for our reception. I never imagined I would ever get to say that again. Thank you, Danny." She pulled my head toward hers and kissed me sweetly. I love you.

We walked over the grounds until we came to a small pond.

"Watch out!" I tugged on Betty's arm because there, next to the pond and under a big tree, was a twenty-foot crocodile watching us.

"That's Roger, our garden mascot. He has been sitting there for as long as I can remember. He was caught in the lake that's up where we are camped." She winked at me, smiling.

"Really? And we swam around in there naked with crocodiles?"

"There are no crocs around here anymore. Taxiplus has stuffed them all—totally illegally, of course. Now we source them from crocodile farms, but they are very expensive. Go on and touch him! He is so rough and smooth at the same time."

I ran my hand down Roger's side. "I see what you mean. He really is huge, an incredible specimen."

Betty's phone buzzed to let us know that our meals were ready; we headed back in and thanked Rita and Penny before taking our trays to the table outside, under the pergola. We both tucked in to our delicious Bucatini all' Amatriciana.

We had just finished eating when Betty's phone pinged again.

It's Peter; he is waiting out front with our things. No hurry, he says.

We may as well go now.

We took our plates in, and Betty gave Rita a little peck on the cheek as another thank-you for the lovely pasta. We walked out past all the taxidermy in the hallway and gave Gertie another pat. Penny nodded and gave us a wink as she raced into the dining room with two steaming meals. Looking out across the car park, we saw a Taxiplus van parked next to Horus. Peter leaned back against it, having a smoke that he quickly put out when he saw us.

"Hey, guys, I have put the heavy case in this locker, so you had better lock that. The big bag of salt is in here." He pointed to the first one, then patted another locker, then opened the side of his van. "Here's a case of nonalcoholic wine and a big box of fruit. Conner also has this big bag of goodies for you, and this other long box here as well."

We shuffled the goods into the camper and thanked Peter for his help. Then, we drove back up to our camp in the foothills.

"What is all the other gear Conner has for us?" I asked.

"We'll check it out when we get there," Betty said, munching on an apple.

I parked Horus near the tent, and we went into the kitchen area. I placed the bag of goodies on the table while Betty opened her wine and poured a glass, then took out the Sinatra Century and poured another heavy slog for me.

Thank you, my darling.

You are more than welcome. Come and sit next to me so I can kiss you.

Betty leaned in and kissed me passionately, then reached into the bag without looking and pulled out a leather holster with my name embossed on it.

Betty handed it to me. "Oh, lucky you: a Beretta 92FS. That is one cool gun."

I took it out gingerly. "Is it loaded?"

"No, he wouldn't have done that." She dropped the magazine and opened the breech to confirm it was empty, then handed it back. "This is an Inox: made in Italy, with the mahogany inlay in the grip. Very nice."

The next item was a small box with Betty's name on it. She opened it, and her eyes gleamed as she lifted a diamond necklace up for me to see.

"Holy crap! This was my great-grandmother's. I had no idea it was still around. Wow, just wow." She immediately put it on.

That is stunning on you baby.

Thank you. Here.

She handed me a large, wooden box with intricate carvings and a small, brass latch. Inside were two dozen Cuban cigars. The smell of these babies was intoxicating.

That box belonged to my great-granddad. Betty took one of the cigars out and smelled it. "Hmm, this one is mine. The rest are yours."

"Okay, baby." I winked at her.

She reached in again, and this time she pulled out a crystal ring box. She carefully lifted the lid to find two dozen rings that she said belonged to her mother, grandmother, and great-grandmother. Betty started to cry, so I put my arms around her as she sobbed.

"It is okay, baby; he gave them to you because he loves you and knows how much they mean to you and your family."

I held her tightly but gently, rubbing her back and caressing her hair until she was quiet.

Thank you darling, I needed that.

She looked into the bag and pulled out an envelope, which contained a card from Conner.

> **Dear Betty and Daniel,**
> **Congratulations on the twins. These gifts are how I've chosen to express my love and gratitude to you both.**
> **Love,**
> **Dad xoxoxo**
> **P.S. Check your bank accounts. You'll find something for your future together. Use it wisely.**

We looked at each other, our eyes wide.

What has he done?

Betty raised her hand, and her phone floated across the cabin. I went to get mine, only to see it floating toward me. I grabbed it out of the air, and we both opened our bank accounts only to gasp in unison.

Is he fucking serious?

Conner had transferred ten million dollars into each of our accounts.

We were suddenly millionaires.

"This is insane. How can he even do that? How much money does he have?"

"Danny, I can't even guess what he is worth, but I heard the term billionaire used in our house when I was still at home. This is a mere drop in the ocean to him, but it could be very useful for our preparations. Then again, after the event, it may be worthless if trade rules the new world's economy."

"I think you should ring him soon and thank him. But first, what is in this box?"

I lifted the heavy, plastic case by the handle and placed it on the table. Betty opened it, and lifted a hunting rifle out of its case.

"What a beauty, this is a Remington Model 700, one of the best hunting and sniper rifles in the world; this one has everything." She swiftly attached the fancy telescopic sight, then pulled out the folding stand and attached that to the barrel and sat it on the table. "These are used by the army and deer hunters around the globe. This shoots .308 caliber cartridges. Look here—there are two other sights, a shoulder strap, a stock munitions holder and a munitions belt. Hell, we could take on Rambo with this asset."

I gulped down my bourbon and stared at Betty. *Who is this gunslinger girl? Oops.*

I got you again!

Damnit, you are getting me horny, playing with that big gun.

Ha, just you wait.

I killed the rest of my drink. *That's just it. I don't think I can. Come here.*

She stood up in front of me; I undid the buttons on the front of her dress until it fell off her shoulders and landed at her feet. I stared at her beautiful body, her sexy underwear. I ran a finger slowly from her chin down to her breasts, pausing long enough to unclip the fastener of her bra. She shrugged it off, and my finger slid down slowly to her navel. I poked it gently, causing Betty to shiver and giggle. My finger paused at the top of her panties, then went right to the thin strap at the side and slid underneath. I gently pulled the right side of her panties down a few inches, and then my finger went left ever so slowly, pausing in the middle.

Betty sighed as it carried on its journey to the left and hooked on the other strap to pull it down, too. Her panties fell to the floor, and I kissed her navel and pulled her to me.

"God, I love you, my Bett," I whispered in her ear as she pulled down my shorts and then pulled off my shirt.

We spun around and Betty pushed me back onto the bed. She was on top of me in an instant, and her motion was so fluid. I was trying to hold back, but no matter—she was already there, screaming in ecstasy as she clamped down on me. I let go, too, and that just set her off again.

She collapsed on me, shuddering again and again. Breathing heavily, she pushed herself up and looked down at me, smiling.

"Well, that was *fucking* awesome. Sorry about your eardrums; I have never screamed like that before. I don't even know where that came from." She squeezed me and then released me over and over again, slowly making me hard again. She winked that wicked wink. "This time I will be gentle. I promise: slow and steady."

Her arms waved slowly in the air from side to side while her whole body glided on top of me and clamping as she swayed so beautifully. I was a rock; how did she do that? I was enthralled by her sexy, slow dance.

You are so beautiful. You are mesmerizing me; you have me under your spell.

I feel all of you now, Danny. I remember us making love eons ago. I loved you then, and—fuck—I love you so much now. I can orgasm at will now, but I am holding off. This feels perfect with you inside me. I wish this moment would last forever. I love you, Dan.

Betty changed her movements and started to lift off me, then slam back down again, squeezing me at the same time. My heart quickened; she sped up and put her face inches in front of mine, wearing a look of bliss and happiness that I will never forget. I let go as she did, too. Her mouth closed, keeping in her cries this time, but it only made it that much more intense because, in my head, she was so loud, so emotional, so joyful. I lost count of how many orgasms she had.

That was crazy, Bett the most intense sex ever. My dick will never go down after that.

Betty smiled and looked at it. *Whoa, you're still hard after that? Did you take some Viagra?*

Er, no, never tried that. Let's go for a swim before dinner. The cool water will fix it.

Okay, Danny. Sorry for breaking your dick.

Ha, don't worry. It's not broken.

We ran out into the cool water; my muscles soon relaxed, thankfully. *You okay, big fella?*

Yeah, but seriously, that was next-level, boss-level sex. Were you serious about orgasming at will? I mean, if you were just out here swimming around...could you?

Come here, where we can stand. Hold my hand, and put the other one on my navel.

Now what? But I could feel her trembling and shaking, then moaning in my ear. *Oh. See, but I need to be touching you.*

Lately, every time you touch me, I shiver. It's like a mini...you know.

I'd better not touch you in public, then. We have a wedding coming up; that could be embarrassing.

Danny, I'll learn control, don't fret. And believe me, it feels so good when you touch me.

What, like this?

I squeezed her beautiful bosom, pushing her nipple in, and Betty started shaking before she let out a deep, rumbling groan and called my name.

I'm sorry, I was just testing you, er...yep, it's true. You look so sexy when you are there, in the moment.

"Thank you, Danny, for every single part of today. Now, I am starving. What are we doing for dinner?"

We went back to camp and dried off. I threw some shorts on and set about getting the fire started. Betty went into Horus to get dressed and to find something easy for dinner. I poured another drink and took a swig, thinking about how amazing Betty and our day was.

Danny, I have you, thank you darling. I am impulsive.

How am I supposed to think about you and all the things I love about you without you eavesdropping on me, Bett?

I'm sorry, but I find it hilarious when you blurt out your feelings in my head. I can't help but call you out on it.

I still cannot get used to this whole telepathy thing. I am impulsive with my thoughts.

Okay, so learn control. Eventually, it will come. Be patient and learn to think to yourself, not out loud.

I'll try. Everything sorted for dinner? Do you need a hand?

I've started tacos in Horus Is that okay with you?

Yes, that is great. I'll be right there.

As I neared Horus, I could smell the Mexican spices cooking; I opened the door and was greeted with Betty's cute butt and that gorgeous apron.

"Damn, girl, you want to get laid again?"

"You wish, jellyfish. Can you cut up some tomatoes and lettuce, please?"

"Yes, ma'am, I'm on it. Do you want some more of that wine?" I asked.

"Yes, please. It's nice, and from Mclaren Vale; they have some good wine down there."

"Yes, I have heard that. Too bad we will never get to see those vineyards."

"No, we will need to learn how to grow grapes and make wine and distil bourbon. We have a lot to learn, and tomorrow we start our survival training."

"Yes Bett, train me as hard as you can. I need to get up to speed."

Betty finished cooking the meat, and we sat and constructed our tacos. They had just the right amount of heat, but, as always, I piled on the jalapenos. We sat and talked about what was in store for Conner and how this could affect him. We had moved our queen into play, and she could be aggressive.

We spent hours drawing up a training schedule and for a plan to use the funds wisely. By ten o'clock, I could hardly stay awake.

* * *

We opened our eyes and looked around. We had no idea where we were. We stood up, our golden bodies glistening in the artificial light. Our atten-

tion was drawn to a large screen or window—we could not tell which—giving us a view of the night sky. Earth was visible in the distance, but it was small, like the moon, in a sky full of stars. We had to be on our moon, looking down on, our planet.

Then we saw it streaking across at a shallow angle: a huge comet.

* * *

Hathor chose a slightly different dream for Conner, part of her own agenda, not the past, but his future.

Conner, you have been chosen by those who love you to witness a travesty to come. Drink the tea of life, while it is hot and steaming; drink your future.

He floated above Earth, and it was such a beautiful world: so busy and alive. Out of the corner of his eye, he saw a huge comet streaking by. It slammed into the atmosphere above the United States, the compression wave flattening every structure, every tree, and all life in an instant. But it was not finished. It skipped through the atmosphere, making contact again above Europe, breaking in half and exploding across Germany. In an instant, all of Europe was gone. The other half traveled on to Asia and exploded in the atmosphere.

Yellowstone erupted with anger at being disturbed by a mighty blast. A wave of water ten miles high traveled south, hitting Indonesia, New Guinea, then Australia and all the Pacific Islands. Mexico, then Cuba and Brazil. The Mediterranean Sea traveled south over Egypt and northern Africa. The wave was only two miles high by the time it hit the Antarctic, wiping all the bases away and breaking the entire ice shelf into a million icebergs. The entire planet went dark in a murky cloud of dust, dirt and smoke, then became a dirty, stinking hell for the next thirty years. Another ice age lasted nearly a thousand years. Pockets of humanity had survived, but most of those did not even last a year. Conner was not distressed at all by what he saw; he was busy making calculations, considering his next move.

* * *

Conner woke the next morning a new man, driven by his will to survive.

He showered and dressed. He called Gertie's and ordered a coffee and a toasted ham, cheese, and tomato sandwich to go. He picked up his breakfast and headed straight to Taxiplus, where he immediately got on the phone and barked orders to ten different suppliers.

I need to get my daughter's wedding sorted, too. Taxi will survive this—thanks to me.

21
The Torture Starts: Training for an Apocalypse

"Good morning, sweetheart." Betty kissed me on the forehead. "Are you ready for today's adventure?"

"I sure am, baby. Bring it on."

"Okay, run, swim, and then breakfast to start," Betty stated as she jumped out of bed.

"Yes, ma'am," I replied.

Betty pulled on some baggy shorts, a tank top, and her joggers; I grabbed my footy shorts and joggers, but no shirt. Betty started slow for the first two hundred feet, then turned to me and winked. In a flash, she sprinted ahead. I tried to keep up, but she remained fifteen feet ahead until she slowed again. We jogged on up the road to the lookout before stopping to catch our breath.

"Okay, give me twenty push-ups, please," Betty said, smiling and with her hands on her hips.

I looked at her and then got down on the ground. The first ten were easy, then I slowed. I hit seventeen and started to struggle, collapsing at nineteen.

"Good effort! I will have you up to fifty in a few weeks. Now it's my turn." Betty did thirty in quick succession, followed by ten burpees. I clapped. "Race you back! You can even have a head start."

Oh, crap. I took off at a steady pace, knowing it wouldn't be long before Bett was right there next to me. I turned and there she was, grinning broadly. *Stay with me baby.* But after another fifty feet, Betty started to pull ahead. I pushed myself to catch up, and I did for about fifty feet, but I was running out of steam.

Nearly there, Betty thought to me, *just two hundred feet to go.*

I stayed about ten feet behind her for the remainder of the run. Betty stopped at the water's edge and stripped before running into the water without a hint of hesitation. I was close behind, so we dove in at the same moment. We swam together across the lake and back five times our strokes almost synchronized.

"Good job! That is enough for now. Stay here." Betty ran out and grabbed the shower gel, then returned to the water. "Come over here and I will lather you up."

I did as I was told and stood still for her in knee-high water. Her hands scrubbed my hair, then my chest and back. As they neared my groin, she started shaking and moaning, then fell forward and had to grab me to keep from collapsing completely.

When she had control of herself again, Betty looked up at me. "Whoa, that was sudden. I hope you don't mind."

She jumped up, wrapped her legs around me, and slid down onto me. I struggled with my balance for a moment since we were so slippery, but leaned back to redistribute my weight and remain upright. She squeezed me tightly until I came, and then she threw her head back as her whole body shuddered.

"Oh, Danny, you are perfect."

She jumped off and dove back in, and I joined her. We swam around for a bit longer, then went to the tent and dried off. I fell back onto the mattresses.

"Whew, girl, you are going to wear me out," I said with a chuckle.

"Er, that last bit was not part of training. I think you will have to lather yourself from now on." She winked and slapped her own butt. "I'm going to Horus to start some bacon and eggs, okay?"

"That sounds great; I'll be right there, baby."

I watched her casually stroll naked back to Horus. *I am so lucky; she is gorgeous.* I kept my thoughts to myself for a change. I stood and pulled my shorts on before running up to Horus. Betty leaned against the table in her little apron, filing her nails while watching the stove. Some tongs flipped the bacon for her; eggs were being spooned onto our plates by a spatula, and a knife sliced tomatoes. Bett winked at me; she had a huge smile on her face. The toast popped up and landed on our plates, where a knife quickly buttered the crispy slices. I watched in stunned silence, shaking my head. The bacon went to the plates, which then lifted and flew to the table.

"Bett, that is amazing. How did you—?"

"That felt easy. Oh, after breakfast we should do some target practice with the handguns," Bett said.

I nodded as I stuffed some bacon in my mouth. *Good idea. This is great, by the way.*

We finished our food and sipped our coffee. Betty flew the two handguns to the table.

"Okay, first things first: disassembly and reassembly. You need to know this in case of a jam and for when it's time to clean the guns. Follow my every move and listen to my mind. The more times you do this, the faster you will get."

I watched her closely, and within ten minutes I had it down pat. I was not as fast as Bett but that would come with time and practice.

"Excellent Danny, well done. Now, when you load them, you have to make sure the safety is on, and then in they go. That's it. Finally, we dress the part."

She stood up and threw her apron on its hook, then went in the bedroom. About thirty seconds later, she came out dressed in some camouflage pants and a black tank top. She threw a similar outfit to me, then grabbed two gun belts and put hers on before attaching her holster and strapping it around her leg. I followed her lead. Two boxes of bullets in our side pockets and some ear plugs, and we were ready.

Bett looked intimidating, but topped the look off with a camo baseball cap and a pair of aviator sunglasses. She handed me nearly identical accessories.

I grinned. "Bett, we look like CIA operatives!"

"Yep, that's the idea, let's go!"

We left Horus; Betty floated five apples away from us and settled them on the ground at different intervals.

"What are they for?"

Betty grinned and pulled out her gun, took aim at the one furthest away, and fired. The apple exploded.

"Do we have any watermelons?"

"Danny, you can use your mind, too. Concentrate and your aim will improve dramatically. Trust me and have a go at the first one. Use the sight, safety off. Breathe out and pull the trigger."

I steadied myself, lined up the sight with the apple, and fired. A puff of dirt kicked up about two feet from the target. It took four shots for me to hit the first, three to hit the second, and two for the third.

"One shot: make it count. You got this."

I lined it up and fired; the apple exploded.

"Perfect! Now, reload, baby." Betty lifted four empty bottles and set them up on the edge of the firepit. "They are probably too far away, but see if you can hit one of these."

I raised my firearm and took aim, concentrating hard before I pulled the trigger. One bottle exploded. I fired again, but missed. Then, I fired again: a hit that time. The third and fourth exploded soon after that.

"Danny, you are a natural! You're using your psychic skills well. Let's go for a walk." Betty led me into the hills. "Food will likely be scarce after the event. We will need to become hunters; to survive, hold still. Up ahead, there are two 'roos to the side of the path. Stay quiet, crouch down, and take aim at the larger one. That is dinner."

"Are you serious?" I looked back at Betty, doubtful.

Betty nudged me. "Take the shot."

I raised my pistol, but I was shaking, so I lowered my gun.

A loud bang made my ears ring. The kangaroo fell due to a shot to the head, and the other bounded away. I looked back to see Betty with her gun still raised.

"Danny, sometimes there will be only one chance and it could be a matter of life or death: yours or theirs. This 'roo will feed us for a week, the skin can be used for warmth and clothing."

Betty walked over to the 'roo, ensured it was dead, slit its throat, and then I helped her hang it over a tree branch to drain its blood.

Damn, I'd lived in the city too long. I was happy to eat steaks at home, but all those animals had to die so I could eat them. I was sheltered from the reality of their death.

Betty was staring at me. "You okay?"

The kangaroo's blood pooled on the ground, staining it dark red. I stepped back.

"Danny, you ate kangaroo your first night at Gertie's. Now, I will show you how to skin and gut one."

Really?

Danny, toughen up. There may come a time when we even need to kill people—people that want to kill us—and we cannot hesitate.

Betty took her hunting knife to the 'roo again and deftly opened it up, removing its intestines, then all the other organs. She cut off its head, arms and lower legs and proceeded to skin it.

"His organs will feed many other animals; we'll dry the skin and eat the meat." Betty grunted and heaved the remainder of the carcass over her shoulder. "Let's go. Take the skin, leave the rest for the dingoes Daniel."

We headed back to camp, and Betty had me lay the skin out on the ground, fur side down and in the full sun, while she dropped the carcass into the shallows of the lake. Then she went to Horus and retrieved a bucket and the bag of salt, filling the former with water before adding a heap of the latter. She took the skin down to a large rock by the lake and picked out a smaller one. I watched her scrape any remaining flesh from the skin carefully, working from one end to the other. She rinsed it off in the water, shook it out, then pushed it into the salty bucket.

"Danny, can you take this over to Horus and put the lid on with a heavy rock on top of that?" Betty picked up the 'roo as I nodded, taking it over to the same rock and using her big hunting knife to deftly carve it up into steaks. "Freezer bags and the shovel next, please."

I headed back to Horus to get what she'd asked for. By the time I returned, she was finished. I handed her the bags and went over to the soft sand to dig a deep hole for the bones and tough bits of sinew. Betty bagged all the meat and washed her hands; I collected the bones and bits and threw them in the hole, then covered up the bloody mess. Most of the meat went in the freezer, and we placed the remainder in the fridge.

We grabbed the shower gel, stripped, and waded out into the lake to wash up. Betty watched me closely.

Was that your first time?

Yes, but I am fine.

You have learned how to close off your emotions, haven't you?

I have—at least partially, anyway.

It's like your thoughts are hidden behind a dark window; I can only see glimpses of them. I think I preferred it when you were yelling in my head. She smiled at me and winked. *We have 'roo steaks for dinner. You're in for a treat. Come and give me a hug, Danny. I will try to behave.*

I hugged my sweet girl tightly, and she kissed me gently. We swirled around in the water together, doing a bit of a dance, and laughed. Suddenly, Betty pulled away with a worried expression. She had her arms wrapped around herself, I could see her trembling and she was trying not to look at me.

"Oh, Danny, I'm, trying so hard to control myself, but it is hard. It feels like I'm sitting on the edge of a beautiful pond and just want so badly to fall in."

The concentration was plain as day on her face, and her muscles were tensed.

"Oh, just give in to it, babe. I love you too much to see you so uncomfortable."

She swam back into my arms, wrapped herself around me and cried out as she began shuddering almost instantly. I held her tightly and kissed her neck. Her whole body went rigid before her quaking subsided and finally stopped. Then she went limp, exhausted. Keeping her head down, she looked away and pulled back, clearly ashamed of her lack of control.

"Wait, Bett, don't be like that," I said with what I hoped she'd see as a reassuring smile. "Please, come back."

"I didn't even make love to you, Danny! I'm sorry."

"Shit, I don't care. Holding you is enough. Read my feelings."

I know you would never lie to me, and that you are deeply in love with me. Betty started to cry. *I don't deserve you; you are too good for me.*

"Bett, that is ridiculous. We are perfect for each other; you know I'm right. You are just confused because your body is going through changes.

So is mine. You will learn control."

"This is so overwhelming. I'm losing control of my own body way too easily."

"Patience, Bett. You will find balance. In the meantime, come on. Let's get out."

We walked out of the water with a few feet between us, went to the tent, and dried off. Betty poured me a big glass of whiskey and brought it to me.

"Here you go, beautiful man. Sorry for being a weirdo before."

I took the drink and had a swig before I thanked her, but she wasn't listening. She slowly went down on her knees in front of me and took me in her mouth. My breath caught; I gently placed my free hand on her head, and she looked up and smiled. Within minutes, I arched my back and let go. She grabbed my bottom and tugged me forward as she moaned and shook, too. I was spilling my drink, so I chugged it and dropped the glass onto the mattress. She had lost all control and was all but biting me at that point, so I pulled out and tossed her on the bed before crawling on top of her. She pulled me in eagerly as her chest heaved.

"Yes, come again, Danny."

We rocked together. She cried out as each wave rolled over her, and I let go again.

I kissed her gently and rolled off, exhausted. We lay there looking at each other, each knowing exactly what the other was thinking and feeling. Betty was happy, and so was I.

Betty raised her hand; my glass soon floated in front of me, and then the bottle of Jack Daniels joined it.

"Ha, thank you." I poured myself a drink as Betty's water bottle floated past me. "What's next? Hatchets, knives, or bows and arrows?"

Betty smiled. "I think bows and arrows. Have you ever used them?"

"Does archery at school count?" I asked.

"That is better than nothing. Come on, bring your drink."

We walked to the edge of the water to retrieve our clothes after Betty pulled out the two hunting bows from the locked cupboard and two quivers full of arrows. When we were dressed, she ducked back inside and returned with a crossbow featuring a scope and a beautiful wooden stock, as well as a small quiver of bolts. Then, Betty pulled out a large, straw target with colored rings and a few books from the manufacturers.

I glanced through the books first. "These will come in handy. They even show how to tighten these bows."

We pulled out the large table from the side of Horus and placed all the gear on it, then pushed the button that would make the awning silently and smoothly extend to give us some cover from the midday sun. Betty looked around, then hung the target on a sturdy trunk of a nearby tree.

She skipped back so I could show her what I'd learned about checking the tension on the bows. When we thought we had a handle on that, she slung the quiver of arrows over her shoulder and then took one out, moved away from the table, and lifted the bow in the direction of the target. She notched the arrow and pulled it back until it touched the side of her jaw, then released it. The arrow zipped through the air and hit the target, but missed the bull's-eye by mere inches.

"Wow, great shot!" I exclaimed.

"Thanks." She immediately notched another arrow, pulled it back, and released it. It landed right next to the other one, so Betty gave the sight a little twist. Her next shot hit the other side of the bull's-eye. "Okay, a little too much."

She twisted the sight back a touch and tried again. This one hit the bull's-eye.

Yes! Elated, Betty fired off three more arrows and hit the bull's-eye every time.

"Okay, you are amazing," I said.

"That target is less than twenty feet away. Wait until it is thirty or forty feet away, or moving as quickly as a rabbit. They are hard to shoot. We need to be that good."

"Well, I'm sorry to disappoint you, but I will need a lot of practice before I bag any rabbits."

"That is okay, just focus. You've got this."

I took a few deep breaths as I stepped up, bow in hand, and pulled an arrow from the quiver. Concentrating on the bull's-eye, I released the arrow and watched it hit the dirt near to the target. Betty was silent, watching me intently. I peered down the sight and adjusted my stance for my next shot. The arrow zipped by and hit the right side of the target. I adjusted the sight again, and my next arrow sank in just an inch to the right of the bull's-eye. I adjusted the sight again slightly. I got this. I drew the fourth arrow back, and this one hit just inside the bull's-eye.

"Yay!" Betty cried. "Excellent."

My next three landed around the inside edge of the bull's-eye, and I was over the moon. There was a long road ahead, but hours and hours of practice could be the difference between life and death one day.

We took turns for a while, watching each other and learning. Then, Betty shifted it back another five feet and we started missing again. We had to relearn it all, but we kept at it for another hour.

"That was great! We have a ways to go yet, but if we practice daily—say, two hours a day—we will get there." Betty was confident now. "We will try the crossbow tomorrow."

"Sounds good. Are you hungry? I'm famished."

"It is nearly two o'clock in the afternoon."

"Really? No wonder I'm so hungry."

Back in Horus, we made toasted sandwiches with thin beef steaks, cheese, pineapple slices, and barbeque sauce. Washed down with some beers.

"Thank you, Bett," I said with my mouth full. "Delicious."

Danny, close your thoughts and listen to me.

I paid attention and watched her as she ate. She was looking down at her plate.

Hathor is doing this. I mean, she is affecting me somehow. I'm certain.

Careful, she might hear you. I downed some beer; she was smiling at me while she ate.

No, she can't. She is the god of sex, reproduction, and fidelity, after all. But, I do feel like she's influencing me somehow. I feel so overly sensitive to your touch, and your electricity drives me wilder than it should. I have had more orgasms in the last few days than I have had in my entire life before now. Sometimes you only need to brush past me for me to lose control. Sure, it feels fantastic when we make love—I am in rapture, on another plane—and maybe Hathor is trying to show me a reality where ecstasy and pure joy can be everywhere. I'm not sure, but that that is how I feel.

Betty, you have been incredible, but I know what you mean. Something has changed; I feel as if you are evolving, and if Hathor is behind it, then we need to be very careful.

Putting our plates in the dishwasher, we headed out to the tent and sat cross-legged on the mattress. Betty floated the whiskey and a glass to me; I poured myself a stiff one.

Your turn.

What do you mean, Bett?

Send me my wine and a glass, please. You can do it.

I looked at her, then her nonalcoholic wine, and back. *I don't think I can do that yet.*

Have you even tried?

Well, no, because I don't think I have abilities as strong as yours.

Danny, try. Please? I'm thirsty.

Yeah, right. Why do you raise your hand?

It helps me concentrate.

Okay, I want that wine to come to my hand slowly.

Concentrate. You are nearly there.

Suddenly, I felt a vibration coming from me. The bottle lifted, shaking, then steadied and started to float slowly toward me. It was like it was part of me.

It stopped in front of Betty; she reached out and grabbed it. *Thank you, Danny. Now the glass.*

The glass is hard.

She levelled me with a stern look, so I sighed and gave it a try. The glass lifted and started to shake. I listened, then realized that its vibration was off. I concentrated on righting it, and then it floated smoothly over to Betty.

Thank you, baby, well done! See? I knew you had it in you. You are stronger than you think.

"Here's to my newfound psychic abilities, then."

"Cheers, darling. You are the best thing that keeps happening to me."

We stayed on the mattresses, talking and laughing for another hour. It was around four in the afternoon when we decided to get up and move around.

"You up for another jog?" Betty asked.

"Come on, girl."

I stood and held out my hand. Betty grabbed it, and we exited the tent.

"Ten miles," Betty said as she pushed a button on her watch. "Just a slow jog, okay?"

"Sounds good. I don't feel like sprinting right now," I replied.

We headed off down the path by the riverbank as the sun slowly started to hide amongst the trees and the hills. This was serenity and true outback beauty; the birds noisily fed, other wildlife was busy drinking and eating nearby, our steady steps lightly pounded the dusty track in unison, our breathing was matched. Without intentionally doing anything, we were totally in sync with each other.

It's time to turn back for a swim and then we'll have some 'roo for dinner. Betty looked over at me. *Love you, man.*

I love you. I held my hand to my heart, looking at her.

We arrived back at camp around five o'clock that evening, panting. Pulling off our clothes, we entered the water to cool off and wash. At this time of day, the water was still and cool. We swam to the other side and back a few times, enjoying the freshness of the water. I could feel Bett's need mounting, but I did my best to ignore her just in case this was Hathor's doing.

"Let's go and get the fire started and dry off," I suggested.

"That's a great idea," Betty replied.

I ran ahead and grabbed my towel, wrapping it around myself before I took the lighter to the firepit. Betty wrapped herself in her towel and joined me. Together, we lit the campfire adding bits of kindling to get it going. We sat on the logs, staring at our fire as humans had done ever since they could harness flames.

A few minutes later, I looked over at her; she had dropped her towel to her waist and was staring at me. I saw her longing, her insatiable need, but I resisted.

Danny, I need you.

Is it you, Bett? Really you? I can almost feel Hathor here, too.

Yes, Daniel, it is me, only me. Come here. I want you.

I was sure I could feel the Hathors, gloating in anticipation, drooling with lustful envy, I pushed them to the back of my mind. Betty opened her towel the rest of the way, and she was beauty defined: vulnerable yet sexy. I was mesmerized, locked in her spell. I wanted her so badly. I pulled her closer to me; she gasped as we embraced. Her hand went behind my head and tugged me to her so her wet mouth could latch on to mine. She gently pulled me down to the ground and climbed on top of me, moaning quietly the whole time, but controlling herself. When I was inside her, I could feel her quivering, shaking, pulsing. I closed my eyes in ecstasy as Betty sped up and moaned louder.

When I opened my eyes, Betty looked different. Her skin was tan, her hair was longer and golden, her eyes glowed red, and her ears were strangely shaped like that of a cow and covered in brown and white fur. Betty had somehow transformed into Hathor. Her huge tan tits swayed in rhythm, but I was on the edge and could not stop. I let go, heaving, pushing upward with so much force that I nearly lifted us off the ground.

Hathor smiled down at me. "That's it. Harder! Come on, Daniel. Fuck me harder and give me your milk. Feed me. Here—I'll give you mine." Her heaving breasts dripped milk all over me, covering my chest in it. Then she squeezed them in my face, and her loud moaning started sounding more and more like that of a cow. "That's it; give me all you have. Feed me good!" She screamed and moaned as she orgasmed on me.

I came again, unable to help it. *Oh, fuck! No, Hathor—stop!* No matter what I did, I couldn't pull away from the monstrosity. *Leave her! Get out of my Betty, Hathor!* I was screaming at Hathor.

Hathor cackled wildly. "No, *you* get out of Betty, Daniel!"

I closed my eyes. She was squeezing me tighter as she moved; it felt like she was milking me, taking everything I had inside of me.

Get away, you horror! Stop! Betty, please, come back to me!

Danny!

I opened my eyes, and Hathor was gone. Betty was back, her eyes looking up to the sky as if she was in a trance, and she kept saying my name between her loud moans. *"Danny!"*

Betty, come back to me. I shook her as best as I could in our current position, but she kept on. "Betty! Wake up!"

"Danny!" Against my will, I came again. She was still lost amid wave after wave of orgasms when I found the strength to sit up, putting my face inches away from hers. I was scared; she just kept going on and on, completely lost. Not sure what else to do, I cupped her face in my hands and gently kissed her lips. Her eyes flickered briefly. I kissed her again, this time more passionately, and her rhythm slowed. I kissed her again; she stopped moving and her eyes focused on mine. She was breathing heavily, and had to be just as exhausted as I was.

She opened her mouth to speak, but I put my finger to her lips.

Just breathe, darling. I raised my hand and pulled her bottle of water through the air. I lifted it to her lips, and she gulped it down. I wiped the corner of her mouth.

What just happened?
I'll tell you later. Just relax now.
Do you want me to get off you?
No, not unless you want to get off.
Lie back.

I did, and she rested her head against my neck, taking deep, slow breaths. She fell asleep within a minute; her body twitched and lightly squeezed me every few seconds. I stroked her hair and back. She felt so warm and comforting on me, and her slight, rhythmic spasms kept me hard.

There was no way I was closing my eyes—Hathor and that whole episode had terrified me—but I let Betty sleep for half an hour before gently waking her with a kiss on the cheek. She roused and moved slightly so she could see my face. She smiled at me and touched my lips with her finger. I smiled back.

"Oh, you are still inside me, and you feel good," she whispered in my ear. She shuddered. "Thank you for looking after me." She squirmed around just enough to make my breath catch. "I feel you throbbing. I can do that, too."

Betty licked my lips and squeezed me gently; it was my turn to moan. She slowly rocked forward, then back. I nearly slipped out, then went all the way back in.

Just let go, babe.

So, I did. I grabbed her butt and squeezed. She kept going as I shuddered, her head buried in my neck. She started to shake and tremble, the slow rhythm making everything way more intense. Betty cried out as she ejaculated and then fell on me, breathing hard.

She very gently rolled off me and lay next to me, stroking my chest. After a while, she raised her hand, and the bottle of Sinatra Century floated gently over, followed by my glass. She poured some for me and handed it over.

"Thanks, baby. Are you up for a quick swim before it gets dark?"

"Okay, but just a quick wash."

She stood up. I had another sip and threw a couple of logs on the fire before following Betty to the cool water. We swam for a while, then Betty raised her hand, and the shower gel bottle came flying across the lake like a little missile. We quickly washed up, rinsed off, and went back to the fire.

"I think we need some fresh towels," I said as I ran up to Horus.

While you're there, can you take the kangaroo steaks out of the fridge and bring a few spuds and the foil? Ta.

I placed the potatoes and foil on Betty's folded towel and raised my hand, watching it all lift like magic and float out the door.

Well done, Danny.

I came back out to her, drying my hair as I went. Betty had wrapped the spuds in foil and found a good spot for them in the firepit. She looked pretty, sitting by the fire and drying her hair. She looked up at me as I wrapped the towel around my waist like a sarong.

"I'll head to Horus to make a salad and gravy, but first, can you tell me what happened before I fell asleep? I can't remember anything, Danny?"

"I need to tell you quietly, okay?"

Yes sure, I'm closed now.

I think Hathor took control of your body and my mind, and it scared me. I was terrified.

Betty stared at me. *Did I try to hurt you?*

No, I don't think so. You were on top of me, and you started to have a big O before anything even happened, but when I came, I closed my eyes. Everything changed when I opened them. You looked and sounded like

Hathor, and she acted as if I was fucking her instead of you. It was disgusting and terrifying. I was covered in milk, and she moaned like a cow, Betty—a friggin' <u>cow</u>! She made me blow a second time and it felt like she was milking me. I just kept coming, and she screamed at me to feed her more.

Betty's eyes were wider than I had ever seen them as she stood up and grabbed my hand. *Oh, Danny, I'm so sorry.*

Don't be. It was Hathor, not you. And when I heard you say my name, I opened my eyes and Hathor was gone. You were there on me, having a seemingly endless run of orgasms, but it seemed like you were also in some kind of a trance. You wouldn't stop moaning. I decided to kiss you to break the spell, and it worked. Three kisses and you came out of it. Then I let you fall asleep on me for a bit.

Okay, wow. I don't know what to say.

You don't have to say anything. Please just go and fix the salad and think about everything I just told you. We need to figure out how we can stop Hathor from doing that again. Although, I'm glad you fell asleep on me; it was a magical experience, I watched you the whole time, and you were having these tiny little spasms that kept me awake and hard. You smiled in your sleep.

Betty smiled and squeezed my hands. *You are welcome.*

She picked up her towel and walked back to Horus.

Nice butt!

She laughed, turned to wink at me, and slapped her bottom. *I love you.*

I love you back. Call if you need a hand.

A short time later, a large tray came floating out of Horus, with Betty walking a few feet behind it, casually sipping her wine and smiling. Betty wore a fishnet t-shirt. She smiled even broader when she noticed me checking it out.

It is warm tonight, and this is the only place I get to wear this sort of stuff. I like it. Is it no good?

Er, well, it is good. You look fabulous in it. Turn around, please.

Betty obliged, extending her arms like a model. The shirt fell just under her bottom.

Yes, Bett, perfect barbeque attire. I raced over and gave her a kiss, then grabbed the tray out of the air. *Oh, and you smell delicious.*

Thank you, Danny. She curtseyed. *Do you need a top-up? I want to try something.*

Er, okay.

She kept her hands down, but the bottle of Sinatra Century rose and went to my glass anyway. The cork came out and floated nearby as the bottle slowly tipped and poured bourbon into the glass, filling it before it tipped back upright. The cork went back in and the bottle went back to the table. The glass lifted and came to me. I raised my hand and grabbed it.

Betty, that was amazing, but are you trying to get me drunk?

She winked and started to prepare the hot plate. "Are you hungry, Danny?"

"Yes, always baby. What are you up to?"

"We have a simple orange and rocket salad with a little goat cheese and beetroot. Our spuds will be finished with wattle seed butter and sour cream. The gravy, should you wish to use it, is an Australian native herb mix with Szechuan pepper and cream. The 'roo will be lightly seared for a few minutes on each side. It's best when served rare."

"Yes, chef, that sounds fantastic."

The 'roo hit the sizzling plate, and Betty watched it like a hawk. She flipped it and retrieved the spuds, opening them with care and cutting them open to dress them. Betty put them on the plates along with some salad. She quickly sliced the steaks into thick, juicy strips, and my mouth watered as she was piling it onto the plates. The gravy was in a small bowl with a lid.

"Dig in, Danny."

"Thank you, my chef. This looks and smells delicious."

Even better was how it all tasted. The 'roo turned out to be a good, lean meat, and since it was freshly killed, it tasted even better—or so Betty said.

"Are you done?" Betty asked.

"Yeah, that filled me up and then some. Thank you, Betty. Do you need a hand?"

Our plates lifted into the air and floated toward Horus; the door opened, as did the dishwasher. Everything went into its place, and the doors closed.

"Well, now we can just sit back and get fat and do nothing at all. Yes!"

"It means I have more time with you—in your pants! Or, your lack of pants."

"Okay, very good, Bett. Keep it up."

We went to the tent and stretched out on the mattresses, but just when we started to relax, the vibrations that heralded Ishta's arrival or departure started up.

"What do they want?"

We are here because you have met our saviors, the Hathors. They will help us both survive. They have united us and led us to our joint salvation. BettDanny, Connerelle is doing a good job to help us, but we need so much more still. Many of us will not survive. You need to trust the Hathors, Ishta and the Lloyds. We know of the struggle you deal with. You will overcome and be stronger together. We will survive, thanks to you two.

Ishta, wait! Do not leave. Please tell the Old Ones about your civilization. Hathor has wiped our memories. How will our skins help you and your civilization?

We know the Hathors are tough on all in contact with them. We have also struggled with Hathors. But our biggest struggle has been with our sun, our star. It has gone through many stages, but now it is dying. As a species, we evolved beyond physical bodies using AI, and exist without the need for property, housing and other physical things. We live as energy beings with no true physical form. When our sun started to die, we did, too. Then the Hathors came to us with their minds when we entered your system and they showed us your skins. The skins are a means to survive on another planet, in another system. We are thankful to you and the Hathors, but our family outnumbers the supply. Too many of our children will die. We all weep as one in anticipation of that day. This is what drew the Hathors to us. They came to feed on our pain. We comply with their needs and let them feed on our suffering; in return, they help us. You are different. You are strong, Old Ones. The Hathors feed on you too but also fear you. You beat them before. That is all we can say, and we may still be punished by the Hathors. Good health, Old Ones.

As soon as we knew they were gone, I told Betty to close her mind to them.

Done, Danny. I think the Hathors are feeding on us, on our emotions and lust—. When Hathor said feed me, she meant it literally—which means they must love the turmoil of an extinction event. Hathor enjoyed my anguish, the terror of not knowing what was happening; she thrived on it. Her strength grew as we felt deep love and sexual joy. With the Ishta race they know many will die, too, but like humanity's future for us, they dangle a carrot of hope—our skins— in front of Ishta so they can feed on those heightened emotions accompanying hope. The Hathors are pitting two races against each other for their own gain, to supplement their damn diet.

Okay, that is a lot to take in. You're saying that Hathor feeds on our lovemaking and death?

I think it's more about lust, love, pain, loss, hope, joy, gratification, hurt, and maybe all the emotions that make it so we cannot help ourselves.

Yes, I think I feel that, too.

Betty, Ishta said we beat them, before. That means we can do it again, maybe even send them back home this time. We need to put beef on our menu.

I couldn't agree more, Daniel.

* * *

Meanwhile, in Taxi, Conner had gone into overdrive. All of his underlings were trying to avoid him. He had organized three separate shifts for the bunker so work could carry on around the clock. His list of supplies grew daily after his prophetic dream, and the roster of farm animals that would join the survivalists now included insects for added protein, as his scientists had advised.

Elon Musk had answered and was interested in talking with him. The earliest opening or a meeting was in December of 2026. Boston Dynamics wasn't available until November of the same year.

Medi-Corp had requested even more Study-Skins, but they are paying incredible amounts of money for that. He was currently pumping out ten thousand a week and raking in more than two million dollars per week from Medi-Corp alone. The skins are stacked high in the freezer, and if there was a federal raid or something, Conner would be the first Aussie in a hundred years to be hanged in public.

The caverns that the mine led to were incredible, and some were as big as theatres and stadiums. Conner had four spelunkers who found more of them each day and reported back. They had also found vast lakes of crystal-clear drinking water, and even evidence of ancient occupation. Conner had the best teams working on more than a hundred hidden shafts to supply filtered air into the caverns. He planned out other secret shafts in case they were needed for escape or reconnaissance, knowing that all entrances needed to be waterproof and have the means to close off areas if necessary. His personal space and the area he'd put aside for Betty, Daniel, and their growing family was huge and luxurious, with ceilings that imitated the sky, day or night. Swimming pools, spas, tennis courts, bowling alleys: he'd thought of it all. Supporting cement pillars would be made to look like trees. There were huge screens that could display vistas of nature they'd film before the devastation.

His pride and joy was the library. The internet would collapse eventually, so for the last thirty years, he had been amassing a huge collection of not just books, but maps, artwork, taxidermy, movies, and music. This would be his legacy: a place to learn and remember what it was like before the apocalypse.

He had created a huge space in the side of a hill next to the runway with a concealed entrance, but it was still large enough to house a few planes, helicopters, and at least twenty cars and trucks of various sizes. Most of that section looked like they were planning for a zombie apocalypse: mounted machine guns, mortars, and reinforced steel armor. He had huge reservoirs of fuel in massive tanks buried underground all over Taxi. In the other, smaller bunkers hidden all over Queensland, he had stashes of food, fuel, water, and a massive stockpile of seed.

Yes, Conner thought he had thought of everything, and of every scenario. When Betty was born, he started this project as a means to protect her. She was a survivor. Thirty-two years later, it was nearing completion. His recent dream just reinforced his sense of urgency. Taxi and the Rage bloodline had to carry on. The crematorium was running at maximum capacity twenty-four hours a day; smoke constantly billowed out across the valley as the dead burned to ashes. Conner Rage had complete control of Taxi's destiny.

22

The Standoff

Betty, how can we stop Hathor? Every single night we travel to wherever they decide to take us. Ishta said they fear us. We need to play on that fear factor, but we don't even know why they are afraid. Should we go to her? Talk about what she did and ask her to stop and not do that again?

She must be watching us every time we have sex so she can feed on our lust and joy. If that has no other effect on us, does it matter? Everyone needs to eat, and Ishta said they allow her to feed off them.

But Hathor made me feel as if she was taking all my bloody sperm and feeding on that, too. I think it was more like my ecstasy mixed with my terror that was really getting her off. The more terrified I became, the louder and more powerful she became. Was she testing me?

I'm not sure; I wish I'd known what she was thinking and where my mind was in the moment.

Betty, do you want to look into my mind and see that memory for yourself? Fair warning: it may terrify you.

I hadn't thought of that, but I don't know how I will react to seeing Hathor in me. Let's try it and see if it even works. Hold my hands and look into my eyes while you recall what happened by the fire.

Betty remained motionless, staring at me intently, but her eyes clouded over and I figured she was witnessing that memory even as it played out in my head. Suddenly, she smiled and moaned. She shuddered and shook in ecstasy. I realized Betty could also feel every feeling that I had then; she squeezed my hand and started shivering, but she never stopped staring at me with those vacant eyes.

Stay in control, Betty.

She slowed down, but her breath quickened as she rocked back and forth slightly, in time with what she was seeing. Then, she sounded exactly like me as she moaned deeply and closed her eyes just as I did when I came. Her rocking increased in time as she too orgasmed, gripping my hands tight. She opened her eyes, and they were wide with horror when she saw Hathor on top of her. She arched back and let out a cry, then tried to recoil. I held her hands tightly, for I knew exactly how she felt. She gasped, then orgasmed again

Right when she saw and felt the milk everywhere, her expression changed to disgust, but she kept rocking. Bett could see and feel it all. She orgasmed again and she closed her eyes tightly and started calling her own name. She opened her eyes with a look of relief, though she didn't stop moving. Her expression changed again to worry. Her eyebrows went down, her forehead creased and then pursed her lips. She shook her head and my hands slightly and blew a kiss. Then another longer one, and finally one more. She stopped rocking, and I knew Betty had woken from the trance.

I squeezed her hands. *Okay, you can come out now.*

Not yet. I want to see the rest of this, please.

I couldn't blame her; the thirty minutes following that freak show were bliss. I let her stay in my memories and held her hands softly. For that half hour, the look on her face was just as sweet as it was while I watched her sleep. she smiled and squeezed my hands very lightly every few seconds. Then I knew when Betty woke up, as she started moaning in front of me; her breathing changed and she licked her lips. She had a quiet, blissful orgasm, and I smiled, remembering that moment. She trembled and threw her head back in ecstasy thoroughly owning this intense orgasm. When she came out of my memories, she was still shaking as she grabbed me by the shoulders.

You beautiful man! I love you so much. Lie down, babe. I need you inside me right now, but you keep your eyes locked on mine: no Hathor tonight.

She undid my towel and sat on me gently. We kissed and made slow, beautiful love. Her body shuddered against me the whole time, and I didn't last long, but Betty kept me hard with her graceful motions so we kept going until I let go a second time a short while later. She squeezed me tightly and then rolled off to cuddle up next to me.

"No Hathor," Betty said softly.

"No, but she was probably watching us like a creepy voyeur," I replied.

"Despite that ordeal, that last forty minutes of your memories were beautiful. I love how you feel about me, how focussed you are on me, and how you felt when I slept on you; *that* was unbelievable. I am keeping that memory forever. Well, that and how your dick *feels*!" Betty said, squeezing my arm.

I kissed her on the cheek and laughed. "You're a ratbag!"

She snuggled in. *The cow sex was terrifying. It really felt like she was using you—using us—for her own sexual gratification. I wonder what she really looks like, or if she even has a physical body at all. She felt different than me from your point of view, as if it really was someone else on top of you.*

Exactly, but she couldn't possibly change you physically…could she?

That creepy milking feeling was horrible. And what was with all that milk everywhere?

Yeah, that was right up there on the list of the weirdest sex I have ever had.

Betty hit me on the arm. *Danny! What other weird sex?*

Ha, I got you. I grabbed her bosom and squeezed gently as she jabbed me in the ribs with her elbow, she grinned as I winced convincingly.

You're the ratbag!

What now? Do we go and see Hathor and show her we are not afraid of her? I'm sure she won't hurt us, but she has already broken our trust. It is up to you; you're the one who got body snatched.

I say let's do it right now.

We lay on our backs, closed our eyes, and mentally told Hathor we needed to talk to her.

* * *

When we opened our eyes, Hathor sat on her throne, but we could see nothing else around her.

"Hello, my children, you are angry with us? We agree that some of us went too far."

"Some of you?"

"All seven of us were present in Betty, but some of us went too far. It has been eons since the last time we entered your body and took control of it like that, and we were too hungry. All the Hathors are sorry for scaring you. That experience alone will last us a century; you are feeding us well."

"Hathors, listen to us, that can never happen again. Never take over Betty again," I said.

The Hathors stood up and glared at us, suddenly split into all seven beings in a row, each slightly different. Some were completely naked, two had the head of a cow, one had cow legs and hooves, one was a large white cow with a human head, one had the head of a lioness, two looked more like normal humans, one sported cow ears, and another still had bare breasts that looked like udders and a cow's tail. They were intimidating when they spoke as one.

"You are our Children You cannot say that to us, we enhanced you. You cannot stop us from feeding."

We stepped forward. "We just did."

They moved back slightly. "But you are our children. We are here to help you."

We stood our ground, and Betty put her hands on her hips as she said, "What you did does not help us. You hurt your children; you are not good parents. Do you treat all your children like this? If you do, then you do not deserve them. You are selfish; you eat feelings because you have none of your own. You watch us because you can't have any relationships. The goddess of sex can't have sex. We were making glorious love together until you stepped in and turned it into your own disgusting sexual fantasy. We do not know how you can help us or this planet anymore. You say you enhanced us, but that is for your own gratification, not ours. Isis took your power long ago, and you went into hiding. You are weak, we can smell your fear."

The Hathors said nothing; they seemed smaller than before.

"We are done talking with you. Leave us in peace."

* * *

We opened our eyes and I raised my eyebrows at Betty. She smiled and let out a little giggle.

"That was perfect, baby. We put them in their place, they could not answer us. Did you see them step back together?"

"Yes, Betty, they do fear us. We must have really whooped their asses last time." I joined her laughter, then adopted a deceptively serious tone. "Bett, I hate to mention this, but you had eight beings' inside you at once if you include me."

Betty got me in the ribs with her elbow again. "Very funny! How about we sleep now and block the Hathors just in case they get any funny ideas."

"Good idea." I glanced down at my watch. "Er, it's four in the morning."

"What? Really? Okay, close your eyes. We can sleep in, anyhow."

We slept like babies, exhausted from the long day and the even longer night. We dreamed only of each other.

23
A New Day, Our Wedding Looms

Betty's phone pinged and woke me from my slumber. I glanced at my watch; it was eight-thirty, the sun was beaming into the tent, and I had to pee. Betty was still asleep next to me with her arm over my chest and a leg over my groin. I did not want to wake her, so I tried to stealthily slip out from under her. Very slowly, I lifted her arm and placed it on her instead. The leg was more difficult, as it was positioned diagonally across me.

"What are you up to?"

She confessed mentally that she had been awake the whole time; I just hadn't seen her open her eyes.

"I need to pee."

"Of course, Danny. Go on then, but first a kiss first." She lifted her own leg and tilted her face up.

I kissed her on the cheek. "Good morning, gorgeous."

"Good morning, my hero." She rolled onto her back, looking stunning in the morning sunlight. "I need to go, too."

She jumped up and left the tent with me. I stood near the lake, looking around as I peed.

What a beautiful day.

Yes, it is. Nice butt, Danny. She came up next to me and slapped me hard on the bottom.

"Ow!"

I spun around and wrapped her in my arms, lifting her off the ground in one smooth move before I spun her around and kissed her on the lips, then carefully placed her back on the ground.

"Oh, Danny, you are the best."

"Before I forget, your phone woke me when it pinged this morning."

"That is probably Dad with some news."

It might've been important, but we just stood there a little longer, watching the morning come alive, our arms wrapped around each other and the morning sun warming our behinds.

I stepped forward, pulling Betty, "How about a freezing morning dip?"

"Okay." Betty shrugged. "Why not?"

We splashed into the cold water, yelping when it doused sun-warmed skin. We headed across the lake and back five times, swimming in perfect time again until we could no longer feel the cold. I summoned the shower gel; it sailed across the lake into my hand, and we washed up and went to our tent to dry off, feeling invigorated. Betty went and sat down near the fire, which was still giving off some warmth. She had her towel around her waist and her phone in her hand.

"Our wedding is booked for two weeks from this Saturday. Dad has already invited all of Taxi."

"Are you happy with that, baby?"

"Only if you are, Danny. This has been a whirlwind, but I know I am deeply in love with you and can't wait for you to be my husband."

"Oh Bett, never again in my life have I ever expected to hear those words said with such genuine love. Thank you."

"You are so welcome. I am looking forward to our wedding and to being your wife. Now, Dad said we can look through the bunker whenever we want; we just have to give him twelve hours to clear the workers."

Betty opened the small fridge with her mind and two small orange juice bottles floated out. She took one, and the other came to me.

"Thank you, miss."

"After our morning run, we should play around with our abilities. See if we are missing anything and how much we can lift with our minds."

"Yes, we need to train our minds, too. Maybe after that we have some more pistol practice?"

"Yes, and we should have a go with the Remington rifle, too. We also have a big crate in Horus full of semiautomatic guns and a grenade launcher."

"You asked for a grenade launcher?"

Betty shrugged and smiled cheerfully. "Sure did. You never know when one might come in handy."

I shook my head in disbelief, but finished the juice and fumbled around, looking for my shorts. "Have you seen my shorts?

"I think we both left our clothes at the edge of the lake yesterday when we had a swim."

Betty pointed off in the distance. Okay I got this; I decided to get a head start on training my brain and raised both hands, concentrating. Slowly, all our clothes and our joggers lifted into the air and shook off sand as they floated over to us. I let them hang there in the air as we took each item and put it on.

"Very good, Daniel."

"Thank you." I bowed to Betty.

"Okay, let's jog ten miles with intermittent sprints."

She pushed the button on her watch, and once again, we fell into rhythmic steps that were perfectly in time with each other's. We headed off down the path by the river, and soon, Betty increased her pace until we sprinted for forty feet, then slowed back to a jog. We repeated this pattern until we hit five miles. We stopped for a breather, walking around with our hands on our hips and breathing deeply for two minutes. Then we headed back, repeating the same pattern until we arrived back at camp. Off with our clothes and straight into the water: we swam slowly across and back ten times. Betty stopped and raised her hand; the shower gel came sailing across to us. We washed and rinsed off, and as we left the water, our towels sailed over to us. As we dried ourselves, our sweaty clothes and joggers flew past us and into the tent. We walked back to Horus to make breakfast and find some fresh clothes. Betty looked to the tent and summoned all the clothes to Horus.

"We should wash all that sweaty stuff," she explained as she opened the washing machine, waited for all the dirty clothes to fly in, and added the detergent.

"Right, I'm thinking some grilled cheese and tomato on toast with a few eggs. Sound okay?"

"Yes, that is good."

I pulled on some shorts and a T-shirt. Betty put on her little apron and laid some shorts, underwear, and a tank top on the bed for later. In ten minutes, we sat and ate our breakfast.

"Whenever we go into Taxi again, we should get some more eggs and drop off some of that frozen 'roo at Gertie's. We are never going to get through all that."

"Okay, Bett, I'll remember that. This Welsh rarebit is nice, as are the eggs."

We finished off our coffee and cleaned up. I worked out how to extend the clothesline and gave Betty a hand hanging up our stuff from the washer. She removed her apron and put it in the washer, then went and got dressed. We stood outside Horus under the awning.

Okay, we know we can shift small, light things—including multiple things at once—but the question is how heavy, how big and how many.

Okay, you first, Bett.

Alright, I'll start with all those pebbles by the edge of the lake.

Slowly, but all at the same time, hundreds or maybe even thousands of pebbles took flight. Betty concentrated, and they started to swirl around, then come together to form a huge heart with a large B at the top, an L in the middle, and D at the bottom.

Betty smiled. *You take over; I'll hold it steady for a few more seconds.*

I lifted my hands to help me concentrate. *Okay, I'm ready.*

The letters started to sag, and the heart looked as if it was melting, but I restored it to how it was before. I brought my hands together and the pebbles formed a huge ball in the air, then started to spin. I took the formation higher, then flattened it out into a huge disk and flew it across the lake so that it looked like a flying saucer. Betty smiled proudly. I flew it around for a bit longer, then spread the pebbles out to how they were when Betty first lifted them off the ground; I gently dropped them back into their original spots.

Betty raced over and hugged and kissed me. *Fantastic, Danny! I want to try something.*

Betty pointed to a small stone; it lifted and came over to within two feet of her, then started spinning faster and faster. Betty swiftly pointed over to the target, and the stone traveled so quickly I could barely see it.

It sailed straight into the bull's-eye and exploded out of the back of the tree faster than a bullet.

Holy shit!

We went over to the target and looked straight through the small hole in the tree; it looked like it had been professionally and intentionally drilled. We followed the line of sight and found the stone embedded in another tree ten yards away.

Danny, we won't even need guns. We have a whole beach of ammunition. Betty took ten apples from the crate and set them flying to random spots around us. After warning me to stand back, Betty lifted ten stones off the beach and flung her hand in the direction of the apples. Almost instantaneously, all ten apples exploded.

Wow, Betty! That was amazing.

You have a go, Danny. Just picture in your head what you want to achieve and follow through.

I tried with a single stone first; lifted it, and flung it at the target, it whistled straight through the hole Betty made and then straight through the tree behind it.

Betty looked at me and smiled. *Very impressive, Danny.*

Stand back. I spread my hand toward the pebbles on the beach and lifted twenty larger stones, then lined them up and spun them as one like a propeller on its side. I picked out a small, dead tree and flung the propeller first at the top, then back and forth through the trunk, chopping the entire tree into small logs. I then lifted them and placed them in our log pile near the fire.

Betty applauded me. *This is amazing! We could take down a whole army with some stones in a few minutes. In fact, we could probably do it with just two stones: one each.*

You're right. It'd be too easy. Let's go find some boulders now.

There were plenty of those along the riverbank. Betty raised her hand; a rock the size of a basketball lifted, followed by one twice its size, and then another. Each one was nearly twice its predecessor's size. Betty stacked ten on top of each other, from smallest to largest; the one on top was as big as a bus.

She put them all back, and I raised my hand to do exactly the same thing. When that took so little effort, we agreed that it was too easy.

Can you throw a big one?

I raised the largest rock we'd collected and threw it twenty yards; it landed next to the lake with a heavy thud. *Easy.*

Betty lifted it and placed gently back where it came from. *It is very satisfying to know we can do all this cool stuff.*

We have become deadly weapons now. Shall we fire a few rounds with the Remington?

We went back to Horus and retrieved the Remington and the pistols from the gun safe. We toted the pistols in gun belts around our waists, as if we were a couple of rednecks. Betty quickly attached the Remington's accessories and showed me how to load and clear it. Then she lay down on the ground in front of Horus and marked her target.

"Can you see the mark? There is a red spot on a tree over by the lake."

"Yes, barely."

Betty fired; the tree all but exploded on impact. She reloaded and shot another round with similar results.

"This I like; it's exceptionally smooth, and perfectly accurate over long distances. Have a go, Danny."

I lay down and took aim at what remained of the same tree. I hit close to Betty's mark. "Oh, I like this gun," I said. Taking aim again, I let it rip, hit right next to the last spot. "Excellent, although I'm quite sure our minds are contributing to our success."

"Yes, it's like we cannot miss."

We took the Remington back to Horus, packed her away, and didn't bother practicing with our side arms. That seemed unnecessary after what we had discovered about our aim and our abilities.

"Let's do something easy for lunch."

"Sure, Betty, anything you feel like."

"Well, I feel like KFC or McDonald's; I haven't had either in about seven years, you know. That's how long it's been since I left Taxi; I had nobody to go with before."

"Do you want to get out of here for a while? Charters Towers has both of those places, so we could just go for a day and have one for lunch and the other for dinner. Tell Conner we'll be back tonight. He will be okay with that; I can feel it."

Betty rang Conner right away. "Daddy, we are going to Charters Towers for some takeaway, so we will be back tonight…Yes, I understand…yes…yes, it has been seven years. He will look after me, you know that…I love you, too. Oh, can we see the bunker tomorrow? Yes, just after lunch will be great. Thank you, Daddy, see you then, thank you, I will." Betty hung up. "He sends his love and said not to get sick from takeaway since I haven't had it in so long."

"I knew he would be okay with it; he trusts us both to be careful. Ready?"

"Sure, I just want to tidy myself up a bit."

Betty went into the bathroom for a while, then to the bedroom to change into a hippy dress that was long, thin, and flowy. I had not seen her in a long dress before, and I was delighted. She had a little make-up on, too, and she waltzed to the front of the camper like a queen.

"How do I look?" she asked proudly.

"Stunning, baby. I think I should have a quick wash and find a shirt. You smell amazing."

I dashed into the bathroom and freshened up, found a button-down, and returned in less than two minutes.

Betty laughed so hard. "Well done, Mr. Fantastic. Let's go, that way." She pointed to the road. "We can go ahead and drop off some 'roo at Gertie's on the way."

Taxi was bustling with activity once again. Cars and trucks came from every direction. We pulled up at Gertie's, and I grabbed the frozen 'roo and headed to the kitchen with Betty right behind me. Rita was busy preparing some late breakfast, so I put the 'roo in the freezer for her. She thanked us and gave us both a kiss and a hug. We jumped back in Horus and headed out of Taxi.

Betty grabbed my leg and looked at me with a tear rolling down her cheek. "Thank you for this. I love how you think of me."

The tunes started with "Roadhouse Blues" by The Doors. Betty was in her element, singing along and just enjoying the drive. She was a joy to be with, and I was loving this drive. Our lunch would be late, but Betty seemed okay with that. She banged on my knee with her hand in time with "Immigrant Song" by Led Zeppelin, screaming the lyrics at the top of her lungs. This was a new and playful side of her, and I enjoyed getting to know it.

Nearly two hours later, Betty's voice was getting hoarse, but she carried on until we pulled into the car park of KFC; she was wrapping up "Livin' on a Prayer" by Jon Bon Jovi.

"Aren't you hungry after all that singing? Bett, you have a beautiful voice."

"Thank you, all those years being coached actually paid off. Come on, Danny. Let's eat one of everything."

Betty was out of Horus before I had even engaged the hand brake. I ran after her, loving every second of her excitement. Inside; Betty's eyes were wide, trying to take in everything at once. Her nostrils flared as she took it all in, and I could feel all her emotions and gratitude at being in such a fun but ordinary place; it was intoxicating. She couldn't turn away from the menu.

Can you please order for me, darling? I don't even know this menu anymore.

Slightly overwhelmed by the responsibility she'd placed on my shoulders with that request, I ordered six pieces of the original recipe, four spicy pieces, a large potato and gravy, a large side of coleslaw, large chips, popcorn chicken, and four sliders with pepper mayo.

Popcorn chicken and sliders?

You'll see.

Our order came out, and I found a park nearby where we could sit under some huge, old rain trees. We went into Horus's kitchen first so Betty could pour me some whiskey and herself some nonalcoholic wine. Then, like a child at Christmas, she unloaded the bag of food and was almost mesmerized by its contents. We ate in silence, but she was so loud in my head as she enjoyed every morsel. I suddenly understood the Hathors and how they fed on love, sex, and lust—just not their methods. I enjoyed Betty's meal just as much as she did, and I was just watching her eat. The chef who could cook such excellent meals herself was scarfing down fast food with unadulterated gusto.

Danny, this is almost the best thing I have had in years.

We thoroughly enjoyed that chicken, then drove to Sovereign Tavern and ordered a local beer for me and sparkling water for Betty. The bartender was a lively chap who had us totally engaged with his retelling of the town's history.

"Have you seen the Longhorns?" he asked. "You should have a look at them."

"Okay, we will check it out."

I enjoyed another beer, and then we left to do just that. Betty and I had never seen steers with horns quite like these. They were so incredibly huge: at least ten or twelve feet across.

A while later we walked casually down the streets of Charters Towers. Betty looked in every window and stopped to browse at the dress shops. She bought a few simple dresses and some lingerie.

We came to another old pub called Irish Molly's. We went in for a beer for me and a nonalcoholic Great Northern Zero for Betty. We sat and enjoyed watching the locals have a laugh; some played pool and joked around. This was relaxing, and Betty had the most beautiful smile on her face, she kept laughing and grabbing my leg or my hand as we chatted. The sun shone in her sparkling eyes, and her glossed lips glistened in the afternoon light. I was awed by her beauty.

"Thank you, babe, this is great." She leaned forward and kissed me on the lips tenderly.

"I love you, darling." I whispered in her ear. She trembled, and I took her hand. "Careful."

She scoffed. "I'm okay, Danny, you just make me, er, you know. I'll be right." She winked that sexy little wink of hers that I loved.

"Do you still want McDonald's for dinner?" I asked.

Actually, I think I want pizza!

"Okay, did you see that little Italian pizzeria?"

"You mean Bon Italiana Pizza?"

"That's the one. How about we go with a large so we can eat a few slices here somewhere, then take the rest home for later? If we order now, it should be ready by five and we can be back at camp by seven this evening."

We headed off to the pizza joint, placed our order for a supreme, and went for a walk while we waited.

"Oh, the smell in that pizzeria was divine. They use good yeast, I could tell."

"Really? You can tell how good yeast is by the smell? You're amazing."

"Yes, I am. Thank you." She squeezed my hand and grinned.

We collected our pizza, drove to a park, and sat at a picnic table to eat. The pizza was great; we had two big slices each and left Charters Towers for Taxi. After a nice, but uneventful drive, we arrived back at our camp.

"Home sweet home," Betty commented.

"Yes, and home is where the heart is." I replied. "Wherever we are together is home to me, no matter where we are." We kicked off our shoes and I took off my shirt. "How about we go down to the tent, light the fire, and chill for a while?"

"I'll be down in a second, just need the toilet and freshen up a bit first."

I took off my shorts in favor of some looser ones, walked to the firepit, and summoned some fresh logs from the pile; they gently flew over and arranged themselves. I poured myself a bourbon and Betty some of her wine without lifting a finger once the fire was going, then sat back on the couch and looked across the lake. My glass floated patently next to me until I reached out and took it. Betty soon came and joined me, this time wearing a pink fishnet T-shirt.

I looked at her and shook my head. "You're incorrigible, but I suppose that is why I love you."

"I'll take that as a compliment, thank you."

"How many of those did you bring anyhow?" I asked as I floated her glass over to her.

"Thank you, and seven different colors. Some with bigger holes, some with smaller. I like it when you look at me. I have spent years and years without experiencing any man's attention. You know I can feel your appreciation, right?"

"If you were to grab my groin right now, you would really feel it." I winked at her.

"*Ha!* No matter what I wear, you like it, don't you? You were turned on by my dress today."

"Er, guilty. I suppose that is part of our magnetism. You just have that effect on me, and I set you off accidentally."

Betty giggled, nodding her head as she sat right next to me. "Cheers, Danny."

"Cheers, Betty"

We sipped and looked across the lake as the light started to fade. I lifted a stone with my mind and flew it over to the edge of the lake, then sent it skipping across the water. Betty looked at me, then immediately back to the lake. She picked up a slightly bigger stone and flicked it all the way over to the opposite shore.

"See that rock on the other side? Hit that," Bett said, pointing to a rock the size of a basketball on the far bank.

My next rock was slightly bigger than the last. It skimmed perfectly and hit that rock she'd chosen with ease. Betty did the same. We could not miss; time and again, we hit it. Then we tried doing it with the rocks going just under the surface of the lake, faster and faster each time until one of mine went so fast that it glowed bright orange and split the target open on with an enormously loud crack.

"Oh, shit. That was fast," Betty said, her eyes wide.

I tried again with a larger rock; this one glowed even brighter, but met our target with an even louder sound before both rocks exploded into dust. "Holy shit! Did you see that?"

Wow, Danny you could take out a battleship like that!

Betty, I believe I could shoot hundreds of rocks like that. Together, we could maybe manipulate thousands and sink a whole fleet—not that I have any intention of doing. Perhaps our power is why the Hathors fear us.

"Feel like eating some more pizza?" I asked Betty.

"Not yet. I'm happy just to sit here and enjoy the dusk and you."

Betty snuggled into me on the couch, and we sat together like that for another hour. We hardly spoke, just sat and enjoyed each other's company. I sent a few more logs to the fire as the night started to cool off, but it was still so very mild and warm.

"Let's go sit near the fire," I said.

Betty reached behind my neck and pulled me down for a kiss. I obliged; because her kisses were delightful, and in the glow of the fire, some ten feet away she looked like an angel. After a few seconds, I pulled away, trying not to arouse her. She seemed okay, but kept her eyes on me as we walked to the firepit. A rug came out of our tent and laid itself out near the fire. I glanced at Betty as I became aware of music; Fleetwood Mac was slowly getting louder.

Baby, I want to dance for you.

A new bottle of Sinatra Century floated over to me as I sat on the rug, as did about seven pillows. Betty slowly started to dance around me, swirling around with her arms raised and gyrating above me like she was feeling the music in her very soul. "Gypsy" by Stevie Nicks was playing, and it seemed so fitting. I almost felt that Bett had the soul of a gypsy, nomadic and free spirited. She glided around me effortlessly, knowing her near-nakedness tantalized me. She was arousing me; she knew exactly what she was doing. When Rhiannon started playing, she pulled off her fishnet shirt, twirled it around, and threw it away with a flourish. Her steps got faster as she moved to the song, and sang along, pitch perfect and if my admiration was a physical presence, it would have neared the stratosphere.

Spinning around, she became lost in the song. Then she slowed down with the music and started to shake. I jumped up and grabbed ahold of my princess, but as soon as I did, her body shook and heaved in orgasmic bliss.

"Oh, it is okay. Just let it out, my girl." I eased her gently down to the rug and held her as her body slowly calmed. "You are okay. I've got you."

"Thank you, Danny. I love you." She smiled and pulled me down to her. "Come here, beautiful, and hold me tight."

She was so comforting and warm, satisfied and joyful; I could feel her love so close to my heart as I did as she asked and held her.

We lay for hours together in the warm glow of the firepit and barely spoke. We had no wants; we were one, an old soul. Our love was complete.

At some stage Betty fell asleep until "Runnin' with the Devil" by Van Halen came on. She opened her eyes as her body started moving again in time with the beat—almost like the music had taken her hostage. Her hand went into my shorts, and within half a minute, she was on me. In time with the beat of "Jump" by Van Halen, she brought me to climax.

Her gyrating on me was ecstasy, and her orgasm rolled in waves in time with the music, her head back and face towards the stars as she moaned deeply.

As the second song finished, so did she. Betty rolled off to my side, her eyes closed, her hand limp on my chest, breathing deeply and asleep once more. I tried to decide if she even knew what just happened; I could not read her at all, but she had a smile on her face and looked content, and that was what was important. I decided to ask her later what she remembered, but I was not sure it even mattered.

I looked down at my watch; it was seven minutes past ten. Time for some shut eye. I closed my eyes and fell asleep within minutes.

* * *

I awoke to Betty shaking me.

"Danny where have you been? I thought you weren't coming."

We were on the shore of an immense, yellow ocean, in a cavern so huge that the ceiling disappeared in the distance. The cavern sparkled like millions of diamonds. This space was so big it had its own weather, we could see a massive storm way out over the ocean. It rained out there with lightning and thunder that echoed deep. We stood, huge, bright blue mushrooms the size of trees were everywhere: a forest of them, as far as we could see. A cool breeze blew against our golden, glowing bodies. The ground vibrated with the steps of something huge trudging nearby. Bright red-and-purple birds flew in circles and out to sea as an intoxicating scent filled our nostrils. We looked out across the ocean and saw seven huge fins weaving above the surface and wondered if they were all part of an immense creature swimming just below.

"What is this place, Bett?"

"I don't know, but it is overloading my senses."

We turned together as a massive lizard-like creature strolled by, totally indifferent to our presence.

"Welcome, surface shadows, to our realm."

We spun around together. Before us stood a hundred lizard beings that had silently snuck up behind us.

"Hi! Please excuse us, I am Daniel and this Betty, we don't mean you any harm, but who are we talking to?" we inquired.

"I am Kraikarr of the Silurians," announced the one we supposed was their leader of sorts. "We have always been here, ever since the first cleansing that took our brothers. We came from the surface eons ago, but now this is our home. You are different; you are not here, yet we see you and feel your presence. You are like shadows with substance, but you are welcome. Please tell the surface man Conner Rage to go no deeper. He is near, and once that door opens, it cannot be closed. We want our peace and quiet, but he is a mere ten of your miles from us. We have taken steps, should he come any closer to discovering us. Our dark realm can have no contamination from the surface. But you cannot contaminate us in this form. Why have you come to us?"

"We did not mean to intrude; our dreams guide our future somehow. They bought us here."

"You are Old Ones, we believed they were all gone, but here you are. You are welcome to visit us. Our city lies beyond the forest. Would you like to see it? Follow us."

The lizard folk moved quickly and eerily with barely a sound. We soon arrived at the entrance of their city, and we were breathless. Before us was a structure without comparison. We struggled to comprehend what we were seeing. It was beautiful, yet indefinable: a honeycomb of structural wonderment that, to us, looked impossible.

"That is grand," we said, "unbelievably beautiful, Kraikarr."

"Thank you, surface shadows. I knew we would impress you."

As we walked through the amazing city, we felt a warmth from these beings; they had been there longer than humans had walked Earth and had survived with no wars or hate or bloodshed.

"We must go now, but thank you, Kraikarr, for everything. We will talk with you again soon. Our love to you and your people; we want you to survive this upcoming event, too."

"We, too, have love for you, but do not waste your concern on us; we always survive the kind of events of which I think you speak. Goodbye, surface shadows."

* * *

I opened my eyes; Betty stirred at the same moment.

"Hey, gorgeous," she said lovingly.

"Hey you," I answered as she rubbed my chest.

The sun was beaming in at seven o'clock that morning, and Betty's body all but glowed in the morning sunshine. I leaned over and kissed her.

"Hmm, thank you, baby," she said with passion. Her fingers were on my nipple, slowly spinning it. "So, a race of lizard people…really? And what was his name? Cracker?"

"I think it was more like Kwaikor, I don't know Bett. Their city was incredible and beautiful and huge."

"How do we tell Dad not to go any deeper without telling him of the Silurians?"

"I think we will need to tell him some of what we know."

"Okay, we can do that today when we see him. For now, it's time for a run, a swim, and breakfast," Betty said as she stood and offered me her hand.

"Thank you, Bett. Where did we leave our clothes?"

Suddenly our clothes floated toward us, followed by our joggers. We dressed and went outside. The sky was full of clouds for the first time since we arrived here.

"Looks like it might rain later, let's get going, we'll do fifteen miles, some sprints, and push-ups today."

Betty pushed the button on her smart watch as we started jogging down the path, in perfect time, we broke into a sprint, then slowed back down to jog, repeating yesterday's routine until we hit the halfway point. We stopped for a brief breather and forty push-ups. I struggled with the last few, but did it. Back on our feet, we sprinted to our lake. Panting heavily, we came to a stop and both planted our hands on our hips, trying to catch our breath.

"Whew, well done, Danny—great effort. I love that you are really pushing yourself. Come on, let's swim."

Betty was out of her clothes in an instant, running naked into the water; I followed her as soon as I was naked, too. We did ten slow crossings, then stopped in the shallows and floated around on our backs for a while. Betty raised her arm and summoned the gel, which flew promptly into her hand, and I watched Betty lather herself up. She was alluring, exciting; I could not stop myself.

Baby, you are gorgeous.

That compliment deserves one of my special hugs.

She winked, one of her deliciously sexy winks that drove me crazy, and came over with her arms outstretched. Instead of hugging me, she pushed me so I fell back in the waist deep water. *Oops, not sorry,* she wrapped her arms and legs around me, waited for me to harden, then guided herself onto me. We moved as one, our lips locked together as were our bodies. Betty quivered all over and moaned louder as I came, pulling me in tightly as her body heaved and shook.

Then she relaxed, but still embraced me tightly. We bobbed around in the water like two corks stuck together, kissing and laughing for another half hour.

Betty finally let go of me and we swam to shore, then went up to Horus, our towels flying to us as we walked.

"Would you like pizza for breakfast?"

"Sure, we can't always be healthy. At least, not while we have that nice pizza sitting there. I'll whip up a few eggs, too, Betty said as she finished drying herself off and pulled on her apron after she laid out a nice skirt and blouse on the bed for later.

I threw on some shorts as Betty started frying up four eggs and made some coffee. Betty threw some slices of pizza in a large frying pan and put a lid on it. Betty saw me looking at her strangely.

"You'll see. It tastes way better than microwaving pizza."

Yep, it did. We ate our pizza and eggs in silence, then washed the dishes and prepared for our trip into Taxi.

"Hey, Bett, I'm going to close up all the flaps on the tent just in case it rains when we are in Taxi."

"Good idea, Danny."

At the tent, I shifted the rugs and pillows back inside and lowered all the flaps telepathically, then covered our log supply and the couches with tarps that Conner had supplied.

That's better. The wind is still picking up a bit; when it dies down, the rain will come.

Probably will. I'm all ready to go, babe.

Okay, I'm on my way back now.

We drove back into Taxi; Betty ordered some battered mackerel at The Dermy for lunch at twelve o'clock, and we arrived at five minutes to twelve, perfect. Davo had seen us pull up and had two beers waiting for us on the counter.

"Hey, lovebirds, how ya doin'?"

"Great, Davo. Thanks for the beers; I'll have both, but can you find a Zero for Betty?" I said, patting her stomach so he'd catch my drift.

His already cheerful face lit up, and a huge smile took over his face. "Whoa, congrats! When is it due?"

Betty grinned at him and replied, "April of next year, and there are two."

"Give us a big hug, B. That's fantastic!" I almost lost sight of Betty when Davo wrapped his massive arms around her. Then he shot his hand out for me and shook my hand rapidly with much gusto. "Come here and take a seat, mum-to-be." He pulled out a chair for Betty. "I'll be right back with your zero."

Betty looked at me and smiled. *All of Taxi will know in about ten minutes, but that's alright.*

He was beaming when he returned. "Here you go, beautiful; your fish and chips will be out in ten minutes." He headed into the kitchen, returning a short time later with two huge plates filled with battered fish, chips, and a hearty salad. "Enjoy."

"Looks delicious," we said in unison.

He laughed his head off as he left. We shook our heads and tucked into our meals.

We struggled to finish it all, but we did. Then we sat back, and I slowly finished my second beer.

Delores and Billie ran out from the kitchen and raced over to us, smiling brightly. "Congratulations!". They chimed.

"Oh, thank you, lovelies," Betty replied as they hugged and kissed her.

They nodded at me smiling shyly and then left again. We stood up, thanked Davo for the delicious food, and went back outside to Horus.

24
The House of Ra

We headed toward the airstrip; the roads were busy, with trucks going in every direction. We drove past the point I had to turn around at last time. I felt as if I was doing something naughty. This area was previously above my paygrade, I felt out of my league. Security was on high alert; we pulled up at the boom gate and were met by two armored guards.

This is new, but it makes sense, Betty thought.

The guard came over to the window. "Welcome, Ms. Rage and Mr. Starr. You can head over to Ra; we will inform Mr. Rage that you have arrived."

"Excuse me, Ra?" Betty asked.

"The building over there," the guard pointed, "over the mine."

"Of course, thank you," Betty replied.

Ra is the god of the sun, and the creator of heaven, Earth and the underworld. Clever, Conner.

He sure is, Danny.

The building was totally unremarkable, but that was probably done on purpose. It looked like a storage shelter, or a pump house, if anything. Conner stood out front, watching all the activity happening on the airstrip. Three planes were being loaded; destination unknown, apparently, Medi-Corp now had their own planes.

We jumped out of Horus, and Betty ran to Conner, her arms spread wide. "Hi, Daddy!"

"Hello, sweetheart." Conner hugged her and kissed both cheeks. "Daniel, thanks for coming."

I held out my hand, but he ignored it and hugged me. "Hi, Conner. I wouldn't miss this for anything."

Conner swept his arm out as an invitation. "This way, please."

He pushed a button on a fob hanging around his neck, and the whole front wall opened, then slid out silently. It was roughly four feet thick and made of steel and cement. The whole building was constructed in the same fashion, this place was totally built to last an apocalypse.

"Welcome to The House of Ra, Taxi's haven and means of survival should any life-threatening event ever occur. I started this many years ago—soon after you were born, Betty—and now it is ready for occupation. Notice the sturdy door with twenty, ten-inch locking pins. We are standing in an airlock; these next two chambers are filled with all kinds of decontamination equipment. Come on through."

"Wow, this is very impressive Conner," I said, wide-eyed.

"Well, thank you, but you ain't seen nothing yet. Through these automatic doors is the old northern mine, which has been totally relined and reinforced and opened up, in fact more than half of this place is like a giant Faraday cage to protect electronic equipment from EMP, which will likely happen immediately after any major kind of impact. We have dug out many rooms off this main shaft: an armory here and another larger one further on, a small hospital with an operating room, and some accommodations. We have really tried to spread those out so we all have our space. Just wait until you see the caverns."

I watched Betty intently as we went deeper in. *Are you okay, Bett?*

I'm okay. When I was a kid down here, I think I must have sensed the Silurians and thought they were evil. I must have misunderstood their protective feelings.

Unaware of the silent conversation taking place right next to him, Conner continued. "Now, here is our first seal. If we were to be breached by whatever, we could close this section off. Seal One." A massive hidden door slid out within a second and sealed off the section we had just left. "Many features and security aspects are coded to only my voice and yours, Betty. Here is our first set of halls, which have been designed for our menagerie of livestock. One of our main staples will be rabbit due to their high reproduction rates. Our chefs are working on as many different recipes as possible, and we are incorporating insects in our diets since they are high in protein and fibre—and surprisingly tasty."

I glanced at Betty, who poked her finger into her mouth and pretended to gag. I suppressed a laugh.

"There are more accommodation and facilities here: restaurants, barbers, and a small chapel."

"Oh, wow, Daddy. You've thought of everything."

"Seal Two," Conner said with authority. Another huge door slid across and closed off the section, just like the previous one. Conner spread his hands as the area lit up. "And now, the caverns."

Before us was a vista that was comparable to our vision from the previous night: an open area with grassy fields, waterfalls, and swimming holes. The light above looked exactly like a blue sky on a sunny day.

"How are you achieving that?" I pointed at the high ceiling.

"We have worked on that marvel for years: hydrothermal generators power most of our lights and air filters in a system that can last generations. The ceiling can reflect the time of day outside." We came to an area with moving vistas of greenery and islands with the bluest oceans. "These huge screens use less power than a light globe, and also run on hydrothermal power. Off to both sides of the cavern are more accommodations and community areas for eating and cooking, as well as a school. There are also swimming pools, gyms, spas, and a tavern."

Betty, are you seeing this? This is incredible.

Danny, tell him.

"Conner, it's amazing what you have achieved in thirty years. There is so much space down here. Your vision is so defined, focused."

"Thank you, I appreciate that. Now we come to our quarters off to this side. Seal Three."

The door slid closed, and Betty squeezed my hand. *This could also be our tomb, the last time we see light. It is fantastic and beautiful, but it scares the shit out of me.*

Conner watched us closely. "You guys, okay? This can be a bit overwhelming at first."

"It certainly is a lot to take in, Dad. Are these our living quarters?" Betty answered, trying to deflect his attention away from her nerves.

"They are, and I have spared no expense. Check this out."

Conner spread his hands again, so proud of what he'd built, and he had every right to be. This was luxury at the highest level. I had never seen such beautiful living quarters as these: plants, water features, bars, play areas for children, tennis courts, swimming pools.

"Dad, this is fantastic. You have put so much into this. But do you really think something so bad will happen that all of Taxi will be forced to come down here just to survive?" Betty said, letting go of my hand and walking up next to Conner so she could gauge his reaction better.

"Many years ago I had a dream about an apocalypse. Recently, I had another. This one was way more vivid, as if I were watching Earth's destruction from above. A huge meteor struck, and only two percent of the entire population survived. I believe that what I experienced is something that will happen, and sometime soon. I'm sorry to unload all of this on you, but I want us to stay together and survive this."

Conner grabbed Betty's hands as a solitary tear rolled down his cheek.

"Daddy, I love you. Listen carefully; we must tell you something profound, that is related to all of this, something fantastic. Please, let's sit for this." Betty and Conner sat on a big wide couch, and I found a smaller seat nearby. Betty searched her father's eyes. "We know of your dream. We have had it, too. Something big and terrible is coming, and life as we know it will cease to exist. Danny and I have skills to help humanity. I will explain a little, but you must trust us both. First of all, do not go any further into the caverns. This is very important. It has been made clear to us that further exploration is forbidden." *Danny, I will show him Kraikarr telling us to stop him.*

Are you sure, Bett?

Betty didn't answer me except to take both of Conner's hands again and tell him to focus on her. She looked into his eyes; Conner's started to blur over as he saw everything we did about the Silurians and Kraikarr's request. He sees the door that cannot be opened.

When his eyes cleared, Conner pulled back out of Betty's grip. "How?"

Betty raised her hand toward the side table; a statue lifted into the air, then the table itself. She quickly guided them back down, not wanting to show off too much and spook him.

"Did you know about this?" Conner asked. I lifted my hand, and the statue lifted and spun around before gently landing in its spot. "You, too? What is going on? I don't understand."

"Daddy, it is fine. We have visions like you, but ours are a little… more. The lizard people are real; do not break their faith in us, please. We made a promise, and you have enough space here to survive. Further exploration must stop today."

"Yes Betty, I will stop, I believe you, but what's with the tricks? How can both of you do those things?"

"It is telekinesis, but we are also telepathic. We can read each other's minds and show others like you things like that dream."

"How is any of that possible? I don't understand, Betty."

For this first time since I'd met him—and perhaps for the first time in his entire life—Conner looked lost.

"Daddy, the important thing is that we know what is ahead. Other races from other worlds are watching our every move. This reset will be the fifth; civilizations have fallen before us, and likely will after this event, too. The Hathors are guiding us on our journey so we can aid humanity."

To anyone else on the planet that would be nonsense, but to Conner, it made complete sense thanks to his interest in Egyptian history. He then sat back and said, "How about a whiskey, Daniel?"

"Yes, thanks," I answered.

"Sorry, Betty, I know you like it, too, and can't have any right now. But hell, I kind of need one after that," Conner stated.

"We are new to this, too. Every single day brings a new revelation." I raised his bottle of whiskey in the air with my mind, removed the cork, and poured out two glasses. I sent his over to him while he looked on in wonder. "Conner, you ain't seen nothin' yet."

I raised my glass. Conner looked at me seriously and seemed unable to speak.

"Daddy, we are here to guide you and everyone else that we can. This will not be easy by any means, but what you have achieved is miraculous. This place is incredible, and Taxi will survive if you stick to your guns and keep everyone calm through all of this. Daddy, you need to stockpile books and seeds, okay?"

"Well, I haven't shown you the library yet. Come on, and bring your drink, Daniel."

We headed out of our accommodation area and crossed the huge cavern.

"Open Library," Conner said to an unremarkable section of the rock.

It hissed and moved inward, revealing two large steel doors that also opened with the unmistakable hiss of an airlock. It was as big as a concert hall with rows of bookshelves, on top of which were taxidermy animals, filling one half of the cavern. There were large leather couches with reading lights and rows of tables and chairs. Monitors and headphones were set up on separate tables, and the entire space was filled with artwork of all tastes and mediums.

"The whole library is a Faraday cage, too. We have our own internet network, but it's more like accessing a large mainframe that contains as much information as my geeks could get their hands on, which they tell me is a lot. We have millions of movies that can be watched anywhere down here, millions of songs and videos downloaded with special backups that I don't understand. The books took me more than thirty years to collect. We have thirty thousand maps stored here, and a printing and binding press, should any aspiring authors wish to write a story about a town called Taxi or The House of Ra."

We looked at him and said together, "This is outstanding!"

We looked at each other and laughed, and so did Conner.

"Do you do that often?"

"Dad, sometimes we sit and talk for hours without saying a single word out loud," Betty said.

"We can talk from miles apart without a phone, too, but we are rarely more than a few feet from each other," I added. "Your daughter is the best thing that has ever happened to me. I love her deeply."

"You are a good man, Daniel, and good for my Betty. You both have an aura of happiness and love surrounding you, and it rubs off on everyone. The whole town is talking about you two, and how happy you make them feel when you are around." Conner smiled in a way I'd never seen him smile before. "Your wedding will be special to everyone; you will unite all of Taxi with your love. I can feel it, too, and it is truly intoxicating."

Oh, wow! Just look at him.

I know, right? "Thank you, Dad, that was very sweet. Almost too sweet for you," Betty teased, causing Conner to roar with laughter. *Shit!*

"See? You guys are having that effect on me. I love it! Come on, let's go."

I have never seen him quite like this before. He almost seems euphoric. This is weird.

Don't worry, Bett, it is a good thing. I can feel it.

"You two had enough? We have been down here for two hours now," Conner stated.

"Really?" Betty looked at her watch.

"Yeah, and I have shown you nearly everything except the stores, which is kind of like a huge supermarket, but with no checkouts and it goes on for about a mile. And there are the crops."

"Crops?" I asked.

"We need to grow stuff if we want to survive. Check this out."

We came to another big cavern, this one with rows and rows of different crops, and even a small orchard with different fruit trees and nuts, and a small vineyard.

"Oh, wow!" Again, we exclaimed together.

"You two are hilarious." Conner laughed, shaking his head. He meant it in a nice way. "Come on, let's get out of here. I am sure you have had enough. Anyway, I have a surprise." He pointed to an illuminated sign: Emergency Exit 4. "Open Exit Four," Conner said firmly. The doors slid back to reveal an elevator. "This is an escape lift. Please enter."

He pushed the top button, which simply said *up*; the other said *down*. The doors closed and the elevator silently went up. It came to a stop, and the doors slid open.

It took a few seconds to realize that we had come up inside of a fake crypt like the ones at the cemetery. This was different, though, in that it had reinforced walls lined with lead.

"Exit," Conner commanded.

The wall to the side slid open silently. Standing there on the other side was one of Conner's goons. He motioned for the wall to close behind us after we stepped out of the elevator and into the sunny cemetery. Soon, we arrived at a car park. Horus was there, as well as an immaculate, black '65 Lincoln Coupe with blacked-out windows. It idled roughly with what sounded like a heavily modified twin turbo engine.

"This is a beautiful machine, Conner."

Conner looked at me and winked.

That's where she gets it from.

Betty laughed hysterically in my head.

Conner turned and took Betty's hand, "Thank you both for coming to see my dream. I really enjoyed showing it to you, and I meant what I said. You are joyful to be with. I can't wait to see you again soon, but I really must get back to work. There is still so much to do."

We thanked him profusely and told him how much we loved what he had created. He shook my hand and climbed in the back of the Lincoln. I heard him tell his driver to floor it as he closed the door. The Lincoln roared like a race car and sped off, its wheels spinning madly and the engine growling like a tiger.

* * *

Conner sat, lost in his thoughts as he stared out at the countryside. His love of Egyptian mythology had been with him all his life, and he'd had visions in the past, so it didn't surprise him that he'd had one now. He was surprised when Betty could show him a vision of her own, one that was as realistic as any ultra-high-definition movie. Silurians lived near his shelter, and they had been there for an eternity—long before humanity crawled from the primordial swamps and were nudged along by the Pleiadeans.

Conner's mind was in turmoil as he tried to assess all the information he was given. He still couldn't get his head around the telepathy and telekinesis. Taxi had way more secrets than he'd realized.

* * *

"Is he always so dramatic when he leaves? That is a next-level car," I said wistfully.

"Danny, his garage is full of old muscle cars and classics: at least twenty on last count."

I looked at Betty incredulously. "How do you even say that so nonchalantly?"

"Probably because I have lived with it all my life."

Betty poked her tongue out at me as we walked to Horus. *Jealousy is pointless, especially now, when possessions will soon become worthless. Muscle cars will be nothing more than a memory. They will all rust away within two or three hundred years. Our whole existence is a mere flicker of an eyelid in the scope of Earth's timeline.*

Okay, I get it, Betty. But it is sad. I'm going to miss cars like that, and a whole lot of other stuff.

"Danny, feel what matters and tell me."

"Bett, you matter more than anything: you and humanity."

"Go buy yourself ten muscle cars if you think that will make you happy; you can afford it now. But you know that is not what you desire. You want me."

Betty moved to the back of Horus. We were still in the cemetery car park, but she removed her clothes and lay on the bed. I started to move toward her, but stopped. My clothing was rapidly being ripped apart, thread by thread. I looked down at what once was my shorts lying at my feet.

Come to me, Danny, take me now.

We made love with no more hesitation. Our desire was more important than anything else. It was perfect: Betty, right there loving me as I was loving her. Our simultaneous climaxes were so intense. Satisfied, we lay back for a bit, looking at each other.

Perfect, baby. We just had sex in the cemetery car park, kiddo. We should probably get moving before Conner sends some goons to check on us.

Yeah, okay, Danny.

I found some new shorts and started driving. Bett returned in a bright blue fishnet T-shirt, which made it much harder for me to focus on the road. Betty soon started rubbing my groin.

"Danny, drive faster."

"Baby, we are only about five minutes away."

But Betty was insatiable again. She started to pull at my shorts, trying to go down on me, but I begged her to wait until I was no longer driving.

I soon pulled into our camp, and my shorts immediately fell apart. Betty was all over me, her mouth around me sucking, taking me. She shook with how much she loved it, too. The Hathors had taken over again, I just knew it, but she kept going, and I could not stop myself from getting lost to it, too.

Betty pulled me to the floor and on top of her. "Come on, Danny. Give it to me, harder." Her eyes were wide open, staring at me as she gasped for breath between moans. "Yes, that's it, baby!"

She pulled me over and onto my back and started gyrating faster, her hands pushing down on my chest. *Fuck!* I came again, thrusting upward, and Betty's head went back as her back arched and she let out an almighty roar—almost sounding like a lion. Then she collapsed, breathing hard and kissing my neck, nibbling my ear.

After a few minutes she said, huskily. "Sorry Danny. I don't know what came over me. I didn't mean to get so forceful, and I don't think it was Hathor because I couldn't sense her. All I could think of was you, of satisfying you. You make me feel so alive, so full of joy and so fucking horny."

Betty squeezed me again, ever so lightly and gradually making me stiff.

"Betty, I thought you were satisfied?"

"Hmm, I am, but you feel so good inside me. Once more: gentle this time. Please, baby."

"You are insatiable today, Bett. Okay, but gentle."

She slowly moved around on me, making the most of every direction, her body pushing on me firmly. She started to moan as the waves flowed through her, her grip on me tightening.

"Come, Danny," she whispered in my ear.

That was enough to send me over the edge. I let go in spasms of shuddering joy. She relaxed, gently slid off of me, and lay next to me with her eyes closed.

We lay there quietly for another ten minutes, and then Betty stirred.

"Swim, Danny?"

We got up off the floor, and Betty wrapped her arms around me and squeezed.

I love you, Danny.

I love you, Betty.

We swam in unison, first freestyle, then the breaststroke, and then the sidestroke. We did ten crossings before we stopped and floated on our backs, holding hands for a while,

Danny?

I knew immediately what was on her mind. *It is okay. Come on.*

Betty started kissing me as her hand slid down my stomach, grabbing me gently. Then she wrapped her legs around me, guided me inside her and kept it slow again, her body shuddering as the first wave hit her, then another, and then another, each increasing in intensity.

Danny, now.

I came on her command; it was intense and highly erotic. Betty was totally in sync with me, and we both tilted our heads back and let out a loud cry across the lake.

As if on cue, it started to rain. It began gently at first, then slowly built up to a downpour. The rain was cold, and we had to fight to keep our heads above water. Holding each other like that in the water and in the rain was magical; we both felt it and knew we had experienced this exact feeling together long ago, on another continent, in another body of water in the rain. Finally, we were spent. That was a first: a complete shared memory from our distant past.

Our noses were touching, but we still couldn't see each other's face in the deluge.

"Do you want to go in the tent?" I nearly had to yell; the rain was so loud.

"Not yet, baby," she yelled in my ear.

We slowly floated around as the rain started to ease up; it was dark with all the clouds around. Embracing each other like teenagers, we could not get enough. Bett kissed me again and again. She reached down and then practically thrust me inside her once more. This time, she couldn't hold back, and went off like a rocket on me. Betty screamed across the lake as she came at the exact same instant as me.

Daniel, you are amazing today—no, every single fucking day. I love you!

When you say stuff like that, you drive me wild. I love you back tenfold, baby.

The rain stopped.

"I'm turning into a wrinkled prune from being in the water so long."

"Hey, you wanted to stay in," I pointed out.

"Yes, and I am glad we did. That was awesome."

We ran to the tent and grabbed our towels, lifting some of the flaps telepathically as we dried ourselves off. Betty poured me a bourbon using her mind and sent it to me.

"Thanks, babe. So, what is going on with you today? I don't even know how many times we did it. Are you done now?"

"Er, okay, last bit first, I doubt it, so be prepared. I think I was like this sometime in our past, and it's making up for lost time. Today has some importance for us, but I have no idea why. I'm sorry for my insatiability. Even now I am thinking of you and wanting you. But first, I need to feed you so you have energy for more, and I am a little bit sore from all the action. Sorry for being so demanding, baby."

Betty walked over and kissed me warmly., she was on fire, I could sense she was still barely in control.

"You have been crazy—that is for sure—but whenever your desires take over, I will do my best to show you how I care for you, how I love you."

"I know. You are everything in my world right now. I am sorry for my weakness, but I don't think our love has ever been fully realized in our past, no matter how many times we have been together. This time our love is fulfilled. We realize that life is not linear. There are many paths, and some are without fulfilment. Some lives we live make no sense, and have no answers. Yet there are others that are so enlightening that we thrive in the afterglow. This is one such life. This time we survive—some of us, anyhow."

"Betty, you are full of surprises, I am just happy we are together now."

Betty thought for a moment. "Danny, I'm going to Horus for a quick shower before dinner, okay?"

"Of course, Betty. I'll come up in a few minutes and find something to cook."

When Betty left, I looked up at the sky. Most of the rain clouds were gone so I lifted the tarp on the logs and thankfully found them all dry. I took half a dozen and lit the firepit. It soon burned nicely.

Betty had just finished her shower when I got to Horus. I could sense how good she felt after having a warm shower, and she smelled delicious.

"I took out two steaks. We can slice them up and serve them in those Turkish rolls with some slaw."

"That sounds perfect: nice and simple."

Betty came out dressed in a purple silk shirt that had one button done in the middle. She lifted her arm and leaned against the doorway. "How do I look?"

"Delightfully sexy."

"Good answer. You're cooking tonight, right?"

I nodded; she poured me a bourbon and herself some wine before she sat down at the table and watched me prepare the slaw. I put the knife down and kissed her on the neck, taking in her perfume. My hand cupped her breast lightly.

"You smell amazing, baby," I whispered and stepped back.

She shivered, then winked and pulled back one side of her shirt, exposing her breast. I just stood there admiring her beauty.

"Thank you, Danny. Now back to work."

I finished up and put everything on the tray. It lifted into the air as the door swung open. We followed it down to the fire and set it down on the table. I adjusted the hot plate, shifting a few smaller logs. The steaks lifted into the air and flew to the plate, sizzling immediately. In a few minutes, they flipped over and continued cooking. We sat back, enjoying our drinks, as the rolls cut themselves in half, buttered themselves, and landed next to the steaks, which then went to a clean plate to rest. I enjoyed watching my handiwork. The rolls were toasted and went back to the tray as the steaks were sliced up and placed on the rolls, followed by the sauce and slaw. Our plates glided silently to us, and Betty applauded me.

Well done! That was fun to watch, and the steak is perfect.
Thank you, Bett. It is good.

About an hour later, we went into the tent and Betty stretched out on the mattress, inviting me. I got down on my hands and knees above her and undid that single button with my teeth. Betty quivered. I kissed each nipple and licked her belly as I moved down her body. I reached the top of her legs and she started to moan, so I pushed them apart and kissed her with my tongue. As she started to orgasm, her hands pulled my hair, and her back arched so much that her pelvis lifted off the ground. Wave after wave racked her body, and I couldn't believe she wanted more.

Suddenly, she pushed me onto my back and climbed on top of me. She moved like a goddess, bringing me to the edge and kissing me passionately until I came. She cried out with me as I pushed up against her, then eventually relaxed. She fell off to my side, exhausted.

"I think I am done now, Danny." She smiled as her hand moved all over my chest slowly.

Betty poured me another bourbon and it glided to me. We sat up, leaning against the pillows, holding hands, and admiring each other's bodies. Betty's purple shirt was open, exposing her breasts; she was aware of my gaze and enjoyed it. Her hand squeezed mine and then let go to rest on my leg next to my groin, and her little finger poked me. I glanced at her from the corner of my eye; she giggled and did it again.

Betty? What are you up to?
I'm trying to wake it up.
Why would you want to wake it? You just said you were done.

She looked at it, and with her finger in the air, pointed at it. It magically stood straight up, fully erect and throbbing.

How are you even doing that?

Then it felt like she was doing something with her mouth, but she still wasn't touching me. She intensified what she was doing.

You had better stop that right now, or I am going to—

A towel flew over and wrapped itself around me, then started moving up and down. When I closed my eyes, it felt exactly like Betty. Betty could feel it as if she was physically doing me. She started to moan again, too. The towel moved faster and faster, tightening and twisting. We both exploded with joy repeatedly, over and over again.

Panting heavily, I looked down as the towel flew out the tent and dropped on the ground. I expected to find my skin red and raw, but everything seemed normal, except somehow slightly bigger. Betty leaned over and kissed me.

That was different. She looked down. *What's happened to you? It is bigger. How? Is it is still engorged?*

I felt light headed all of a sudden and slightly off. *Someone is watching us!* I sat up and peered out; Betty could sense it too. *Up, there!* I pointed to where, about thirty feet above us, a flying saucer sat silently. *What are they doing?* As we watched, the towel that Betty used on me lifted and was immediately pulled up into the saucer, which then zipped away silently. *Betty, they've taken that towel full of my sperm. They did this to me somehow.*

I looked down, my cock was now soft but even bigger and my balls seemed huge and heavy. I fell back on the pillows.

Danny are you okay? She leaned over me and kissed me on the cheek.

I'm alright. I'm a little dizzy and my body just feels a bit weird. What did they do, put some chemical in that towel? Why would they take my sperm, and why would they want me bigger? Bett, how did you do that without touching me?

Betty thought for a second, unconsciously staring at my cock. *I'm not sure why they did that, but I thought of doing that to you with my mind, concentrated, and then it happened. I had no idea it would be so pleasurable to both of us.*

How is your mind controlling my body now?

I don't know, but I had better be careful with that. It could get out of hand—excuse the pun.

She squeezed and let go of me, but kept staring at it.

Betty. Stop.

She snapped out of it and kissed me again, lovingly.

Betty jumped up to go to the bathroom, and I decided to go, too. We both left the tent; Betty went to the outdoor toilet and I stood near the lake. As I peed, I thought of what she did, and wondered if I could do to her what she'd done to me. When she started to open the door, I

— 215 —

imagined suddenly entering her. She let out a loud gasp and nearly lost her balance. My rhythm built up as she tried to walk. She knew exactly what I was up to and was enjoying it, but she was also trying to get back to the tent. I turned and watched her slow progress as she kept stopping to moan and shudder.

Danny! Please, oh, stop it.

But she didn't want me to; I could feel her like she had with me, and it was incredible. I looked down at myself; I was big, hard and pulsing. Betty stopped trying to walk altogether and cried out in bliss; I let go at the same moment, shooting out across the sand, it went on and on. I moaned as I finished and removed myself from her, and she sat down where she was, moaning softly. I ran over to her and knelt down. She smiled at the fact that my big cock was still hard and dripping cum.

"What a surprise! I can't believe that you worked it out so quickly." She punched me softly in the arm. "Ratbag."

"It felt the same to me; I felt you even when you were one hundred feet away."

I picked Betty up and carried her back to the tent, imagining she weighed the same as a feather to make the job even easier. Betty's head fell to my shoulder. I could sense every feeling that passed through her: admiration, love, joy, bliss. We were so in tune, it was crazy. She just watched me silently as all these feelings ran through her. I felt her joy, too, and it was beautiful.

Gently, I set my goddess down on the mattress and summoned drinks for us both. Betty was silent in my head.

Hey, you, are you good?

Thanks, Danny. I am just resting, I think I had about a thousand orgasms today and my body is tingling all over, as is my mind. I am sure you feel the same. We cannot do this every day; we will wear out some of our bits! Thank you for putting up with me.

Exhausted, we closed our eyes and slept.

* * *

The Hathors all looked at each other, smiling.

"Send them somewhere nice. We have gorged ourselves today on their lust and we grow fat on it. Let them rest. They have given us a hundred years of food today, as we hoped they would. They are nearly there; full enlightenment is near. Betty is very close and Daniel, the leader, is as strong as we expected he would be. Their power grows, so we need to stay hidden and benevolent when they request us, or they will easily stop us.

"Pleione and Maia: stop messing with Betty. She could hurt Daniel, and we don't want that. Stop with Danny, too. Don't make him too big, you gave him something else- pheromones, didn't you? Women will soon find him irresistible. Oh, and did you steal more DNA?"

* * *

We awoke as the ground rumbled beneath us. We sat up and immediately knew that we were on Earth, but this was at the dawn of time. Earth was still quite old, but dinosaurs had only been there for one hundred million years, they would carry on for another seventy-seven million years.

We stood up then lifted off the ground; our golden bodies glistened in the dawn's sunlight, and we swirled around each other like swallows dancing. We flew high through the morning sky, breathing air that was pure and clean, but dense with water vapor. Holding hands, we looked down as herds of dinosaurs roamed forests and swamps

We became aware of dwellings and order, streets and towns, inhabited by bipedal lizard people. They waved as if they knew us; their civilization had existed for ten thousand years. They started playing music, something we recognized, but could not remember. We spun through the air, dancing to their tunes as they all started to mimic our sky dance. They were intelligent and happy beings, and we were happy with their existence.

We sailed on, swooping low over the oceans. Many creatures swam beneath us; many were malevolent, but some showed great intelligence, like the primordial whales singing their songs of love. This was a beautiful planet.

On the shore of a huge lake, we watched fish jump out of the water. The sun slowly set behind two active volcanoes spewing lava and fire. We sat in bliss, enjoying each other's company at the dawn of life. As night brought a million stars and lit the heavens, we became aware of a familiar sight: a single craft with two occupants, our slimy friends The Octo. They swooped in low and landed near us, they have come to sit with us on the shore. To chat, and watch the stars.

* * *

Our hands were tightly clasped together as I awoke. She was a vision of beauty, and her eyes flickered as she slowly awoke.

"Hey, babe," I whispered.

She snuggled in and pulled me closer. "Come here and give us a kiss." I kissed her on the cheek lovingly. "What was that? Kiss me, baby."

So, I really kissed her with everything I had.

"Now that was a kiss! Thank you, baby."

We didn't need to move, get up, or do anything that day, so we lay together and gently caressed each other—not sexually, just because we were enthralled with each other's bodies. Our breathing naturally matched up with each other's. We were one, as we had been many times now. Betty and Daniel: a force to be reckoned with.

25
Wake Up, Guys

"Betty, when I carried you back, I imagined you were as light as a feather, and it took no effort—none at all. What if I imagine that you or I weigh nothing. Could we fly?"

In the next instant we shared the same thoughts of flying and just like that we lifted off the mattresses and hung in the air. The tent flap pulled back, and we zipped out into the morning sky totally naked, our arms extended outward not from necessity, but pure joy. The higher we went, the cooler it became. Birds looked at us curiously as we circled and dove, spinning around each other. Within minutes of learning to fly, we felt like masters; it was easy and fantastic and gave us so much pleasure.

We stopped and held hands, watching the beautiful clouds slowly float by. We slowly spun around and looked each other up and down in total admiration. We were two beautiful phoenixes, and we were madly in love.

Betty let go and assumed the classic Superman pose: one fist outstretched and one knee lifted, her toes pointed down. She smiled and gave me one of her sweet winks, then zipped away in a blur. I immediately gave chase, but she was moving fast—nearly a thousand miles an hour, if I had to guess. I sped up and caught up. We approached the Coral Sea, slowed down, and flew lower to glide across the perfect ocean and over the Great Barrier Reef.

Humpback whales migrating north breached below us and called out in their minds, *Greetings, Old Ones. Good to see you are awake.*

Hi, whales. It's nice to see you, too. You are beautiful souls, and your songs are joyful.

We swim north to warmer water to make love and become pregnant; we are all happy that you are blessed with twins. Most humans do not care for this planet. We know you are different; we sense you, and you sense us.

Whales, something bad is coming: a big space rock. You need to go very deep underwater to stay safe. We will warn you when we know more, but you must alert all the others in the sea.

Thank you, Old Ones. We trust in you, for you have always looked out for us and bring us so much joy with your beautiful love. We will tell the orca, dolphins and the octopi.

They disappeared below the waves; we spiralled up and headed inland, careful to avoid any aircraft. Two naked, flying people might have caused an awkward accident. We sped up, going as fast as we could, and arrived back at camp within minutes. Gently landing by Horus.

That was unbelievable. These last two days have been incredible. This must be due to our enlightenment, as Ishta said. And yet, I feel there is still more to learn.

Betty looked so innocent and vulnerable as she nodded. *I agree. We have grown so much, and our feelings have grown, too. Our sexuality has matured and gone next-level crazy, but in a good way. Then there is the elephant in the room.* She raised her eyebrows and pointed down at my groin. *Or should I say, the elephant trunk in the room? Is that part of your enlightenment? When you fly slowly, it hangs down as if it is erect.*

I pulled her to me and hugged her, lifting us both off the ground and spinning us around a few times in the air before dropping down. Betty kissed me with all the love she had, and I felt it. Everything about us was changing, growing, developing.

"We should have some breakfast," I said.

"What will satisfy you, my dear?"

"Apart from you? Maybe just bacon and eggs?" I replied.

Betty donned her tiny apron and swiftly made breakfast using all her newfound skills to cut, dice, and cook bacon, eggs, mushrooms, onions, tomatoes, and potatoes all at once. She had it on our plates in less than five minutes.

"Is that a record?" I asked.

"Yeah, maybe," she replied with one of her tantalizing winks. She sat next to me in her tiny apron, and I could not take my eyes off her. *What?*

Where do I start, Bett? This food is amazing, and you look amazing in that apron. Every time you wear that, it excites me, and you know it. And that makes me love you even more. God, I am crazy about you, baby.

Betty smiled. *My only desire is to make you happy, darling.* Her phone pinged, and Betty flew her phone over to check the message. "It's Dad. He says his jet is free tomorrow if we want to go to the city and get anything for the wedding."

"Which city?" I asked.

"Sydney. The pilot is available the whole day, so we can have dinner there, too."

That meant Betty could pick out a nice wedding dress, and we could find some wedding rings as well as her engagement ring.

"He thinks of everything, doesn't he?"

"Yes, he sure does." Betty looked up at me after accepting Conner's offer via text. "I haven't been to Sydney in more than twelve years! We'll have to split up at some point, though, or you will soon get bored with my shopping. You can buy a suit for the wedding, and I will pick out a dress, but we can do the rings together. We can have a nice feed at a top restaurant and go to a couple of good bars. Woo-hoo!"

Betty stood up and started jumping around me like a little girl, clapping and hitting my bum each time she went behind me.

"Okay, that is enough. Relax, or I won't be able to sit down."

"I'm just so excited." She grabbed me around the waist and hugged me. "What a whirlwind this is. I love it all, and I love you."

"I love you back."

She kissed me and squeezed my bum; I did the same to her. We laughed until Betty stepped back a little.

"Do you want to make love to me now?"

I picked her up and threw her carefully onto the bed. "Yes, baby, I do." Her heart was racing as she watched my enhanced cock slowly stand erect, I was so aware of being careful with her. I laid down next to her, allowing her to climb on. She slowly lowered onto me, taking me all in slowly. She gasped and bit her lip.

Every single time was different, and we just keep getting better at it.

This time it lasted an hour, with us changing positions and resting in between multiple orgasms.

"You are bigger, and it's perfection." Betty winked at me, smiling. "Come on, big boy. Time to run." Betty quickly dressed as I threw on some shorts, a T-shirt, and my joggers. "Twenty miles today, with sprints and push-ups Go!"

Betty took off; I chased after her, and we fell into rhythm. She sprinted faster and faster until we were going at least forty miles an hour. We slowed back to a jog. I looked over at Betty, and she was not even sweating.

Betty, we can probably go way faster, but I don't think it is a good idea. We might injure ourselves. Our muscles may not be ready.

You're right: normal sprints from now on.

We came to a stop and hit the dirt for push-ups. We were certainly getting fitter, but by the time we arrived back at camp, we were huffing and puffing. We stripped off and ran into the water, crossing the lake ten times before stopping to float on our backs.

Betty looked over at me and raised her finger. Suddenly my penis was fully erect, sticking straight up like a periscope. Betty swam over and stopped next to me to do things to me with her mind. It felt amazing. She smiled and watched it quiver and move by itself. I looked at Betty and started in on her with my mind. She gasped and started to shake. I grabbed her, and she slid onto me. We moaned and groaned for ten minutes straight.

When we finally let go of each other, Betty summoned the gel. I took the gel and guided Betty into shallow water so I could cover her in soapy bubbles. My hands gently slid over her soft skin, as she watched me. I felt her shiver every now and then, but she kept herself together. My hands focused on her thighs as I used my mind to gently caress her nipples. Her eyes widened.

Not fair!

She gasped and let out a squeal as I took her hand and pulled her down onto me. She cried out in ecstasy and threw her head back as I thrust in. I held her tightly as I started to blow, and she kept going in orgasmic bliss. I let go and completely gave into her. She grabbed my head and locked her mouth on mine. She let go and fell back into the shallow water and just floated there smiling and watching me watch her until the gel floated through the air and stopped in front of me.

I took the hint and lathered up my body while Betty watched me, letting out an occasional moan and shudder. I rinsed off as Betty finished washing herself and swam around. Fresh towels flew to us as we got out of the water, and we dried ourselves as we walked back.

The gel flew to shore and landed at the edge of the lake. We went to the firepit, lit it, and sat on the couches in our towels to watch the flames. It was nearly noon.

Betty suddenly tensed. *Do you feel them creeping around?*

Yes…I do now, two men with guns: pig hunters. How did they get here undetected? Get dressed.

Too late.

Two men walked into our camp with their guns raised.

"Well, what do we have here, Marvin? Two naked hippies with a fancy camper and a tent. Looks like you have some money. Perhaps you would like to share that with us poor folk. Marvin and I could never afford all this shit. Is that Jack Daniels? Hope you don't mind sharing."

He grabbed the bottle and took a huge swig, then passed it to Marvin, who was staring at Betty.

"What are you wearing under that towel, missy?" he said, pointing his gun at her. A few feet from her face. "Drop the towel, slut."

Betty lowered her towel, exposing her breasts. *It's okay, Danny. I've got this.*

Meanwhile, Marvin's eyes widened. "Well, would you look at these sweet titties, Harry? You're going to love it when I put my dick in your face."

"Oh, really, Marv?" Betty mocked.

"Shut the fuck up, bitch!"

"Don't talk to her like that," I said.

"Oh, now you have a fucking voice. Shut yer pie hole before I give you some of my lead. I'm gonna fuck your missus, then I'll probably fuck you, too, cunt."

Betty stood up; her towel dropped to the ground, and the two idiots stepped back.

"Well, have a look at that! This bitch has attitude to match her body and I'm about to fuck the shit out of her."

"Oh, really, pencil dick?" Betty took a step forward. "Why are you wetting yourself, Marvin? Are you scared of me?"

The front of his pants were suddenly wet, and Betty looked rather pleased with herself.

He was shaking as he raised his rifle. "Stop it, you *fucking witch*!"

He will never pull the trigger.

Careful, Bett. These guys are loose cannons.

But Betty was on it already. She spread her arms out as if in invitation. "Come on, then. Fuck me, dickless!"

The men didn't notice as two small stones rose silently from the edge of the lake behind them and started spinning. Marvin was preoccupied with undoing his fly as he moved closer, then with pulling out his stiff little cock.

Betty said, "Take another step, you creep, and you are dead."

He laughed loudly. He either didn't hear her or didn't believe her, because he moved forward, dick still in hand. One of the little stones came up in front of his face spinning fast. He stared at it, perplexed, but he didn't have to wait long for what came next. Betty sent it through his temple faster than any bullet, and he fell to the ground. Harry looked on mutely as blood slowly seeped from his partner in crime's head.

"What the fuck have you done, you bitch?"

He raised his gun quickly, ready to shoot me, but I spun the other stone in front of his face; he stared at it with wonder and in bewilderment as it spun there for a few moments before it went straight through his brain, shattering his skull and killing him instantly. He collapsed to the ground in a heap.

I looked to Betty to see if she was okay, but she was already busy. The two men lifted into the air and floated over to the fire. The blood-soaked dirt joined them, followed by about a hundred logs. Betty intensified the fire with her mind, forming a powerful vortex and we stepped back to watch as they burned to ashes. Their guns flew out to the middle of the lake and dropped in. Betty found their truck with her mind. She telepathically drove it from far off in the bush to somewhere even more remote, until it almost ran out of fuel and went over a cliff; the impact set it on fire.

There was nothing left. No evidence of these creeps. Betty stood near our firepit, still naked. "It was us or them. You know that, don't you?"

"Yes, baby, I know, but how did they get in here?"

"Their truck was on the far side. All they had to do was cut the fence and stay off the roads. I need to tell Dad about this so it doesn't happen again. If we didn't have our powers, everything would have ended very differently."

Once the fire died down, Betty lifted the ash and all solids from the pit and flew it all downstream, dropping it in the fast-flowing water, just to be sure. All that was left of those creeps were their keys, some coins, and belt buckles.

I went to Horus and grabbed another bottle of Sinatra Century. When I came back out, Betty sat on the couch by the firepit with her legs up over the armrests with a small glass of Moet in her hand.

"What's all this, then? Are you comfortable? You look quite relaxed."

"Just one glass before I ring my dad."

I went to the cigar box and took one, lit it, poured myself a bourbon, and sat next to Betty; she lay back with her head in my lap. I was careful to direct the cigar smoke away from her.

"You are a nice pillow, Danny, as long as you stay soft."

"I will try, but your hair feels so nice on me," I said. Betty squirmed around on purpose, lifting her head slightly and shaking her hair on me. "Baby, stop."

"Don't you like that?" she asked even as I started to harden beneath her head. She squirmed around some more. "Hmm, there seems to be a lump in my pillow now."

"Ratbag," I whispered as I shook my head at her.

Her hair tickled me, and she could sense my delight. She moved her head and rested her cheek against my erect penis.

"It looks massive this close up," she said, staring at it.

She tickled me with her eyelashes this time, giggling, then ran her tongue down my length and wrapped her mouth around it. Ever so slowly, she started to bring me to the edge of bliss, her eyes on me the whole time. My hand slid down to her crotch, where my fingers rubbed her clit, then gently slid inside. Betty groaned and was soon shaking in delight, too. Minutes later, we both moaned loudly as we came together. I lifted a towel and wiped my cum from Betty's mouth and chin as she pulled back smiling up at me gorgeously as my cock drooped.

Betty lay back and stretched out and took a sip of her Moet, grinning up at me. "You make loving you easy, Danny."

"Thank you, baby. Are you going to ring your dad now?"

"Yes, in a minute. I just want to calm down first. My heart is still racing, and Dad might ask why I'm out of breath." She laughed softly, then sat up and summoned her phone. "Hi, Dad…Yes, all good, but there was a breach…we dealt with them. Two redneck pig hunters that wanted to rape us and take our stuff…yes, we burned their bodies. I made sure it was hot enough…no nothing, we scattered the ash in the creek. We are fine, and their truck is about a hundred miles away at the bottom of a ravine…No, I did, with my mind. Yes, it was easy. No, we did that together, with our minds…yes, we used little stones, spun them fast straight through their heads. Yes instantly. I know, yes, Dad the fence on the far side somewhere…okay, yes. Love you, bye." She hung up and took a deep breath. "Danny, Dad sends his love. I think we impressed him. He will send a team out to check the whole fence, but they don't need to come anywhere here. For now, what would you like for lunch, babe? How about hot dogs with chilli beans? We have rolls in the freezer. I can whip them up in no time."

"Sounds good to me, darling."

I followed as Betty went to Horus. Her apron flew to her as she walked and tied itself. The door opened, and things started flying around the tiny kitchen before we even entered it. Like a sorcerer or the maestro of an orchestra, her hands moved, but barely touched anything. I just stood in the doorway, looking on in awe. Suddenly, a pair of board shorts flew at my face. Betty roared in laughter at my surprise.

Put some trunks on that trunk.

Ha, you are hilarious, ratbag.

Careful, mister.

One of the hotdogs flew over and started slapping my cock as if they were in a dick fight; mine lifted, thanks to Betty, and returned a few blows before the dog flipped away.

That one's yours, I thought as I pulled on my shorts.

There was so much going on at once that I could hardly keep up. Betty was in total command of her abilities and had the dogs on the plates and overflowing with hot chilli beans in seven minutes. As I sat down, a Corona floated over to the table.

There you go, my sweet. She winked at me beautifully.

Perfection on a plate: thank you. That was amazing to watch, and these are delicious.

Thank you, and you're welcome. She telepathically squeezed me hard as she bit into her hotdog, and I nearly lost it.

Stop it, you. That nearly felt like your teeth.

Oops, sorry. Too much?

Just let me enjoy this without fearing for my manhood.

Okay, but just so you know, the look on your face was worth it.

We finished our dogs and sat back as the dishes silently cleaned themselves. We stood together and walked to the tent; Betty's tiny apron undid itself and flew back to Horus as a green fishnet shirt flew out. Betty raised her arms as it dropped onto her. This one had big burn holes in it, as if it had been in a fire—very punk.

That's better, I felt naked.

Er, Bett, you are still basically still naked. But yeah, this is better.

Thanks, baby.

We sat on the mattresses in the tent, leaning back on the pillows. The fire raged once we added some logs.

"Why so overdressed, Danny? Relax." She undid the threads of my shorts and put them back together beside the tent. She winked at me, and I did relax; lying next to her felt like home. A glass of Jack Daniels floated to me. "Here you go. Chill, baby."

"It is one-thirty on a Thursday afternoon—I think—I am lying naked next to the most beautiful woman in the world, who is practically naked, and she is making me drinks. How relaxing and chill is that?" I leaned over and kissed her. She felt so warm and beautiful. "Now what, Betty?

What is our plan?"

"I think we should talk with Hathor again. She is supposed to be our guide, even if we can't really trust her, and we really need a timeline for when all this shit will hit the fan. We have fed them so much, so they should have no reason not to help us. We must demand it; lay back baby, Hathor please speak with us."

* * *

"Hello, children. We feel your hunger for knowledge…time. You want to know about time. Why is this so important? Your journey is important, not when anything happens. Time is irrelevant. It is true that we enjoy your love and you feed us very well, but we learn from your love, too. This is your gift for all of humanity as well as all others like us. You have a love everlasting. That is the binding force of your world. Above everything else, that is what draws us all in. All the whales in all your oceans are singing songs of joyous love for you two again. Beings from other worlds are here because of you. Every time you reemerge, they are all drawn in. They sense your presence and want to feel it, to share in it. You are so humble and yet so strong; we love your innocence. You would struggle to understand our connection with you, but we are bound to you both.

"Time is before, as future is past; now is then, as dusk is dawn. Repeat the futures that have passed as we remember all that is yet to come.

* * *

Hathor was gone, but I was confused.

What just happened? And that time riddle—what was that?

"I don't know, but is everyone watching us when we do it? That is plain creepy. We're never doing it again." She looked at me and winked. "Just kidding, I still can't get enough of you. Every time we talk to her, we end up with more questions. What happened to your cigar?"

She held her hand up; it lifted off the side table by the couches outside with the ashtray and lighter and sailed in through the open flap and gently landed on the ground near me. She looked at me, "It'll be okay if you're careful; I don't want you to burn the tent down either." We sat back and smoked the cigar together, Bett only having a tiny bit. I sipped on Jack and Betty had some NA wine. We finished the stogie and Betty stretched out on her back, and I did the same. Very slowly, she lifted into the air horizontally. Her fishnet shirt flew off as she rolled over to hover above me, her eyes locked on mine. Her hair floated up and away, as if there was no gravity, her hands at her side, looking down at me, and she smiled as she lowered herself until her nipples were just touching me. They felt electric and very erotic, and she quivered as she kissed me passionately; only her nipples and lips touched me. I could sense her excitement, and my erection grew until it tapped her ever so lightly just below her navel as it throbbed. She giggled and licked the tip of my nose. Taking hold of my hands, she lifted us both away from the mattress and maneuvered onto me, wrapping her legs and arms around me.

Lifting us higher, with no sensation of gravity we rolled and gyrated, upside down, vertically, and horizontally, bouncing and pumping in the air, our excitement reaching new levels of orgasmic bliss. We both moaned loudly as wave after wave hit us, shaking our bodies, until we fell onto the mattress, exhausted and, looked at each other in amazement. We were panting hard, trying to catch our breath.

Danny that was fucking incredible. That is my new favorite position; I'll call it air fucking.

I laughed at that and took Betty's hand, kissing it gently; she moaned again and closed her eyes smiling as another orgasm rolled through her body. Every sense on her was heightened, I looked at her body as she lay there and admired her beauty. She opened her eyes, still on edge, and let out a deep, roaring moan as she squeezed my hand tightly her body trembled all over. Her eyes closed again, her hand relaxed, and she sighed.

Are you okay, babe?

Betty opened her eyes slowly and gave me a tiny wink. "I'm so good."

"How about we rest for a while? Just lie back, no dreams: just rest for an hour or two," I whispered in her ear.

"Okay, baby." she whispered back.

We slept quietly and peacefully for a change, with no crazy dreams or interruptions.

Later, I slowly woke to Betty kissing me lightly on the cheek.

Hey, it is about four o'clock. I think we should go for a short run to wake up and then a swim. By then we can organize some dinner. That was a great nap I'm full of energy.

We stood up and dressed, pulled on our joggers, and set off. We crossed over the creek at the dam and ran up the hill to the lookout, then turned around and jogged back. We stripped off and ran into the water, diving in together; we swam back and forth across the lake, stopping after about twenty minutes. The gel sailed over to Betty, and we managed to wash ourselves without fooling around. We left the water as our towels flew to us, and our clothes followed us to the firepit. I sent a few logs spinning through the air and into the fire as Betty lit up some kindling and soon we had a nice fire going. I turned to see a glass of whiskey floating behind me. I took it and looked at Betty where she sat on the couch and thanked her.

"My pleasure. Come and sit for a second."

She patted the cushion next to her. I sat and ran my fingers through her hair. She pulled her towel down, exposing her breasts and tummy, and gently placed my hand on her belly. We closed our eyes; I heard Betty singing softly to the twins with her mind. They were singing, too—not with words, but little noises with their minds. Tears ran down my cheeks. It was the most beautiful song I had ever heard. I opened my eyes as Betty cradled my face with her other hand and wiped under my eyes, but I couldn't stop. I laid my head on her shoulder and kept listening as she stroked my head, singing to our twins and me.

Don't cry, Danny, we all love you. Don't you cry…

I had never experienced anything so wondrous. Tears of joy kept running down my face and dripping down Betty's breast. She pulled the towel to my face and wiped gently. She stopped the song once they fell asleep and held my head in her hands.

This is the joy that I live with all the time now. It is not just them; it is you, too. This is what's driving me, making me want you constantly and feel you inside me. You beautiful man, I love you.

I didn't have words, so I closed my eyes and lay for an eternity in her arms.

26

Eve and Siris

One hundred years later, Eve and Siris—third-generation descendants of Betty and Daniel ventured out of Ra in survival suits. They flew into the dense sky effortlessly, searching for life or any change in the atmosphere. The air had been slowly clearing since the event, but was still full of dust particles and ice. The entire planet was frozen, and had been for decades, in the throes of another Ice Age. New generations of scientists aided by AI worked on methods for clearing the atmosphere. Huge purifiers worked tirelessly to this end, but at this rate it would take centuries.

The Silurians had made contact decades ago. They monitored the surface closely and agreed to help with their fantastic technology. They offered more space as families grew. There was a search for pockets of humanity, but they were very scarce; they'd only found one on the western coast of Australia. It was a military-style compound that the survivors of Taxi wished to avoid. There were a few scattered throughout the former US and around the equator. Mexico also had some bunkers that had survived, but all struggled. Life was very difficult.

The Octo had returned from space to search for survivors with us, they had loved Betty and Danny, and shared things that would aid humanity.

Stories of the Old Ones were passed down as everyone awaited their return. Betty and Daniel had left The House of Ra after only seven years. The twins—Arora and Renner—stayed with Conner. Their path was there, and they communicated with their parents for years and years as they traveled, teaching and providing seed for crops.

They returned after twenty years with another set of twins: five-year-old Ailia and Rayar. They stayed another seven years and met their first grandchildren, but they had more work to do. Eve and her brother Siris were blessed with their enlightenment, and had used their skills as their parents had to aid the survivors of Taxi. The history books that Conner had lovingly collected were rarely used and collecting dust, but he would still be proud. The more popular books were works of poetry and art, fictional tales about love and humanity, and stories of Betty and Danny's life in Taxi.

Conner's Taxidermy body stood proudly on display in the library, looking down on all those he had saved; his vision had been perfected with outside guidance, but it was his dream to save his family. Eve and Siris were grateful that he did. Their partners had also gained enlightenment through them, and their children would, too. The new world would be very different when it eventually emerged from the current ice age. Eve and Siris were in command of The House of Ra; they decided everything together, as their grandparents did.

Hathor had always been in their dreams, offering advice, but Hathor waited for the return of the Old Ones, too. They sat quietly in the background. Their hunger had been satisfied by Betty and Danny and the apocalypse, so they would rest until humanity crawled out of the caves again and started to rebuild and procreate. That wouldn't be for another thousand years; they had plenty of time to plan their next dramatic appearance.

But future history had not yet occurred, and now was not over just yet. Betty and Daniel had a few more tricks up their sleeves and had worked hard on solving Hathors riddle about time and destiny. Now was their time to shine—whenever now was. They were truly awake, more so than the Hathors understood.

Eve and Siris suddenly heard their voices calling to them, but this was one of many tomorrows and we needed to get back to today…whenever that was.

27
One Hundred Years Ago

Betty, I feel so much stronger for hearing you and the twins singing to me. I feel indestructible now; your strength, beauty, and joy have enveloped me, and I am eternally grateful.

We sat quietly by the fire, sipping our drinks and chatting about children's names and palindromes, like Hannah, Bob, and Eve. Their start was the same as the end—a little like the riddle the Hathors shared. Back was forward, the past was future. We thought more about time and our dreams; they seemed to last only minutes, but we'd wake to find we'd slept for hours and hours.

Even our time together so far has seemed like months and months, but we've only known each other for fourteen days. Every moment is filled with new experiences. This is living, Bett.

Yes, Danny, it is. We are living such full lives.

Betty, we really need to think about what is coming. The Hathors avoided all answers about when it will arrive, Conner's urgency, Ishta's demand for skins: it seems like it is just around the corner, and yet we are still in the dark. Betty, can I have a drink please, I looked up and found a fresh glass of whiskey floating in front of me. *How did you do that?*

As soon as you thought about needing another drink, I reacted. Simple. Betty shrugged.

This could be useful at some point. I need to relax; it feels like my mind is traveling a thousand miles an hour.

I took a sip as Betty looked at me and squeezed my leg, then leaned in and kissed me. I took another swig. Looking in my eyes, she rested her hand on my penis as if it was done unintentionally and kissed me again so sweetly. She winked at me, all faux innocence, as I stirred under her hand.

Hmm, Danny, you are delightful. A light squeeze and she just sat there holding onto me firmly. She kissed me passionately and swung her leg over me, guiding me deep inside her. She came in close and kissed me as she moved around on me. Moaning sensually in my mind as she held my face.

You are perfect, Danny.

Betty started to lift and squeeze as she climaxed, bringing me with her. I cried out in bliss and in tandem with her joyful scream of ecstasy. Betty relaxed and settled on my lap.

Relaxed?

I am, baby, thank you. That was beautiful. My drink floated over to me, and with each sip I took, she squeezed me gently, lifting slightly and watching me closely, knowing exactly how to arouse me again. Within minutes, she had me close again.

Now baby.

I dug my fingers into her hips as I thrust up, her muscles squeezed my cock like a vice as we erupted. This time, my cry was as fervent as hers. Our bodies shuddered with bliss, and Bett fell back on the couch grabbed my glass, and poured me another drink. She took a tiny sip and handed it to me. I knocked it back, and she poured another. I drank that, too, but slowly this time. Her legs were all tangled around me, and her breasts kept rubbing against me as she moved; she felt so sexy.

Bett, I...

Yes, Danny, I know, exactly how you feel. Relax, and free your mind from the clutter. This is us, now and then.

Our future is not certain, Betty. I feel we can change something, something big, but I am uncertain as to how to proceed. The Hathors are misguiding us, covering up the truth, whatever that may be. They hide behind a wall, and there is something sinister going on behind the scenes. I feel it in my bones Bett. Everyone seems to think that we bring joy and love and are powerful together, but what if there is more to it? We easily killed people together—not that I am proud of it—but we stopped something bad from happening together.

Okay, but this is a major catastrophe we're talking about, not two pig hunters, and the Hathors have not even shown us what or when it's happening. They did show my dad a single huge meteor.

Somehow, we need to improve humanity's odds. Two percent of the population is nothing. How can we possibly change any of this?

Kind of wish I could drink to relax, too, but no matter. I have you, and a little loving later will relax me.

"I think we should eat. It is nearly seven-thirty," Betty said. It was the first sentence spoken out loud between us in nearly three hours. "I have already started cooking; can you smell it?"

I lifted my head and inhaled through my nostrils. "Something Italian?"

"Yes, baby, I know you like pasta."

"How do you concentrate on all the steps involved in preparing a meal while you are just sitting here quietly talking with me? That is amazing, Betty."

"Thank you, darling. It will be ready in another ten minutes."

The bottle of Jack Daniels came sailing over and refilled my glass.

"Thanks, Bett." I leaned over and gave her a big kiss.

"Your kisses are so sweet, Danny." She hugged and snuggled into me.

"How is it that you can make me hungry for your food and for you so easily?"

"Simple: I know you now, and I understand your needs and mine. I am in tune with you and our family. I can hear you all at once and I can feel your emotions. It fills me with joy."

"Betty, have you been communicating with our twins other than singing?"

"Kind of. It feels like they listen to me and settle when I talk to them."

Could you talk to them as if they were older, like future them? Close your mind immediately; I don't want anyone listening in on this.

I have never even thought to try, but I could—

No, not yet. If this is possible, we may be able to change the future.

I don't get it. What are you trying to say?

Betty, if we can reach their older selves, maybe we could leave something for them, some kind of message so they can help us in their past. If they all have our powers, then, united as a family, we might have the strength to change the future. This could be the answer to the riddle the Hathors told us. But, their present could change dramatically if they change the past. It's easier and safer to change the future. Wait, now I'm wondering if we have been here before. Could we possibly communicate with ourselves in our past? Did they wipe our memories to stop us from doing exactly that? If we all joined forces to change something in the future, we could be super powerful. We don't even know who we were; we certainly were not Daniel and Betty. But how would we find ourselves?

"Danny, I hate to interrupt your line of thought, but the pasta is cooked, it is coming out to us now with some Grange Bin 95—only one glass for me, of course. You get the rest. Bon Appétit sweetheart."

I looked up as a big tray came to us, along with two smaller ones lifted that settled on our laps. The glasses of the superb wine came directly to our hands.

"This smells amazing, straight from Italy. Thank you, gorgeous. You are the best chef, lover, and fiancé. I love you, Bett. Cheers."

"Cheers, my Danny, and here's to a good life."

I couldn't take my eyes off my goddess. She glowed as she felt my appreciation for the food, the wine, and her beautiful body.

I finished my bowl quickly; I was starving, and our day had been full of action. I sat back, and Betty kept my glass full. We had been sitting there for hours, still naked from our earlier lovemaking.

Betty washed the dishes with her thoughts. We sent a few logs into the pit to keep the fire going, then sat back and digested our meals. So much had happened that day, and we felt the weight of it.

One of Betty's playlists was on quietly in the background. "Isn't It Time" by The Babys came on and instantly transported me to the back seat of my car in high school with a girl I thought I loved, but didn't really. Then "Time Is on My Side" by the Rolling Stones came on. This song sent my train of thought in a whole new direction. Time was on every side; it was never linear. It was a personal thing, not a mutual thing. We all perceived it differently. Were we out of time with the music, or just dancing to a different beat—one we can't hear?

Danny? Are you still thinking about time? I can't read you at all.

Sorry, I've fallen down a rabbit hole. I'm sure the Hathors gave us a clue by mistake.

Well, I'm a little sleepy. Can we go and float around in the tent for a while before bed?

We lifted off the couch with our arms around each other. She held me, making me hard and we slowly floated into the tent. Betty's legs wrapped around me and she guided us together.

She was trying hard to be calm and cool about it all, but she was already climaxing and trying to bring me to do the same as quickly as possible. We cried out together as one again and again, rolling around above the mattresses effortlessly, Bett's hair floating everywhere except in our faces. We shuddered and shook in ecstasy until gently we fell onto the mattresses, tightly locked together, and fell asleep instantly. We embraced each other all night without release or weird dreams but we were beautifully content the whole night.

I felt a stirring, a slight squeeze. I opened my eyes. Betty's face was close, smiling at me. We were a few feet off the bed, and I was throbbing. Somehow, I had stayed inside her the whole night.

What a nice way to wake me. I kissed her sweet lips. *How did I manage that, baby?*

Bett looked at me and gave a wicked little wink. *I kept you in even as I slept. I didn't want you to leave, so I kept it warm and wet and a little hard, so I could wake you like this.*

*Well, that was nice of—oh.*m I pushed up with so much force we hit the top of the tent and nearly lifted it off the ground. I let go with a tremendous roar, and Betty held onto me tightly, grunting and moaning in time with me. She flew us out of the tent and we went straight up as I continued pushing up into her. I didn't even realize we'd left the tent until I heard a bird squawk nearby. I opened my eyes, and Betty laughed, shuddering as she buried her face in my neck, her arms still wrapped tightly around me.

Shit, Betty, stop. What is happening?

You have to stop, Danny.

I stopped coming at last, and we stopped going up. *Are you okay? I didn't hurt you, did I?*

No, I stopped you from hurting me. I'll be fine when all these orgasms stop. God, that was intense. Look how high we are!

I looked around for the first time; we were at least five hundred feet up.

Danny, I must let it all out. It's natural, so don't be grossed out. Just pull out, fly straight up, and don't look.

I did as she asked as she spread her legs, releasing all of our juices.

Betty squeezed my hand. *That was a lot of you, more than you have ever done, but a lot of me, too. Let's just fly down to the lake and have a swim.*

We swooped in like a couple of eagles, coming in low and fast, skimming the water with our hands until we dove in. We swam around for an hour, when I suddenly felt a sting on my cock and then my balls. I yelped; it felt like the prick of a pin prick. My cock started throbbing in the water, but it wasn't Betty's doing.

Are you okay? What's the matter?

We swam to the shallows. I felt lightheaded again, and slightly dizzy as I rolled to my back. I grabbed myself; I was soft, but numb. Betty suddenly pointed.

Look, the Grays are back. Up there.

As I looked, a small drone lifted out of the lake. It had three arm-like appendages and flew up into the saucer, which then swiftly and silently disappeared. Betty came over and sat next to me, her wide eyes drawn to my groin. She took hold of my cock and lifted it, cupping my balls in her other hand. I started to stiffen in her grip as I looked down and realized it had increased in size again.

What have they done? It is way bigger, and so are your balls.

She slid her hand up and down my shaft, feeling its girth and tugging on it slowly and sensually. She kissed me, speeding up gradually and watching my body tense until I came loudly in the lake. Bett's eyes were wide in wonder as my cum went flying; I had never seen so much. I stopped and took a deep breath. Bett kissed me and swam away quietly. I took hold of my cock, staring at. I was slightly worried that I was too big now, and wondered if she was thinking the same.

We swam away from all my jizz and washed up with the gel. As our towels flew over to us, Betty kept staring at it.

Danny how is that even possible? Did the Grays do that?

I think they are working for the Hathors. That small drone did something, or injected me with something. It's the only thing I can think of. It's not like it can be enlarged by our thoughts. It's not like I'm thinking about it. Maybe it's you; you think about it a lot.

She laughed out loud. "I do, but I don't wish for it to keep growing. You know how to use it well, and that is all that matters to me. Oh, and your love—that matters, too."

28
Sydney

"We should have a bite to eat, get dressed, and pack for our flight. Did Conner give you a time?' I asked as we walked back to camp.

Betty summoned her phone. "He sent a text message that said the jet is ready and the pilot's just having breakfast. Dad will send a car in a while, be ready."

She had already made coffee and some toasted ham and cheese sandwiches by the time we returned to Horus.

"Betty, how have you done this in the three minutes it takes us to walk from the lake to here?" I asked.

She looked at me and smiled. "I started before we left the lake."

"Oh, you're not superhuman, then?"

She looked at me grinning.

"I sure feel like it when we are flying through the air and fucking at the same time!"

We laughed and sat down at the table. Sipping on some coffee, I saw things flying into a backpack and a handbag in the bedroom as Betty picked out clothes for both of us. She sent a text to her dad asking for some coats, as it was only sixty degrees in Sydney. He answered immediately

"He said the flight will only last seventy minutes since we're taking the fast jet. We will take off minutes after we arrive, and there is a limo on the way to collect us in seven minutes. Let's get dressed; we can take the toast on the jet. We spent a little too long this morning messing around, but it was totally worth it."

Betty was ready, complete with make-up, in four minutes, waiting for me to finish doing up the buttons on my shirt. We stepped outside as Conner's Lincoln roared in. Conner was driving,

"Hop in, kids!" he called out from the driver's seat.

"What a nice surprise, Conner."

I'd leaned forward to talk to him, but was thrown back as he hit the gas, nearly landing on Betty in the process. We laughed, and Conner joined in when he realized the chaos he had created.

"Hang on," he said as the car slid sideways in the dirt, throwing us to one side. He watched us in the huge rearview mirror and laughed.

Once the car was on the road, he activated cruise control, dropped the speed, and lowered the whole car. The music became louder: "Low Rider" by War. We shook our heads in unison and burst out laughing again.

"Great to see you guys, you crack me up." Betty leaned forward and asked, "Are you coming, too?"

"I am, but I'll be working. I have a full day of business, might be able to have dinner somewhere nice with you around six before we fly home, if you are free," he said sincerely.

"Absolutely, that would be great," we said in unison.

"Oh my god, an hour and a half of listening to you two talking as one on the flight is going to kill me," he said as he laughed again.

Betty side glanced at me. *All the way, okay? And let's keep it light. I love him like this.*

Alright, I'll follow your lead.

"Love this car, Conner: it's a beauty."

"I thought you did; I'll show you all my others and you can take your pick. Any car, even this one: my favorite. You've got to make the most of one while you can, you know?"

I dare not refuse, Betty,

No, Danny, take it.

"That is so generous," I replied.

"Daniel, in the days ahead, there will be a lot of change. Unfortunately, some things will become irrelevant, like muscle cars and classics, so be sure to take one for a spin soon."

"Thank you, I can't wait," I said as we pulled into the airstrip. Ahead of us sat a fancy, compact jet. "Is this yours, Conner? How beautiful."

"It is a Gulfstream G650, one of the fastest and most expensive small jets available. Just wait until you see inside."

Conner strode across the tarmac and bounded up the stairs. We followed closely behind and raced up the stairs like a couple of kids. We were overwhelmed with opulence once inside: leather everything, beautiful walnut inserts everywhere, screens, and a bar.

Conner claimed a seat and said, "Welcome to Isis, my pride and joy. Isn't she beautiful?"

"Incredibly beautiful," we said in unison.

His head tilted and he guffawed. "Seriously, this is a thing? You talk together always?"

Betty said, "Not always. It depends on the conversation, I suppose."

Conner walked to the bar. "Who wants a drink before take-off?"

"Thanks, Conner, I'll join you, and Bett will have a nonalcoholic wine if you have it."

"I always have the best for her. Betty, I also have mocktails."

"Wine is good, thanks."

He poured our drinks as the pilot announced we were ready for take-off. Conner strapped in just as the jet lurched forward, gaining speed and lifting off effortlessly. Soon, we were cruising at Mach 0.925, according to the small speedometer above the door. A screen next to it showed our flight path. We were flying above commercial airlines and overtaking them. Betty opened the little bag on her lap and passed around three toasted ham and cheese sandwiches.

Conner smiled as she passed one to him; we both thanked her and sat back, munching on our toast. Conner looked at Betty, and said it tasted just like her mother's toasted sandwiches.

When Conner's glass was empty, I lifted the bottle and sailed it over to him.

"I hope you don't mind?"

"Daniel, it is seven o'clock on the seventh of July. What more could

I want than a glass of old No.7, Jack Daniels?" We raised our glasses. "Here's to the Rage line. Long may it last."

We clinked our glasses, content in the knowledge that it would indeed last a little longer. As we started to descend, we looked out the window. Beautiful Sydney Harbour sat below us, the iconic Opera House and Sydney Harbour Bridge. It was always a welcome sight returning here.

Our jet arrived at the airport a little later and requested landing space, which was granted. We disembarked and headed across the tarmac to two waiting limos. Conner kissed Betty and shook my hand.

"See you guys a bit later. Have fun, but stay out of trouble. I will meet you for dinner."

And just like that, he was gone. I looked at Betty; her eyes were wide, but this was a lot to take in after so many years spent in Taxi, where there were hardly any people or traffic.

Are you okay?

Yes, Danny, this is just a little overwhelming: too many people with so much anguish and pain. Everyone is screaming out in one way or another.

I feel them, too, but we can't help them, so we have to shut them out.

We rode in the limo through the city for a while, but when Betty expressed interest in visiting a clothing shop, I decided it was time to separate.

"You have an hour and a half to shop before I want some lunch with you, will you be okay?"

"Okay, Danny, I'll be fine, see you."

She practically ran away. I watched her disappear into the masses, her mind making lists for wedding dresses and other things she desired. I did things the old way by googling. Pitt Street had a shop where I could pick up a suit. I just had to find it.

It took me ages to find a good tailor, but Betty knew exactly where to go and knew what she desired. Money wasn't an issue, but we both wanted these things settled as soon as possible. It felt like time was running out, but was it?

Time is before now, after then, and ahead of us. Or is it all happening at once, Quantum mechanics, a questionable dilemma and we are just aware now? What is ahead or past, what we see is relevant: think Schrödinger's cat in a box. It is dead and alive at the same time because we are unaware of the truth until we open the box and see for ourselves. Until we open the box. The cat sits there alive, but we open the box, and it is dead. Until we open it, the cat can be alive or dead. It exists in two states. This whole idea links us to multiple universes, linked to ours, Quantum physics enables us to envision realms in which we are all the same, yet slightly different, alive and dead until observed. The Mandela Effect, or déjà vu: we have all felt it, one way or another. These could be memories of ourselves in other dimensions, or reflections from that existence. Is there a multiverse, as the comics say? Could we communicate with our other selves in other dimensions?

All this went through my head silently as I walked between the masses. I sat on a bench and thought of myself sitting on a bench in another Sydney, where there was no impending comet or meteor, and yet we were still enlightened. Anything was possible until we observed otherwise.

That is all we need to do: look for ourselves. It hit me like a sledgehammer. *Even right now, if I concentrate, I can see an endless mirror where there are hundreds or even thousands of versions of me sitting on this bench, all slightly different, but all suddenly aware of each other. We all think this is staggering at the same instant.* At that moment we all pulled back, knowing this was not the time to try this, but that it would come soon. I wanted to tell Betty what I had discovered, but I knew I must wait; Sydney was not the place, and this was not the time. *Patience: we have some time.*

I stood up and got moving. I could see Betty in my mind's eye, her hands clutching bags of fancy clothes, but all I kept thinking of was her not wearing any clothes most of the time, and how happy that made me.

Ha, I got you!

Did you hear that, Bett?

Of course, you nearly yelled it in my mind. You are so cute; can we look at some rings together now?

Stay there. I am about six hundred feet from you, and there are three good jewelry stores right there, I'm on my way.

At the shop, we explained that the rings must be available immediately; they said that it was not possible until we said we were willing to pay extra and the boss agreed. We left with two wedding rings and a beautiful, diamond-encrusted engagement ring. We went to Sakuratei Japanese Restaurant, where they gave us a nice, quiet corner table. I reached into the jeweller's bag and pulled out Betty's engagement ring.

"I have waited way too long to give you this ring, a symbol of my love, and you know how deep that goes. Bett, you will never be lonely again. I love you."

Tears rolled down her cheek as she held out her hand; I took it in mine and gently slipped the ring on her finger. She immediately leaned forward to kiss me and hug me tightly.

"Oh, Danny, you are perfect. Thank you, baby. I love you, and I love this beautiful ring." Betty could see the waiter coming, so she looked into my eyes and said with conviction, "I can shield them, our babies. I worked it out. My mind is way more powerful than I imagined. I can keep them safe from all my vices: liquor, nicotine, raw fish. Danny, trust me on this. I don't ever want any harm to come to our twins, you know. And we will never be ill, ever. Neither will they."

She was interrupted as our saki arrived. I knew she was telling the truth; my rheumatoid arthritis was totally gone, I had never felt better, and our minds were sharper, capable of looking after our bodies for us. So, we raised our glasses and toasted our love for each other. Our gourmet banquet platter arrived, full of Japanese sashimi, sushi, and tempura delights.

The food was amazing and a great change for us. I could see Betty analyzing each mouthful, trying to work out how they did each dish, and knew she would be serving me something similar sometime soon.

"What do you reckon, Bett? Pretty good, eh?"

"This is the best! In fact, it is so good it's making me horny; I think we should get a room for a couple of hours: one with a king size bed and a stunning harbor view."

"I can't tell if you're being serious or not."

"Absolutely serious, if we go soon, we could stay there until two thirty, that gives us nearly three hours." She shot me a sexy wink, and I only thought about it for about two seconds before I agreed

Betty booked the presidential suite with a harbor view and a king bed at the Four Seasons Hotel. It was only five minutes away, so we walked there, checked in, and went up to the thirty-fourth floor. Betty kept grabbing me and rubbing on me in the elevator, trying to excite me before we even entered the room. Finally, we went in, and I was gobsmacked.

"Check out the view!" I couldn't take my eyes off the harbor, but by the time I turned around, Betty was totally naked with four mini bottles of bourbon and two beers walking towards me as my clothes started to remove themselves. "Not wasting any time, my sweet?"

"There you are, big cock. That is much better. Clothing is so uncomfortable lately; I don't even know how you tuck that in. Here, let's start with these." She put the beers down and handed me two little bottles of Jack Daniels. "The bar fridge is included in the rate, so we had better not waste it. Here's to Sydney."

We clinked our little bottles and stood arm in arm, looking out the full-length windows, totally naked as we sculled Jack Daniels. We felt amazingly good.

"Bett, I thought today was going to be just boring shopping, but look at us. This was a great idea."

I looked down; she smiled and looked at the effect she was having on me. We lifted into the air and she pulled me toward the bed. All the bedding pulled down and we landed gently with a kiss. She wouldn't let go of me, "Easy does it Bett, take it slow." I pulled her on top of me and slid inside as gently as I could. She immediately let out a deep, long moan and shuddered as an orgasm hit her. She gyrated around on me beautifully until I came, too.

She let out a cry of pleasure and kissed me over and over, keeping me hard and loving every second. First five minutes passed, then ten; we had orgasm after orgasm until she finally slowed down, kissed me a final time, and ran to the toilet.

After a few minutes, she returned. The bottles of beer sailed over as she jumped on the bed. She lifted her drink and sculled it; she was just staring at me. Two more little bottles and two more beers came out of the fridge and landed on the bed. Finally, she said, "Danny, you are fucking amazing. I have never felt this way ever. You bring me there instantly and hold me there the whole time. In about five minutes, I want you again, if you'll have me."

"You think I'd say no? Besides, I think all this is you, not me. It is incredible, and I never considered what we are experiencing now could even be possible. Like what just happened: we have never done that before."

"That was so good! My body is still buzzing, and your huge cock feels alive in me—in a good way, obviously." She stopped to open another and took a swig.

"Okay then, let's get drunk." Suddenly, the bar fridge door opened, and all the alcohol joined us on the bed. It was quite a cache. I looked at Betty and arched a brow. "Really?"

She shrugged and started drinking, so I grabbed a couple of little bottles, too. Soon, we both started to slur a little. I entered her with my mind. Her eyes opened wide, and she gasped loudly.

"I did not expect you to do that."

She crawled over our empty bottles to get on top of me, but she was facing the other way. She took me in her mouth as she dropped down until her lower half was just above my face. I obliged her, kissing and licking until she howled around her mouthful of dick. Meanwhile, in my head, she was screaming in ecstasy.

She started to push down on me and moved back and forth against my mouth. She kept going as a towel flew over; she was nearly choking as I came, so she pulled away. A geyser shot out of me and into the air, but the towel expertly caught it before landing on me. She wrapped her hands around me and the towel as more and more came out of me. Her own orgasms were so intense that her back arched, her head tilted back, and she ejaculated all over me.

When she realized what she was doing, she quickly got off me. Her hands slowed before stopping so she could float us both into the huge shower, which was already running when we entered. She dropped the soaked towel and stood out the way since I was somehow still going, but it tapered off after she released me. She stood under the showerhead, watching my dick slowly droop, but it wouldn't go down all the way. She was still having one or two orgasms herself, but they, too, were easing as I leaned against the wall and let the water hit my head and run down my back.

I looked at her after a few minutes, and said, "Well, that got messy pretty quick."

"I'm sorry, I didn't think it would end up like that. What do we do with that towel?"

"We can't leave it for some poor cleaner to deal with. Perhaps we can rinse it under the shower with our minds. By the way, how did you move your hands like that? It felt incredible."

"I'm not sure, I just thought about doing it fast and I did. I loved every second, too. I could really feel your pleasure. Hopefully that goes down a bit more before you have to put your pants on."

"Me, too."

We washed and dried off while the towel washed itself. We were fully sober by then, so we started drinking again. It didn't seem to affect us as much now anyhow. It was nearly two we sat in the big chairs by the windows and looked out across the harbor. We were still very naked, and I was still semihard, but trying not to think about it; a few more drinks would probably take care of it.

"What is to become of this beautiful city and the millions who live here? It's sad to think everything will soon turn to shit."

"We will think of something, Danny."

"I have thought of a few things, but I won't get into it with you now. Later, at camp, I will tell you."

Betty looked down at me. "That needs one more round. This time, I will control myself, be gentle and slow. We still have plenty of time. Come on, Danny, please."

She took my hand and led me to the bed, urging me to sit on the edge. She straddled me, wrapping her legs around my back and planting her hands on my shoulders before she slowly rocked back and forth. After a few minutes of passionate kisses and squeezes, we climaxed together. It was long and intense, and as soon as it stopped, Betty relaxed and rolled off to my side.

"You never fail to satisfy me. That was beautiful and sweet."

"Oh, Betty, it was, and you are fantastic. And look!"

She poked at my finally flaccid member. "See, I knew that would work."

All the bottles flew to the waste bin, nearly filling it, and we sat by the windows with fresh drinks as Betty tidied up the bed as best as she could.

"Dad will ask us what we did all afternoon, and we can't say we spent it in bed."

"How about we say we did a pub crawl? We can go now and have a look in a few so we won't be lying. Plus, we still have few hours to kill."

"Great idea, Danny! Let's get dressed and go. Thank you for the last few hours in your arms. It was magical and sexy and beautiful."

"Thank you, too. I never expected today to be like this, but this was perfect," I replied.

We stood at the window naked and shared a tight embrace before we pulled apart for a quick wash and to get dressed.

We went down to the lobby and handed back our key card. The concierge asked if everything was okay, and we looked at each other and said in unison, "The room was perfect, and the view amazing."

Less than two minutes away we came to the first bar: The Push. It had just opened, so the barman came right over when we sat down.

"What can I get you two nice people?"

We said in perfect unison, "Two Gentleman Jacks, straight up."

He chuckled. "Okay, is that two or four?"

"Four, please."

He smiled and lined up four shots, I paid him We lifted our first and downed it together, then the second. I took out ten dollars tip and put it under a glass as we stood, called out our thanks, and walked hand in hand out the door. At Eric's Bar, we ordered the same drinks. Then we came to The Doss House. It had a very nice atmosphere and served Whisky Apples, so we had two of those with a Scottish Whisky in it. They juiced a green apple in front of us and mixed it with whisky, very addictive. Betty had never had one before, and she loved it. Next stop, The Keel, served us some more Jack Daniels. At The Cruise Bar, we ordered whiskey sours and sat outside facing the Sydney Opera House.

Betty looked so radiant and glowing: my beautiful goddess.

"Thank you, Danny. I am blessed to be with you, my love." She patted my knee and kissed me. "How are you feeling?"

"I'm feeling great, so alive, I love the smell of the ocean but it is making me a little hungry. Want to split some hot chips?"

"Perfect, I'll order them and another cocktail each. How does an old-fashioned sound?"

"Sounds great, thanks."

Betty jumped up; and I stared at her bum in those tight jeans as she walked and watched her lean against the bar as she ordered for us.

Damn, girl, I so love you.

She turned and winked and mentally squeezed me gently but firmly. While she ordered, I entered her slowly from behind with my mind. Her back straightened and her voice got a little higher, trembled slightly as she spoke with the bartender. I pulled out when he turned away and started making the cocktails.

Danny, that's not fair while I'm talking to someone…but fuck me, it did feel nice.

I can do it again,

Go on, just do it quickly, like before.

I did, and after a second, I saw her shudder in delight and close her eyes, trying to control herself in public. My cock was throbbing in my pants.

Oh, you're a ratbag! I love you, but no more here, okay?

Got it. Your face was priceless, though. I love you. Soon Betty returned with our cocktails and told me the chips would be out soon. We sat there watching the ferries, and our chips were delicious, nicely salted, crunchy, and made with good oil. We devoured them while they were nice and hot.

"I wonder how Conner's day has been. Business meetings sound boring," I said.

"He often needs to come down here for boring meetings." Betty stopped and looked at me. "Danny, I can sense him somehow, it's like a movie in my mind, he's with a gorgeous woman right now. It is a meeting, but certainly not about business. Ew!"

"Betty, don't invade his privacy. He has needs, too. How can you see him?" Still, I couldn't help but try and peek. Suddenly they were right there, naked in bed in my mind, I closed it immediately.

"Yeah, I just never thought about it, I suppose," Betty said. "She is extremely pretty. He has known her for years, but recently his feelings have changed. I can sense all of this. Danny, I think he is in love with her, and that she has genuine love for him."

"I can feel that, too, Bett, but we mustn't let on what we know at dinner."

"No, absolutely not." Betty knocked back her cocktail. She went back to the bar and ordered two double shots of Jack Daniels. "I am happy for him. It is a good thing; he has found someone."

"I agree. Cheers to Conner's new love."

We raised our glasses and toasted Conner Rage, then sat back to enjoying our vista as a large sailboat full of young people partying passed by. We could hear music thumping, and some of the passengers were dancing on deck.

As the sun sank, shadows grew longer. The sun reflected off all the high-rise windows across the harbor hitting the small waves and reflecting a million points of golden sunlight in all directions. A myriad of smaller boats and ferries skittered across the harbor; a large cruise ship off in the distance was being guided by tugboats. Quiet music played in the background as we watched the world, and it felt surreal, almost melancholy, since we knew a huge rock was headed toward this planet. All these beautiful people going about their lives had no idea. We both felt a huge weight on our shoulders and looked at each other.

I think we need a few more drinks before we meet Conner for dinner.

We'd had a lot to drink, but we were still sober, our minds defending our bodies so I went to the bar and ordered two more doubles. We had twenty minutes left before dinner, when Betty's phone pinged with a message from Conner.

"Hey, guys, I sincerely hope you don't mind, but I would like to bring a good friend of mine along to dinner. She is dying to meet you both," Betty read aloud and then typed back swiftly to agree and ask where to meet. His response was quick. "He said he booked a table at Cirrus Dining in Barangaroo at six o'clock." Betty looked up from her phone and finished her drink, "Wow, I didn't see that coming, but I'm looking forward to this. We have time for one more."

I got us two more doubles and couldn't help but wonder about Conner's mystery woman. How did Conner even have time for a relationship?

We ordered an Uber since we didn't feel like walking to the restaurant, and Bett and I still had a handful of bags, which I carried all. We stopped briefly at my tailor to pick up my suit and still arrived early.

"A booking for Mr. Rage," Betty said.

"May I take your bags for you? Come this way, please." The waiter led us to a large table set for four and brought us some water in no time at all.

They are here.

Yes, I feel them. He's nervous. Be nice to her, Betty. She seems like a nice soul.

Conner said, "This is Elouise, my close friend. Elouise, this is my daughter Betty and my future son-in-law Daniel."

Betty stood and gave Elouise a slightly awkward hug, after which I shook her hand.

"Pleased to meet you both, and congratulations on your recent engagement," she said with confidence.

We replied in unison. "We're pleased to meet you, Elouise, and thank you."

She smiled warmly as Conner grinned broadly. We all sat down, and when the waiter came over, Betty made Conner forget about alcohol affecting the twins.

"Two bottles of your best Moet, please."

"Yes, sir, right away." He left quickly.

Conner looked at us, and said, "Please let me order for all of us. Head chef is my friend."

We agreed, and from then on, Conner was on fire. He told Elouise about our whirlwind romance and our upcoming wedding, and all the while, Betty was busy analyzing Elouise, searching for flaws and untruths but couldn't find any. It seemed she was genuinely in love with Conner, and was not a gold digger, as Betty had initially feared.

This could work, she loves him—really loves him. "How did you guys meet?" Betty asked.

Conner's hand went to Elouise's. "It was at a business meeting years ago; we locked eyes and a fire lit, but circumstances beyond our control kept us apart until last year. We could finally open up to each other and express our love. These days are crazy—you both understand—so we decided today that we are going to get married two weeks after you two."

"Congratulations!" Betty jumped up and hugged him with such genuine joy that I felt it, too. She immediately went to Elouise and gave her an even bigger hug. "Welcome to our family, lovely."

I hugged Conner next. "Well done, Conner."

He hugged me back, and when I turned to Elouise, she embraced me warmly, too. All I felt from her was joy. She is totally in love with Conner, and it felt right.

We sat back down as our bottles arrived. The waiter poured our first glasses and left us to it. I raised my glass for a toast.

"Here's to love and the unity of family."

"You got that right son," Conner said proudly. The waiter came back to take our order, and Conner said, "Just send out your top-tier everything: lobster, steak, swordfish, bluefin tuna, abalone, kingfish, South Australian pipis, Coffin Bay oysters. Oh, all the good stuff, and tell Brent Savage that Conner Rage is here."

"Yes, sir!"

"You have been here before, I take it?" I asked.

"This chef is one of the best. His seafood dishes are top-notch, yes, we have been here many times." He looked at Elouise and smiled.

We sat back and engaged in small talk as we waited for our meal. Elouise was incredibly nice and a perfect buffer for Conner's stiffness, but he was changing, too; even I could feel that after only a few days of really knowing him. Our food soon arrived; the waiters struggled to fit the massive feast of Australia's best seafood on the table, and I couldn't wait to sample some things of which I had never before experienced. The flavor and taste of the ocean was present in every bite, and it was all so good.

As good as your cock.

As good as your lips.

With her mind, she squeezed my cock, so I went in and then out of her. She gasped, but covered it well by saying how delicious everything was. The food was truly amazing, regardless of our games. The head chef came out and said hello, we all praised him on the food, he thanked us and left but sent out a couple of complementary dishes. Conner's lady seemed perfect for him; she was nice and straightforward, just like him, and we all chatted together as if we'd known each other much longer. Elouise would join us on the flight back, and she was going to stay for a few days.

Conner has been so busy lately.

Yeah, I know, Danny; I don't see how this will work out.

We all had plenty to eat, such an amazing feast, and after Conner paid up, we went for a short walk along the wharfs at Barangaroo, to get in some fresh evening air, knowing we would soon be sitting in the jet for a while. Conner had spoken with the pilot; he is ready and waiting with a runway booked for forty minutes from then. We climbed into a limo Conner had commissioned and drove through security and straight out onto the tarmac; we boarded the jet with just ten minutes to spare. We conversed lightly on the return flight with drinks all round. Elouise knew all about Taxiplus and was excited to go on a tour; Conner invited us to come along the next day, too, which we accepted eagerly.

When we touched down in Taxi, Conner's Lincoln was waiting for him next to a beautiful '56 Buick Roadmaster.

"Here's your ride, guys. Thanks for coming along. See you tomorrow!"

"Thank you very much, we had a ball. Nice to meet you, Elouise," we said in unison.

We all hugged and kissed and then jumped into our respective rides. The Buick roared down the road under our driver's direction, and we arrived at camp within minutes. Thanking him, we climbed out, got our bags, and watched as he jetted off.

We stood hand in hand and looked out at our camp, grateful for the solitude. Being in the city was nice, but this was way better. The camp was very dark apart from the dim solar lights around the tent, so I turned a few more on with my mind.

Betty looked at me, smiling. "That was great. Elouise was very nice, and I had a lot of fun with you today, but now, I just can't wait to get these tight jeans off and get naked with you by the fire. What do you say?"

"I say, hell, yes and let's get naked."

As we walked slowly to Horus, all our bags flew ahead of us to the door, which Betty opened so they could fly in. I prepared the firepit sending logs and kindling and then lighting it, while Betty poured two stiff drinks. Her blouse lifted off, followed by her bra, and then my shirt. Just before we reached Horus, we both lifted off the ground, facing each other and holding hands, as our shoes came off, our zippers came undone, and the rest of our clothes slipped off effortlessly. We embraced as we floated there and kissed.

Our clothes floated inside, and our bourbons floated out. We caught them and had a drink as we drifted down to the couches by the fire. Betty started up some soft tunes in the background as she kissed me, one hand in my lap, lightly tickling my head and then stroking me. I started in on her in much the same way, both of us enjoying the electricity between us for a couple of minutes. Then, Betty lifted us off the couch and wrapped her legs around me, guiding me in. We hovered a few meters off the ground near the fire, slowly rocking and pumping and squeezing and kissing, totally immersed in each other. Our hearts beat faster, but Betty was in total control and stayed right at the edge of bliss. My hands gripped her hips tightly as I pumped into her.

My back arched as I thrust, moaning deeply as I came, and Betty pulled me in tightly, her fingernails digging in to my bum cheeks deep and screaming out as she clamped down on me. We were horizontal and spinning slowly in the air, both moaning and quivering as our orgasms went on. Slowly, the sensations subsided. She kept me inside her as we slowly turned until we were vertical. We kissed but didn't say a word, and the fire's warmth on our bodies felt amazing.

I kissed her some more as her hands moved all over my body. She started squeezing me, gradually making me hard again, then let go of me and sat up, gyrating on me as we slowly spun. Her legs locked around me as I caressed her breasts and nipples. I could feel her as her pace increased and she started moaning loudly as she climaxed. I exploded at the same instant; she fell onto me and rocked back and forth, up then down, faster and faster. Betty cried out in bliss and came to a stop. We hung there for a few more minutes before Betty let go of me and flew up like a ballerina, spinning and turning. She was screaming at the top of her lungs.

"I love you, I love you," she chanted as she landed next to me looking perfectly gorgeous.

We sat on the couches, and Betty winked as full glasses appeared by our sides.

"You ratbag!" I said, pinching her nipple lightly.

"No, Danny boy, you are the ratbag, baby."

She grabbed my balls and squeezed them firmly, kissing me before I could complain. I pinched her nipple again and she let go with a squeal. We relaxed, sat back, and sipped our drinks, looking at each other in admiration.

29
The Infinite Mirror

Betty close your mind. The Hathors cannot overhear this. I saw something in my mind today, something fantastic. I was sitting on a bench, surrounded by a million shoppers. I started to think about alternate universes. Do you know what I mean by those?

Yes, Danny, I've seen some of the Marvel movies.

Well, forget them. I read a lot, and the concepts of quantum physics deal with many possibilities, including multiple universes all existing at once. As I sat there, I could see myself in an infinite mirror. There were hundreds or maybe thousands of me sitting on that bench, and we all became aware of each other at the same moment. These Daniels were all like me: awake and enlightened and aware of each other. Betty, if we can communicate with them, we might find that there are a thousand Bettys, too.

Betty frowned. *Why do we want to talk to ourselves in other universes?*

If we can sense each other, communicate, maybe we can interact with all the versions of us that have our powers, we might be able to alter our future, the coming disaster, and save the earth. Together we are stronger, so imagine us times a thousand. Maybe this is what the Hathors fear.

That is amazing, but what about all the other Earths facing the same catastrophe as ours?

I'm working on that. If my theory is correct, many Earths are safe from the meteor, all who are safe can concentrate on those who are not. We have family that can help, too, and we have lived many lives, so maybe we can help ourselves.

"Oh, Daniel, you are incredible," Betty said before she leaned over and kissed me warmly. "We have some work ahead of us, but now you need to rest. It is nearly eleven o'clock."

"Yes, you are right," I answered.

Betty brought our drinks, into the tent and set them on the low tables. We floated just above the mattress as Betty embraced me tightly, her hands wandering so much that I knew she wasn't ready for sleep at all. "Thank you for another fantastic day."

"Oh, Bett, you are the ratbag." I whispered as she spread her legs.

She guided me straight in and wrapped her legs around mine, but she remained motionless and just kissed my neck. She was doing something to me that felt sublime; my breath caught. She was concentrating, her body quivering slightly, as a vibration traveled through it. I could feel the little ripples along the length of my penis, flowing like little waves. Betty's nipples were hard points rubbing against me, tingling, and she was holding me tightly.

Danny, I feel you; I know you feel me.

Wave after wave crested through our bodies like miniature orgasms, and the feeling was beyond words. It did not increase or intensify, but it was a steady vibration endlessly flowing through us. Bett was trying to kiss me, but couldn't close her mouth as if she were taking one continuous breath in. We gasped in bliss, slowly dropped onto the mattress, and I started to really pump into her. I came like a freight train, and Betty cried out in ecstasy as she climaxed and buried her face in my neck to muffle a scream. I collapsed onto her as she was shaking, and all but cried with joy.

I pulled back and lay next to her, holding her hand. She was sobbing, but her body almost seemed electrified, she smiled at me as a tear slid down her cheek. I shook my head at her in bewilderment, having no idea what had just happened. I looked down at myself and saw that I was still rippling, throbbing, vibrating, and standing straight up. I thought I was done. Betty looked at me, eyes wide.

Let me fix it.

Betty, no. You have had enough; I can feel it.

Close your eyes.

I did as she asked and felt Betty's mouth around me, but knew that it was a towel that she'd silently retrieved. I groaned, and Betty could feel my pleasure. Faster and faster it went, twisting and turning at the same time.

That's it, Danny, feel me.

She kissed my mouth and sucked me with her mind; it was amazing. I lifted off the mattress, and my back arched as I exploded, crying out with Betty as she felt it, too. The towel kept going for another few minutes, gradually slowing down before releasing me, and then flying off. Betty kissed me tenderly on the lips and face, but my eyes were still closed as I drifted off to sleep.

* * *

The towel floated out of the tent and was silently pulled up into the upper atmosphere, where a saucer waited. A small hatch opened, and the bounty was taken. They zipped away silently, heading for the moon. They had taken his sperm and DNA; Danny had been enhanced again.

* * *

"Baby, are you here?"

"Yes, darling, I am," a thousand voices replied. "We are all here in the infinite mirror: . We all look as one to the left, Betty and Daniel as far as the eye can see, we all look to the right it is the same, endlessly. It is too overwhelming for some, and they blink away, out of our vision. Others are amazed, we all blink together as one, we are the same, yet different, as are our worlds."

Betty and I looked to each other, then next to us, unsure who we were because we'd become many. Were our experiences the same? Our feelings mixed as we searched for the answers, but none were clear. The mirror went on and on. Suddenly, we realized that while we were many, there are only seven Hathors in all the universes, they were unique to ours. They could not see all of us across the universes. Their games would be over once we united *to save all the Earths in danger. United as only two, we became the focus of all the others; our love was our strength uniting all.*

Slowly, all the other faces turned and looked only at Betty and me; it was unnerving.

"We are with you," they all said together. "Watch out, Hathors, you ought to fear us because you are next on our hit list. We are in love, and that is our power. We look across the wide expanse and understand the need for unity. Can we all pull it off? This is unknown, so we must be silent. The cow must not know. It will become clear; we have got this."

* * *

I woke to Betty licking my ear.

Hmm, good morning, my king.

Good morning, gorgeous. That is…nice, but my ear?

Yes, baby, your ear. I hear you; I see your mirror, and it is unreal. You are the king in this chess game. The queen Hathors move against you, but I am your queen, and I will protect you. They are powerful; I see that now. Your pawns and knights and bishops are nearly ready to close in on her, Danny we can do this; I can see it in you. There is a strength in you that I have not realized. We will outmaneuver the Hathors and hopefully save the Earths. Oh, yeah, and what do you want for breakfast?

Such a nice, normal conversation.

Yes, Danny, normal: do you want to talk about that?

"What?" I looked at her, and she was pointing once again at my groin. I had increased in size again: at least a few centimeters in length and girth. I grabbed myself in disbelief. "I'm going to pass out from the loss of blood to my brain the next time I get an erection. If this keeps up, I will need longer shorts. What the fuck?"

Betty wrapped her hand around me and, for the first time, could not touch her thumb to her first finger. "Pretty soon, you will be too big for me, and that will be the end of all our fun."

"I understand completely. This is scaring me, too, I have no idea why or how this is happening, but you be careful when you're with me. I would hate to hurt you."

If this is the Hathors' doing, they are in deep shit. We need to talk to her again.

Oh, Danny, I hate talking to them. They are so full of shit. But, I do agree they are playing us for their own needs. Do you think they want to feel our pain?

We need to work out how to shut the Hathors out entirely. We can close them off from our mental conversations, so this should be easy.

She or they are always so close that sometimes I feel them take over and I have no control over what is going on. I want to stop for fear of hurting you, but sometimes I can't, Danny.

Betty, we need to take back our lives. What we share is incredible, but we need to be ourselves again. Close them off completely, or at least try to. Do not let them see anything, okay?

Okay, done…I think.

Betty, what are you up to? We, the Hathors, see you trying to hide, but it is no good. We want you to feel his growth; he is the leader, after all, the steer, and should be bigger than most. You can cope with it, we know you can; your time to reproduce and make lots of love is now, just as this is our time to feed generously on your lust. Do it, Betty. Grab his horn. You want him.

Betty, close them off completely. I still feel them close.

"Done, Danny, now come here and fuck me with that huge cock." She grabbed my dick and started tugging on me, kissing me hard and squeezing my balls with her other hand. "Come on, baby, you need you to fuck me now. Come, my alpha steer."

Hathors, leave us alone, Get out of her! We know what you are trying to do, but you have fed enough on us. Soon you will fear us, and will never try this again. Feed on your own fear!

The Hathors retreated, but before they left, I could feel that they were scared.

Betty released me and looked around with a bewildered expression. "What's going on? Did they have me then?"

"Yes, they did. The Hathors have been playing us. They did this to me for their pleasure, but they won't do it again. Somehow, I will make them pay for what they have done. I think I'm stuck with it, though, so, yes, I have a big dick, but don't get obsessed with it, okay?"

We stood up together and went out to the firepit. Betty sat on the couch while I retrieved some logs and found Betty staring at me again.

"Stop, baby, please. It is just me."

"Can we have sausages for lunch?' she asked innocently. "Danny, can I just hold it in my hands? I want to see it fully erect."

"No, and I'm going to put my shorts on."

"Oh, Danny, how could you?"

"Betty, snap out of it!"

She had to be in a trance; the last few days had overloaded her senses or something. I summoned some shorts and put them on as I stoked the firepit, Betty sent me a glass of bourbon. I reached for it as she pointed at me and drew in a deep breath without saying whatever was on her mind. Biting her bottom lip.

"What now?"

"Danny, you are sticking out of your shorts. I can see it, and I want you; I know what you said, and I am good with that. I'm not obsessed. I will be very careful. Sorry for my lust, darling, but I want to know if we can still do it." She walked up to me and placed her hand on the tip of me, just rubbing it lightly. As she slowly moved her hand around on me, kissing me tenderly, I grew so hard. She undid the stitching on my shorts; they fell to the ground and she stood back to admire my erect penis. Even I was impressed. "Oh, Danny you are beautiful. I will start calling you Horse," she winked at me and walked forward, slowly reaching out and gliding her hand down the length of me, "Please lie down."

I lay on the rug by the fire. "Bett, baby, please. Easy does it."

Betty carefully lowered herself onto me and ever so slowly allowed all of me in. She gasped and moaned in pleasure; she was close, but stayed in control, gently moving back and forth, and around on me. As I slowly lost it, I thrust up into her, trying hard not to move too much, and she groaned deeply as she pushed down onto me.

We came together, rising and falling as one. It did feel good—really good. Betty was shaking wildly, smiling and moaning as she carefully bent forward and kissed my forehead, my nose, and then my lips. Her warm, luscious cunt clasped tightly around me.

"Oh, Danny," she whispered and groaned.

I caressed her breasts, but tried not to move so Betty could explore my new size. When she came again in a rush, it surprised her, and she cried out and clenched my cock firm.

I grunted and howled as I suddenly climaxed a second time, thrusting up so hard I lifted Betty into the air; she kept rising, and, to save herself as cum went everywhere, she managed to contain it in a bubble. I grabbed myself, trying to make it stop; Betty lifted me off the rug and placed the huge bubble of cum above me.

"Betty, oh, the lake," I moaned.

She squealed in delight; I was sure I looked absurd.

"Time to swim, Danny!" She dropped me gently in the water and sent the bubble of cum downstream. Then, Betty flew over to me and floated beautifully above me smiling, giggling, moaning, and shaking all at once as she watched my face. "Are you done yet?"

I floated on my back to show her, and Betty moved back as it was still shooting out in waves, my cock hard and throbbed in time, she moaned quietly and quivered.

Oh, it's you. Stop, Betty! You're doing this to me with your mind—oh—and you don't even realize it.

Betty looked at me and frowned; I stopped coming at last. Betty shook her head slowly in disbelief.

Oh, Danny, I'm so sorry. How did I not know? I felt so good, but I thought it was because of you.

I tried to stop as soon as you lifted off me, but you were still on me in your mind, still going strong. Betty, you felt unbelievable, but I warned you; you must learn to control yourself. No more sex until you learn some control, okay? No matter how long that takes.

I got out of the water and dried off, watching as Betty dove in and cleaned herself up. We walked back and sat on the couch with the fire low and some whiskey in our glasses.

I'm sorry I let you down, but you just feel so fucking amazing. Control was not an option then, but I will learn it. I can't wait to be on you again.

Betty! We have a job to do. You know, save humanity—remember? I need you to concentrate. Our love is our strength, not our sex. Our sex is great and erotic, but our love will save the day. Baby, I love you, but sexual satisfaction is not the answer.

I can't agree, because sexual gratification is the answer to love, especially at the start of something new. It is how trust is built in a relationship. When I gratify you with my body, how do you feel, knowing I love you?

Oh, Bett, you know I feel loved, complete, and like I am a part of you when we make love.

That is what I'm telling you; I am here to be with you. That is the reason for my existence. Please let me love you as we are meant to. Together, we will save the Earths and save Ishta and the Lloyds, and we'll send the Hathors back to their star cluster if that is what is required. Are you hungry baby, I'm starving, give me a few minutes and I'll fix us something for breakfast. I think together, loving each other, our journey will be immense. This path is meant to be, Danny.

I am hungry, too, and I agree that we share this path for a reason. We are meant to be one, as we always have been. I can never put limitations on your love. You can fuck me whenever you want to, just control your mind. Agreed?

Agreed, Danny. That will not happen again.

A few minutes passed in silence as we sat and watched a flock of cockatoos fly low over the lake. Then a tray gently floated out to us, and the breakfast Betty had prepared looked delicious; I was starving. She had made Eggs Benedict on sourdough, salmon, and creamed spinach. "Thanks, babe, this looks awesome. I can't wait, so please excuse my manners."

"I love your enthusiasm for just about everything, including me."

We ate our breakfast, sipping whiskey and tomato juice, each of us with a towel wrapped around our waist.

"I had better check my phone," she said as she raised her hand. Her phone came flying out of the tent into her hand, and she had a message waiting for her. "Dad wants to confirm we'll be there today at eleven for the guided tour through Taxiplus with Elouise. Then he's invited us back to his house to look at cars so you can pick one out. He will collect us at ten-fifty in the Lincoln."

Betty answered him and we sent our dishes to the dishwasher and stood up.

"Can you run, Danny?"

"Of course, let's go."

We dressed, and I remembered what I said earlier about needing longer shorts.

Yes, Danny, you are barely covered in those. Twenty miles again, sprints, push-ups, and then a swim, okay?

Betty clicked her watch and we hit it, starting with a one-mile jog, three-mile sprint patter that we repeated until we reached ten miles. At the halfway point, we stopped and did seventy push-ups. We sprinted back five miles, then jogged the remainder; our fitness levels had doubled in the last few days alone. We came to the lake, panting. Betty pulled off her clothes in a flurry and ran in naked; I took care of mine as quickly as I could and ran after her. She powered ahead of me, but I soon caught up and fell into her rhythm. We crossed twenty times with ease, then stopped and floated around on our backs.

Danny, you are way fitter than before.

Yes, and I feel stronger. Even my muscles are bigger and tighter. Your training is paying off.

It is all your exercise on me that is paying off. I made out a wink from her just before she disappeared below the water. I looked over where she had been, and her hand raised out of the water and pointed in my direction. I was immediately erect.

Betty surfaced next to me, "What is this huge periscope doing here? Who are you, Captain Nemo?" With her dripping face level with my groin, she grabbed hold of me, went under, and then came back up, sputtering. "Danny, I've got you, no matter what comes our way, and I am never letting go."

She went under again, holding me tightly, only to resurface sputtering again.

"Betty, are you okay?"

"Danny let's move to shallower water."

"Sure, no problem," I said through laughter because I realize Bett had been trying to make a statement and wound up almost drowning while hanging on to my cock.

She did the sidestroke, pulling me through the water by my stiff periscope. We were soon in shallow water, and Bett still had a firm grip on me. Her mouth lingered above me and planted the occasional warm kiss on my head.

"Danny, how do you feel?"

"I feel like you are in total control of me right now—in a good way."

"I am, aren't I? Do you like this?"

"Yes, I do. Do you like what you are holding?"

"Oh, yes, I love this." She moved down, gripping me tighter but not moving her hands, and kissed my head tenderly. She glided up to my face and kissed my lips. "Danny, you are perfect. Can I?" She had me super excited by now and she knew it.

"Whatever you want, baby, just stay in control and be careful, please."

Betty moved on to me in the water and slid down around me. Once she was there, we lifted out of the water and went high up in the air as she pushed down on me. I pushed up toward her; she went this way, I went that way, and gradually our tension grew. We suddenly climaxed together, crying out in unison and bliss, totally immersed in our own private heaven amongst the clouds.

Rolling around. Betty took us back down to the water and let go of me so we could float over by the fire and add some logs. We slowly rotated and dried off, then embraced each other warmly. I just know that we would always remember that morning as a day we felt truly in love and totally in tune with each other.

Betty released me gently and sat down on the couch. I followed her and checked the time: eight-thirty. Suddenly, we felt Ishta's presence.

Good morning. We have been busy on our new world and apologize for not contacting you sooner. We feel your love grows stronger, and it feels grand. We have had a request from the ones you call a jelly-octopus; we call them The Octo. They remember the Old Ones and wish to communicate with you. We understand you have no memory of them; however, you had a strong bond before, and you may need their help later. Do not dress, for they are naked, too. To them, it is a sign of strength. They will arrive in five minutes. Prepare yourselves for further enlightenment. Good health and love. Your strength grows daily; we will leave you in peace now.

And just like that, they were gone.

"Bett, how the fuck do we prepare to meet aliens?"

"Stand proudly in front of them, show them we are the boss—but in a nice way. You take the lead, okay? This is slightly terrifying to me."

"And to me, Betty? Do we really have to be naked?"

"Remember that they were our friends in the past. Maybe you should mention that all of our memories from other lives have been wiped away."

"Good idea. Wait, I think I can feel their craft."

We looked up and around, but could see nothing. In an instant, some kind of craft came straight down and hovered three feet above the lake. It shimmered as if it was not really there; the surface of this slightly flattened, football-shaped vehicle, its surface was constantly moving, swirling with a golden hue. It was miraculous and mesmerizing.

We stood near the edge of the lake, holding hands nervously. Silently, the craft came forward, but stopped about five yards away from us. We could feel it humming quietly, and it was incredible to see a craft from another world sitting right there. At the same time, we felt so vulnerable, naked and waiting for something to happen. A circle appeared on the craft as it changed colors like a light show. Betty tensed beside me.

Relax, Betty.

Yes, relax, Betty, a voice warbled in our heads.

We looked at each other, then back to their ship. The circle opened and two creatures jumped into the water with a splash before we could get a good look at them. The water swirled in front of us as they approached.

Do not fear us, Old Ones. We are your friends. We have known you for thousands of years.

Two sets of big, purple eyes on long thin stalks came up out of the water, and Betty started to pull back.

It is okay, Betty. Feel them; they are in love with us!

It really is okay. Yes, Danny, we do love you both, the voice warbled in our heads.

They used their many tentacles to lift themselves out of the water using two tentacles like legs to stand, they did look like octopi, but their heads were larger and separate to their bodies by a thick long neck. Their eye stalks really set them apart and their mouths were surrounded with tiny tentacles too. They had six tentacles filled with suckers, and two tentacles with three-fingered hands at the ends, which also had suckers on them. They were bright orange, covered in purple rings, and stood as tall as us.

Hello, our old friends. We understand you have no memory of us, but we can show you all your lost memories if you'd like. Or, we can only show some: whatever you feel comfortable with. In any case, we have missed you, Old Ones. A thousand years have passed since we were together; your bodies are so beautiful. We see a Hathor has been harvesting you again, Danny, stealing your DNA while you sleep, make love, or swim in the lakes. That process enlarges you and increases your wine production; we have seen them do this to you before so some of them can clone you for their own gratification. You need to tell all the other Hathors; they will stop the thief. You can tell them The Octo told you. They can't touch us, but you have the power to stop them from causing total destruction this time. Your infinite mirror is the answer; together with the others, you are all-powerful. The Hathors cannot hear us, so we can show you their lair in your moon. They are not what they used to be. They are mere shadows of their former selves.

You two are now much stronger, but you need to hide that fact for now, as they are blinded by your love and lust. They gorge themselves and guide you for their own benefit. Please trust us, old friends; we are here for you. The love of the Old Ones spreads across this universe and to many other races. We love your joyful bliss, so please share more of it. We feel your offspring, and they are powerful and beautiful like you. Anytime you wish to join us on our travels through the stars, you can; you have done this before, and we enjoyed your company. Long ago, you saw hundreds of planets. We have kept your starship safe, and we told her you are awake, so she is excited to meet again soon. You talk together and decide what you wish to know or experience, we are happy that we can talk with you again; you make us feel truly alive. Our love for you is endless. Call out to us with this device at any time, and we will acknowledge you. We thank you for your time; it's great to be alive with you again.

They passed us a small, flat egg-shaped communicator.

Thank you, you are too kind, and you have given us a lot to think about. We are sorry that our memories were wiped, too; we wish to remember you as you do us. You are beautiful beings, with beautiful souls. We thank you for remembering us, and we look forward to talking again soon.

Satisfied with our reunion, The Octo waved all their tentacles at once at us, then retreated into their craft. It immediately lifted above the lake and shot into the atmosphere.

Betty and I stared across the lake, lost in our bewilderment, unable to talk. Finally, Betty squeezed my hand. I looked at her and she smiled at me.

"I need a drink." I pulled Betty toward the couch while she poured two full glasses of bourbon and floated them over to us.

"Here's to us owning our own starship!"

"Cheers, Betty. Oh, and apparently, I have clones?" We took a swig.

"Imagine you and one of those cows doing it, Danny!"

Betty laughed, but I grimaced at the thought.

"No, Betty, let's not—yuck. We need to tell the other Hathors what has happened after this drink."

"Okay. It sounded like The Octo can tell us anything we want to know."

"I'm not sure if I want to find out how either of us has died each time; that might trigger other unpleasant memories. I would like to see what is headed for Earth, so maybe they can show us that so we can see what we are up against."

"Yes, getting a look at what is headed our way is a great idea."

"Are you ready for the Hathors? Let's get this out of the way."

"Okay, Danny, I will follow your lead."

We lay back on the mattresses in the tent, closed our eyes, and concentrated.

* * *

"Hathors, we need to talk with you."

"You are upset with us. Oh…we see why. You, sister Pleione, are in trouble. *We warned you, not to misbehave. Leave here now! You have stolen from Daniel again, and this behavior is unacceptable. We will confer with you soon, Old Ones, but rest assured that her harvest will be terminated. No clones are allowed. We apologize for your growth, but it is irreversible. You are the alpha, after all. However, you will not increase again. Please trust our judgment of our sister, one mother who has lost her way. She will live in solitude for an eternity. You have our word. Please just enjoy each other's beauty, sex, and lust. You feed us beautifully; that is our purpose, and yours. Betty, his horn is worthy, so do love it, but do not concern yourselves about anything else.*

* * *

They were gone.

Betty, do you believe them?

Yes, that was genuine. Not all Hathors are evil; some know compassion and empathy, like their leader. They live off our lovemaking, and I am more than happy to feed them that way. Babe, she said your horn is worthy, ha, but I can't wait to have you inside me again.

She was lying on her side looking me up and down, and her fingers slowly slid down my chest to my groin and back up again. I turned onto my side and kissed her as she took hold of me, squeezing me, and her other hand gently stroked my face. I let my hand wander from her breasts to her crutch and gently tickled her. She giggled and opened her legs wider for me, then rubbed my tip against her clit as I stiffened.

Oh, Danny, you want me?

Of course.

She maneuverd closer and pushed herself on to me, groaning as I went in. With a hand on my buttocks, she pulled me all the way in. Her muscles contracted on me as her whole body vibrated, and she started to twitch as the first orgasm hit her. She held on and moaned, kissing my neck as she pulsed. Slightly adjusting her body around on me as my own body started to build, careful Danny, I told myself, relax, not too hard on her. I let go suddenly and held her in position so as not to hurt her, she gripped me even tighter as another orgasm racked her body, and she cried out in ecstasy.

We had hardly moved at all, but Betty went off just with me inside her and it felt amazing. She kept kissing me and moaning, squeezing my cock with her muscles and then relaxing over and over. I could hardly breathe as I kept climaxing. Betty lifted us off the mattress and flew us out over the lake, where we hovered just above the water as my essence started leaking out of her. She couldn't let go of me; she could feel my bliss, as could half the universe, it seemed.

"It's okay, Danny. I love you so much. Keep going, baby!" Betty cried out as another wave hit her.

Eventually I slowed and stopped. Betty relaxed and let go of me, then dove into the lake. I looked down at myself; I was still quite hard and big, so I hoped the cool water would fix that. I rolled over and dove into the lake, too. Betty swam around slowly, smiling.

"Come over here and give me a big hug, you amazing man. That was incredible, baby." When I swam over and hugged her at arm's length, she frowned and asked, "What do you call that?"

"Sorry, I just didn't want to stab you with my baguette." I flipped onto my back in the water and showed her what I meant.

Her eyes widened. "Oh, okay then, but give me a proper hug anyway. I will push it out of the way if I have to." She laughed and squeezed it gently once, then wrapped her arms around me. "That doesn't hurt you, does it? It is still very hard."

"I'm okay. It is a bit weird that it stays so hard for so long, and that was the longest orgasm ever, but felt amazing. *You* felt amazing."

Betty just held on to me as I continued kissing her lips and her beautiful neck. She reached down and slowly massaged my balls as she kissed me back, then ran her hand along all of me. I shivered and moaned as she resisted the urge to climb on. I closed my eyes and could see in my mind that she was thinking about me being inside her again, so I imagined I was. She moaned as she realized I was in her mind. Her hand rubbed the tip of my head; I was nearly there, and she knew it. She lifted us out of the water as I blew, and it went flying, but she kept on gently tugging and rubbing as she orgasmed with me. I opened my eyes as we turned slowly around a few feet above the water. A stream of cum continued pumping out of me in waves, marking a circle below us in the water. Betty let go of me, kissed me, and hugged me tightly as the sensations subsided.

We were exhausted as my penis finally drooped and went soft. We floated away from the ring and dropped into the water. Betty summoned the shower gel so we could wash up and then we walked back to camp and sat by the fire. Our numb bodies were still dripping wet, but we couldn't be bothered with drying ourselves.

Betty sat on my lap sideways, rested her head on my shoulder, closed her eyes and fell asleep. I felt so complete. My beautiful Betty: I wrapped my arms around her and held her as I, too, drifted off to sleep.

30
Taxiplus

We awoke at the same moment and said together, "Shit, Conner will be here in about fifteen minutes."

Betty raced to Horus to dress; I slowly stood up and looked around, not even sure I knew what day it was.

I strode up to Horus, where Betty had just had a quick shower. I quickly jumped in and did the same. Feeling refreshed, I quickly dressed; Betty was ready to go. We headed outside and waited for Conner. Soon, we heard the roar of the Lincoln, and then the car flew up the road with Elouise hanging on and laughing her head off the whole way. They pulled up near us in a cloud of dust.

"Hi, guys," they called out as the car came to a stop.

"Hey, look at you two groovers in your hot rod." Betty laughed as we climbed into the back seat.

"Hang on!" Conner called out as he floored it.

The car's wheels spun in the dirt as we went sideways. Elouise seemed to be having a great time watching Conner drive like a sixteen-year-old. We sped along River Road, flying past Gertie's, and soon arrived at Taxiplus. Conner brought the car to a screeching halt. We jumped out and all hugged each other warmly. Conner stepped back to address us regarding what we would see inside.

"Okay, so I will show you all the steps from start to finish, including the human cadavers. Try not get grossed out; think of the skins as only skins, and nothing more. This is a factory, folks, so please watch your step, definitely do not touch anything, and always stay within the yellow lines." We all nodded. "This building houses the main cold room. All cadavers and untreated animals come here to await treatment, and we can store up to five hundred units here.' Conner opened the door to the cool room, the lights immediately lit up the rows of specially designed shelving containing hundreds of cadavers. In one corner sat a small forklift type contraption used for retrieval and insertion. I noticed small tags that hung from the big toes of feet that stretched off into the back of the cool room. He closed the door and we moved on. The cadavers that are to be stuffed go through this 3D scanner so we can get accurate measurements and print their interior armature. The cadaver lies here and this fancy camera moves all around it in every direction. That is the printer, it can print a full armature in a few minutes. This here is an enclosed heated conveyer belt for the human subjects to be transported for skinning. This thaws the skin so it can be pulled off. Then it goes into the De-glove room, through here. The De-glove 101. is this beast of a machine over here. Our engineers designed it from the ground up, so it is the only one in existence. You can observe the process through this window if you'd like, but it is a little grizzly. The cadaver is sliced open across the shoulder, up the neck across the head to the other shoulder. The skin is then pulled slowly back down the length of the body in one piece."

We all declined, but Conner looked in as I imagined he did every day.

"Cadavers for dissection go into that cool room, we won't go in there. The inside out skins travel on this conveyor into the sandblaster, if we wait a minute one will be on its journey, here it comes now." Bett and Elouise looked away, I could not, but almost wished I had. A fleshy, bloody skin left the De-glove 101 and floated eerily across the ceiling and entered the sandblaster room. "This carefully removes any flesh that may still be on the skin. We cannot enter that room as it is in operation. They are then turned outside out and proceed to this next room, where all the tanks of our special water are. Come up here, Daniel, and have a look in the tank."

Conner climbed a ladder to an observation deck; I followed him up, but Betty and Elouise opted to stay put. I peered into the well-lit tank somewhat reluctantly, concerned with what I might see. Below me were about fifty flat skins suspended by chains. They were mounted in frames so they wouldn't float. I found the ones with longer hair a bit creepier than the rest; their hair just drifted out from their flat faces and heads like seaweed.

"This soaking process lasts seventy-two hours, after which they are raised above the tanks, and these blowers remove any water before they exit through this door into the drying room. We cannot enter that one, as we would disrupt the controlled humidity. The skins are dried for another seventy-two hours, then go in different directions, depending on their eventual purpose. Study-Skins go in here, and those that are here for stuffing go through here. The stuffing takes place in this next room."

Conner pushed a buzzer on the wall, and all the staff left the room through another door. Conner pushed it open and ushered us through.

"Here are our new armatures, 3D printed with full articulation. There were rows life size plastic stick- figures, before us. All are printed to suit specific skins. The stuffing is a liquid foam that firms up as it is pumped in." This room was quite large with about twenty tables each had a cadaver covered in a plastic sheet. He lifted a sheet on one of the many tables covering a partially stuffed skin so that we could clearly see the progress, it was slightly terrifying. Elouise and I gasped, the top half of the cadaver was peeled back showing the interior armature and half-filled cavity, he lowered the sheet quickly. My hand tightened around Betty's.

It's okay, Danny. That is a normal reaction.

"The eye sockets are filled with a special polymer, and the glass eyes are matched perfectly to the deceased's original eye color and shape. This is the blue eye drawer, but there's one for every hue." Conner pulled open a large drawer, revealing hundreds of sets of blue eyes that were all slightly different shades. There were at least twenty more drawers by my count. "We have a special make-up that is permanently applied by our extremely talented makeup artists, and then the skin is stitched back up so neatly that it is usually imperceptible.

"Now, this next room is where all the animals are worked on; that is true art. The taxidermy artists we employ here are the best in the world. I sourced them myself. The animals are treated the same way, but in their own tanks. See? All the various sized tanks: this big one had elephants at one point. This tiny one is for small mammals, birds, and insects. They are dried in the room through that door there, and their armatures are printed here. Most animal eyes can be printed on this special printer here. The tables here were filled with all manner of beast in various stages of taxidermy. This door takes us to the Study-Skin storage; they are stacked on top of each other in wooden crates floor to ceiling. No refrigeration is required once they have been treated, ready for transport to their destination. You probably don't want to see that, as most of the Study-Skins are left open with their eye sockets empty, but about twenty percent of them get stitched up.

"That brings us back outside. That building is where we manufacture display cases, cabinets, and clear coffins for those who request them. Obviously, the crematorium is where all the left over remains are disposed of. We have a device in there that compresses the ash using very high pressure to form synthetic diamonds that we sell for a huge profit, so nothing is wasted."

Conner looked so proud, and he had every right to be. It was quite the operation, even if it wasn't everyone's cup of tea.

"What you have here is amazing, and very high-tech. I didn't expect all that." I fed his pride.

"Thanks, Daniel. I'm glad you enjoyed it. Now, let's go and find you a car."

He motioned toward the Lincoln; Elouise had him tightly by the arm and stole a little kiss as we followed them to the car.

"I shifted my collection to Ra's hangar since there is plenty of room there and it is very secure. You can pick one out today, Daniel, but if you're not happy or change your mind, just have Betty call me and I will swap it for another."

We pulled up at the hangar as the huge door slid open. Conner drove in and turned off the Lincoln. Off to one side sat his jet and a light plane; the helicopter was outside on the tarmac. He had his armored cars next to the jet, all decked out with machine guns and flamethrowers; they looked like they belong in a Mad Max movie. Off to the other side of the hangar were all the chrome and brightly painted cars of his collection. There were twenty-four altogether. I whistled in appreciation.

Conner smiled. "Take your time! Sit in them, start them, rev them up, whatever. Elouise and I will be over here at the bar. Would you like a drink to take with you?"

"Yes, thank you. Are you sure, though? *Any* car?" I could see some beauties here that were worth more than two million dollars.

"Absolutely, Daniel, any car. Here's your bourbon." He handed me a full glass.

"Thank you. This might take me a while."

"No problem."

I was sure he could feel my delight, and so did Betty. I pulled her along with me. Conner had all his supercars together: a stunning Lamborghini Revuelto, a Mclaren F1, a Porche 911 GT3, a Ferrari 812 Superfast. These were awesome, but very impractical on the roads near Taxi. Next were his fifties American cars: a 1953 Studebaker Commander, a '55 Chevrolet Bel Air Convertible, a '56 Ford Thunderbird, a '53 Buick 10, and a 1950 Ford Woody.

"Where does he find all these classics?" I looked at Betty, stunned.

"His money finds them."

"Got it."

Next was the sixties collection: a 1960 Corvette Stingray, a classic Alfa Romeo Giulia, a silver '63 Aston Martin DB5—James Bond's amazing car—a late 60s Datsun 240Z, a stunning red Ferrari 250 GTO, a '64 Ford GT40, and the classic '65 Ford Mustang Boss sat quietly next to that. Muscle cars came next: the Eleanor pre74' Fastback Coupe and a Shelby tuned GT500. I opened the door and sat in her, grasping the wheel with both hands as I looked at Betty and grinned. I turned the key, and she roared to life. I held the clutch in and changed the gears. The sound was unreal. It would be hard to top.

The very next car was a Chevy Chevelle SS with a 454 under the hood in classic red with matt black racing stripes. I sat in her, too, and started her up. Conner smiling broadly; she must have been one of his favorites, too. The engine sounded incredible, and the decision just kept getting harder. Sitting next to that was a matte black '63 Shelby Cobra with shiny black racing stripes: a truly beautiful machine. I started her up, and she felt good, but I turned her off and looked at the next car. It was a 2020 Bentley Continental GT V8. The sound that engine made was unreal.

Sitting next to that beauty was an Aussi classic: a HG GTS Monaro in canary yellow with orange pinstripes. Then, I saw a '77 Torana SLR 5000 A9X in red with a black bonnet and a massive scoop. Next to that was a fully restored original '54 FJ Holden in sky blue. I opened the door of this classic and looked in, amazed at how well it had been restored to its original out of the factory look.

The very last car was one of the biggest and meanest out of the bunch: a matte black Hummer H1. Looking it over, I lifted the bonnet. It was fitted with a 6.6-liter Duramax Turbo Diesel V8 and fully tricked out with a leather interior and all the bells and whistles. A truly beautiful beast.

"Bett, let's take this for a spin."

"Yes, this is very *you*, isn't it?"

We climbed in and I started her up. The engine roared to life and I pushed the horn, which sounded more like a truck horn one might find on a semi. Conner gave me the thumbs-up.

"Go for it, Daniel. Floor it!" he yelled. We pulled on our seatbelts.

So, I did. The wheels spun and squealed, as we lurched forward and spun out of the hangar; the boom gate was already raised for us. Betty connected her phone to the sixteen-speaker stereo and played "Fortunate Son" by Creedence Clearwater Revival so loudly the doors shook. We flew down Poison Valley Road, barely in control of the hunk of metal, and skidded sideways onto the Flinders Highway. Betty laughed along with me, and all I could think was that, as much as I'd wanted Eleanor first, this was such an exceptional and awesome ride.

Yes, Danny, this one is perfect for us.

And it might come in handy.

Turn into the creek now.

I didn't think twice about her command and shot down the dry creek bed. We bounced around as we hit some rocks, then came to some shallow water. I powered through it, then slowed down a short time later and turned when we came back up to the highway to head back to Taxi. When we pulled into the hangar, Conner stood and came over to greet us.

"So, what do you think?"

"We love it! Truly, it is amazing."

"I thought you would say that. The engine in this beast is excellent. I spent a lot of money on this car. But don't worry, he has a twin; the other is in storage. Take it. I will organize for fuel to be sent to your camp. If you wish to change to Eleanor or any others, just say so."

I jumped out of the Hummer and hugged him tightly. "Thank you, sir. You are so kind."

"Thank *you* for loving my daughter. Your wedding is only five days away, and we can't wait. Enjoy the H1, which is actually known around here as Osiris."

Sure, enough there was a black chrome plate on the front fender that displayed the car's nickname proudly.

We hugged Elouise, who promised she was returning for the wedding and would move in with Conner soon after that. We climbed back into Osiris and drove it back to camp. Conner had been busy even while we were at Taxiplus; his men had erected a sturdy camouflage tent for us to store Osiris under so as to keep it out of the sun. Betty spun her huge front seat around; directly behind us was a huge bed, a double bar fridge, and a ton of storage spaces. It had a large TV screen that gave us access to all the security cameras and Ra's mainframe.

Betty jumped onto the bed and rolled around playfully. "Come on, Danny, feel how comfy this mattress is."

I climbed through and jumped on the bed; Betty grabbed me and kissed me.

"Any excuse to have you in my arms again."

She didn't mess around we were still fully dressed, but she managed to get my pants open and climb on top of me, moving around until I was fully inside her. She felt so good, and we both came almost immediately, but Betty sped up anyway. She moved faster than she ever had before, pushing down on me and moaning in time with her rhythm. With her mind, she somehow managed to slow my ejaculation soon after I started. She was in rapture, her eyes fixed on mine, and smiling sweetly between moans. She slowed and stopped to kiss me, breathing hard as she continued to contract and shake. I wrapped my arms around her and hugged her close.

She whispered, "We should get out of these clothes and go for a swim while I make us some lunch. That was fantastic, Danny. I love you so much."

"I love you, Bett."

She carefully climbed off of me, looking all disheveled. I laughed at her, but she winked as her dress flew up and off, displaying her new sexy bra and knickers. My eyes widened as she stepped out of the car and casually walked toward the lake. I followed, and she turned toward me as she unclipped her bra, then dropped it on the ground. She slowly pulled down her knickers until she stood there with her hands on her hips, smiling beautifully.

"Damn, girl, you're gorgeous," I said, pulling off my shirt, kicking off my shoes, and pulling down both my pants and my boxers. I stood up straight and put my hands on my hips, and staring back at her. There was no way she's missed the fact that I was fully erect again.

"You are going to have to catch me."

And just like that, she was off, sprinting into the water and diving in. I raced after her, but I was nearly ten yards behind. I lifted out the water and flew just above it; by the time she realized I was flying, I had caught up. She turned to her back and grabbed hold of my shoulders so we could fly together. Wrapping her legs around me, she guided herself onto me and gasped as we broke through the clouds. Her hands on my bum pushed me in and out, and we came together as we spun around and around in the clouds.

She would not let go even after we were both finished, so I stayed in her as we floated around, kissing and caressing each other; it was very sensual.

"Hmm, Danny, your dick is unreal. I have made lunch. Are you hungry?"

"Oh, yes, baby."

She kissed me and let go, swooping down into the lake. We swam to shore and some towels flew over as we walked to Horus. At the table, bacon, eggs, hot coffee, and toast awaited us.

"Excellent, Betty, thank you."

"This is getting too easy," Betty said.

"Well, I've been thinking about The Octo's offer to go into space and see if we can find the asteroid or meteor that is headed for Earth. Maybe we could use our minds to push it off course with the help of the infinite mirror. Does that sound like enough of a challenge? Granted, this is not something I would ever have considered before that conversation."

"It is crazy, for sure. I don't know, Danny. For starters, what do we wear? I'm fresh out of space suits."

"We would go into space naked, just like them."

"That's too weird, isn't it? We will be the first untrained astronauts in space, totally naked and accompanied by two big, happy octopi."

We both laughed at that mental image.

"Their spaceship might be full of water, anyway, so we need to ask them a few more questions before we commit ourselves."

"I agree. Danny, do you really want to do this before our wedding?"

"Darling, we just don't know how much time remains before impact, do we? We might not even see next Saturday. I feel that everything is ramping up, gaining momentum. Do you feel that, too?"

"I know what you mean; I feel that, too, but I feel it everywhere, all around us—almost like Earth itself knows something is coming. Even when we are together, we have an urgency that we didn't have before."

"We need to talk to The Octo now. I'm going to call them."

Betty patted me on the knee. I summoned the egg and squeezed it until it vibrated rapidly. In my head, I could hear them answer the call.

We hear you, Daniel, and we are close. We will be with you in minutes, as we waited nearby for your reply.

Betty and I went outside and walked to the lake to wait. We felt their craft just before it zoomed in and stopped a few yards away from us: a beautiful, shimmering orb of many colors. The circle appeared on its surface as the colors shifted through the spectrum, and The Octo jumped into the water and swam around for a moment, enjoying our water; we smiled at each other, feeling their joy. Their wobbly warbled voices soon filled our heads as they rose up in front of us and waved madly, happy to see us.

Thank you for calling to us. We understand your conflicts, and we wish to help you. We will take you and the infinite mirror to the big rock, but we must go far, and a small shift far away can make a big difference here. Do you understand?

Yes, and thank you. You are so smart. We trust you, but will we be safe in your craft? How long will our journey take?

You will breathe our jelly into your lungs, then breathe our water like fish. It is uncomfortable at first, but you have done this before. It will keep you safe. It will take two sunrises to return here. You will have ample time to prepare for your uniting ceremony. We do not want to interfere with that joy. We will be there in mind, if not in body. But we must leave now.

Octo, we must have an excuse for Conner. We cannot just disappear for two days. I understand the urgency and we are prepared to go, but can you hide it from him?

He will not perceive your absence. Will you come now? When you enter, immediately breathe the water in. It will feel uncomfortable and unnatural to you, but you will survive it. Come.

31
In Space

Betty and I lifted off the shore as The Octo jumped up and into their craft. We came up to the circle, and Betty gripped my hand tightly. Their water was warm and thick like unset jelly, and it had a sweet taste as we started swallowing it, gagging. We were drowning in it, but not. Betty looked at me frantically.

Relax, baby.

Yes, please relax, Betty. You are okay. Breathe in.

We lay prone in the jelly holding hands, The Octo floated above us. As I took in our surroundings, I realized their craft was transparent, as if we were floating in the air just above the lake, but there was no sensation of movement when the lake started to shrink below us. The sky went from bright blue to black, and stars appeared. It was as if we were flying unaided through space, but The Octo glowed, giving off their own golden light, and I thought that maybe that was part of the way their crafts worked. I looked at Betty; her body was golden and glowing and sparkling like it did in our dreams. When I looked down at myself and saw the same thing was true for me, it hit me that their jelly had turned us gold from the inside out. We held our arms out as if we were flying holding hands, rocketing through space naked and gold. Everything seemed so surreal as our moon loomed bigger and bigger up ahead.

The Hathors lair is nearby on the far side of your moon. They cannot perceive this craft. Look at them, cowering in their crater.

The four of us floated above the surface of the moon and looked into a dim crater. There were two massive doors, barely perceptible at its base, and suddenly we saw them in our minds. They were not beautiful women or cows or hybrids, though; they were small beings that stood shorter than three feet high, and appeared weak and frail and extremely old. They were almost like hairless Lemurs with large heads. Six sat on tiny electronic thrones that seemed to be keeping them alive, while the seventh was strapped to a secluded bed and connected to some kind of machine by wires.

They are not what they seem in your minds. Tens of thousands of years ago, they were mighty and ruled your planet. They were big then, taller than us, but as their power over humans decreased, so did their size. This is why they orchestrate resets: to feed on anguish and grow strong again. This is not fair on you humans. You are beautiful beings, but you have been guided by a race that is using you for its own gratification. We will help you break their control over humanity.

We ascended at an incredible rate and hurtled through space, but our bodies detected no sensation at all. We just floated in the warm jelly with two big, orange-and-purple octopi.

Do you like this flight?

Octo, it is incredible, we had no idea it would feel like this. Betty smiling at me, and we mentally shared the euphoric state the journey had granted us; it was close to orgasmic bliss, and just as joyful.

We will arrive shortly; the rock is near.

Where are we, exactly?

We are at the very edge of your solar system; it has been twenty Earth hours since we left.

But it feels like we have only been gone about four or five hours. That makes no sense.

Time travels differently at this speed. We have arrived now. Look! The immense, icy rock blazes through space toward your Earth. Summon your infinite mirror. Talk to the universe. Join together to strengthen your minds. Please, try and save your planet.

Betty and I were in utter awe as a million stars surrounded us. We could see galaxies and nebula and interstellar clouds as if a colorful and magical painting surrounded us. There ahead of us was the meteor, traveling through interstellar space toward our planet as surely as a magnet. We looked at each other for guidance and realized we needed to hold each other tight before reaching out for our mirror. The Octo watched us closely, enjoying our embrace as we wrapped each other up in our arms and legs with no shame and kissed in front of our alien friends. Betty reached down and pushed my semihard cock inside her warm wet cunt and moaned.

We closed our eyes to our universe and opened them to the others. We looked from side to side; there were a million of us embracing as we all looked to each other.

Push the rock, we all said together in our minds.

All of our counterparts joined us in concentrating on that one rock; we only had to shift its trajectory by a few yards in order to save all the Earths across all the universes from impact. That had to be enough to miss the Earths. All the Bettys and all the Daniels channeled their willpower on shifting that rock through the universes; as far as I could tell, none of them had ever done something like this before.

The Hathors stirred. *What is happening? No, you cannot deny us our feed. This is impossible; you are not this strong. What are you up to? Quickly—we must act now! They are pushing it off course. Make your calculations quickly, Sterope, or we will be too late to intercept it. Hurry, before it is out of our reach.*

Together, we all pushed in our minds at the same instant across the universes, and then we all climaxed as one. Betty and Daniel times a million times a million. The meteor shuddered and veered just enough to miss Earth. We had moved it a few yards off course, by the time it would reach Earth it would be thousands of miles off course. We all cheered, and the Hathors crumpled under the weight of defeat, mourning the fact that if they could not feed this time, they would become dormant for a millennium.

The Octo rejoiced. *You have succeeded in thwarting the Hathors! You are legends!*

We felt so good as we watched the meteor zoom though space, knowing for certain that it would miss Earth, that we had saved humanity. There would be no reset, and life would carry on.

But fate was a fickle thing, and the Hathors had a hastily devised contingency plan. We had already started our journey back to Earth, having closed the infinite mirror. Bett and I were locked in a tight embrace, kissing joyfully, while The Octo quietly squawked to each other in their own language, their tentacles tapping each other's in some kind of dance. We were passing close to Jupiter when the craft came to a stop, spun around, and then sped back toward the rock at incredible speed.

What is happening? What's going on?

The Octo were frantic as they pointed. *Look, Old Ones! Another rock approaches the first at an unthinkable speed. They will collide in a few moments This second rock has shifted trajectory, its path has been altered, only the Hathors could accomplish this feat.*

Up ahead, there was a mighty impact as the two meteors collided. The first rock exploded in a brilliant flash and now it had many smaller pieces surrounding it, hundreds of them, and all traveling together straight toward Earth, according to The Octo and their calculations. There was no way to deflect them all in time. Earth would, without a doubt, be impacted.

We need to get you home. You should fly into space in your starship, which we will bring to you today; we just have to retrieve it from the bottom of the Mariana Trench. Do not go in the caves; Conner will understand if you tell him the truth. We need all iterations of you to survive, so you must go off-world. There are only five days until Armageddon, and only three days until your wedding. There is still time to save more of your people, but you cannot save all now. Your weddings need to proceed; humanity across the universes depends on it.

The Octo raced us back through space, past Mars and the moon toward our Earth, gleaming like a round sapphire. Soon, Australia was directly below us, and we zoomed in on Queensland, then out past Charters Towers. From up there, the town called Taxi really did seem tiny, but it had changed my life and reunited me with my Betty, my forever soulmate, who would be my wife in three days. Betty, who carried our twins and loved me madly.

I looked over to her as our lake loomed below. She was stunningly naked, with golden, glistening skin, and she was smiling at me lovingly. The craft came to stop a few feet above the lake.

See you soon, Octo. Thank you for everything you have done.

Old Ones, we will return in thirty minutes with your starship. She became very excited when we told her she would be meeting you again. She was like a child who is only thirteen thousand years old and has slept for the last two thousand of them. We know you will take care of her. See you soon.

We floated out above our lake and threw up the foreign contents of our lungs as The Octo zipped away. We dove into the lake to wash off the gooey jelly water. Our shower gel flew out to us, and we washed our bodies.

"Come here, baby." Betty reached for me. "The end of our little town is near. We need to make love right now."

Betty started kissing me, her hands all over me under the water and making me hard. She wrapped her legs around me and started slowly rocking up and down, gradually speeding up until we climaxed together, crying out over the lake.

After all that had happened over the last weeks, and all our intense love and adventures, we floated in the water, content to hold each other and kiss in that space while we still could.

"Thank you, Danny. I can't wait for the next crazy chapter in our lives."

THE BEGINNING

This lesson will stay for an eternity, written in folklore for the new world.

> *Materials lost, humanity found,*
> *binding love forever gained.*
> *Humanity's loss, it engulfs all.*
> *In turmoil we are to survive,*
> *with the guidance of the Old Ones.*
> *Their light shines bright as a new dawn.*
> *We awaken on new shores.*
> *A deep love guides us; it is their love that guides us all.*
> *They show a new path, one that has not been trodden.*
> *This is their duty to their children.*
> *The Old Ones find direction where there is none,*
> *but never divulge the destination,*
> *as that is the purpose of our journey, the struggle,*
> *and that is worthy.*
> *The Old Ones know of true love.*
> *They live it.*

Acknowledgements

Firstly, I would like to thank my Mum, for she allowed this young boy to sit up to all hours on weekends watching all the early black and white science fiction films of the fifties and sixties. It was this experience that inspired me and led to my fascination with science fiction.

A special acknowledgement to my loving Birgitta who had to put up with my incessant nights of writing. She would often have to wake me up so I could go to bed as I had fallen asleep at my desk. It was her who helped me come up with this whole crazy idea for *A Town Called Taxi*.

A huge thank you to Lucille who's own writing inspired me to get a move on and start tapping keys to get my story down.

A big thank you to Isaac who had to put up with me at work and nudge me along when I was tired from staying up late on a work night.

You all inspired me to put in 110%. Thank you, my family.

Books by S J Rose

The Old Ones Saga

A Town Called Taxi

The House of RA

The Dawn of Isis